Inspector Camberwell

By

Kevin Steward

Chapter 1

Lewis Hamilton

At last, his day off he so longed for, had arrived, finally allowing him to actually have time to relax, and do some of the things he really needed to. Shaving was one of the things on his list, although standing in front of the mirror in the bathroom, he was unsure whether to shave it all or not, but deep down he knew that his wife would insist strongly that he did, but now as usual it was time to actually start shaving.

It became the usual seemingly extremely long drawn out affair that it normally was, because with razor in hand, staring back at him from the mirror, was a half shaved face and the rest covered in shaving foam.

Looking into the reflection of his own eyes, he became drawn into an all too familiar state of mind, where all he could think about was the beach where he grew up in Jamaica. He always seemed to have the same daydream whenever he had no work to do, a day off, a day spent alone with his wife, which nowadays was a very rare thing, so when the daydreams revisited him he always seemed to get lost inside them.

Then the sound of a deep voice screaming at him, suddenly snapped him out of his daydream, whilst in reality he was subconsciously cursing, wishing he could stay inside it.

After what seemed an eternity in him being able to perform the task of actually getting to the kitchen after being screamed at again, the voice continuously saying his breakfast was ready, he was finally seated at the table.

He picked up his fork and was just about to literally tuck into a traditional Jamaican breakfast, (which consisted of Ackee, salt fish, fried plantain and dumpling) when the front door bell rang.

His wife Marshita, (A big buxom Jamaican woman) answered the door with a stinging scowl.

"What do you want?" Only to be responded by,

"Is the Inspector there, please Ma'am?"

"Who is calling? Wait don't tell me! Why can't you damn people leave him alone!" She replied scornfully, whilst slamming the front door shut in the man's face

"Paul McIntosh" she yelled at the top of her voice. "Come here!"

He put a handful of Saltfish in his mouth and got up warily from the table, and began walking down the hallway towards the front door. He had not even taken three steps before Marshita, with her hands on her hips like some famous Grecian urn, let rip with typical Jamaican fury.

"You may be some high flying Metropolitan Police Inspector but I am sick to death of people in authority just turning up whenever they feel like it and disrupting our lives. Don't you and the Metropolitan Police understand that today is the only damn day off you've had for a whole month? I am sick and tired of playing second fiddle to those bluebottle babies of yours!"

With that she stormed off and walked into the front room, cursing to herself as she went, followed by her slamming the door hard behind her, so hard in fact that the whole house shook.

Vance "Paul" McIntosh, who was better known as "Inspector Camberwell" because there was nothing he didn't know about the place in South East London, quickly opened the front door again apologising to the person who stood outside. As the door opened, he paused to look at the person standing there, but he didn't recognise the man that stood before him.

"Sorry about Dat, Inspector Camberwell at your service young man, how can I help you?"

"My name is Perkins, I am from MI5 and I have been sent to collect you. A situation of national importance has arisen and we need your assistance!"

For some reason he was taken aback by the man's name and the MI5 thing, that he seemingly missed half of what the man had said, and then he asked quizzically "Perkins? What sort off a name is dat? Do you have a first name? Who wants me? What skills do I have dat can possibly help out the nation and MI5? What the hell is going on? Damn, my wife is slowly killing me already without dis sort of stuff going on."

Perkins interrupted him and replied "Sorry Inspector, we are wasting time, I will try and fill you in as we go."

A jet black Ford Galaxy people carrier pulled up sharply with a squeal of tyres, and along with it came, a real stench of burning rubber. "In we get sir,"

Camberwell looked at the vehicle and thought to himself. "With all the windows blacked out, how the heck can the driver see where he's going?"

Once seated he didn't even have time to do his seatbelt up, because the precise moment his bottom touched the seat cover, the car sped off again with a squeal of tyres and yet even more burning rubber, and seemingly filling the interior with a putrid rubber smell.

With his seatbelt finally done up, Perkins finally answered one of Camberwell's questions. "Perkins is all you'll need to know about me sir, the rest you'll be briefed about at The House," With that he stopped talking and just looked forward.

"The House, where is dat?" Camberwell queried, but as he got no response, his thoughts returned to his wife. "She is going to be well miffed"!

Down the road they went, at times seemingly flying through the air, especially when the driver went flat out over the speed bumps, leaving the car then suddenly crashing down from the mid-air ride, which had the effect of sending everything crashing about them inside the car's interior.

At the junction at the bottom of the road, they turned left towards the roundabout, all of a sudden the car started sending out a wailing, beeping scream, the blue lights on the top of the car were flashing like they would never flash again. Up the hill, continuing through to the traffic lights by Kings College Hospital, then right towards the main Camberwell Green crossroad junction.

The driver then speeded up even more as he went the wrong side of the road, Camberwell thought he was going to die and then screamed at the top of his voice. "Stop! Stop! Da driver is going to kill us, he is a damn maniac!" Still he received no reaction from either the driver or Perkins!

Turning left, still on the wrong side of the road, making many of the oncoming vehicles swerve to avoid them, onwards towards the Oval Tube Station, round past Surrey Cricket Club, continuing down the road towards the cream and green windowed building at Vauxhall Cross.

Camberwell again had to scream at the top of his voice, because of the noise the sirens made. "Why didn't you say Thames House?" But as usual Perkins just sat there saying nothing.

"Jesus! Man, you are insane!" exclaimed Camberwell to the driver again. The car never bothered to go round the one way system at Vauxhall Cross. It just went straight through the tunnel the wrong way against the traffic, scattering all the oncoming vehicles all over the place. Skidding! Slewing!

Somehow the car missed all the oncoming traffic then turned right onto the Albert Embankment. How the driver made it he never knew, but somehow he did, then they turned left and continued down a ramp at what he now knew to be Thames House, through some awaiting open gates that slammed noisily, then closing immediately behind them.

The sirens finally went quiet which allowed him to speak normally. Turning to the driver he said "Dat journey should take about 10-15 minutes, but you have done it in three minutes twenty five seconds. I know Lewis Hamilton has just recently won another Formula One World Title but I didn't know he worked for MI5?"

"Just follow me," Perkins stoically replied.

Still none the wiser, Camberwell followed Perkins through a maze of corridors, up steps, down steps. "Perkins, stop a minute Man, all dis damn maze walking is making me feel dizzy!"

"Was that supposed to be a joke? If so we have no time, so please hurry up and follow me," came Perkins reply.

Finally he was led into a darkened room that was only lit by the white light from the projector that stood on a table. Next to it was an ash tray, which had a large cigar protruding from the edge of it, cigar smoke was wafting around the room.

"Okay, enough is enough man, I don't know what is going on but dis is just getting more and more ridiculous. The damn cold war finished years ago, so what the heck is going on?" He exclaimed.

Suddenly a side door opened and in walked a tall but balding middle aged man.

"My name is Tomlin, Bob Tomlin," said the man. He made his way to the table where he picked up the cigar, then after taking a long drag from the cigar, he continued.

"Inspector, sorry for any inconvenience caused to your day but an extremely serious situation has arisen. We have reason to believe that a dirty bomb is going to be placed within the Camberwell and Peckham borders."

Tomlin took out a piece of paper from his jacket pocket, and began reading it out loud. "Slovakia, 28th October 2018, Two shells containing 481.4 grams of enriched uranium powder was seized by Police in east of the country. Two Hungarians and a Ukrainian were arrested whilst trying to sell it. The uranium had come from the former Soviet Union and we also understand from the Slovakian Police, that it was enriched enough to be used in a radiological 'dirty bomb'."

He continued "I am personally convinced that somewhere someday, it is going to happen, but anyway that's beside the point.

The world's press finally got wind of the story and everyone worldwide was alerted. But what the world's press and public don't know is and hasn't been told, is that last month, one of these shells went missing. Intelligence leads us to believe that the shell is now here in London! We think we know who is behind it, but we don't know why, but we believe the threat is serious and real."

Pointing to the projector screen that was standing in front of a wall, Tomlin continued.

"Perkins, start the film." He barked. Turning back to Camberwell he added. "Watch the footage and you'll get a better idea of what is going on!"

The projector flickered into life, onto the screen came footage of a place he knew intimately. Peckham High Street, suddenly the face of someone Camberwell knew very well appeared. The footage followed him for about 20 seconds before it showed him going into a shop door.

"Dat's Daniel Nelson! What does he have to do with all of dis? He's just a small time thief, the highest criminal ranking he's ever had is a batylicker!" Camberwell said. All of a sudden Nelson came back on the screen with another person he knew. "Dat's Russell McDonald, now man, he's a special sort of criminal! He would turn his own mother over, to find dat extra one penny to make sure he had one pound!" With that the film stopped.

"Lights, Perkins!" Tomlin snapped.

"As you correctly stated, they are the people you know. But with one massive difference! Daniel Nelson is now dying in Kings College Hospital with severe Uranium ingestion poisoning.

We were alerted by the staff late last night. Kings have a policy that whenever someone comes in with a radioactive type of poisoning, protocol says that they have to notify MI5. We went to see Mr. Nelson late last night but he refused to speak to us saying he would only speak to you. So that's why you're here, to find out what he knows and to help us resolve the problem."

Drawing deep on his cigar then blowing even more smoke into an already smoke filled room, he continued "We have been in touch with the Metropolitan Police Commissioner Cressida Dick and your Borough Chief Superintendent Simon Messinger, both of them have agreed that you will now be working with us until this situation is resolved. In fact your boss said that as you know the area better than anyone else, plus you know the local toe rags very well, where they go when times are rough etc. You are to take charge of this investigation. This is now especially important because it seems that Mr. McDonald and his family have gone missing. This footage shot the day before yesterday, was the last sighting of him."

Tomlin looked at his watch. "We should get to the hospital, so you can talk to Mr. Nelson!"

"Well I hope you have someone who drives a bit slower than Lewis Hamilton out there!" Camberwell replied,

Tomlin replied "What?"

"Don't worry about it, Jamaican humour!" Camberwell said.

This time they walked down the maze of corridors at a more sensible pace, as they walked Tomlin asked.

"What if anything do you happen to know about dirty bombs Inspector?"

Camberwell said nothing for a few seconds and then replied. "Dat is a good question."

In the car on their way to Kings College Hospital, Camberwell started to tell Tomlin, not only what he knew but more importantly how he knew about it. "A dirty bomb is better known as a radiological weapon or a radiological dispersal device. RDD for short. It is contains conventional C4 explosive, which has been extensively packaged together with radioactive materials."

Without pausing for breath he continued. "It kills or injures through the initial blast of the conventional explosive, and then by all the airborne radiation and contamination. Hence the term "dirty", if you took a small measuring cup of radioactive material, dat would be enough to cause devastation in the area where the explosion took place. God forbid it gets detonated on a windy day, because then all hell could break loose, because the wind would enlarge the area of exposure. It is more commonly known by people as the fall out fear factor."

He waited for Tomlin to take in what he said before continuing. "Also no real special assembly to make the bomb is required, the C4 explosive simply disperses the radioactive material. The hardest part is acquiring the radioactive stuff, but nowadays it seems as if that is no longer a problem for these guys. It can be made into a very small package which makes finding it very difficult."

"Well that is where you come in!" replied Tomlin.

"Anyway you know a lot more than I thought you knew, how do you know so much?"

"Back home, I served in the army as a military policeman before coming here from Kingston, Jamaica. After arriving, I then spent about three years, as a security guard at the

Sellafield Nuclear processing plant, during the early eighties. It is amazing what you learn from boffins whilst you're all having lunch. You say I know more than I think, but let's see what you know? Can you tell me what damage can a dirty bomb do, apart from the fall out?"

Tomlin replied "The actual explosion of a dirty bomb would kill or injure people in the immediate area and contaminate them with radioactive material, exposing the general public to risks of cancer in the future. The radioactive exposure is not likely to cause immediate harm. Extreme versions of dirty bombs would not kill as many people as those who died on September 11th 2001, in New York City. A worst-case scenario, if there was an explosion at midday, say in the centre of London. It would cause more than 2,000 deaths and the radiation poisoning affecting thousands more."

Taking another long draw on his cigar and exhaling for about 20 seconds, his cigar smoke filled the car interior. It was starting to make Camberwell feel very sick, Tomlin continued oblivious to the discomfort that his cigar was causing Camberwell.

Tomlin continued. "A radiation safety officer of the University of London said recently, that the use of radiological weapons would result mostly in deaths of people as they fled the scene and would kill more with anxiety-induced heart attacks accounting for many more.

Also that the average dose of radiation within a half-mile of a typical dirty bomb would be the same as a person's annual exposure from natural sources. The damage and injuries from a dirty bomb would vary considerably depending on the amount and form of the radioactive material used, the means of dispersal, how many people there are around, weather conditions and how long the public were exposed to it."

When he finished, Camberwell queried "How did you find out dat the Uranium powder was here in Peckham? Also, how long have you been watching McDonald?" "Because I knew he was up to something, I just didn't know what.

Tomlin answered "we asked about quietly and found out that he's been a very active member of the Rye Lane's so called "Bouncers from Mothercare brigade." We have been watching him myself on and off for about two weeks, now with what you have told me, certain things are starting to fall into place."

Tomlin continued. "I can't tell you how or where we got our information, but suffice to say it has proved to be correct. What makes it even worse is that we have only recently found out that Prince Harry and Her Royal Highness the Duchess of Sussex are due to visit Peckham Library in 3 days' time. They are coming to unveil the new statue at the Queen Elizabeth the Second Wing in the library, total screw-up if you ask me anyway, the Palace people say that we lost the paperwork and we say that they never sent it. But what we do know is that after being told of the threat, they stated they will not cancel. What was it he said, Have to keep the British stiff upper lip, let that public know that no-one will scare us away! Apparently the Duchess also agreed!"

Camberwell thought for a second then said.

"Young Nelson is one of the most active local toe rags, I have nicked him for almost everything dat you can nick someone for, so why and how has he got involved in dis? There must be something very weird at hand. He is not religious so it won't be martyrdom stuff. If McDonald is involved then it could be revenge, but revenge against the government? The royal family, why? Have you at MI5 or any other government departments had any sort of run in with him or his family recently?"

Tomlin said nothing for a few seconds before replying. "We are waiting for a home office report to come through, but apart from that, there is nothing that we can see! Until then we will just have to wait and hear what your Mr. Nelson has to say!"

Chapter 2

Daniel Nelson

As they approached the isolation ward at Kings College Hospital, Camberwell turned to Tomlin and said.

"Right now listen man, me don't care if you're from MI5 or from Sainsbury's online shopping. We going to have to do dis my way, so let me speak to him for about ten minutes before you come in, and when you do come in, come in like a bull in a china shop. As far as he is concerned, we have not ever met and I am only there because, I got a message to come and see him. Remember you have to create a scene, where you insist dat no matter how ill he is, he has to come with you for questioning."

Camberwell knew that he had to get the information super fast, because although Tomlin had just stated the fact that MI5 had only just found out about the visit of Prince William and the Duchess. He in fact had known for some while, and this was because his granddaughter was one of the children chosen to present them with some flowers.

As he walked along the corridor, he didn't need to ask where Nelson was, because outside a small room on a side corridor were two men that were suited and booted at least, they obviously thought that they were in the FBI, even down to wearing sunglasses in a dimly lit corridor, Camberwell said to himself. "Typical Men in Black wannabees"

A nurse came up and told them that they had to go into a clean room, and put on protective clothing due to the danger of radiation. After scrubbing up they then had to put on the special gowns they had been given before entering Daniel Nelson's room.

Gowned up, he walked towards the door, one of the "Men in Black" special agents stepped in front of him and blocked his way. Camberwell glared at the man who then said. "What do you want?"

With the other one talking over him saying "Where do you think you're going? You're not allowed in here, because this man is not allowed visitors. Access is only for nursing staff and my boss!"

Camberwell just stood there for a second then replied "Man, I may be wearing this mask and gown but if you don't move out of my damn way, you will need those glasses to hide your black eyes. "For your information I am Inspector Camberwell and I am now in charge of dis whole operation and if you cause me grief, I will see to it dat the only job dat you will be fit for is to guard the elephant shit house at London Zoo!"

Just at that moment Tomlin came out of the clean room and into the view of the two men and instantly, both men stood to attention, and the nearest agent quickly apologised, saying "Sorry sir, we did not expect a black man to be Inspector Camberwell!"

Tomlin responded with venom with. "What's up with you pair? Do you think he is going to try and eat you? Put a blow dart in your arse? Or send you to Sainsbury's for some bananas? We live in Britain and we don't act like that! Even in America they have previously voted in Barack Obama, not only that! He's a black man! Get a grip, just because someone is black, it doesn't mean he can't be a better man than you! Because if you think that, you're in for a damn shock, because soon, Black, Asian, or Russian they all going to be running this country. Then where you are gonna be then man? People like you make me sick. Man I don't care if you are black, white, pink or green.

We are all human beings!"

Camberwell just stood and with a massive grin, smiling to himself.

Tomlin grabbed his radio and requested that both the men be replaced immediately, then turning to them he told them to report back to Thames House when their replacements arrived, as he walked away from them and towards the door he shouted back to them. "And take off those stupid glasses!"

When Camberwell entered the room, Daniel Nelson was sitting upright whilst being tended by a young nurse. He was obviously extremely sick, he knew he had to act fast, from what he could see, he didn't think that Nelson had long to live. He quietly asked the nurse about Nelson's condition, who replied "I am not sure how long he will survive, so please take it easy on him. We have given him morphine for the pain but it is incredible that he has lasted as long as he has."

Pulling up a chair to the side of the bed. "Daniel man, what you been doing? I got a message to come and see you urgently! So what's up?" Nelson was so barely audible, Camberwell had to lean right over to hear what he was saying. "He stitched me up! He told me he was my friend and we would make a lot of cash, but all he's done is, kill me!"

"Daniel, who's stitched you up?"

He didn't reply so again he asked him "Daniel, who's stitched you up?"

"Mc…. McDonald," He said very weakly.

"He asked me to go and collect a package, a week ago from some marina near Lowestoft, from some Russian yacht. Its name is written down on some paper, which is still in my wallet."

Camberwell opened the wallet and withdrew a small piece of paper, which had, Royal Norfolk, Suffolk Yacht Club Marina "отравитель" berth twelve written on it.

Nelson continued "He told me that he would pay me twenty thousand pounds for doing it. So I obviously thought it was drugs, but hey ho, I was in the dough." He tried to laugh but was obviously in too much pain.

Then he started to whisper again, but it was obvious to Camberwell he was getting weaker by the minute and Camberwell knew that if he didn't get the information now, he never would.

"Daniel, come on tell me more, come on man, tell me!"

After a few gasps for breath Nelson continued.

"On the way home I had to break hard to avoid hitting a child that had run into the road. The package on the back seat shot forward and split open. Thinking it was drugs I started to scoop all the powder up and put it back in the split bag and in all the confusion, it went everywhere and I started to inhale it."

"Yes, but where did you take the damn package, come on I need to know!"

Still gasping for breath, he carried on.

"Chadwick Road Print Village Industrial Units, which is where McDonald met me. When I told him what happened, he refused to pay me. He said that the money would be no good to me now as I would soon be dead from the Uranium powder. I met him again yesterday in Peckham High Street, but he still would not help me. Afterwards I was feeling so ill that I came straight here to the hospital and I ended up here. When the other men came late yesterday to question me, I told them that I would only speak to you. I may be dying but I want revenge on McDonald!"

"Did he tell you what he wanted the Uranium powder for? And why he is doing what he is?" Nelson just laid there staring at the ceiling. "Damn man…..Come on, talk to me Daniel, talk to me man!" The desperation was now really noticeable in his voice.

All of a sudden the door burst open and Tomlin strode in, and went straight onto the attack by saying "Nelson, we're going to take you somewhere and you will die in complete agony and you will be allowed no relief from it, just tell us what we need to know or else!"

The nurse yelled at Tomlin, that Nelson was almost near death now and that they should be left to treat him and let him die with dignity. But he refused to let any treatment be given, saying.

"Then let him die in agony then and with no dignity, all I care about is getting the information from him."

Meanwhile Camberwell, who was still bending over towards Nelson, heard him whisper very quietly.

"McDonald found out that his brother Ralph had been killed by the British Army. They left a group of soldiers unprotected in Afghanistan and the soldiers including his brother were killed by the Taliban. The army refused to send a rescue party saying, we cannot afford to upset the local militia by sending in people to get them, so unfortunately as what normally happens in war, they became expendable even at the cost of their lives. McDonald swore revenge on the government by killing Prince Harry and the Duchess when they come to Peckham."

Gasping for breath even longer he added "He chose Prince Harry because he had been to Afghanistan as a soldier in the army. Now he wanted the royal family to grieve as he was grieving."

Suddenly his intake of breath became incredibly long and laboured "……. He is, he's going to, to place the bomb innnnnnnnnn…….."

With that his head rolled to one side with his mouth open and his eyes staring at the ceiling. Tomlin screamed at the nurse "Get a doctor in here quickly and try to resuscitate him, now!" "But he's dead! Can't you see that!" she cried.

Tomlin continued screaming at her. "You don't know that, you stupid cow! Now go and get a Doctor!"

A Doctor came rushing in and after a few minutes of trying to resuscitate him, he pronounced Daniel Nelson dead! Cause of death was "Massive Internal Uranium Poisoning caused by ingestion of Uranium Powder."

Tomlin turned to Camberwell and asked "What did he tell you? Will it lead us to McDonald and his people?"

Camberwell thought for a second then turned to Tomlin and said. "Yes it will help!" pausing for a few more seconds he added. "Get a team from Thames Water Board to meet us at the Old School car park in Bellenden Road. Get them to bring extra protective overalls, we will need to use them when we go in."

Using his radio, Camberwell called the control room at Peckham Police Station, then talking to both Tomlin and the person at the other end of the mobile. "We need a team of our own to meet us at us there as well, then we can get someone to check out the Print Village. We can make out we are doing water and drainage inspection, then we'll be able to use radioactive meters to see where the Uranium Powder is or was. Once we know where to start, we can go from there, but remember, the people you send must dress and act sensibly, not like Joe 90 and his brother Bert outside here, sunglasses in a hospital corridor!"

Tomlin replied "Who's Joe 90? Who's Bert and what's that about sunglasses?"

Camberwell ignored him and continued. "Just hurry up man! We need to get someone to those industrial units! When you have arranged dat, we will talk and I will tell you, what he told me."

Tomlin barked out orders via the radio to some unknown person, then when he was finished he walked over to Camberwell who then started to tell him what he knew.

"It turns out that seemingly all Nelson was, was a damn patsy!" He explained about Nelson being sent to Great Yarmouth, about the collection and the damage to the package containing the Uranium powder.

"Get the coastguard and the Royal Navy to look for a boat called dis." He gave Tomlin the piece of paper that had been in Nelsons wallet.

"Nelson said it was a Russian boat, so we need to find out where it is now and who it is registered to. We could do with finding out what dat means in English, also have you heard from the other government departments yet, because it seems as if we now know the reason for all of dis? Dat reason is the British Army, McDonald wants revenge on for leaving his brother to die in Afghanistan. Killing Prince Harry and the Duchess is his way of getting his revenge, an eye for an eye so it seems."

Tomlin, pointing to the name written on the piece of paper added. "Well if you translate the name from Russian into English, it means "The Poisoner".

Suddenly there was a sharp crackle and Tomlin barked another order into his radio and told the person "Let the palace know about the intended attack on Prince Harry and the Duchess, that way they can try and call off the visit to Peckham."

Almost immediately Tomlin's mobile phone rang, he kept acknowledging statements from the caller. When he finally hung up, he started to explain to Camberwell, who had called and the info he had been given.

"It seems as if Nelson was telling the truth about McDonald's brother. The MOD has just confirmed that the brother was in a small group of soldiers that got misplaced in Afghanistan and the army did nothing to save them. So you can understand why he's really pissed off!"

Seemingly ignoring him, Camberwell just said. "Let's make a move to the Old School."

On the way to the car he told Tomlin "Depending on what we find out at the print village, it will dictate what move we make next. McDonald will almost certainly have gone to ground, he would have guessed dat Nelson went to the hospital and eventually gave the game up, and he'll know dat Nelson will have also given up the industrial estate address, so a lot depends on what we find.

People always make mistakes, So far he has been predictable in all his dealings, so we may stand a chance of moving dis further along."

Tomlin queried "Who are his acquaintances?"

Camberwell replied. "Well he did have a close knit group of friends that he grew up with, so they will have known his actual brother as well. His closest ally is James Dillon."

Continuing on he added "Dillon has a record for armed robbery, he was convicted for a raid on the Lloyds Bank branch at West Dulwich. He was caught on CCTV, after the security guard there managed to grab the mask dat he was wearing, pulling enough of it off so dat he could be quite clearly identified. The security guard then got shot in the chest and leg for his trouble.

After the raid Dillon laid low for about three weeks before he went shopping in Rye Lane. The police followed him back to a house in Kings Grove just off the Queens road in Peckham. So dat's one place to check out after we have finished at the industrial estate."

With that Camberwell's mobile phone rang, stopping him in mid-sentence. The sound of Bob Marley's One Love filled the car, after letting it ring for about five rings he answered

"Camberwell here! Hello Bab…"

He was cut short by the tirade that everyone else in the car could hear "When you coming home for your dinner? Why you still out?" then the phone went dead, basically because Camberwell was so embarrassed, that he had turned it off completely.

"The wife?" Tomlin asked. Camberwell said nothing, he just sat there fuming to himself.

The fax machine, come printer, that sat between the seats in the Galaxy started to churn and two photos appeared as if by magic from nowhere. "Well at least we have some photo ids of McDonald and Dillon to give to the troops on the ground." Camberwell didn't need to be shown any photos, he would know those two faces anywhere.

He opened his mobile and dialled, speaking clearly into the phone.

"Camberwell here, can you get a Specialist Hart Hazardous Area Response Team from Kings College Hospital to meet us in the car park of the Old School in Bellenden Road. We will need it as back for up for anyone who needs it, and ensure dat when they attend dat they don't use sirens or blue lights. They will probably want to send a major incident unit as well, but if we can have them and a few ambulances on very close standby just in case, I don't think they will be needed. Also I want to get a specialist Fire Brigade Unit, it will only be as back up, to meet us there as well, again no blue lights or sirens. We don't want to alarm them if they are still in the estate. Right we will be there in approximately seven minutes."

Camberwell remembered something he had forgotten, so barking out orders on his radio again, he said. "Please get McSloy and Critchley to meet us at the Old school, dressed in Peckham skivvies, as soon as possible. Ok thanks!"

With that he calmly closed his phone, turned to Tomlin. "Paul McSloy and Dave Critchley are two very important people who can help us loads, they are part of my crack team of surveillance officers."

He paused to cough then turned back to Tomlin and continued "I'm certain dat McDonald is long gone."

As the Galaxy pulled into the Old School car park in Bellenden Road, some people had already arrived. Two short haired men in obviously brand new jeans, tee shirts and what were laughable dark glasses.

Both men approached them. One of the men said to Tomlin "Ready to go sir, the Thames Water van has just arrived and we're just about to gear up and go."

Tomlin started to reply with "Okay let's be having you in and out as quick as possible"

When Camberwell interrupted and barked at Tomlin "No do not send them! We are not dealing with amateurs!"

His head turned sharply as a beat up old Vauxhall Astra pulled into the car park with a cough and a splutter of dying engine noises.

Camberwell walked over to the car and spoke to the passenger through the open window.

"Right you two get changed then take the Thames Water van, get down to the print village and start checking those units. The Thames Water guys are in the van, they have all the equipment you will need. Get in and out as fast as you can. We have an open mike to you, so once it's either clear or you find something, we'll know."

After stopping the driver got out and looked around their surroundings, then turning to Camberwell he asked.

"Have you seen how most of these men are dressed? Jeans and tee shirts under the overalls are fine but FBI sunglasses and brogue shoes, any Peckham brother worth his sort, will spot them a mile off. It's bad enough hearing that you had Joe 90 at the hospital let alone now having Bill and Ben & Little weed here as well now!"

Camberwell turned to resume speaking to Tomlin but he was now over in the far corner of the car park berating the two men from before. As he turned round again to look at his own men who were already pulling out of the car park and turning right into Bellenden Road.

Turning round again to begin his walk back towards Tomlin, he thought to himself "Where would they go if they aren't there?" Tomlin was suddenly right by his side and asked Camberwell who the two men were.

"I told you five minutes ago, McSloy and Critchley, they are my two most trusted Peckham skivvies undercover people, they never, ever under any circumstances enter the police station, and they never call or never meet anyone from the station, unless it is dat important they have to. So apart from me, they are only known to one other person at the station. If we'd have sent your guys in, the whole thing could have been blown in seconds. Now all we can do is sit and wait, it should be no longer than fifteen minutes."

Whilst waiting, Tomlin walked off to speak to the ambulance officer in charge about what to do if anything untoward happened. He just stood there listening to McSloy on the radio, when there was a tap on his shoulder. A young female police officer stood there holding a steaming cup of something along with a sugar bowl.

"Coffee, Sir? If so how many sugars Sir?"

Chapter 3

Russell McDonald

Meanwhile in a small flat above the Ivanhoe public house, Russell McDonald was deep in conversation with James Dillon and Shaun Jackson. "Well I hope you both ensured that the industrial unit was clean, because they are almost certainly there by now, Nelson would have talked. We need to be very precise and careful in what we do or say now, because everyone will seemingly be staring at us all the time and if we give them one hint of a clue, we'll be for it."

"That's okay, I'll just blow them away with me Uzi" Jackson laughingly replied.

Shaun Jackson was a flash but instantly antagonistic sort of man. His answer was the way of the gun, he is a fantastic friend until you crossed him and even then sometimes when you didn't.

Dillon replied with.

"Sit down and keep calm, by the way Shaun, did you collect the stuff from Makro's? More importantly did you get it all? Remember, we have Neil Lawrence coming very soon to make the package up, so we need to have it all ready for him, and we don't need to have the hassle of going out to find more stuff at short notice, and especially when we have had time to do it right first time!"

Jackson nodded and pointed to the corner of the flat. "That's all the important stuff, all the big bits are locked away in the van, and that's garaged off the street."

McDonald spoke slowly make sure he was clear and precise.

"Remember there should never be more than three of us here at any one time, that way we can keep suspicion and rumour down to a minimum, so when Neil gets here Shaun, get lost for a few hours. Remember to keep your mouth shut and keep cool and as much as possible stay out of sight, so be sensible"

"Right let's go over the plan again. Prince Harry and the Duchess are due at 11:00 am and information leads us to believe that he will watch a group of local young Afro Caribbean dancers perform, and then they will get presented with some flowers. We know that it will be the interfering idiot Inspector Camberwell's Granddaughter, who will present them with the flowers. That should all take about fifteen minutes to complete, their visit will live be on the telly, so when they leave to enter the library, that's when detonation will happen. We will be miles away and the world's mobile phone system will be used to detonate the package. Which means the package has to be in place the day before, so not to attract any unwanted attention."

With that there was a loud knock at the door, a voice said. "I got a visitor for you, downstairs Russell! A guy by the name of Mr. Neil Lawrence! He says that you are expecting him?"

"Cheers, please send him up!" he replied. Turning to Jackson. "Time to go and get lost for a while Shaun, we'll go over everything with you when you get back, take this and while you are out, oh remember to pick up the twenty disposable mobile phones we spoke about, not from the same place mind you! Now remember, keep your mouth shut and don't do anything that will draw attention to yourself."

Handing over a large bundle of twenty pounds notes, which Jackson stuffed into the inside pocket of his jacket.

"Okay, give me a call when Neil has gone, tell him I said hello. Cheers!" He quipped, and then with that, he was gone, out the door!

McDonald turned to Dillion "I try to tell him everything at the last minute, because as you know he can be a loose cannon, and if we give him time to think, who knows what he will do!"

30 seconds later Neil Lawrence entered the flat and made the usual acknowledgements to both McDonald and Dillon. "Tea?" Asked Dillon. "No milk and two sugars please" Lawrence replied curtly." McDonald then pointed to all the equipment in the corner of the flat.

"We have everything that you asked for and we got a couple of extra items just in case, is there anything else at all that you might need?"

Lawrence glanced quickly at the stuff and mentally ticked off all the items that were there from his list. "Superglue, I will need some superglue! We'll need that to seal the package once it's made."

McDonald called Jackson on his mobile. "Ten tubes of super glue and again get them from different places, no need to rush them back. We can take care of what we need them for when you return. Then remember to lose the phone when we have finished, so call me when you are on your way back, remember now lose it properly, I don't want anyone finding it!"

Turning back to Lawrence, he asked "Do you need us to leave the room whilst you make it up? I've seen what damage this stuff can do on its own, up close and personal!"

"Yes and when you come back in try not to make too much noise. We are not arming this today, but we still need to take great care."

McDonald and Dillon slowly and deliberately went to the door, and carefully closed it behind them. As they walked down the backstairs of the pub into the public bar area, Dillon commented. "Well we'll soon be ready and then it will be payback time for Ralph and all of the troops that recently have complained that the military brass, are not providing the correct equipment for their protection!"

McDonald interrupted him. "Don't let us forget that, they also they leave soldiers in the lurch because some bloody do gooder is afraid to upset the local Taliban leader, even at the cost of our own troop's lives. When the royals are dead, the higher echelons of military personnel will be the ones to blame and as much as I don't want innocent people to die, their blood will be on their hands as well."

McDonald thought very carefully before saying anything else. "Look James, I may have made millions from the internet and have almost everything that money can buy, but I don't have the ability to bring Ralph back. Every time we approached the British Army and the government, they have fobbed us off with one excuse after another and it has taken three years to discover the truth, because they all denied it. The Prime Minister was forced to make a statement in the Houses of Parliament acknowledging the fact that my brother and his troop were left behind to die. And what did he say specifically? Oh yes "Acceptable loss for the long term good of the country of Afghanistan." Well that is unacceptable to me and now they will pay and pay dearly. If it means that I have to die achieving my aim then so be it, because there will always be someone else in line behind me, waiting to take their turn for justice and revenge."

The mood changed, when the giant television in the public bar, showed Queens Park Rangers score a goal in a football match versus Crystal Palace.

McDonald screamed with delight. "Get in there my son!" He had always followed Queens Park Rangers since he was a boy and because of his physique, he always styled himself on Sir Les Ferdinand. He whooped with delight as two minutes later, when Rangers swept another ball into the net, giving them a two goal advantage. "It's all over now, those poxy Palace poofs are finished." He shouted!

Dillon just sat there and said nothing, his beloved team, Millwall had lost earlier in the week 5-0. He just said. "Another game that's par for the course, one day we'll actually win one."

Neil Lawrence appeared as if out of nowhere and called them over to him. "Your kettle is now fixed, remember to be very careful with it, it may just be a kettle but like all electric equipment you have to be treat it with respect. Any problems give me a call later tonight! See you later man, tell Shaun hi!" He then calmly walked out of the public house door.

As Dillon went to get up, McDonald whispered to him. "Don't be in such a rush, give it ten minutes or so, otherwise it will look suspicious. Look we can't do anymore tonight or at least until Shaun comes back, saying that, I'd better phone him, give him the all clear to come back when he's finished shopping."

Whilst calling Jackson, McDonald had to turn the television down, as a large rush of noise restricted him from listening to Jackson properly. "Hello man, how's the shopping going? Do we have it all? Okay, how long do you think you will be before you get back here? Okay man, see you then."

He turned round just in time to look at the television and see the ball in the back of the Queens Park Rangers net "Shit, they've scored!" He said,

Dillon then took the opportunity to comment. "Sorry Russ, but in the time it took you to speak to Shaun, Palace have scored two, so it is now two each."

McDonald swore under his breath and growled "I know it's only a repeat of the match from the previous weekend's fixtures. Let's go back upstairs, because this shit has already pissed me off once this week and I don't want it to piss me off again!"

About an hour later Shaun Jackson returned to the flat and found both McDonald and Dillon deep in conversation about a backup plan, should the royals visit be cancelled?

"We can wait for a little while before deciding, but I honestly believe that they will still come to Peckham, he's that sort of arrogant snob!" McDonald scowled.

They then set about getting ready to finish off the container that would house the package. The superglue would stick the bottom of the container together, so when it was dry the container looked just like new. More importantly there would be no evidence of any tampering of it at all.

Very carefully McDonald moved the container onto an old padded chair.

"Right that should give it some protection until Neil finishes it off, so remember no unnecessary banging in this room According to Neil it should be quite safe and we now know the telephone number needed to set it off. Just to remind you, all three of us are going to call the number at two minute intervals, just in case there was a problem with any of the other two people on detonation day."

Jackson asked "How long had Lawrence been in the military before being busted out, it's just that I want to feel safe whilst moving around that thing?"

Dillon answered "He served with Ralph for three years, mainly dealing with explosives until he got busted for bedding the commanding officers daughter. The commanding officer then made his life hell when his daughter became pregnant, eventually he got him kicked out of the military on a technicality."

"Which explosives was that?" McDonald queried.

"Well he got accused of stealing five pounds of C4 explosives, which he denied obviously! But funnily enough, he found enough C4 explosives for us to use. So anyway the daughter ran back home to daddy and had an abortion, he got kicked out and his military life was over, so he says this is his way of getting revenge. He told me afterwards he did a bit of mercenary work in the Baltic countries, learning about how to handle and make this sort of device terrorist style!"

"Enough of this guys, let's get down to business! Shaun brought twenty disposable mobile phones. Now the most amount of calls we make from each phone is two, then it has to be disposed of. Once we have received a call on any phone, it is then disposed of. That way it will make it harder for anyone to track our calls.

If you run out of phones, immediately go and buy five or six more new ones then notify every one of the new numbers. But remember to dispose of the phone used to notify us of a change of number. It is long winded I know but it is the best way to keep us untraceable. Is that clear?

Right we tell no one, irrespective of who they may be, the number to trigger the device. That way it is only the three of us that can set it off, understood? Good, any questions?"

"I just want to confirm where we make the call from?" Asked Jackson.

McDonald opened and began to read from his pocket diary "Well it makes no difference where you are as long as you make the call dead on time. I will make the first call at 11:14 am, followed by James at 11:16 am, and you make your call at 11:18 am. We are putting the bomb in place the day before and that will be at around 3pm, which gives us time to separate to different places. I will be at Manchester Airport heading for Banjul-Yundum in Gambia, James will be at East Midlands Airport, heading to Ljubljana in Slovenia, and you will be at Gatwick Airport heading to Agadir in Morocco."

Continuing he said. "None of these countries have a Bilateral Extradition Treaty with the UK. Remember your money has already been placed into your accounts there, and we will all meet up in five months' time in St Lucia. Cathy and the kids will be waiting for me to arrive at the airport, we will then disappear into the local countryside and watch the fall out on the world's television and the worlds press."

McDonald took a mouthful of water before continuing

"With my Caribbean roots they will look for me, Cathy and the kids there. James is London born and bred so anywhere outside of the UK is good and they speak a fair amount of English in Slovenia. For you Shaun, the best place to get lost is Morocco as you can speak basic Arabic and you already have a girlfriend who comes from in the middle of nowhere over there.

Remember the money is for living, so don't go around buying flash stuff that will bring unwanted attention on yourselves! The time to celebrate will be when the job is done, the heat is off and we meet up in St Lucia."

"Okay guys I'll see you tomorrow, about what time is best for you both?" asked Jackson.

"We need not to be seen together too much, so I suggest that we make it Thursday, say about 10:00 am if that is suitable. That way we can double check everything, get Neil to arm it and get ready for the drop off of the bomb later in the day as we have arranged. Is that okay? Okay, goodbye Shaun. James, hang on for a few minutes before you go!"

McDonald looked at James Dillon with concern, and said. "The unit at the Print Village is definitely clean isn't it, the last thing I want to do is have to worry about anything there?"

Dillon replied "It is like a new born baby's bottom, immaculately clean. We both checked and double checked again to make sure it is fine. Is that all? If so I'll be making a move home? Cheers then, see you Thursday."

McDonald just replied "Okay, take care."

Chapter 4

Radiation Exposure

Paul McSloy and Dave Critchley turned into Chadwick Road, off of the Bellenden Road one way system, before driving a few hundred yards then turning right into the Print Village. "Still the same!" remarked Critchley

"Never changes does it, still a dump!" replied McSloy sarcastically.

The Print Village industrial estate is quite a dirty, dingy little industrial estate. It is not that large, it only houses eleven units and mostly they are taken up by small printing firms. When you enter the estate, it seems to have the stench of printing ink hanging heavily everywhere. If you were to run your fingers down the front of most of the units, you would probably end up with ink stained fingers.

The industrial estate consisted of, ABC Bet printing at unit one, followed by The Press printing at unit three and so on. On the other side of the courtyard you have the Plumb Drain that also uses two massive silvery grey containers that jut out into the courtyard, like two fingers stick out from a hand. Coming back towards the entrance there are two units that did not look like they were in use at all.

"You start at the Plumb Drain!" McSloy said to Critchley. "Work your way towards unit eleven, if you find anything or need help then give me a shout across the courtyard. Right let's get cracking! Oh yes, we need to find out if anyone has the keys to units ten and eleven! Normally the firm that has been here the longest usually help out the estate owners by showing prospective new clients around."

McSloy called in at unit one, a place he knew well. As he walked into the unit, one of the workers called out to him. "Oh we're working for the water board now are we, what happened to the postman's job?"

"Shut up and get on with printing you're My Little Pony Life Story." He replied, with the person he was talking to, sarcastically responding with "How many different jobs have you had in the last two years? Postman, Bus Driver, Joiner, Electrician, Roofer and what was the other one?"

"Painter and Decorator!" was the shout from someone else, everyone then started laughing out really loud.

McSloy thought to himself. "Do they know I'm a copper? I think so!" "Enough of this rubbish. Where is Mr. Dalgliesh please?" someone pointed to the office. Entering the office door, without even knocking, interrupting the person on the phone, he said. "Morning! I need to look around as we have had a report of noisy pipes on the estate and we need to check them out!"

Colin Dalgliesh looked at him with a quizzical face, then just waved his hand in acknowledgment then returned to speaking to someone on the phone.

With that he walked out of the room closing the door behind him and then started towards the back of the unit, the smell of freshly used ink filling his nostrils. It seemed to be clinging to his nasal hair, which to him intensified the putrid smell.

With the water meter detector unit in his left hand and an Ortec portable radioisotope identifier meter clutched in his right, he started working his way through the unit, but apart from some very tiny movements being registered on the identifier meter, there was nothing at all in unit. So on to the next one, it took a few minutes to check each one.

When he had finished his side of the industrial estate, he waited in the centre of the courtyard for Critchley. Soon Critchley was walking over to McSloy commenting "well that took a bit longer than I thought, it was a right pain getting in all the nooks and crannies of those two silver containers, but there was nothing in there."

McSloy spoke directly into his radio mic. "Boss we are just going into the last two units, but so far there is nothing out of the ordinary. If you want to start making your way down, we should have finished by the time you get here!" They then started to walk towards units ten and eleven, both had large foldable concertina metal doors that were shabby in appearance. Unit ten was locked, so they tried unit eleven. It was unlocked!

Critchley spoke first. "Well we don't need to worry about a key then! My meter is reading a little above normal but we will find out more when we get inside." Walking into the warehouse area, they both remarked how immaculately clean it was.

He then walked into the office space and apart from a few bits of paper in the waste bin and a small pile of rubbish in the far corner is was clean. Talking out loud he said. "Clean! It is way too clean! Especially for an unused unit. Someone has gone to a lot of trouble to tidy up, which means they will have made mistakes and left evidence behind. If they have been out here, evidence will also be easier to find."

McSloy Answered. "You carry on checking the office and I'll check out here."

McSloy's radioisotope meter started to show strong indications of the presence of Uranium radiation. The reading suddenly shot up high, in fact dangerously high.

"Dave, let's get out of here, The meter is now going mad, I want some back up and get some protective clothing, so come on….. Out, Out! Now no messing OUT!!"

As they came out of the unit, Camberwell and Tomlin's car pulled up outside the unit, Critchley came over and told him

"Better not leave it there sir, it could end up being contaminated! We will need to evacuate the whole industrial estate, and probably even some of the occupants of the houses across the road from the entrance as well. The readings inside unit eleven are dangerously high, but the metal framework of the unit has acted like some sort of box and sealed most of the Uranium radiation inside it. But for safety's sake we need to get everyone on the estate, and it would not hurt to get the people across the road checked out by the Hart Team (Hazardous Area Response team)."

McSloy was now dressed in his PPE (Personal Protective Equipment suit) with a light on one side of the helmet and a video camera on the other. The helmet had a wide, clear visor to see through.

Tomlin walked over to both men and said. "Your Critchley aren't you? Well either way, your suit is now ready for you, and remember to check the oxygen supply before you go in. We'll be taking video footage as you go, and at the slightest sign of any issues come out immediately." Turning to McSloy he added. "The same goes for you, no heroics!"

McSloy turned to Critchley and said "I'll bag and tag anything I find, you do the same."

Turning to Camberwell he said. "Sir, the video will send a live feed back to the control van, if you see anything you're not sure about or want to ask questions, I will be live to you via the headset by the screen. We will obviously be recording what we see and do, for future evidence. We have decided to use the blue tags for what I collect and the red tags for what Dave collects, that way it should help when checking through any evidence in relation to the video."

The head of the Specialist Hart Team, Roy Askell walked over to Tomlin and Camberwell, who were in conversation with McSloy and Critchley. After attracting their attention, he started to recount the protocol for suspect materials that the HPA (Health Protection Authority) had put in place.

"We need to inform CCDC (Consultant in Communicable Disease Control), who in turn will contact the HPU (Health Protection Unit). Someone will come and collect contact details of everyone potentially exposed to the risk. We will need to decontaminate any persons that have been exposed to the radiation here at the scene. So when people exit the units, we will collect and bag all clothes and personal items. If necessary we will refer any persons we deem to have been highly exposed, for immediate medical treatment."

Rather rapidly he continued. "Some people may have to have Prophylaxis treatment here at the scene, in the form of antibiotics until the results of samples taken from inside and around the unit are known. Oh yes! Can we get all the units in the estate that have air conditioning to turn them off because that will help stop the spread of any radiation?" With that he walked away, calling to someone across the estate.

They both looked at him and then after a moment Camberwell turned to Tomlin and said.

"Did you understand a word of dat? I think he means dat if anyone needs help here, they will get it here initially."

Tomlin just stood there with a perplexed look on his face and said nothing. Camberwell continued "We'll isolate the main area and get samples taken straight of to the nearest National Specialist Laboratory. Right, it is time to see how McSloy is getting on!"

McSloy was moving through the warehouse part of the unit, and giving commentary as he was going along. "Very clean so far, but way too clean, it seems as though the place had been cleaned with a toothbrush? Hold on what's that?"

In the far corner of the warehouse, right next to the fire exit door were some form of crystals lying on the floor. He noted "They were definitely too big to be any of the Uranium powder and to me they look like soap powder crystals."

Stooping down to collect some samples of the crystals, he became aware of a torn piece of cardboard that had got caught by the bottom of the door. Someone had obviously swept dirt and stuff out of here through the fire exit. Having collected the piece of cardboard as well, he then started using his meter to register if there was any Uranium radiation. The meter flashed across the screen immediately, showing dangerously high dosages of the radiation right there. "Boss!" He shouted in to his mouthpiece.

"We need to get someone to take samples from the other side of the fire exit door, at the back of the unit. My meter is going crazy."

Camberwell answered "Okay, we'll get the fire brigade to spray some decontaminate foam around the scene, once we have taken some samples."

Tomlin then shouted quite loudly.

"Have you found anything that might tell us where they have gone too?"

McSloy replied through the headset. "Apart from this bit, it is cleaner than a baby's bottom after a nappy change, but the radioisotope meter is registering a lot of stuff."

Just as they turned to the other screen that was showing Critchley in the office area, they heard him saying "It is immaculate in here as well! By leaving it so clean they will have obviously missed something and that will make it easier for us to find., for instance, they have missed this rubbish in the waste bin."

"Camberwell replied." Okay, bag it, tag it, then bring it out, we can go through it once it has been photographed and recorded as evidence."

Roy Askell had returned to their side after finishing his conversation across the estate. Tomlin said. "When they come out make sure that they have a clean bill of health, and then send them over to the other control unit at the Old School. We can leave an officer here with you and the fire brigade. Go through this place and get it sorted out, anything that you need to complete the job is yours, just ask. Okay! Right speak to you later."

"Let's walk back to the Old School, I want to clear my damn head. It feels as if Maxi Priest is playing drums on me skull!" Camberwell said, as they were walking back down Bellenden Road, Camberwell's mobile rang. "Times like dis Bob Marley gets on my damn nerves" he said. Taking it out of his pocket, he looked at the number calling.

"The wife?" Tomlin asked.

"No! The station. Camberwell here!"

"Okay, I will speak to them when they get to the Old School, cheers."

He stopped for a moment, thought and then spoke to Tomlin "Two of my officers were walking down Rye Lane, when someone stopped them and gave them some information. They think dis information is very important to dis case, so we'll get dat when we get back to the Old School."

Having bought a cup of coffee each from the local coffee shop, they continued back. "Where do you think they've gone now?" Tomlin asked.

"Well they have gone to ground somewhere local, someplace where they are revered enough, not to be grassed up, but it will be local. McDonald is a very clever person, he personally won't make mistakes but it is the other idiots with him dat will make them."

In the Old School, the caretaker of the building had opened up some rooms, so that they could use them. The two of them had been sitting around for about two minutes when two uniformed men walked in the door. "Excuse me Sir." One the men commented.

Camberwell responded with "Doris and George, what news do you have?" Tomlin just stood there looking totally bewildered not understanding why all the nicknames were being used?

Simon Cox and Glen Cox had both wanted to be police officers all their lives and finally after passing out at Hendon Police College, they had both been posted together to Peckham Police Station. Simon spoke first.

"We were walking our beat down Rye Lane, when we approached by Raj Singh. He owns two shops and a stall in Rye Lane Market, selling mobile phones and other small electrical bits and pieces. He told us that a very strange thing happen today."

"Yes, hurry up spit it out boy, we don't have all day!" Tomlin said.

Leaving Tomlin looking extremely angry, Simon retorted sharply. "Well, if you give me a chance and shut up I'll tell you. Anyway as I was saying before I was rudely interrupted, because he owns all three shops as previously explained, he obviously cannot be in three places at once. So he gets a phone call from the small shop at the Peckham Rye end of Rye Lane, asking him for seven extra disposable mobile phones, when he queried why? He was told that someone wanted to buy them. Great he thought, bit of profit, anyway, he sends the mobiles to the shop."

Glen interrupted him and said "About fifteen minutes later he gets a call from the stall in the indoor market in Rye Lane, asking for six more disposable mobile phones. You can see where this is going, can't you? Then fifteen minutes later someone walked into his shop and asked for seven more phones. So being very community minded, when we walked past he told us what happened."

"When did dis happen?" Camberwell asked.

"About two hours ago. We tried to contact you earlier but the station told us not to disturb you, due to the radiation scare incident." Simon answered.

"Thank you, right now dis is what you two have to do, is go back to the shops in your Peckham civvies and find out everything you can about the person who bought them and anything else of relevance. Get back to me when you find something! And oh yes, well done the pair of you, good work!"

As the two brothers walked off, he heard Simon say. "Well thanks for that bro! You made me look like a right Pratt!"

"Well you never gave me a chance, and I didn't want you to grab all the glory." His brother replied.

Simon continued "You wait till I'm the Commissioner, I'll have you put in charge of the school crossing patrols."

Glen quipped in return. "Yeah, and when I'm the Commissioner, I'll have you put in charge of traffic light control." Then they both started to laugh and carried on walking.

Tomlin turned to Camberwell, who seemingly had steam coming out of his ears with rage. "Do you normally let your young officers talk to high ranking staff like that?"

Camberwell turned to face him. "Look man, if you calm down a bit and take off your rose tinted glasses, you'll see the bigger picture, let people finish then you might understand more. The information they found out, given, whatever you want to call it, is of vital importance. We are getting closer and the net is closing. And yes for your information my people can talk to people like dat, if they have something important to say! I thought you would have learned by now, dat we don't work on a higher rank system, we work on doing a damn good job system!"

"What does that mean, how does that information help us?" Tomlin asked, still obviously very angry.

"Dat is why you work for MI5 and I am a real policeman, you remind me of a Arsenal fan, who is so jealous of clubs richer than them. They find every excuse to belittle other clubs. Come on the evidence from the Print Village should be back by now."

Chapter 5

Home Life

Russell McDonald turned into the driveway and drove slowly towards his temporary lodgings, his mind going at 10,000 miles per hour, trying to reconcile all the different things that were going through his mind, it was made worse by the problem that seemingly it was all at the same time.

It seemed an eternity in reaching the end of the driveway, the 200 yards seemed to be a mile and after finally coming to a halt, he didn't make any attempt to get out of his car. He just sat there thinking about what was going to happen and his internal rage about the reason why it was going to happen grew even more stronger.

Finally he started to calm down, as he knew he could not enter the house, see Kathy and the girls in the mood he drove home in, they had no idea about what was about to happen and they thought their upcoming trip was just a holiday, he hadn't told them he had sold the house and these dingy surroundings were just temporary because they would be emigrating.

As he entered the house he was met by Kathy standing there holding an envelope, as he closed the door behind him she stretched out her arm. "You might want to open this? It is from Downing Street. It was dropped off by Felix"

He felt himself snatching the letter from her and his internal rage started to rise again as he started to open the envelope, suddenly he stopped.

"Actually I think I need a drink first" He retorted snappily.

He walked into the kitchen, Kathy following behind him, and drank a soft drink that he retrieved from the fridge.

Before continuing to open the letter he looked at her and said. "I am not expecting good news in fact it will only be more lies just like the ones before."

"Just open it" she replied. The envelope fell to the floor as he removed the letter, first thing he noticed was the Downing Street logo at the top of it, then when his eyes fell upon the start of the letter itself he started to read out loud.

"Dear Mr McDonald, The Prime Minister has asked me to write to you and convey his condolences but once again states that it would not be in the public interest to the people of the United Kingdom to hold enquiry into…………"

As his voice trailed off after saying the last words, the letter like the envelope fell to the floor, landing on top of the envelope. As he walked out of the kitchen, she bent down to pick it up, then she continued reading. "Mr McDonald this is the fourth time that we have notified regarding this issue, and we shall not be corresponding with you any further regarding this issue, once again the Prime Minister sends his condolences."

Walking out of the kitchen herself, she went looking for him, when she found him sitting in front of the open fire in the front room, she softly asked. "What will you do now? They have made it quite clear, that no more correspondence about this issue will be entered into!"

He just sat there and said nothing for a few seconds then quietly but firmly answered. "If they think that they have heard the last of this then they are very much mistaken." Changing the subject he asked where the children are, to which she replied "In bed!"

"Anyway I am sorry to you all, that we are staying here but it gives them a start on doing the building work at the house, the new garages will come in very useful, anyway changing the subject, how is the packing going? Hope it is almost done remember we only have a few day before we are away" Turning to walk out of the room she replied,

"It is all done, the girls and I are really looking forward to this holiday and it'll do them and especially you the world of good."

Under his breath he said. "It will turn my life around, and turn other people's lives around too!"

The silence again was broken a few minutes later when she popped her head around the front room door and politely said. "I am going up to bed, will you be long?" He never replied and just sat there silently, she sighed to herself, then after turning the light off which left him shrouded by the glow of the open fire, then she quietly closed the door and walked up the stairs towards the bedroom.

Picking up his mobile he called his solicitor and asked whether or not the house had definitely been sold. "The purchaser is ready to wire through confirmation of the funds for the purchase, but I asked him to wait until tomorrow because I needed to check with you about the price! Now are you sure Russell that you want to sell at this price? It's crazy, I mean your house is worth over 4 million pounds and your selling it for five hundred thousand pounds, it's no wonder that people are queueing up to buy it." Again he said nothing for a few seconds, the things on his mind were starting to weigh heavily.

"I don't need money, and we're emigrating in a few days so I just want it gone, the British Heart Foundation are coming the day after tomorrow, as for everything that gets left behind. "Just sell it!"

With that he cancelled the call. Replacing the phone back on the arm off the chair, he remained seated and staring at the fire, suddenly tears started to fall from his eyes, but he did not wipe them away, he just sat there and eventually started gently sobbing to himself.

The silence was broken when his phone rang once more, finally wiping away the tears he answered "Hello"

The voice on the other end asked "Russell, are you ok? It sounds like you have been crying?"

He ignored the question and replied with. "What news do you have for me?"

"I have been in contact with the other families from the squad and none of them have got anywhere in relation to getting answers, most of them want to go to high court again to force the issue and there was even talk of going to the International Criminal Court with charges against the Prime Minister, but they have been as have we to the high court so many times only to be told no, that maybe the International Criminal Court maybe the next answer for them!"

Continuing on the unknown voice added "In 2012 the Judges at the Court of Appeal in London ruled that the families could sue the Government for negligence - saying the Ministry of Defence had a duty of care over its personnel even when they were on the battlefield. A woman recently went to the Supreme Court, claiming her case that soldiers like her son should be protected under the European Convention on Human Rights."

"Article one of the convention says everyone has a right to life, additionally, she believes the MOD as her son's employer has a duty of care to those it sends into battle, and as I bet you can gather, the MOD disagrees and believes combat immunity absolves it from providing a duty of care to its personnel"

McDonald felt his inner rage start to surge again, and just simply replied. "Well that doesn't surprise me in the slightest!" After thinking for a few seconds he added, Give them a helping hand with some funds but make sure it is done anonymously please!" then just as before he cancelled the call and went back to staring at the fire.

Chapter 6

The Old School

"Are McSloy and Critchley back yet?" Camberwell asked the young WPC who just walked in the room. "If they are, could you ask them to come in."

Turning to face her he added. "Please if it is not too much trouble, could we have two more coffees and then when you're back I have an important job for you!"

"Yes Sir" She replied with a smile on her face.

Tomlin looked at him quizzically? "What important job can she do for you? She's just a new WPC, obviously not important that's why the station sent her here. Someone to do the general dog's body work!"

Camberwell turn and glared at him. "Look. Listen. Learn. Just because someone is brand new in the job, it does not mean to say they have no use in the case. New people can see things dat we older coppers or copper wannabes from MI5, just over look. Man look, remember when you first got the job at MI5? Didn't you think dat there where some things you could do but no one gave you a chance?"

Tomlin tried to interrupt him. "Yes, but."

Camberwell was having none of it. "Yes but nothing. Man cut people some slack and let me do what you are unable to do, or otherwise MI5 would have you solving this case not me!"

"Right, can we get to work? Good! Right just so you know. When Critchley was bagging the evidence from the office, did you see what he took out of the waste bin?"

Tomlin answered very sheepishly "No"

"Well then you should pay more attention, one of the items was a torn piece of receipt. Dat receipt was from Makro's, more importantly although it was only a small piece of paper, it looked like it had yesterday's date on it plus the store code as well. So dat new WPC will go to the store and collect any evidence from them, as well as a description of the person who shopped there. If possible she will get some video footage as well. Now who's the stupid, useless one? Unless want to go yourself?"

Tomlin said nothing, just standing there looking at the ground. He had been put in his place and he knew it. The tension was broken when McSloy and Critchley walked into the room carrying some sealed evidence bags. After laying them on the table, Tomlin picked up one of the bags then said.

"Well this is one of the items you found in the small waste basket. This piece of paper is from an A4 notebook. It looks very much to me like it was the copy beneath a master copy. We will need to send it to the laboratory to see what comes up when it has been treated by the Indented Restoration Method."

He continued "McSloy and Critchley listen and you'll learn something. The Indented Restoration Method is formed by using The Electrostatic Detection Apparatus (ESDA). This is a special instrument which is capable of restoring handwritten impressions on piece of paper that are completely invisible to the naked eye. A document which needs be tested is placed on the instrument and covered with a sheet of transparent film. The film and sandwiched document are then given a strong electrostatic charge.

The charge dissipates quickly except in those areas where indentations occur. The final step involves applying black toner to the surface of the film which sticks to the charged areas rendering the indented writing visible."

"Impressive, you said all dat without pausing for breath." Camberwell laughingly replied.

McSloy turned to Tomlin and said. "We already knew that Sir, we are in the police force and they taught us that at Hendon Police College. Anyway back to the torn piece of a receipt that's from a Makro's store, and yes it did have yesterday's date on it along with the store reference number. We checked it out and the store number referred to the branch at Charlton."

Camberwell responded by saying "Dat's good, we are going to get the WPC to go and check it out and get a copy of the whole invoice plus any other information and video footage if possible. Anything else I need to know?"

"The rest is only normal run of the mill rubbish, nothing of importance, Sir." He replied.

McSloy then went through the video footage that he took in the warehouse. "Right Sir, the warehouse itself was immaculate and we found nothing in there of any note, well that is apart from this. At first I thought that it may have been actual Uranium powder, but upon closer inspection it looks more like soap powder to me. But why would they have soap powder on the floor when the rest of the place was perfectly clean? Beats me? As I said on the video, this piece of cardboard was trapped in between the fire exit door and the floor. It is as if it got caught whilst someone was sweeping the rubbish out through the fire exit. Again we have taken samples from the other side of the door and they are being checked out."

They looked at the piece of cardboard in the bag, it was about five inches long, three inches wide and lilac in colour, when they turned it over there was no residue on the bottom of it.

"Well it doesn't look like much to me" said Tomlin.

"Well, make sure dat everything is resealed, tagged and photographed again and put the photographs into a folder. It is to be carried with us at all times. Dat way we can go over them now and again to see if we can make any sense of any of it, as we move along." Remarked Camberwell.

Tomlin turned to the dry wipe board and prepared to write. "This is what we know so far."

1/. The suspects names are, Russell McDonald, leader. James Dillon, a convicted bank robber. Who is the third suspect we believe to have bought the mobile phones from Rye Lane? We need to identify him as soon as possible, name is preferable, but a photo will do.

2/. Reason, is revenge on British Army for the death of his brother.

3/. Bomb is a "Dirty Bomb" which needs C4 explosives. Where did they get it? Any been reported missing from anywhere?

4/. Target is Prince Harry and the Duchess of Sussex, who is visiting Peckham on Friday.

5/. They used the Print Village industrial unit as a first port of call. Why?

6/. What is the lilac coloured cardboard from? And does it have any relevance to our case?

7/. What are the crystals found at the Print Village industrial unit? If it is soap powder, again, do they have any relevance to our case??

8/. What is written on that piece of paper from the waste bin, is it of importance?

9/. They went shopping at Makro's at Charlton, for what?

10/. Someone bought 20 or more mobile phones, why?

He continued "At the moment these are the things we have to go on, agreed! Are we missing something, is there a common denominator there that we cannot see?"

With that the door opened and in walked the WPC with a tray of coffee. "Sorry Sir, I did not realise that there was now four of you, I'll go and get two more cups."

Camberwell called her back. "No don't worry about dat at the moment, I have an important job for you to do."

She looked around the room, trying to see who he was talking to, suddenly she realised that he was talking to her. She felt her face go flush red as she replied. "You're talking to me sir! I mean, are you sure you are talking to me, Sir? I thought when you said you had an important job to do earlier I thought you were talking to someone else?"

"Yes, you! What is your name?"

She replied stuttering "Name? Whose name? Oh sorry Sir, my name! My name is Maureen .... WPC Maureen Lackey, sir!"

"Calm down, don't be so nervous. Right I want you to go to Makro's in Charlton, when you get back to the office, use the internet for their full address. When you get there go and see the manager and explain the situation, without explaining the situation. Understand? Okay, get a full copy of dis numbered invoice, then see if they have any video footage of the time of day when dis person signed in. If they haven then bring it here to us."

Continuing he said. "Find out if they have any other information about the person and the items he bought, did he speak to anyone? Did he ask for things dat were out of stock? Because if they were out of stock, we need to find out if and where he got the stuff he needed. Right, let's have you off to the station, then to Makro's."

He asked thoughtfully. "You'll need a car, do you have clearance to drive?"

"A panda car Sir!"

"Okay I'll call the station and ensure dat a car is ready and waiting for you and you tell nothing about what is going on to anyone, anyone at all, irrespective of rank. If they keep on at you, then tell them to contact me. Go on then, what are you waiting for?"

"Yes Sir!" With that she was gone.

Turning round he said. "McSloy, I want you to go and sit on 105B Kings Grove in Peckham, the Asylum Tavern end. Make sure dat you have a mobile printer, just in case we find out whom the new suspect is. Dat is of course, if there is a third suspect. If you need to pee, you get another person to come and take watch but it has to be watched twenty four hours a day, so take the Gas Board van or something. You will need to take a backup video as well and ensure dat your live link is secure, go on then, go!"

Continuing he said. "Critchley, same detail for you but dis time I want you to go to 95 Rainbow Street in Peckham. Now be careful because dat address is two flats, A and B but the same rules apply to you."

Turning back to face Tomlin and his dry wipe board Camberwell said. "To get close enough to plant a bomb dat will cause the maximum blast devastation. It will need to be planted I think, within two hundred yards, three hundred at the maximum. Would you agree?"

Tomlin answered. "Well, a dirty bomb is not a "Weapon of Mass Destruction" but a "Weapon of Mass Disruption, where contamination and anxiety are the terrorist's major objectives. But with enough C4 the radiation cloud will go miles but I think that your right about the blast distance. I think McDonald is trying to cause the maximum disruption along with the maximum damage."

He continued "If we go down to Peckham Square which is where the events start. It is also where Prince Harry and the Duchess will be able to pull up right alongside. We need to measure a three hundred yard radius from there, because that is, somewhere in that area the bomb will be planted."

"I agree, we need to get the local CCTV cameras there to monitor the entrances to the Library and the surrounding area on a twenty four hour basis." Camberwell replied.

Using his radio, he called CCTV control and had them move all the cameras in the area around the library, to focus specifically on Peckham Square. That way they could basically watch the whole area nonstop.

He also confirmed with the control room at Peckham Police Station that WPC Lackey was about to leave for Makro's.

"Right, let's take another look at number ten on your list, why would they want twenty mobile phones?" Camberwell's chain of thought was broken by the sound of Tomlin's mobile telephone ringing. After a few minutes of chatting to the person on the other end of the phone, Tomlin finally spoke. "The Crystals are definitely Soap Powder, Surf Soap Powder to be exact."

Camberwell reacted quizzically by stating. "Why would the unit be totally clean apart from soap powder and why was it only in one area? It does not make sense!"

"Well I don't know how soap powder helps McDonald? He must know sniffer dogs can track the stuff, so what else could it be possibly used for?" Tomlin replied.

"Back to your list, I think dat we can only assume dat the phones are going to be used possibly once then disposed of. We need to get all the local mobile phone shops to notify us should anyone come in to buy a large quantity of phones. For a disposable mobile, even five is a large for any individual to be buying."

Tomlin then went over to the chalkboard and wrote alongside number seven. "Surf Soap Powder! Why? What for?"

"What we need now is to identify dis piece of cardboard. I will assume dat it is from a packet of Surf Soap Powder, but we will need to get it confirmed. Hang On! Do you know if soap powder has any explosive capabilities? If it does it, makes the scenario even worse."

With that they both reached for their mobiles at the same time. When connected they both asked the same question.

"Does soap powder have explosive qualities and we need to know fifteen minutes ago!"

When they had both finished, they just stood looking at one another. Both obviously distraught at the thought of the new and even more deadly angle. After what seemed hours but was only in fact minutes, Tomlin's phone rang.

"What did you find out? Shit! That is the last thing we need to know." Putting the phone down, he said to Camberwell. "Apparently if you mix soap powder together with household matches it will become a highly combustible device, put that together with the dirty bomb. If the damn thing detonates then half of Peckham will be wiped out. Could he have filled the soap powder boxes with matches and other household items, that'll give us a reason for the torn piece of cardboard and the soap powder crystals?"

Camberwell was already reaching for his radio.

"WPC Lackey, can you hear me?"

"Yes Sir!" She answered

"When you get there and get the copy invoice, look at it and tell me immediately whether or not there are matches on the invoice. Immediately, do you understand? Immediately, it's dat important."

Lackey replied. "Yes Sir, I'll be at Makro's in about thirty five minutes, the traffic is quite bad."

Tomlin who was standing next to Camberwell shouted at the phone. "Use the horn, blue lights anything you can but get there in ten minutes. I'll back you up if there are any problems, just get there girl!"

Camberwell added "You heard the man! Get there as soon as you can, okay? Come on Tomlin, let's get to Peckham Square and try to work out what's what! Time is not on our side."

Chapter 7

Makro's

WPC Lackey after finishing her conversation with Camberwell, thought to herself "Oh yes, I can see the headlines. "Unqualified Police Officer Mows Down Six Family Members Including Two Babies!" What was it that the idiot from MI5 said? "There will be no comeback if something goes wrong! Well I am taking no chance."

Using her radio to call control, she asked to be patched through to Greenwich Police Station. Once through, she requested some help to beat the traffic because the way it was going, it would take forever to get to Makro's.

Informing the Chief Inspector that was on duty at Greenwich of her needs and should they wish to confirm that it is a real emergency, the people to contact, she then asked for two police motorcyclists to come and help her get through the traffic.

After a few seconds the Chief Inspector acknowledged her requirements and she was told to wait until her support got there and then proceed with their help and a lot of caution, she thanked him then settled down to wait.

"Why would Camberwell be so desperate to know whether or not the suspect bought matches? These day's people use mobile phone technology to detonate bombs not household matches."

Her train of thought was broken by the sound of police sirens wailing and screeching further up the road. She had turned her engine off as the queue she was in was not moving, so she restarted her engines in readiness to pull away when her escort arrived.

She was frustrated and disappointed to see two rapid response police cars speed past her like speed itself was going out of fashion.

Talking to herself. "I wonder where they are going in such a rush. Could it be anything to do with what Camberwell and Slim Jim from MI5 are working on? Well, all I can do is sit and wait for assistance."

Ten minutes passed and still no sign of the motorcycles and to make her feel even worse the traffic queue she was in still had not moved an inch.

Suddenly from behind her came two police motorcycles, their sirens sounding like hell itself. One pulled up behind her leaving her enough room to pull out, the other indicated to the car in front of her to move up so that she could pull out into the opposite side of the road.

Off they went, forcing oncoming vehicles to pull into the kerb and sometimes the escort behind her would shoot off into the distance to what was obviously the next major junction, to keep it clear so that they could just drive straight through it without the necessity of stopping. They had covered more distance in the last two minutes than she had on her own in thirty minutes.

As they approached the old Greenwich Hospital, the rear escort once again shot ahead to clear the way. Suddenly a van pulled straight out into the path of her car forcing it to skid and it hit the nearside front of a parked vehicle, from what she could see in the brief moment she passed him by, he wasn't happy!.

Her escort who was in front of her stopped and then waved her on through, then he set about berating the van driver over his driving standards.

After reaching the old Greenwich Hospital the road became quite clear and even though now she only had one escort, they easily reached Makro's with no further trouble at all.

When they pulled up outside, the remaining escort walked over to her and informed her that the van driver thought she was being chased and decided to help stop her.

All he got for his good deeds and trouble was a ticket for driving with undue care and attention and a hefty repair bill, because of the damage to his van and the parked vehicle. When WPC Lackey stepped out of her car, she went and spoke to the police motorcyclists and asked him to wait for her, just in case she needed help getting back to Peckham in a hurry.

Walking into Makro's, Lackey was distracted by a garden furniture set that was in the entrance. She stopped to look it over. "Not bad and only one hundred and twenty five pounds, that's cheap. I may have to see if I can afford to come back and buy that." She thought to herself.

Suddenly her radio barked into life. "WPC Lackey, have you arrived at Makro's yet?"

She replied. "I am just going in, Sir, I will give you a call back in a few minutes."

At the help desk she asked to speak to the store manager. After being told he was on his break, she started to lay the law down to the staff. "What do you mean, he's on his break? Do you think that I have come all the way here just for the good of my health! Now go and get him and tell him that if he refuses to come and see me, that I will arrest him for perverting the course of justice! Now go and get him here quick!"

The member of staff nearest to the entrance of the help desk, shot off like a scalded cat.

The manager came rushing to the helpdesk. "Mr. Ravi Younis, Makro Charlton Store Manager. How may I help you?"

Lackey replied. "Firstly do your staff understand that when a uniformed police officer enters your store and asks for you, that it is for a reason?"

Younis answered "All members of staff have been trained to accommodate any police officer in any situation and I will be dealing with all members of staff when I have finished with your inquiries. Shall we go to my office?"

Once there, she then produced a copy of the piece of receipt that Critchley had found in the waste basket. "We need very urgently a complete copy of this invoice, and we need it like ten minutes ago!" Younis picked up his phone and asked a member of staff to come in, he then asked "Why, was the request not phoned through?"

She replied. "We needed to come and try and get descriptions of the man who actually came and did the shopping. Also we need to collect any video footage from the tills area at the time that the invoice was timed at. I wanted as well to speak to members of staff. I need to check their reactions when asked about the man, you never know there may be someone here who knows him, and we cannot take the chance of them alerting him to the fact that we have been investigating him."

There was a knock at the door. "Enter!" he said. A young Asian lady entered and he told her what was needed and asked her to get back to him as soon as possible, with that she left the office. Lackey sat down in the chair and whilst waiting for the person to return she asked Younis about the possibility of being able to purchase the set of garden furniture.

"Most definitely, we can do a deal for you. Officially you are meant to be a retailer as the general public cannot walk in and buy, but as a special favour for the Metropolitan Police, I will work something out. Don't worry about the cost, we shall do a special deal just for you! Come to see me Saturday and we shall sort it out! Come on whilst we are waiting let us go and have a cup of coffee, we sell really nice coffee here."

She radioed Camberwell and told him. "It should be no more than five minutes until I have obtained a copy of the invoice. They are also searching for any available video footage as well.

Once I have given you the details about the contents of the invoice and any video footage that is available, I am going to send it back with the police motorcyclist. That way it will be returned to you a lot quicker because of the traffic. Then I am going to speak to any members of staff that were working yesterday, to see if I can get any further information. I will report back to you when I have finished, if that is okay with you?"

She was just about to start drinking her coffee when the young Asian lady came back with a copy of the torn invoice.

"Nothing special on it, were you looking for anything in particular?" she said.

Lackey answered curtly. "Don't worry about that, just pass me the copy invoice. Thank you very much."

She opened up the folded piece of paper to reveal a copy of the invoice. The suspect had bought the following items.

40 big boxes of Surf soap powder.
30 boxes of mixed walkers crisps.
30 sleeves of salted peanuts.
30 sleeves of dry roasted peanuts.
10000 Benson and Hedges Cigarettes.

She checked out the name of the person who had actually been and done the shopping. The Makro card itself was registered to a Company called McDonald Internet Enterprises.

Also the woman had copied the details of the trade card application form. Mr. Shaun Jackson was the name on the card. The registered address was in Camberwell.

She reached for her radio and then called Camberwell. "WPC Lackey here Sir, I have the copy invoice here and there are no household matches on it. But I have the person's details that they registered with when they joined Makro's… Yes Sir, that person's name is Mr. Shaun Jackson, aged 39. The card itself was registered to a Company called McDonald Internet Enterprises. Registered address is 52 Rainbow Street, Camberwell London SE5." She then read out the list of items that the suspect had bought.

Camberwell said to her. "That's the address we have under surveillance, it was a hunch so glad we got someone there." Then he asked her. "How long before your get back?"

Answering Camberwell's question she said. "I am just waiting for the video footage! Hold on, here it comes! Right away Sir, I am going to give it to the motorcyclist who will get it to you straight away. Then I am going to get on and start interviewing the staff here, thank you sir. Speak to you soon, sir. Goodbye!"

Turning to Younis, she told him that she was going to give the stuff to the waiting police motorcyclist, then she was coming back to start speaking to any staff who were on duty at the time that Jackson was shopping.

She requested that he find her a quiet space to work in and could she have the first few members of staff there waiting for her to return.

When she returned she found that the space that she was given was a large broom cupboard. As she entered the cupboard, she thought to herself. "Great, I know I asked for a quiet space but a cupboard? Oh well better get on with it.

"She beckoned the first member of staff in. "Please may I take your name? How long have you worked here? Do you know this person?" She asked the same questions to all the members of staff that were sent to see her. They all replied with the same answer. "No!"

After forty five minutes of questioning people she felt like a break. How many more members of staff are waiting to see her outside she asked?

"Three" was the reply.

"Can you please ask them to wait for a few minutes more as I definitely need a coffee and toilet break!"

After she had finished her coffee she returned to the luxurious splendour of the broom cupboard. Speaking to a young lady, she said. "Please give me one minute to get myself sorted then come in."

Entering the office she radioed Inspector Camberwell and asked whether or not he had received the package yet? Good.

"I shall be about thirty minutes before I leave here to return to Peckham.
Should I go to the station or should I go straight to the Old School? Old School, yes sir! I'll let you know when I am leaving or if anything comes up I will get back to you sir. Goodbye."

There was a knock at the door. "Come in." She then started to ask the same questions that she had previously asked the other members of staff. "What is your name?"

"Karen Westbrooke." The lady replied.

Showing her a picture of Shaun Jackson, she asked. "Do you know this person?" She was taken aback when the lady answered.

"Yes he is my partner, well partner of sorts. We meet up three to four time a week. Why?"

Lackey said. "Please hang on here a second, I will be back in a minute." She then left the room and went and found Ravi Younis.

"Sir, I need you to baby sit one of your staff for about five minutes while I finish questioning the last two members of staff. I do not want her speaking to, or telephoning anyone. She has to be incommunicado, is that understood?"

He just nodded and she turned and walked back to the broom cupboard.

Lackey called Inspector Camberwell, explaining that she was bringing Karen Westbrooke in for him and Tomlin to question. Then she called Greenwich Police station and asked for an unmarked car to come and collect herself and Karen Westbrooke and take them to the Old School, as well as a spare driver who could drive the panda back to Peckham Police Station.

Returning to Younis's office, she politely asked him to leave as this conversation was confidential.

Westbrooke asked her what was going on. Lackey replied by asking. "Do you have any young children at home that would need to be taken care of?"

"No!"

Lackey continued "What can you tell me about Shaun Jackson? Where do you meet? Had she ever been to any of the premises in the Camberwell, Peckham and East Dulwich area? Had he ever abused her?"

Westbrooke who was obviously upset replied. "Am I under arrest? I have done nothing wrong, and he has always been a perfect gentleman to me. No I don't have any young children at home. What the hell is going on? Do I need a lawyer?"

Lackey responded by saying that "You would need to come with me, as there would be more questions that you could help our enquiries with."

Karen Westbrooke was quite composed, not seeming to get upset in any way. "I will help you all I can, I have nothing to hide but you have to explain to me what is going on!"

Lackey said. "Well they will explain more to you when we get back to Peckham and see Inspector Camberwell.

When the transport arrived, both women were lead out the back entrance of the store. After getting into the car, Lackey told the driver. "Hang on I'll be back in a second." Rushing back into the store she went and found Ravi Younis.

She saw him in the stores reception area, as she approached him she said. "Sir, I'll be coming back on Saturday morning about the garden furniture."

He replied "No problem, I will be more than happy to see you then and again don't worry about the price, I'll do a really good deal for you!" With that she was gone again, straight into the car and on their way to the Old School at Peckham.

Chapter 8

Peckham Square

As WPC Lackey arrived at Makro's, Camberwell and Tomlin were walking to Peckham Library, when he received the message from her. "The name of the person who bought the goods was a Mr. Shaun Jackson. The address registered at Makro's is given as 52 Rainbow Street, Camberwell London SE5."

Camberwell recognized the name at once, turning to Tomlin he stated. "Shaun Jackson, I thought he may have been involved but I have to say that we have had no run ins with him lately and I haven't seen him around dis area for almost a year, but have been hearing loads of rumours. Last time he was around here, he got arrested and sent down for ABH (Actual Bodily Harm). He assaulted three young boys aged thirteen who were taking the mickey out of him, he broke two of the boy's arms whilst giving the third one a clip round the ear. He got eighteen months with six months suspended for dat. He was out within three months because of time served. He always claimed dat they tried to mug him, so he dished out his own form of justice. He was quite possibly telling the truth too, as the three boys were also local toe rags."

He continued. "We already have his address under surveillance because of the rumours that have been circulating. Critchley is watching there, so should anything untoward happen we are already on the scene."

Tomlin responded with "Nice class of new young thugs then growing up here in South East London what? Anyway at least no household matches were on the invoice, which eases my mind a bit.

Thing is though, why would he need 40 big boxes of Surf soap powder but no matches? Why would he need loads of peanuts? Why would he need all those crisps and cigarettes? This is getting weirder by the second! We also got the registration number of his van SRJ 2008, which comes back as a white Ford Transit Van."

Upon arriving at Peckham Square, they both stood and surveyed the area. Tomlin was the first to speak. "Where would you plant a device close enough to ensure that the royals were killed? It would be easy to plant it with the intention of causing the maximum damage and confusion but they are out to kill them, not injure them. I mean this area will be full of people and performers, so they are also potential fatal casualties. It has to be somewhere up close and personal. We can obviously use the sniffer dogs all over the place, even up to the minute that Harry gets here, but I cannot see anything that looks like a possible place to plant a device aimed specifically at killing him, and if soap powder is going to be part of it, then there's an issue all of its own as almost every shop here sells it, so what are going to do? Take all the soap powder away from all the shops until the royals leave?"

Camberwell responded by saying. "From tomorrow onwards all personal entering or leaving the library will be searched and have their hands swabbed for explosive residue. Every single item dat is carried in there will also be searched and sniffer dogs used. Basically you will have to be whiter than white to enter the library no pun intended, so I don't think the attack will come from there. All the waste bins around dis square are going to be removed for the day, so dat solves another problem. The local traffic will be diverted around the area whilst the royals are here."

Continuing he said.

"Buses will be held up for the fifteen minutes dat they are outside the library here in the square, once they are in the library they will be allowed through again.dat is until they are ready to depart. Then they will be stopped again. So dat solves a third problem, mind you though, dat is if they still come!"

"They'll still come." Tomlin answered. "They will not want to let anyone down, but although we are still waiting to hear from the Palace, I can feel it in my bones, they'll still bloody well come!"

Camberwell stood there looking around, trying to visualize a rough radius of three hundred yards. Nothing behind him seemed dangerous.

Speaking out loud. "Whitton Timber is just over there, but although a blast would cause damage, there are buildings between there and here. Prince Harry or the Duchess may get injured, but it has to be a lot closer than dat if it is aimed to kill him or her!"

Looking at the shops across the road from Peckham Square, Tomlin asked. "Any idea of how long those shops have been there? Are any of them overnight businesses?"

Camberwell looked at Tomlin with a quizzical look on his face. "Overnight businesses? What do you mean by dat? Do you mean, have any started up in business, say in the last three months or so?"

Tomlin nodded. "Well in answer to your question, no! They have all been here for at least five years, so I don't think the threat will come from them. We are missing something, something so simple dat when we find it, the case will be blown wide open."

Tomlin had a sudden urge to call the two young PC's that had earlier given him the information about the disposable mobile phones.

"I'd better give the young Cox brothers a call to see if they have found out anything else from the mobile phone guy, if that's all right with you?"

With that he borrowed Camberwell's radio and called them. "Hi Tomlin here, which Officer Cox am I speaking to? Ok. Anyway have you managed to find out anything else at all from the shopkeeper? Okay. Well that's a start, keep at it and let us know if you come across anything. I am going to have to think of some nicknames to call you two, otherwise it will be murder trying to remember who is who whilst this is going on."

There was obviously a response because Tomlin then spoke out loud so Camberwell could hear. "Oh the good looking one! If you say so!" With that he handed the radio back to Camberwell.

Looking at Camberwell, he said. "Well the shopkeeper cannot remember anything new, but the. "Good looking one" and his brother will stay on his case in the hope dat he remembers something."

"Don't you mean Doris and George? "Doris is the nickname for Simon Cox and George is Glen Cox's new nickname, I gave them those so I'll remember who I'm talking to."

Camberwell's radio crackled and interrupted the silence, Oh, hi Officer Lackey. What is her name? Karen Westbrooke! Well, get her back to the Old School. We have about another thirty minutes here then we will start making our way back there. Ok and by the way, well done indeed!"

"See what I mean about trusting in the new blood in the force? Instead of just going to Makro's and getting the copy invoice and video tapes, she went in and asked questions. She has discovered dat Jackson's supposed partner, girl friend or whatever they call each other nowadays, works at Makro's. So she is bringing her in for questioning." Camberwell remarked.

"Let's just hope she will be of some use." Tomlin mumbled under his breath.

Tomlin started to say. "McIntosh, changing the subject....."

"Hold on, call me Camberwell, everyone calls me dat and I seem to respond to it easier than my actual name. Now you were saying?"

Tomlin squirmed with embarrassment as he started to say again. "Camberwell, do you know where or if any drains run under here? If not I can get onto Southwark Council Planning Department, for any plans that they have, we will also need to find out if there are any maintenance tunnels going underneath here, also whether or not it they are accessible for humans. I think we better get someone to check out and guard the man holes from today onwards. I now it is a bit of overkill but we have to take drastic preventative measures in this case."

"Well you had better have the man power to baby sit manholes, as we don't and how do we explain to the tax payers dat we spent thousands of pounds in overtime for officers just to sit and watch man hole covers for three days. Also I don't know anything about the sewers."

Tomlin didn't reply he just out his mobile and phoned Southwark Council.

After finishing speaking to the planning office at Southwark Council, Tomlin said. "Have you heard back from the laboratory regarding the piece of paper?" Camberwell didn't answer him, he just stood there obviously deep in thought. "Camberwell!" Tomlin shouted "Did you hear me?"

"Sorry! What? Sorry I was miles away. I was thinking about something, what did you say?" "Have you heard from the laboratory yet?"

"No. It is on my list of things to check out when we get back to the Old School. By the way I was thinking back to what WPC Lackey said was on dat invoice. If you were buying such a big quantity of snack foods, they would need to be for someone, correct?" Camberwell queried.

Continuing to think out loud, he said. "Sweet shops possibly, corner shops or public houses, but we cannot check every single shop or public house within dis area, we'd be still checking them out dis time next year."

Tomlin was really listening and he carried on saying what he had started to say. "Oh yes, by the way, the council are going to get back to us, regarding drains and any plans of them that they have."

Turning round Camberwell said. "Let's try and look at dis logically. We have the Mantis Bar just round the corner, close enough to cause injury but close enough to kill the royals? I think not, on one corner of Rye Lane we have the Subway Sandwich Bar and then on the near side of Rye Lane we have Mk1 the clothing shop. Then we have Kumasi Markets at no 74 followed by The Flower Shop at 76. We have the Jewellers at 78. At no 80 there is LLC Nails. The rest are just normal shops, all selling a variety of goods and again it would be just like checking all the local public houses. Pointless!"

Tomlin started to walk away from Peckham Square saying "The only one with anything outside is the Flower Shop and even then there is nothing there that is big enough to hide a five to six pound bomb. Where on earth can a device of that size be hidden? Come on Camberwell let's get back to the Old School. You never know, the walk may clear our heads. By the way do you want a coffee if we find a café on the way back? By the way it's your turn to pay!"

They were taking one last look round Peckham Square before starting back when Camberwell noticed something very strange, something that seemed really out of place too him. Attached to the telephone junction box that was just round the corner was a small metallic box about fifteen inches wide by six inches deep and fifteen inches tall. Part of it had started to come away from the actual junction box itself. He made his way over to it then after kneeling down to have a closer look he noticed some wires going from one box to the other.

After getting Peckham Police Station control to contact British Telecom, asking them to get their chief maintenance supervisor to call him on his mobile, Camberwell turned to Tomlin. "Well I wonder what it is for. I have never seen anything like dis before."

Camberwell's mobile phone rang. "Yes, dis is Inspector Camberwell speaking! Hi. Question for you, I am in Peckham Square and I have come across one of your green junction boxes dat has something attached to it, when I inspected it closer, there seems to be some wiring going from one box to the other. Is it a new thing dat you at BT are bringing out? Okay, dat's fine. The serial number on the attached box is PM23FR678. Okay I'll wait."

Whilst waiting for the person at the other end of the phone to come back to him.

He started to tell him what he had been told. He was just about to explain about the serial number when he was interrupted by the telephone.

"Hi, yes I am still here. Right okay, do you have anyone local who can come and deal with dat immediately as we are checking the place out for the royal visit on Friday. Okay I will wait for them. Oh by the way please can I take a note of your name and telephone number? ……Got dat! Is dat your direct number? Okay, many thanks, speak soon."

He turned to face Tomlin and said. "Right where was I, oh yes. Apparently it is a new system dat they are currently trying! It is a visual thing dat allows the engineer to be signalled dat work needs doing to the junction box. It is supposed to send an engineer an automatic signal saying what work needs to be done or if there any new faults in the junction box as they drive past. It flashes up on a machine dat has a display unit fitted to the dashboard of the van. A yellow signal is for unfinished work, red is for a new fault and green means dat everything is okay and the box can be removed."

He continued seemingly without pausing for breath. "They are also given a serial number dat can be referred to online. Apparently dis box is due to be removed Friday at 8am but I have asked for it to be removed today. Mainly it is used for housing extra telephone line numbers, until the engineer comes and fits them in properly. They are sending an engineer any time now."

Within five minutes a BT van pulled up and out of the passenger door stepped an engineer. As the van went to drive away he could be heard shouting to the driver. "Be back in ten minutes to pick me up!"

Camberwell and Tomlin stood across the other side of Peckham High Street and watched as the engineer fiddled with the wires and then finally started to take the extra box off the side of the junction box.

Precisely ten minutes later, the BT van was back again it then picked up the engineer and then they were gone. Tomlin added. "It's a pity we can't catch crooks or terrorists as quick as that!"

Camberwell just laughed then added. "Come on let's get back to the Old School because we have got work to do!"

Chapter 9

Polite Interview

By the time Camberwell and Tomlin got back to the Old School, the police car containing WPC Lackey and Karen Westbrooke had already arrived. Tomlin went off to check with the laboratory about any possible results on the notepaper. Camberwell asked a uniformed officer what room the two women were in. "Classroom four, Sir." Came the reply.

Entering the room he was surprised about the appearance of Karen Westbrooke. For some reason in his mind she would be about five foot two inches tall, overweight and most definitely quite obnoxious, but she was actually five foot eleven inches, approximately 130 pounds, quite pretty without the need of make-up and she seemed to have a lot of self-confidence. She seemed to glide around the room not walk.

Eyeing her up for a few seconds, his train of thought was thrown out of the window by Westbrooke. "Please sir, could you explain why I am here?" There was no anger in her voice, just firm politeness which threw him a bit.

"Please sit down. Thank you, before we start, would you consent to having your house searched?"

"Why do you want to search my house, you say you have only brought me here because I know Shaun. Now you are asking me to give permission to search my house. Why? I want answers before I say any more or I want my call to a lawyer!"

WPC Lackey interrupted. "You say you have nothing to hide, so why can't we search your house?"

Westbrooke just sat there and said nothing.

Camberwell asked. "You know Shaun Jackson, yes? How well do you know him and I mean really know him?"

She replied, again with no hint of anger, just firm politeness. "When you answer my question I will answer yours and in the scheme of things I asked first!"

"Just answer Inspector Camberwell's questions and then we can all go home." WPC Lackey, interrupted again.

"Officer would you please, go and get me a nice cup of coffee, I think I'd better have two sugars please. Karen, would you like a drink as well?"

She nodded and said. "A can of caffeine free Coke would be nice, thank you." Lackey turned round and looked stony faced at Westbrooke then left the room without saying a word. Westbrooke then turned to Camberwell.

"Look I don't know what my Shaun has done, but it cannot be as bad as all this seems to make out. So as I said, if you answer my question I will honestly answer yours."

Camberwell studied her, thinking to himself at the same time. "She is definitely not what I thought she would be like. She is obviously very bright and has been brought up well. From dis area, I think not! Do I dare trust you with the truth? It would mean dat for a few days that you would be kept here, unable to contact anyone until dis is resolved. We cannot take a chance on you letting him or anyone else dat knows him, where you are and why!"

Sitting back in her chair with her arms crossed she said. "Look I told you, you tell me the truth and I will tell you the truth. So it is up to you? You have a choice!"

Camberwell knew that he needed to confide in her, otherwise this would take too long and time was running out fast! Feeling frustrated that they were backed into a corner he spoke. "We believe dat Shaun is part of a group of people dat are going to try and kill Prince Harry and the Duchess of Sussex!"

Showing the first signs of anger and frustration she jumped up and protested. "You are having a laugh! There is no way he could be involved with that, no way at all! Also why would he want to kill Prince Harry and the Duchess? Sorry but you are mistaken!"

With that she sat down again only this time she slumped down more than sat down. Camberwell went on to explain all the evidence that they had against Jackson. Every time he outlined the different evidence, she protested even more.

Camberwell asked her whether or not she knew about the visit to Peckham by Prince Harry. She replied. "She did know because her niece was a member of one of the dance troupes that was chosen to perform a Caribbean dance who for the Prince. Why was that important?"

"How long have you had a relationship with Jackson?" He queried.

"About nine months, as I told your WPC He has always been a perfect gentleman to me!"

He continued to question her about their relationship.

"Did you ever go to Rainbow Street in Camberwell? Did you ever meet his friends? Had she ever met Russell McDonald or James Dillon? How did she meet Jackson?"

Westbrooke snapped back at Camberwell. "I don't even know where Rainbow Street is! The only place apart from my own home that I have met Shaun is in East Dulwich and no she had never heard of either McDonald or Dillon. When we meet, we normally spend the nights at home or at his house in Upland Road alone. Are you sure that were talking about the same Shaun Jackson? And before you ask it is no 36 Upland Road, it is just a normal house and Shaun has nothing flash in it at all."

Camberwell then asked her about her background. "Where are you from?"

"I was born in Morocco but came here when I was twelve years old. I had a bad marriage but apart from that, there is nothing special about me at all."

The door opened and in walked WPC Lackey with the coffee and the coke. "Mr. Tomlin said that he will be with you very shortly." Do you want me to stay or is there anything else that you would like me to do?" She asked.

Camberwell did not answer, instead he turned back to Westbrooke and said. "So now I have now answered your question I ask you again, are you willing to have your home searched? We can arrange dat a neighbour or relative is present whilst we do it?

Westbrooke replied by saying. "Yes okay but I do not want anyone going there in uniform, I do not want any neighbours getting wind of what is going on. My private life is personal to me. And I want to be there whilst it is being searched. I have nothing to hide, plus I want to get a change of clothes."

"Well we cannot let you leave here just in case you are seen with us and it gets back to Jackson. If you write your address down and a list of clothes dat you want and where they can be found, WPC lackey will bring them back for you. Is dat agreeable?"

"Well it seems as if I have no choice in the matter, doesn't it? My front door keys are in my inside jacket pocket. What will happen about work? Is this going to cost me my job?"

Lackey replied. "Well if you have done nothing wrong as you say, there won't be a problem. How far do you live from work?"

"I live about a mile away." Westbrooke replied.

Camberwell asked her what sort of car Jackson drove. To which she replied "As far as I know, he does not drive a car he drives a white transit van." Camberwell said nothing else for about two minutes, instead he just stared at the notes he had taken."

"Please wait here for a second. WPC Lackey would you step outside with me for a second?" With that they both went outside and Camberwell reiterated to her that.

"Everything is to be thoroughly searched, ensuring dat everything is put back tidy and under no circumstances is there to be any damage at all."

Continuing he added.

"If you find nothing, call back into Makro's and speak to the manager and explain dat she will not be back to work for a few days. Tell him that she is not under arrest but helping us with our enquiries. If you find anything at all dat is out of place and you think may be important, then radio Me, now get changed at the station and get going.

Take somebody else with you, but get a move on. It is getting late and we need any information dat we can get."

Using his mobile phone Camberwell called Critchley, who was on undercover duty at Rainbow Street.

"Camberwell here, have you anything to report? Okay, we are going to change people around as we have got a new address that needs sitting on. Got a pen and paper? 36 Upland Road, SE22, we have reason to believe dat Jackson will be holed up there. So we need you to go there, we'll get somebody else to replace you at rainbow Street. What I suggest is dat you get Mick McCarthy to replace you there and get Glen King to initially go to Upland Road, until say midnight. It means you can go and grab a couple of hours sleep. Okay, if anything comes up let me know and tell King to do the same."

Returning to the room, he continued to ask Westbrooke about how and where they met. "We first met at Makro's while he was shopping and after a few meetings, he had asked her out. Because of my shift work, we only meet two to three times a week and we are both relatively happy with the arrangement."

Tomlin walked into the room and said to Westbrooke. "We have seen from the video footage taken from Makro's that he drives a white Ford Transit van, registration number SRJ 2008. Do you know where he keeps it at night?"

She said. "He had told me that he had a lock up garage somewhere close by, but I do not know where."

"When was the last time that you saw him? When are you due to see him next?" Tomlin added.

Westbrooke answered. "I last saw him yesterday morning at work but socially, I saw him last Saturday in his house at Upland Road. We have arranged to meet next Saturday, because he told me that he was going to have to work away for a few days and his return to town would be in the middle of the week, but that coincided with me working late nights."

Reading out the list of items that were on the invoice from Makro's, Camberwell asked her "What would he want all these items for? You have to admit dat it is a hell of a lot of stuff, especially the soap powder! Do you know what he does for a living?"

She said nothing for a moment, thinking before she answered. "Well he told me that he buys and sells things like that to local shops, he goes and does the bulk buys for shops. Which in turn saves them the time and cost of going, he adds on about fifteen percent for doing it, he earns a good living doing it."

"Does he work for anyone or does he work with anyone else?" Tomlin queried.

"No, he does it himself and he is self-employed, I think." She replied.

Tomlin added "Did he tell you that he owns the van? It's just that the van is registered to a Mr. Russell McDonald. Also it's registered to an address in Rainbow Street Peckham!" For the first time in the whole of the interview her voice, became a little bit strained.

"Look I don't know who you are, but I am going to tell you the same as I told him over there! I don't know nor ever heard of someone called Russell McDonald or James Dillon. You can either believe me or not! I have tried to be totally honest with you in all my answers, so enough is enough now. I am hungry, tired and want to sleep. You guys want me to stay around, to which I have agreed. So now this interview is over, any other questions will have to wait until tomorrow."

As she go up and went to leave the room, Camberwell asked her to wait here and he will get someone to take her, eventually she left the room escorted by two WPC's who took her to a room where she relax and wash and change clothes.

As the WPC's started to leave Camberwell said to them to get her anything she needs but she must remain incommunicado and there must always be 2 WPC's with her at all times.

Then he turned to Tomlin and asked about the results from the paper test. "They said that the paper was really badly creased but they are hopeful to have something by tomorrow or worse case scenario Thursday."

"Thursday! Dat's pointless, can't they do it any faster? Dat will give us just over a day to investigate anything written on there!"

"They are working on it, is all I have been told and they are going as fast as they can. They have managed to show some words but nothing at all that makes sense. Those words are, Banjul something? Further down the page the word Agadir appears. But more than that they can't tell. I have sent someone back to Thames House to see if any of the people there can make head or tail of them, but in truth we really need more."

Continuing on he added "We seem to be going nowhere fast, everything seems to be tempting us but giving us nothing complete to work on. For instance, soap powder and loads of it. Crisps and loads of them. Peanuts and loads of Benson and Hedges Cigarettes as well. Now I know Miss Westbrooke says that Jackson resells them, but it just seems very strange and do we visit every shop in Peckham asking them if they deal with Jackson."

Camberwell took his usual thought process pose before speaking. "No dat is correct, but we only need to check with all the shops along the part of Peckham High Street dat faces Peckham Square! We can do dat tomorrow morning. What I need to do now is get some sleep. So do you. Come on I'll please the wife by letting you crash at my place, then if anything comes up we don't waste time get back to here. Everyone knows what to do. McSloy and Critchley are house watching. WPC Lackey is searching Westbrooke's house and she'll call if she finds anything, but to be truthful I don't think she will, so there's not much more we can do today."

Chapter 10

Bats

As he was sitting in his van outside 105b Kings Grove, Paul McSloy became desperate to go to the toilet. Even though the Asylum Public House was right behind him, he knew it was more than his life was worth if he got caught. But he was seriously considering it, that was how much discomfort he was in. It didn't make any sense to him at all, the Asylum was definitely serving after hours and he was sure that it would make no difference all to the surveillance operation that he was on. For Christ's sake, it was 2am on a cold and wet Wednesday December morning.

It was no good, he just had to go to the loo and it wasn't like he just needed to pee, that he could have done in one of the empty coke bottles that littered the van, but he needed to go number two's. He slid open the side door of the van, stepped out into the bitter cold and driving rain. It hit him just like someone was slapping a wet fish across his face. Sliding the door shut again, the rain already starting to run down his face.

For some reason he stopped and paused to look at the sign writing on the side of the van. In big bold letters were the words, London Bat Mobile Research Vehicle. Hmmn he thought to himself. "I know they were out of British Gas vans, but London Bat Mobile Research Vehicle! Where the heck do they dream up these names? I mean they have even gone as far as having leaflets made up depicting what it was all about."

If anyone asked him, he just answered "Sorry this is my first day and I have drawn the short straw and been given the night shift."

Mind you it made sense really because it would explain all the video cameras and night vision equipment.

He was just about to walk away from the van when a car turned into Kings Grove.

Turning round as if to open the passenger door, just in case the person driving wondered what he was doing. Next thing he knew, the car pulled up alongside his van. A slim man got out of the car, turned as if to walk away. As McSloy went to open the door of the van he noticed that the man had turned round and was now approaching him.

When he got closer the man said. "Well you have a great job! Been here long?"

McSloy replied "Too long! New to the job today, typical, give the new boy the night shift. Are you interested in Bats? You can have a leaflet if you want one? It gives you all the details about it. The species we are researching tonight are the Noctule, Nyctalus Noctula. Tell you what? Somewhere on here they say you can even sponsor a bat! Don't really know how you can sponsor an individual bat. It's more likely to be a colony of bats."

"Err, thanks but no thanks, well I hope it is worth all your effort. Goodnight!" Dillon replied. With that he turned and walked across the road into 105b. Well that was with no doubt James Dillon, smart, so smart in fact that he is still using his old address.

McSloy got back into the van, forgetting everything about the fact that he needed to go to the toilet. Picking up his notepad he made a note. Suspect entered the premises at 2:05 am Wednesday morning, the car the suspect was using is a Citroen C2, registration number JPD 1967.

Obviously it had to be a private plate. Still I'd better check with station control too see if it is registered to him.

So straight away he got onto station control at Peckham Police Station and requested a registration check, he also asked if someone was around who could let him have a toilet break.

"No was their response, there was no one. All available units have been sent to sort out a fight outside the McDonalds Hamburger Bar in Camberwell Green."

"Typical, I bet McDonald has something to do with it. He always has something to do with everything illegal that goes on in the Peckham and Camberwell area." He said to himself.

He was taken aback when station control told him that the registered owner came back as Russell McDonald. "Mind you that does not really surprise me, as there is nothing like keeping it in the family" he thought. Making a note of it in the notebook that he was using, he wrote. "Does McDonald own the flat as well? Check land registry in the morning!"

Realising that he still needed to go to the toilet, he exited the van. Ensuring that it was locked, he then walked around the corner to the door of the Asylum Pub. By the time he got there, he was soaking wet from the driving rain. When he returned less than five minutes later, he stood dripping wet and frozen with horror. "The car had gone! Shit! How was he going to explain that?"

He started to write down what had happened on a new sheet of paper, he had to take a toilet break but due to unforeseen circumstances, there was no one to come and relieve him, whilst he went.

But he had become so desperate to go, that he had no choice but to leave the van and go to the toilet in the Asylum Public House. Upon returning to his van found the suspect's car had gone.

Suddenly a car right turned into the Cul de Sac from Meeting House Lane. Jumping into the front of the van and making out he was entering some details into a logbook, just in case it was Dillon. He was relieved to see it was.

Where had he been? He had not been gone long! All sorts of thoughts were going through his head, when he heard a tap on the window.

"God man, you look frozen! Are you ok? I had to run to the all night store, to get some milk, because it is such a really cold, wet and miserable night, I thought you might like a cup of hot coffee and a salad roll! Especially if you're going to sit there and freeze your rocks off all night. Sugars are in the bag, hope it is all right. Seen anything of interest yet? Blimey, you're dripping wet. Hope it was worth it! Do you want to borrow a towel?"

Thinking quickly, he replied. "Yes more than you know. The interesting thing is that there is one particular bat that keeps flying in and out of the street. I was just wondering where he goes, so I got out to have a look, to see if I could see where he went? You must have just missed him, because he's literally just flown back. Getting absolutely drenched for all my time and effort, I'll be lucky if I don't end up with pneumonia, mind you I do have a drop of brandy in a hip flask so I will add that to the coffee and make a hot toddy. Anyway, how much do I owe for the stuff? It really is very much appreciated."

Walking away Dillon answered. "Well if he has any sense he'll stay at home and go to bed, just like me. Don't worry about the coffee, just doing a nice turn to someone that's all."

McSloy was visibly shocked, could this really be a potential terrorist bomber? This man had taken the time and trouble to think of someone else on a night like this. Hold on! Has he sussed me out, have I blown my cover in anyway? Is the coffee drugged? Is the food poisoned? But how could he have sussed me, when it is the first time that he has been here all afternoon and night. It does not make sense. I'd better write that down just in case, even though no one in their right mind will ever believe me.

At 4am the phone tap machine in the van clicked loudly, and it made McSloy Jump, he had started to nod off. Suddenly a voice made the van come alive. McSloy jumped up and banged his head on the roof of the van as he was rushing to put his headphones on.

"JD, is everything all right? When you went home yesterday, did you make sure that you went the long way and you were not followed?"

Dillon replied very sleepily "Russell, do you know what the bloody time is? Of course I went the long way home and yes I ensured that I was not followed! For Christ's sake Russ! Could this not have waited until we spoke in the morning? I am absolutely knackered and I really need my beauty sleep."

McDonald answered. "Sorry, I just could not sleep, so thought I'd just phone you. Go back to sleep, I'll speak to you properly later. I'm just going to check in with Shaun!"

The phone line went dead, turning to look at the phone tracer it could only point out that the call came from the

East Dulwich and Camberwell borders. McSloy made a point of writing in his notebook. "Well we now know that his other friend is called Shaun, Shaun who?"

Whilst writing down the latest received information, he listened to the conversation over again and over again. Apart from the name Shaun, nothing else at all was really of any relevance. Hold on! He thought if they are using disposable mobile phones, they now have at least two different numbers. If they could possibly get a list of numbers from the shopkeeper then they may be able to cross these two numbers off the list, then we may be able to monitor the remaining numbers. Reaching out for his radio, he then called Camberwell. After waking him up, he explained to him what had happened.

Camberwell told him. "Sorry we didn't call you earlier but we now know that the person's name is Shaun Jackson! Make sure you put a tracer bug onto the car somewhere. Then stay where you are until about 10:00 am, then meet back up with me at the Old School. If by any chance Dillon leaves the flat before then, do not follow under any circumstances, but call station control and have them follow him."

McSloy went back to his note book and scribbled out the questions about Shaun who? Looking at his watch, he saw that he had about five and a half hours to kill before he would get relieved. He needed something to help him stay awake, it was that cold that it was starting to snow.

He relieved himself by peeing into another empty coke bottle, then stacking it with the rest of them. "Ten green bottles filled with my piss, ten green bottles filled with my piss, then if one green bottle should. Stop! That is disgusting!

There has to be something better to keep me occupied than rubbish like that!

In total frustration he picked up the nearest booklet that he could find. "Great! More Bloody Bats!" Well if Dillon comes out in the morning he could at least make his cover a bit more credible if he knew a bit more. He started to read the leaflet out loud to himself.

"The Noctule Bat is one of the largest bats found in Britain and is often the first to emerge from its roost, sometimes before sunset. Weighing some 18 to 40 grams and with a wingspan of 32 to 40cm it has a sleek golden coloured fur and broad brown ears. Although still a fairly widespread species in London, the Noctule seems to have declined in recent years. This is possibly due at least in part to over management of trees where it exclusively roosts in wood-pecker or rot holes. It feeds on moths, beetles, mayflies and typically feeds high over woodland, parkland and water bodies. Good sites for seeing Noctules are Hampstead Heath, Berwick Ponds in Havering, over the Thames in Teddington, Oxleas Wood in Greenwich, and even in Hyde and Regents Park in central London, now because of McDonald and his cronies, here in Peckham!"

"Okay, too much of this stuff is boring my brains out. Surely there must be something else that someone left in this van." It was so cold that he decided to sit in the passenger seat and have the heater on full blast.

Pulling down the passenger glove compartment, he found a DVD case, With Millwall's Greatest Matches written on it. "Good I could do with a laugh," he said to himself. When he went to open it, he found that it was empty.

"Typical Millwall, this DVD case is just as empty as their trophy cabinet!" Going back to the glove compartment, he finally found something that he read, a copy of the Daily Mirror Crossword Book.

Going through the book until he found a puzzle that had not been started, he got ready to start. One across. Dracula's favourite mammals? Four letters? "Bloody Bats! Isn't that just bloody typical, Bats! Please clock speed up and save me from this fate worse than death!" Looking at the clock, he saw that only fifteen minutes had passed since he last looked at the clock. "Oh well back to the crossword."

It seemed to be getting colder by the minute, he looked through the windscreen and he saw that it had started to snow heavily. Grabbing a load of blankets from the box in the back of the van, he covered himself up really well. "Thank God, someone had the sense to leave these in here." He thought to himself.

He must have drifted off to sleep because the next thing he knew was that he was awoken by a loud tap on the window. He woke with a start, unsure of where he was, rubbing his eyes to help him see more clearly, he turned to look at the person tapping on the window. James Dillon!

"Bloody hell! What the heck did he want?"

"Morning, when I woke up I looked out of the window to see if it was still snowing and I saw your van still there, smoke belching out the back, so I decide to bring some coffee and toast. When you've finished just leave them on the window sill of 105 and I'll collect them later when I come back."

Still waking up, McSloy answered. "Brill! Many thanks. God it's absolutely freezing, the heater must have packed up and trying to stay warm under all these blankets must have made me fall asleep. Many thanks once again!"

"Damn!" He said to himself, why did I fall asleep? Did he say he was going out? Where is he going?" Getting straight onto his radio, he called station control and asked them to get a car ready as soon as possible so that they could follow Dillon's tracer bug.

Then he called Camberwell, told him everything new that had gone on. Then he was told to go home and get some sleep and meet at 2pm at the Old School. He turned his wrist over, so that he could see the time on his watch. "Shit it is nearly 9am. I must have fallen asleep for hours."

Chapter 11

The Feeling of Hatred

Camberwell was up and attempting to cook breakfast when Marshita thundered into the kitchen, spitting fire as she breathed. "Oh, so you finally bothered to come home last night den or was it dis morning? Did you finish changing them damn baby's nappies yesterday? Who Da hell is sleeping on me new couch? What time you gonna be home today?"

"Ssh woman, else you wake him up!" That incensed her even more. "Don't tell me to Ssh in my own damn home. Dis is my house and I do what I want in it!" Turning on her heels she slammed the kitchen door so hard again the whole house shook violently again and then she started to go upstairs, Stomping and cursing as she went.

The front room door opened and Tomlin staggered out to the kitchen, looked at Camberwell. "The wife? I think we'd better go! She slams the door so hard I'd hate to be on the receiving cnd of all that fury personally." Camberwell brushed past him then strode to the bottom of the stairs and shouted "Dis is my damn house as well and I'll have in it, whoever I damn well like, why I damn well like and whenever I damn well like."

Walking back to the kitchen, making sure that he had turned the gas hob off, he then said sheepishly. "Yeah I think your right, we'd better get out of here. We will go and get breakfast somewhere quiet and most definitely safer."

When they both arrived back at the Old School, Camberwell was telling Tomlin about the strange goings on in Kings Grove with McSloy and Dillon, when there was a knock at the door. "Enter" Camberwell said.

A uniformed officer knocked at the door and said. "Sorry to disturb you, but we have a gentleman called Mr. John Nelson to see you both!"

Looking at each other, Tomlin quipped. "Well this is a turn up for the books!"

"Okay, take him to classroom one and we'll be there in two minutes." Camberwell replied.

Turning back to Tomlin, he continued. "So what do you think about dat? A cold bloodied mass murderer's parent with a conscience."

Tomlin's retort was swift and to the point. "Personally I could not care less, all I want is to get people like him off the streets and behind bars. To his family, Jack the Ripper was a nice guy!"

Entering classroom one, John Nelson was pacing around the room like he had hot coals on his feet. The anger on his face was intense. Camberwell seemed to recognize the face. "Mr. Nelson?   Hmm I know you face from somewhere, but I just can't remember where?"

Nelson replied "Well you should, your one the coppers who attended the scene of my accident at Crystal Palace! Don't you remember? The one where the bus crushed my car! They had to cut me out of the wreckage!"

"Of course, how are you healing?" Camberwell replied.

"Well enough, anyway enough of that, I have come here is to find out who killed my son? I am led to believe from my informants, that I know from local people hereabouts, that it was Russell McDonald and his cronies Dillon and Jackson. I need you to confirm that before I go and kill someone innocent!"

Tomlin said. "Look you must know that we cannot divulge any information concerning this case and you certainly cannot go round killing anyone that currently takes your fancy!"

Camberwell interrupted. "Look Mr. Nelson, What we…"

"Before you go on my name is John, when I have done something to earn the title Mr. I'll let you know until then call me John!"

"Okay John, What we do know and can tell you is dis much. Daniel went up Great Yarmouth to retrieve a package for someone. He knew full well dat whatever the package contained it was illegal. The exact words he told me before he died in hospital were. "Hey ho I'm in the dough!" Having collected the package, he was almost involved in an accident on the way back, dat accident caused the package to open and spill its contents everywhere.

Without pausing for breath he continued. "Young Daniel thought the powder was cocaine or some other form of drugs, but it was not. It was worse, much worse."

"Yes, the hospital told me that it was Uranium powder and my Daniel died because he ingested it. Who sent him to collect the powder? Was it McDonald and his cronies? Because if it was, I swear to God, I will kill him! Then I will kill them!"

Looking at him intently Camberwell reacted to his remark. "Mr. Nelson... Sorry John! We told you before that we can't officially tell you all we know apart from what we have already told you.

Suffice to say dat we are working night and day to solve dis horrible crime, we have fantastic people working on the case and some of them are even putting their own lives at risk, trying to do just dat.!"

"With all due respect to them, I couldn't care less, all I am interested in, is finding out who killed my son!" was Nelson's angry rebuttal.

Tomlin was sitting there quite quietly then he started removing a large cigar from his inside pocket, then he started to smoke it. The smoke billowing across the room, turning the small classroom into a foggy smoke filled box.

Camberwell turned and glared at him then walked over to the windows and started to open them. Tomlin finally realized what was happening and took the hint, stubbing out his cigar without saying anything, knowing that in reality he had overstepped the mark.

Tomlin rose up and walked towards a chalk board and started to write, as well as asking questions of Nelson. "Did he know McDonald? If so how? What about as you put it, his two cronies, Dillon and Jackson? Had he had any business dealings with them?"

Nelson jumped up from his seat and snapped back. "I knew it! You are after McDonald and his cronies!.. I'm going to…"

Camberwell stopped him in his tracks by stating. "Stop, wait a minute. We are only asking because you introduced those three names to us, so we need to find out what you know about those particular individual people. It certainly doesn't mean dat they are the ones we are looking for. You have just opened a new line of enquiry for us to pursue."

That seemed to take the wind out of Nelson's sails, then after sitting back down he added. "Okay fair point but I still say it is them!"

"That may be so, but just answer the questions!" Tomlin replied.

"Well I know all three of them. I may be fifteen to twenty years older than them. In 1995 we all played football for the same Sunday Football League Team, Centra FC. We played in the Brockley and District League. My Daniel grew up with those boys, he always seemed to style himself on McDonald, young boys have their heroes, McDonald was Daniels."

With the chalk scratching away on the board, Tomlin wrote, Daniels hero was Russell McDonald and Daniel personally knew James Dillon and Shaun Jackson. Turning back to Nelson he asked "When was the last time that he knew Daniel had met or had any contact with any of the three men?"

"He met McDonald about two weeks ago. When I asked him at the time, what job he did for McDonald. He told me that he flew to Banjul-Yundum in Gambia to deliver some personal papers. He stayed for two nights at the Ocean Bay Hotel and Resort in Baku. Then he flew back the following morning. He took great pride in telling me the hotel because it was a five star hotel. The week before he went to a place called Agadir, somewhere in Morocco. Again he went for the same reason. McDonald had become a millionaire overnight supposedly by using the internet, but I personally think it was drugs but I couldn't prove it. Daniel would not hear a word said against him, as I said before he was Daniels hero and he would do anything for him!"

Camberwell's world spun in an instant. "Did you just say Agadir Morocco?"

"Yes!" Nelson replied. Tomlin then proceeded to write on the board, Agadir in Morocco, followed by Banjul-Yundum in Gambia at the Ocean Bay Hotel and Resort. Speaking back to Nelson he added "Do you happen to know what room it was?"

"No, but it had a beautiful view across the Atlantic Ocean."

Camberwell interrupted them. "Did he say who it was he met?"

Tomlin added. "McDonalds Father in Law, Mr. Demba Danzo, more than that he did not say, before you ask he never mentioned anything about the Morocco trip apart from the fact that he went there as well!"

Camberwell who did his usual thing of stopping and thinking before saying anything, turned his back on Nelson but still asked. "Was he due to go anywhere else for Mr. McDonald in the very near future?" John Nelson opened the zip on his inside pocket and withdrew a small black leather diary.

Thumbing through it he added. "According to this entry in his diary he was supposed to go last Saturday to in Ljubljana in Slovenia, but he crossed it out with the word cancelled."

Tomlin very politely asked John Nelson if they could have Daniels diary, to help with their enquiries so to speak.

"No problem Nelson replied, I have a photocopy of it all, so it will come in handy for my own enquiries."

Speaking slowly and what was in a very obvious and deliberate manner, Nelson added "Let me tell you, if my own inquiries lead me to prove that McDonald and his cronies are behind Daniels death, I will not only kill them, I will tear them to bits, so you and your people had better not get in way, because if it means that I have to go through you to get to them, so be it. You have been warned!"

Tomlin remarked "We could have you locked up, and then you won't get to anyone, then what would that achieve?"

Nelson replied "I couldn't care less, you may have the police force to assist you but I have the whole of South London to assist me, so again I am telling you, you have been warned."

Camberwell, who was still standing by the window because of the still lingering cigar smoke, looked cautiously at Nelson and asked "Do you know who is due to visit Peckham on Friday? Because if you go round like a bull in a china shop, loads of innocent people will suffer and die, including my granddaughter! How many young Afro Caribbean children and innocent people will have to die to make up for the loss of Daniel"?

Tomlin, was stunned, Camberwell had said nothing at all about his granddaughter being in the firing line. Now he knew why Camberwell was so good at his job. He was impervious to anything personal, it may be his own family at risk but the bigger picture to him was that the local area and all its inhabitants are his family, and they relied upon him and his officers to keep their family safe, at all or at any cost.

Camberwell continued. "Don't you think dat because of my granddaughter that I want to kill whoever is behind dis? I want to kill him now!

But every single innocent, man, woman and child who died or would suffer in the long term, would haunt my every sleeping moment and live with me forever. And all just because I did as I felt and went and killed the main suspect. Could you live with dat? Because I couldn't."

Nelson's response came with such ferocity, that even Tomlin was taken aback. "My life has been ruined and I have nothing to live for. So if it means that others die then so be it!"

Tomlin interrupted and asked Nelson. "How many nieces and nephews do you have? Do any of them live in Peckham? Are any of them in the Camberwell Children's Afro Caribbean Dance Troupe? How about the Sainte Afro Caribbean Dancers of Peckham and New Cross? They will be performing for Prince Harry and the Duchess on Friday."

That seemed to sting Nelson and suddenly you could see fear in his eyes. Camberwell knew he had started to get his point across when Nelson asked.

"Who's coming Friday? And yes I have nieces and nephews who live in the Camberwell area, and yes they are in a dance troupes, although I don't know which ones."

"Well would you want them to suffer or at worse die, just because you want to go and kill someone who ultimately may not even be responsible for Daniels death?" Camberwell replied.

Tomlin added to the mix by saying "We have a total of two and a half days to solve this. Personally I couldn't care less if main suspects were blown away after Fridays visit, but no one including McDonald and his cronies nor anyone else can be touched until the royals had left Peckham and everything was back to normal."

Nelson had tears in his eyes and Camberwell knew he was on the ropes. "Look someone is planning to explode a bomb when the Prince and Duchess are visiting Peckham. Anyone who is within three hundred yards or so will be killed or very badly injured. Dat is why no one can be running around trying to kill people until after they had left. So do you want nieces or nephews blown to pieces?"

Camberwell knew that he could not afford to have a loose cannon running around after McDonald, because if anything happened to him the chances of solving this problem would be non-existent and then all hell would be let loose. If the papers go hold of it, there would be no chance at all of avoiding a catastrophe.

"We have no choice but to offer a solution to your problem and ours, Tomlin you're not going to like this but realistically we have no choice! If Mr. Nelson... sorry, if John is running around like a loose cannon, you know what will happen! We cannot legally lock him up, without creating a situation that may ultimately cost us more. So this is what I propose!"

"Wait." Snapped Tomlin. "Mr. Nelson please could you wait outside for two minutes? Thank you." Turning back to Camberwell with a face like thunder he said. "You cannot be serious! There is no way we can tell him anymore, we really have told him too much already."

Camberwell countered. "Stop, take a look around us. We are getting close now but we are running out of time. We cannot stop him legally from causing mayhem without creating such a storm dat the media will be on us like a ton of bricks, so it leaves us with no choice but to bring him onside. We both know dat CO19 will take all three of them out if they get a chance. So if we secretly offer Nelson the chance to do it before CO19 does, I think he'll accept dat, because realistically it is the only option we have!"

While Tomlin used his mobile to call his boss at MI5 headquarters, Camberwell contacted his Borough Commander and the Acting Metropolitan Police Commissioner.

Tomlin snapped his phone shut, he spoke with dismay and obvious resentment. "We have been given the go ahead, with one proviso. If Nelson interferes with us, then he has to be eliminated from our enquiries, no matter what the cost!"

Camberwell's reaction was just as flippant as Tomlin's statement was sincere. "Fortunately I have been given the go ahead, but I was going to go ahead anyway! It is the only way of continuing this investigation and no grey haired trout from your lot or a do gooder of a senior officer from my lot would stop me. So let's get it done and get some work done."

Asking John Nelson back into the room, they asked him about helping their investigation on the proviso that when it was finished, he would be given preferential information before CO19 got it.

He agreed on the proviso that he would be allowed to take them out given the chance, even if it meant doing it on British soil, so between them Camberwell and Tomlin then started to tell him everything single bit of evidence that they had.

Chapter 12

Information

WPC Lackey decided to go and recheck Karen Westbrooke's flat in Aldeburgh Street, Greenwich. She was certain that she had missed something, she couldn't put her finger on it but she just knew something was wrong. The premises had been searched inside and out but she just had this nagging feeling.

She parked in a parking space right outside the front door and was just about to enter the flat when the neighbour from downstairs stepped out of her front door and was surprised to see someone she didn't know entering Westbrooke's flat.

"Hello can I help you?" She asked.

"I am Karen's new domestic, she is working such long hours now, that she asked me to come and do her housework." Lackey replied.

The neighbour gave a real snooty look on her face and passed the comment. "It's alright for some people, they can afford a domestic, me I can't afford a cup of tea!" She then stormed off, heading towards the Greenwich flyover.

She started to go up the stairs to Westbrooke's flat, after opening the front door and closing it behind her, she stopped to take a look around. Ticking things off her mental task list as she went, then it hit her! Jackson's photograph! We needed one, she missed it yesterday.

Upon the mantelpiece was a double photo frame with a base of marble, which was about nine inches long and five inches wide.

The photos were about four inches by four inches. A picture of Westbrooke on one side and a photo of a man, whom she assumed was Jackson was on the other

Taking care not to damage it, WPC Lackey was carefully removing the back of the frame so that she could take out the photo of Jackson. She noticed that the felt on the actual bottom of the frame was split all along one side.

Upon closer inspection she noticed that there was a piece of paper that had been placed in between the felt and the physical bottom of the frame.

She tilted the frame over towards her so she could easily remove the paper. When she looked she found that it had written on it. "Banjul-Yundum, Gambia, Russell. Ljubljana, Slovenia, James. Agadir, Morocco, Shaun."

Using her radio to call Camberwell, she apologized to him for missing it yesterday, but she had followed her instincts and made a call which turned out to be a good one. After telling her to fax through the picture of Jackson, he then told her return to the Old School and drop off the piece of paper she had found.

"You'll find a folder left on my desk with your name on it. If I am not there follow the instructions and report to me when you have finished. Tell no one else at all. I don't care if the Commissioner asks you about it. Just say nothing to no one."

David Critchley was back on duty outside Shaun Jackson's House in Upland Road. He read the report from the person whom he replaced and there was not much on it. So all he could do is sit here and wait then wait even more.

Whilst he was waiting a Parcel Force van turned up and tried to deliver a small package that was unable to fit through the letter box. When he started to write out his PO739 "Sorry you were out card" Critchley walked across the road and spoke to him.

Flashing his police warrant badge, he took possession of the package. On the PO739 "While you were out" form, he changed the telephone number from the one printed to the telephone number at the Old School, then posted the card through the letter box.

Calling up Camberwell on his radio, he found that only Tomlin was available. He started explaining what had happened, he then asked for someone to be sent to collect the package from him and warned him that Jackson may call as he had changed the telephone number on the form. Then he settled back and started watching the house again.

Camberwell was talking to Tomlin when Critchley called him to tell him what had happened, then no sooner had he finished and walked away when Tomlin's mobile phone rang.

It was the Prince Harry's press office from Clarence House. Paddy Haverson spoke to him on the phone and said that "In the best interest of the British public, Prince Harry and the Duchess have decided that they will still visit Peckham Library on Friday. Prince Harry says has the fullest faith in your ability to keep them safe from harm, we will get back to you tomorrow morning to confirm times and places."

Thinking to himself. "The stupid idiot doesn't understand that by actually attending, it could cost the lives of countless innocent people and all because of his bloody stupid stiff upper lip!" Now he had to find Camberwell and tell him the good news.

Camberwell was back in the classroom where the main dry wipe board list was. Adding to the bottom he wrote.

11/. Banjul-Yundum, Gambia – Russell McDonald

12/. Ljubljana, Slovenia – James Dillon

13/. Agadir, Morocco – Shaun Jackson

Suddenly the fax machine started to whir and hum and out came a report from the laboratory about the paperwork that they were trying to look at. It showed that the information that they had gathered was correct, and through John Nelson and the piece of paper that WPC Lackey had found, this part of the riddle had come together.

WPC Lackey knocked on the door and Camberwell told her to enter. "Well done for using your common sense. So many people will not take the chance and admit dat they felt like something was missing, let alone go and take a second look just to make sure. We believe dat the piece of paper that you found was the physical top copy of the paperwork that was sent to the laboratory, to try and see what was written on it.

Continuing on he asked her. "Do you think Westbrooke has anything to do with dis at all?"

She replied "No Sir, the flat was immaculate, apart from the photo of Jackson, you would not know that a man had ever been there. I personally believe that Jackson hide the piece of paper there himself."

"What leads you to dat conclusion?" He asked.

"Well as the flat was so clean and the only thing about him in there was the photo. I would have expected to find other things about him all over the place but there was nothing. Call it female intuition but she is alright, just mixed up with wrong people." She replied.

He said nothing until he thrust a folder into her hands, he said. "Right what I need you to do now is to go and check these shops out. Take the picture of Jackson that you found, see if anyone knows him. Check to see if he supply's anyone with goods dat he buys at Makro's and sells them on to them at a profit over cost. It is possible dat he will get someone to do the deliveries for him but if he does supply anyone, he will have had to go and visit them himself to start the process in the first place. If in any of the shops dat are applicable, check to see if anyone has bought a large quantity of household matches from them recently. Oh do me a favour will you please. I need some decaf coffee from Lidl's when you're on your way back." Throwing a two pound coin in the air for her to catch.

As she stooped to catch it, suddenly the classroom door burst open and in strode Tomlin, with a face like thunder.

"Who upset you then?" he asked.

"Those stupid people at the palace, they are still going to let them come. I have just received a call from the press office at Clarence House, a Mr. Paddy Haverson, who is some form of press secretary, told me, what were his exact words? Oh Yes." He said angrily.

"In the best interest of the British Public, Prince Harry and the Duchess have decided that they will still visit Peckham Library on Friday."

"Well, all it means it dat we will have to work even harder, as time is not on our side. Turning back to the dry wipe board, he was about to start writing when he snapped.

"Lackey, you still here?" "No sir, I am just a figment of your imagination, I have already left!"

With that she turned on her heels and was gone. Camberwell smiled to himself and then continued working on the dry wipe board.

"Right let us go through dis list again. We now know the name of the third suspect, which is Shaun Jackson." Crossing off the unknown suspect part of number one on the list, then at the end he ticked it, and wrote DONE! "Number two is done, so we can tick dat off, number three. We still do not know where they got the explosives from?"

Tomlin added. "Four and five, we now know about so they can be ticked off. Six, seven, eight and nine can also be wiped off completely. We need to add more to the list." He approached the dry wipe board, took the pen from Camberwell and started to add to the list.

WPC Lackey was standing in Peckham High Street, right outside the MK one store. "I cannot see what Jackson would be able to provide for this store, but I'll check it out anyway."

Two minutes later she was outside having been unable to gather any information at all, next she went into the shop next door, until she had finished all the shops that Camberwell had put on the list. No one knew the man in the photograph and everyone seemed to be doing their own shopping, where wholesalers were concerned.

After radioing back her report, she started her way back to the Old School. Calling into the Lidl store in Peckham High Street to buy some decaffeinated coffee, she thought to herself. "I might as well ask if anyone could identify the picture whilst I am here."

As she approached the till she saw the store manager and showed him the photograph, then asked him, if he knew who the person was?

"Of course! That's Shaun Jackson! He comes in two or three times a month and buys lots of different items. Then he sells them to other stores for a profit. It saves them going to the wholesalers themselves. Mind you though! You won't find him here at the moment, last thing I knew, he was away on holiday in Morocco."

"Sir, many thanks for your help." She replied.

After paying for the coffee, she resumed her journey back to the Old School. As she walked she started to think to herself. "If he was supposedly on holiday in Morocco, how could he be at Makro's shopping yesterday. So he was obviously hiding out somewhere." She knew that Critchley was on surveillance duty at Jackson's home and he had not gone back there.

She also knew that he had not been to the flat in Aldeburgh Street, because she had been there as well. She felt confused and somewhat dismayed by her inability to solve this issue.

Speaking to Tomlin and Camberwell after she had returned from Peckham, she said.

"Sir I would like to go and replace that piece of paper back inside the photo frame, because if by any chance

Jackson returns there and is unable to find it, where it should be it might actually give the game away. She requested that Karen Westbrooke should be allowed to return to the flat with her. I will stay with her and if Jackson comes back we can make up a cover story about who I am. I think she knows now that we have told her the truth about Jackson."

Tomlin declared. "Good idea, but I think you'd better have a plain clothed unit as backup outside and before you say anything Camberwell, yes I will ensure that they are properly dressed for the occasion. No Joe 90's and definitely no Bill and Bens, I finally took your point."

Camberwell laughed out loud, which seemed to ease the tension that had been building in the room. He agreed. "Okay but stay in touch, no radios just mobile phones and make sure you call in once an hour, at all times. Is dat clearly understood?"

She answered. "Yes!" then left the room to collect Westbrooke.

On the way back to Westbrooke's flat, Lackey asked her about the photo frame.

"That old thing, Shaun told me that it was his great grandmothers and he wanted me to have it. Strange though now you come to mention it, he told me never to clean it as it was fragile and never, ever move it. Some parts were really sharp he said."

Lackey then asked her. "Did you know a Daniel Nelson? I ask because he was sent by Russell McDonald and Jackson to Agadir, to meet someone and deliver some papers there."

Westbrooke thought for a second, then replied. "Yes, I know Daniel, only very slightly mind you. We have met a couple of times at Shaun's house in Upland Road. Why would this McDonald or Shaun need to send Daniel to Agadir and what papers would he need to take? Sorry I cannot tell you much more than that."

As they were being driven back to Aldeburgh Street, WPC Lackey outlined a plan that would come into effect, should Jackson return to the flat whilst she was there.

"Did you go to school in this country and if so where did you go? When did you go there and who were your closest friends? We have arranged with the IT department to set us up as school friends on the Friends Reunited website. What are your parent's names and are they still alive? Do you have brothers and sisters, alive or dead? Are any of them living over here in the UK? Does Jackson know any of your other friends?"

Westbrooke took her time and then gave her all the relevant information. WPC Lackey started to try and learn off by heart, the answers that Westbrooke had told her.

When they got back to the flat and whilst Westbrooke was getting changed, Lackey replaced the piece of paper back into the base of the photo frame. Now all they had to do is sit and wait.

The telephone suddenly rang, and after turning the television down, Westbrooke answered it.

"Hello Karen here….Oh hi Shaun, when am I going to see you next? ….. Where are you going? When will you be back?" With that the phone line went dead.

Westbrooke turned towards WPC Lackey with tears rolling down her face. "He said that he was going away tomorrow and he would not be back for a few months, when he got settled he would send for her. Then he put the phone down on me."

She then broke down in tears, Lackey rushed over to comfort her.

She radioed back to Camberwell and told him about the phone call, and asked whether she should return to the Old School, but he told her to stay with Westbrooke just in case anything changed. Should she be needed back at the Old School then she would be told to return.

Turning back to Westbrooke who was in floods of tears, she went over to console her, with Westbrooke continuously saying softly, why? Why? Why?

Chapter 13

Tickets

Dave Critchley was sitting in his observation vehicle keeping an eye on 36 Upland Road, when suddenly a jet black metallic Audi R8 cabriolet pulled up outside the house.

A slim built black man got out from the driver's side and after making sure that the roof was properly in place, he made his way to the front door of the house. He stopped only briefly to check the post box on the wall. After letting himself in, he walked through to the kitchen at the back of the house and put the heating on.

Through the uncurtained window at the front of the house, Critchley watched him withdraw a small package from the rucksack that he was carrying and drop it on the sofa. He then walked back into the kitchen and returned with a hot drink, sat down and started to read a magazine.

He had been reading for about ten minutes before he started to unwrap the package. His mobile phone rang and after speaking for barely a minute, he threw his jacket over his arm and left the house.

Critchley knew that he did not take the package with him and he was desperate to find out what was in it. He had to get into the house to have a look and the only way to do that was to delay Jackson wherever he was going. Using his mobile, he called Camberwell at the Old School and asked him to arrange for a traffic stop to be made.

"The registration number of the Audi is JAC 2008 and would they delay the suspect driving it, until after I have checked out the house, please do a check on the registered owner."

Critchley watched him as he drove off towards North Cross Road and then he went straight across, which meant he was heading for Lordship Lane. Camberwell told him that he would arrange for it to be done and he was to radio back in when he had finished his search of the house.

Waiting until he was told that the stop had been made, he entered the house. Once inside he immediately saw the package on the sofa. It had been half opened by Jackson and after carefully looking he saw that the contents were a passport and airplane ticket. Carefully withdrawing them, he saw that the passport was in his own name and the airline ticket was to Agadir in Morocco. It was dated for 9pm tomorrow, Thursday night.

Making a quick note of the ticket and passport details as well as using his mobile phone to take a picture of them, he carefully replaced them in the package.

He then took a very quick glance around the house, nothing! Then he went to take a quick look upstairs, nothing! Nothing in the entire house seemed out of place.

When he was back in his van, he phoned Camberwell. "I have finished, so the stop can end. Has Jackson called about the package that Parcel Force tried to deliver?"

Camberwell replied. "No not yet. We have had a look inside the package and all dat is in there, is a model of his own car, but it was worth a try, and regarding your question about the registered owner? That's Russell McDonald, which is of no great surprise." With that he hung up.

A few minutes later, Camberwell phoned him back to ask what he had found in the packet and in the house. Checking his notes,

Critchley replied. "Jackson has already pre-booked his flight to Agadir, Morocco with First Choice holidays at 9pm from Gatwick Airport tomorrow night. That's all I can tell you at the moment, Sir."

Camberwell, after telling both Tomlin and Nelson what he had just been told then added. "Well if Jackson has been stupid enough to book his flight in his own name, what are the chances dat the other two have done the same?"

Nelson replied. "Well it's worth checking. I mean, we know where they are going and it seems now as if we know when they are going."

Nelson continued. "Tomlin, you check out Dillon and I'll check out McDonald."

Tomlin looked at him with eyes that had total anger and fury in them, thinking to himself "Who the hell are you to tell me what to do!"

Camberwell's reaction angered Tomlin even more. "Dat's a great idea! Okay let's get cracking!"

Nelson was finding it really difficult to find out if or indeed how McDonald was getting out of the country. No one seemed to have any information on him. Speaking out loud he said. "Do you think that McDonald will use a private Jet, I mean he's rich enough?"

Camberwell said. "Problem with dat is dat the pilot will have to file a flight plan with the Civil Aviation Authority and if anything goes belly up, he will have attracted a lot of unwanted attention to himself."

Tomlin, after trying all the London airports with no joy, then had no choice but to phone round different airports to see if they flew to Ljubljana. Eventually he tried East Midlands Airport, he found out that Brussels Airlines flew to Ljubljana but with a stopover in Brussels.

As Tomlin spoke to the operator at Brussels Airlines, he repeated what was told to him, So Camberwell could write down the details on the dry wipe board.

"Dillon's flight leaves East Midland Airport tomorrow at 18:05pm UK time and gets in to Brussels Airport around 20:20pm local time, which is 19:20pm UK time. The flight number is 5264. The connection onto Ljubljana leaves Brussels at 20:30pm local time. It arrives in Ljubljana at 00.10am Thursday morning local time. This flight number is 5135. It's an open ticket? So far no return date has been booked. Okay many thanks." With that he hung up.

For Nelson, it seemingly took forever until he finally managed to track down McDonald's flight. Again he repeated it out loud so that Camberwell could again write down all the details.

"He is departing Manchester Airport on a Air France flight at twenty to seven, tomorrow morning. Its flight number is 5297. It arrives at Brussels Airport at 9am in the morning local time then the connection leaves Brussels at 11.30am local time. The flight number is 5261. The flight arrives in Banjul-Yundum at 6.25pm local time."

Just before Nelson hung up, Camberwell interrupted him and got him to ask if they could possibly tell him whether or not in the last few days anyone else with the same surname has made the same trip.

After putting the phone down he turned to Camberwell and said. "A Mrs Cathy McDonald and her children, Susan aged 9 and Rebecca aged 6. All had made the same trip three days ago and as they had open dated return tickets the same as McDonald, no return date yet had been booked"

Camberwell wrote the last bit of information on the dry wipe board, when he had finished he then turned to Tomlin and Nelson who were standing round drinking coffee.

"Tomlin, can you arrange for someone to be on the same flights as the three of them. Then arrange for a local agent in all three countries to follow them when they arrive. We need to find out their final destinations!"

Tomlin got on the radio to his office at Thames House. "Ah Collier, Tomlin here, get onto First Choice holidays and book someone on the 9:00pm flight to Agadir in Morocco for tomorrow night. Then get onto the embassy in Agadir and have someone meet the plane, flight number TOM 693. I want full surveillance on a Mr. Shaun Jackson, 24 hours a day. There will be an agent shadowing him on the plane from the UK, we will forward their details to you prior to them getting on the flight." With that he hung up.

Nelson turned to him and snapped. "What! Are we not following the other two?"

Tomlin had forgotten. "But why did it have to be Nelson who told him." He was getting more and more upset and angry with the Nelson situation.

Getting back onto Collier at Thames house he asked for the same thing to happen to both Jackson and McDonald.

Nelson, speaking to both Camberwell and Tomlin said. "If all three of them are going to be out of the country and travelling by plane, how were they going to detonate the bomb? To me, it would make a bloody good alibi. "Sorry your honour, it wasn't me because I was not even in the country at the time."

Tomlin nastily snapped back at him. "Not that clever now, are you? Nowadays you can detonate a bomb from anywhere in the world, simply just by using the mobile phone networks, all it takes is a G2 mobile phone. That will allow you to call from even an airplane flying at 41,000 feet."

Nelson just nodded, leaving the nasty remark from Tomlin unanswered. After stopping to take a drink from his coffee cup, he asked them both. "Is there any way we can stop the three of them leaving the country. I mean you must have enough evidence to arrest them surely?"

"What can we arrest them for? At this moment in time, we cannot prove that they have done anything wrong. Everything else is just hearsay, I can just imagine their solicitors going to town on us for unlawful arrest." Tomlin answered.

"We need to get a couple more things to fall in place then we can turn the heat up on them. We need to find that bomb." Camberwell added.

Back at Upland Road, Jackson had returned and was getting ready to have something to eat. When a young black man about five foot five inches tall walked up the path and rang the doorbell. Jackson opened the door and too his surprise Neil Lawrence was standing at his door.

Gesturing to him to come in he said. "Hello Neil, I wasn't expecting to see you until tomorrow! What can I do for you? There is nothing wrong is there?"

Lawrence replied. "No! I just popped into see if you could get something for me for tomorrow. What I need are a couple of rolls of black vinyl electrical tape. I have tried numerous places today but I cannot get them anywhere."

"Hold on!" Jackson said. "I have a couple of rolls here. What do you need them for?"

"Well, they will hold the mobile phone to the side of the soap powder box, which means that it will not rattle about whilst being moved. The last thing that we want is for the phone to come loose and break the wires, it could cause a premature detonation!" Was his reply.

Lawrence's answer went over Jackson's head, so much so, that his only answer was. "Would you like to have something to eat or drink? I was just doing myself some smoked salmon and pasta? It is no problem, there is enough for two!" Jackson queried.

Shrugging his shoulders, Lawrence replied. "Go on then, I may as well. I don't have much on tonight."

Whilst eating, Jackson asked about the actual making of the detonation system.

He added. "To be truthful, I don't have a clue about how it works, can you explain it in a way that it would make common sense to me."

Lawrence told him. "The long and the short of it is that the ring circuit is used to trigger an electronic impulse that makes the explosives detonate. That really is all there is to it."

Again Lawrence's answer went over Jackson's head, his response being. "Oh okay."

In the van parked opposite the house, Critchley had written down all the information about the visitor. He also managed to get a clear photo of him without having to use the flash.

He faxed through the photo to Camberwell, hoping that someone there would be able to recognize the person.

Nelson was standing next to the fax machine when the photo came through. He had to take a double look at the photo, then he exclaimed. "What's Neil Lawrence got to do with all this? He used to play football with McDonald, Dillon and Jackson for Centra. Where does he come into the picture?"

Camberwell responded. "He has just visited Jackson at the flat in Upland Road. He and Jackson seemed to be having quite an intense conversation at this moment in time."

Turning to Tomlin has said. "Well dat saved us some time, can you get onto your mob and get Lawrence checked out. I will check with control to see if he has a criminal record."

Nelson left the room to go to the toilet, and that gave Tomlin the chance he had been waiting for. He felt that Nelson was getting in the way and overstepping his authority.

Turning to Camberwell he said. "What do you think about this idea? To try and force their hand just a little bit? If we get Nelson to accidentally on purpose call into Jackson's home on the "I was just passing pretence." It would be like standing beneath an olive tree and see what falls off after giving it a good shake!"

Nelson entered the room to be met with the question. "Tomlin has come up with a really good idea, but it will need you to keep your cool, if you decide to go through with it. Did you know where Jackson lived before all dis blew up? Excuse the pun."

"Yes" He answered. "Why?"

Tomlin then spoke. "We want you to go and pay an "accidentally on purpose visit", just to see if we can shake them up a bit, but you have to make them believe that you know nothing about any of this! If they ask you haven't spoken to Daniel for over a week."

Camberwell added. "Remember, really McDonald is the one you're after, do you think dat you can keep you cool enough to stay for about ten minutes?"

Nelson just stood and stared at the pair of them, with nothing but hatred in his eyes. "Yes, with no trouble at all!"

Chapter 14

John Nelson

As Nelson walked up the path to Jackson's house, in his van, Critchley was using a video camera to zoom up really close to monitor Jackson's reaction when Nelson knocked on the door, also the micro microphone that was virtually invisible to the naked eye, would allow him to record everything that was being said.

He watched on the monitor as Jackson opened the front door. The shock and horror shown on his face was so intense, that Nelson commented to him. "What's the matter Shaun? You look like you have just seen a ghost?"

Jackson just stood there for what seemed forever before asking Nelson to come in.

"Are you alright? Do I have that much influence on you that I keep you dumbstruck?"

Jackson mumbled. "No… No. Sorry but this is just such a surprise, how are you?"

Nelson said, whilst trying to keep his cool. "Okay, it would help if I saw my son once in a while! I haven't heard from him for over a week now."

Turning round he saw Neil Lawrence was in the kitchen making a drink. "Hello Neil, I didn't realize that you lived here as well? How are you doing?" Nelson asked. Before Lawrence had chance to answer, Jackson offered him a cup of tea. "Still one Sugar?"

Nelson accepted and then added. "I was just passing and wasn't sure whether to call in or not, then as I drove past I saw the light on, so then I decided to stop, and knock."

Jackson asked. "What have you been doing with yourself?"

Before he had a chance to answer, Lawrence interrupted and said. "Where are you living now?"

Nelson answered "In the Crystal Palace area still, I haven't moved since we were all playing football for Centra, why, where are you living now then?"

Lawrence replied in a manner of fact way. "Nowhere in particular. I have the use of a really nice mobile home. I go wherever I feel like going."

Walking out to the kitchen to replace his cup, he asked Jackson. "Have you seen anything of Russell McDonald or James Dillon? I heard that Russell made it really big through the internet. It would be nice to get in touch with them both again soon."

Jackson's face hit the floor and looked really nervous and fidgety. He kept pacing up and down the front room. You could tell by his demeanour that he was lying.

"No… I haven't spoken to him for a while. Err…… I saw Dillon about a week ago. And err…. I haven't even seen your Daniel for a while either!"

Nelson knew that he was lying because Daniel had told him that Jackson was the person who dropped him off at the airport when he went abroad recently for McDonald.

Turning the screw on Jackson a bit more he added. "I hear that Cathy and the kids have gone on holiday, did they go anywhere nice?"

Again Jackson's reaction was that of an extremely nervous person, not knowing what to do or say.

Critchley, who was recording everything that was being said, made a mental note to congratulate Nelson about his acting. Talking to Camberwell on his mobile, he said. "He's not letting the situation get to him and he's keeping his cool. I think that it is a bit of a masterstroke sending him here. I think this will definitely rattle Jackson's cage."

Back at the Old School, Tomlin started to rant and rave about Nelson taking the piss out of him and. "Who does he think he is, speaking to me like a piece of shit!"

Camberwell bit back at Tomlin. "Man, look who's talking. At times you treat people even worse, you have to learn to treat people the way you wanted to be treated. We have had dis conversation before, one day you will learn and if you're not careful you'll learn the hard way! Trust me you'll learn the hard way!"

Continuing on he added. "Let me fill you in about Nelson. I have been doing a bit of research about him." Tomlin just looked at him with a, who cares less sort of attitude.

"John Nelson used to be a paramedic with the London Ambulance Service. One day he was working in Lewisham and he got a call to an incident involving a train at Ladywell When he arrived he found dat eldest son, had been hit by a train. Denzil, his son was a bit slow. He was playing with some other children on the railway siding, when someone dared them all to play chicken with an oncoming train.

It transpires dat they got away with it a few times, but on the last go Denzil tripped and fell directly onto the track. The train cut him in half."

With sadness in his voice, he recalled. "Nelson was the first person from the rescue services on scene. Can you have any idea what he must of felt like seeing his own son cut in half lying there on a railway track and to top it all he was the one dat actually picked up the two halves of his son. The other paramedics there tried to stop him but he said dat as it was his son he did not want anyone else to do it."

Tomlin just stood there, his mouth wide open with shock and pure embarrassment, not knowing what to say or to do, he felt so ashamed of himself.

Camberwell hammered his point home! "Could you just imagine having to go home to your own wife and family to explain dat you had found him and worse of all, tell them how he died? It must be a soul destroying job at the best of times with the tragedy and sadness dat you come across on a daily basis, but to have dat happen to your own son, well I couldn't start to explain. He must have a really strong character, because most people would have quit their job.

After stopping for some more mouthfuls of coffee, he continued. "Not Nelson, within two days of the funeral he was back at work. His first job was a "One under" Which is where someone is under a tube train. Dat's takes some balls to do dat. Just after your own son has died the same way! Now you know why he feels so bitter and wants revenge at no matter what the cost and why I am going to help him get his revenge, no matter what the cost to me!"

Tomlin just simply said. "I never knew!"

"It doesn't stop there!" Camberwell added.

"Do you remember the Clapham train crash on the 12th December 1988? It was 8am in the morning, AA patrol man called Peter Kiddle was on duty when he came across the accident and was the person who alerted the emergency services. The first vehicle he flagged down had Nelson at the wheel. Nelson was on his way to work. Fortunately like most London Ambulance Service Paramedics, he carried his own emergency first aid kit in his car.

Pausing for breath then continuing. "The scene he found was so horrific but being a Paramedic enabled him to perform basic emergency surgery at the scene. The ability to do dat definitely helped to save people's lives. Using Mr. Kiddle as his assistant they treated nearly twenty injured people before the first ambulances and doctors arrived.

Both Mr. Kiddle and Nelson won commendations for their heroics. Without the actions of those men, who knows how many people would have been added to the list of fatalities."

Again he stopped for another mouthful of his now tepid and luke warm coffee. "I think dat you should cut him some slack. As heroes go, he really is one. Does any of your heroics come close?" Camberwell asked. Tomlin's reply was full of sorrow and remorse at the way he had treated Nelson.

"No…. Nothing I have ever done comes that close."

The silence was broken by the sound of Bob Marley coming from Camberwell's mobile phone. "Camberwell here! " He said. "Okay if anything else happens let me know."
Turning round to speak to Tomlin. "Nelson has just left Jackson's, so he will be back here very shortly, then we should be able to find out if he's managed to rattle Jackson's cage!"

About 20 minutes later Nelson had arrived back at the classroom and after grabbing a cup of coffee he started telling them both about what had happened in Jackson's house. After he had finished he added. "Do you realize how much I wanted to kill them both? I wanted it so bad, I could taste it in my mouth."

Tomlin, who had now warmed to Nelson added. "I would not blame you one bit, but don't worry we will make them pay for what they have done to Daniel."

Nelson looked quizzically at Tomlin and thought to himself. "Hello, why are you being so nice?"

Once again the sound of Bob Marley filled the room. It just was the control room at Peckham Police Station advising Camberwell that Lawrence had no criminal convictions, not even a parking ticket against his name.

Tomlin was just about to respond when the fax machine started to whir and hum again, by the time it had finished printing there were eight sheets of A4 paper.

He read the fax then spoke. "This is from British Army Personnel Office. They had sent through a copy of Lawrence's military service record.

Again he started reading it out aloud, so that Camberwell could write down the important parts on the dry wipe board.

"Lawrence joined the British Army's 52 Infantry Brigade in December 2002. His basic training took place at the School of Infantry's, Infantry Training Centre at Catterick in Yorkshire.

After he passed out of basic training he went to the Infantry Battle School at Brecon in Wales, from there he went to the Army School of Ammunition at Shrivenham, near Swindon.

Whilst he was there, he qualified as an Ammunitions Technicians Instructor. He taught new recruits how to deal with explosives handling and other things.

He became a bomb disposal instructor and again taught new recruits about the basics of bomb disposal."

Camberwell interrupted Tomlin whilst he was in full flow. "So dat could be where the C4 explosive for the bomb has come from! The next question is where did he get it from?"

Tomlin waited until Camberwell had finished writing then said. "Well there's more to this story. He was posted to the 2nd Battalion the Royal Gurkha Rifles at Shorncliffe which is just outside Cheriton in Kent, in late 2003. He rose to the rank of Staff Sergeant. He has done two tours of duty in Afghanistan, where he was awarded The Military Cross for services above and beyond the call of duty.

Again he stopped to take in a big draw of his cigar. He then let the smoke billow out into the already stuffy room.

"Three months later he was mentioned in dispatches, which is a great honour for a soldier. So he had served with Honour and Distinction. That is until early 2007, when he was caught in bed with the base Commanders daughter. Officially he was court-martialled and discharged late in 2007, the court martial was told that five pounds of C4 explosives went missing from an area that he controlled. The court martial found him guilty of gross misconduct and negligence. He was discharged from the Army in disgrace."

Camberwell again interrupted Tomlin by saying. "We definitely know now where they got the explosives from."

Tomlin reacted with. "Well not quite. The court martial found that there was no evidence to prove that Lawrence had anything to do with the theft of the C4. Unofficially Lawrence has always protested his innocence, claiming that because the Commanders daughter became pregnant, he was railroaded out of the service. The base Commander couldn't have his sweet seventeen year old daughter put in the family way by a twenty seven year old black man, No matter how much of a hero he was! The daughter has since had an abortion and gone back home to daddy. So there in fact lies the reason for Lawrence's part in this little get together. Revenge!"

"Do your guys have any idea where he's been since he left the service? Do they have a home address? We need to find out about him pretty darn quick.

While I was at Jackson's he made some reference to a mobile home that he bought this year. So it is possible that he moves around a lot in that!" Nelson asked.

Camberwell in his usual thinking pose, said. "Well I have never had any dealings with him in dis area at all. We will have to get onto DVLA to see if there is a mobile home registered to him or McDonald. Both the other two have cars registered to him, so it is possible dat Lawrence's vehicle is also the same."

Again getting onto the control room at Peckham Police Station, he asked them for the contact details for DVLC at Swansea. After calling them, he was put through to a senior supervisor, who after getting all the details from Camberwell, informed him that he needed to go and check it out and that he would call him back as soon as possible.

Ten minutes later Bob Marley started to sing again, this time it was the man from the DVLA.

Camberwell was getting a bit paranoid, thinking that his wife was calling about "Why wasn't he home for dinner yet!" He could see by the look on Tomlin's face that he thought the same as well.

"We found nothing at all under the name of Neil Lawrence, but you have to bear in mind dat he may have purchased one but not registered it. However under the name of Russell McDonald we found a Fiat Carioca Motorhome was registered on the 1st of January dis year, 2008.

Registration Number is NL 2008. Registered keepers address was given as 36 Upland Road, East Dulwich, London SE22 9EF."

Nelson snapped quite bitterly. "Well as we can see McDonald likes to spread his wealth around, I wonder if he will like me spreading death around."

With that he walked towards the classroom door. "Sorry guys, I am absolutely knackered, so I'm going home to sleep! I'll see you both tomorrow morning about 7:00 am." Camberwell and Tomlin both wished him goodnight, but when he had left the room they looked at each other with a worrying stare.

Chapter 15

Preparation

It was now 8:00 am on Thursday morning. Shaun Jackson left to go to the garage where his van was parked, but for some reason he had the strongest feeling that he was being followed. Having left his house he walked on foot along the side streets then up and down other side streets, retracing his steps to ensure that if anyone was following him they would be seen.

Walking down Hindmans Road for the third time, he noticed that a man was also walking down the same road. Now this was nothing unusual but he felt sure that he had seen him twice already this morning.

Using his own personal mobile he called Dave Lansdale, to come and collect him from the end of North Cross Road at the junction with Crystal palace Road.

Having to time it to the exact minute, Jackson knew that if the person had been following him, they would have been on foot and they would not have expected any one to come and pick him up. As he reached the North Cross Road junction with Crystal Palace Road, there was a Renault Clio with its engine running waiting for him, as soon as he turned left into Crystal Palace Road, he jumped straight into the passenger seat of the car and it sped away.

Dave Critchley knew he was in trouble when Jackson kept walking up and down the same few roads. When he finally started to walk towards Crystal Palace Road, he radioed Camberwell for help. But by the time he reached the end of the road, he had the feeling that Jackson was going to have been long gone.

Having to radio back to Camberwell and explain that Jackson had already given him the slip, filled him with dread. Camberwell will not like this one little bit, he knew that he didn't take kindly to losing suspects when they are being followed, especially when those suspects were on foot.

Jackson was picked up from the corner of the street by Lansdale. Lansdale was the delivery driver for his business. As far as he was concerned today was just another normal day, with just one exception! He had to make a delivery after 3pm to Peckham High Street. It was unusual today that his boss had asked him to come and collect him, but he never gave it another thought.

They pulled into the garages behind the parade of shops at the junction of Croxted Road and Park Hall Road in West Dulwich. Upon opening the garage door, the stench of soap powder was quite over powering, looking around Jackson saw that a couple of the boxes had been nibbled at by mice. Looking closer he saw that some of the soap powder had leaked onto the floor of the garage.

Turning to Lansdale, Jackson said. "Remember you must be back here by 2pm, there are only two drops today. He also reminded him that he was going away for a couple of weeks from tonight and when he collected payments from today's deliveries, that money was to be used for the next lot of orders that were required from Makro's."

Once Lansdale had left, he phoned McDonald and after deciding not to tell him about the visit by John Nelson, because he was sure it would upset him. He told him that he would be waiting at the garage to receive the parcel, when it was ready. McDonald reminded him that he had to go and buy three more Tri Band phones and give Dillon two of them, then the three of them would have one each.

McDonald was already up and dressed when Jackson called. Sitting back at his table he started to check over his plans.

"If things went belly up, we will all be out of the country, more importantly we will be outside of British jurisdiction. The detonation call would be made on Tri Band phones. The phones then would be broken up and flushed down the airplane toilet."

Getting up, he retrieved a rucksack that was lying on top of the single bed. He removed a long white envelope that contained his passport and airline ticket. He had no problem with using his own passport, he had done nothing wrong. He was just a business class passenger on his way to the Gambia on a business trip.

Checking his airline ticket, he made a mental note to be ready for the chauffeur tomorrow at midnight. The trip to Manchester Airport should take about three hours, which will give him time to chill out before boarding.

Using business class he would be able to check in and then board right at the last minute, so should there be any problems, he could change his plans right up to the time of boarding if required.

He checked his note pad, to confirm what time he had to make the call. If it leaves Brussels at 11:35am. That will make it 10:35am over here which gives me 39 minutes in the air before I make the call, by then we should be well away from all the shit that is going to hit the fan.

He would phone Cathy and the kids using a phone at Brussels Airport, to advise them about whether or not he was leaving on time and what time the flight should arrive at Yundum International Airport.

Talking to himself out loud. "The kids and Cathy have no idea what is about to happen, she knows the pain I am in but she would not agree with me doing this."

With that he put everything away and went and turned the television on. The BBC news was on and they were talking excitedly about the forthcoming visit by Price Harry and the Duchess to Peckham Library. Showing some footage of the new Queen Elizabeth the Second wing, he said out loud.

"That it was nothing but glass! Typical, this country is becoming more like America every day, what was wrong with being British, with British style homes, even our troops are becoming more Americanized, and they are being given the same sub-standard equipment."

He screamed out loudly in anger! "They left him to die, all because some faceless do gooder of a bureaucrat in Whitehall didn't want to upset some stupid frigging Afghanistan leader, even at the cost of British lives. I bet if it was his son left behind to die, that would be different!"

With that he threw his cup of coffee at the television, with a loud bang and sizzle of electricity the screen smashed.

Meanwhile Lawrence was woken up by the sound of a lorry rumbling past his motor home. Looking at his watch through sleepy eyes, he saw that it was 7:45 am. It was so cold that he did not want to get up. Getting dressed he put on a set of thermal under wear.

After making tea and toast he sat down and started to read The Book of Incendiaries and Blasts by Sherman Pollock. This book was the Holy Bible of explosives in his old regiment, no one travelled anywhere when working without it.

This book was used in his training days at Shrivenham. It was the book that he told his students to buy when he was an explosives instructor. It covered everything that needed to be covered. Taking notes as he went along.

"When connecting to the phones ringing circuit, ensure that the defragmenter is connected to the battery at two points. That should cut out any chance of a short circuit." After reading further down the page, he started to write.

"The detonator needs to be connected to the pink and blue wire before you connect the yellow and green wire, failure to do so would almost certainly cause a premature detonation."

After thirty minutes of reading the book, he had finished researching everything he needed to know, all he had to do now was get out and check his tool kit to ensure that he had everything that he would need, the last thing he wanted was to turn up without an item.

He emptied his kit bag onto the small camping table and started to replace items back into the kit bag after writing the list down.

Miniature Screwdrivers – Check

Tweezers – Check

Miniature Pliers – Check

2 Rolls of Pink and Blue wire - check

2 rolls of Yellow and Green wire – check.

He always took two rolls of each just in case one had a break in it.

20 boxes of match worth of ground down match head powder.

He had obtained the matches from the pub, he knew that no one there would say about about them even if the police came a calling.

So his list went on. Until finally, he had all the tools that he required! They were all neatly packed away and ready to go. He then remembered that he had to take the two rolls of black electrical vinyl tape that Jackson had given him yesterday. Getting them from his jacket pocket he dropped them into the tool bad as well.

Leaving the motor home, he wrapped up well against the cold, even to the point of wearing gloves. He knew that he could not afford to turn up with freezing cold hands, he needed his fingers to be supple and warm for all the delicate work that he was about to do.

He had parked well away from the pub, as he did not want the vehicle to be seen there, so it meant that he had to walk to Forest Hill train station, then go to London Bridge then get another train from there to East Dulwich and walk up to the pub.

He could have quite easily got a no 176 bus from Forest Hill to right next to the pub but after an incident in Afghanistan where a bus load of young children were killed, he had a severe fear of buses. Thirty children from the ages of four to twelve were blown to pieces. No one on either side of the conflict would admit that it was their bomb, but they all blamed one another for it. Fragments of bombs found there were from both sides of the conflict.

James Dillon had just woken up in bed, next to him were two young ladies that he didn't even know the names of. One was about five foot eight with dyed blonde hair. The other was an Asian looking lady, roughly the same size. Her thought to himself. "Her skin looks so beautifully soft and light brown, A bit like a very milky chocolate. She looks nice enough to eat!"

When he opened the curtains, he found that he could not look outside because the glare of the sun blinded him. Turning back and facing the two ladies, he noticed that their bodies shimmered with sweat as the sunlight hit their backs.

God! His head was spinning and when he tried to focus his eyes, he found that they hurt like hell! Giving the ladies a shake, he said. "Come on girls, it's time for you to go!"

The girls washed and dressed and then with a wave of their hands and a cheerful "See you later James" they finally left, he then set about making some breakfast for himself.

When his eyes were accustomed enough to the sunlight, he looked out of the front room window to check what the weather was like. Returning to the kitchen, he noticed that the clock on the wall said 9:15 am.

"Christ, I am late, I bet Russell is panicking like mad!"

Turning the gas off, he ran to the bedroom and threw the dishevelled bedclothes back trying to find his clothes.

After getting dressed, he grabbed his keys and jacket and went to exit the flat. When his mobile phone rang, it was McDonald! "James, where are you? Have you left yet?"

Thinking quickly to find an answer, he replied. "I was just going out the front door, but I had to come back because I forgot something, I am just leaving now!"

McDonald snapped at him. "What do you mean? You were just about to go out the front door? You have been told enough times that today you have to leave your car there and leave by the fire escape at the back of the flat. Have you ordered the cab to collect you from Montpelier Road?"

Dillon was so hung over and in such a rush, that he had forgotten everything about the plan for leaving his flat today. "Sorry Russ, I forgot. I'll order the cab now and be with you in about twenty minutes!"

McDonald just hung up the phone, leaving Dillon to say out loud. "He is not a happy bunny!"

After ordering a cab to collect him from outside number 52a Montpelier Road, he left the flat through the fire exit. When he was in the back garden he climbed over the wall and went through the alleyway at the back of the flats and come out right where the cab was supposed to pick him up.

In the cab he phoned Jackson. "Shaun, is everything ready for us to go?"

Jackson told him "Everything was ready here, and I am just about to go to Rye Lane to buy the phones. Is there anything else that we need whilst I am there?"

Dillon told him that there was nothing else. When Jackson asked him where he was, he replied. "I am in a cab on the way to meet Russ! Watch out if you speak to him, he seems as if he has the right hump already."

Neil Lawrence, now he had a total fear of buses! He always told people. "I would rather do twenty miles by train than do two miles by bus." The journey was nothing special apart from listening to two old women berating some old man over something frivolous.

Walking to the pub from East Dulwich station he said to himself. "I hope they have the kettle on its absolutely freezing out here. At 9.50 am he knocked on the door of the Ivanhoe pub, and was shown upstairs to the flat where McDonald and Dillon were waiting for him with interest and anticipation.

As he went to enter the door, he suddenly thought about John Nelson's visit to Shaun's house? Calling Jackson quickly he asked him if he had said anything about Nelson's visit?

Jackson reply was short and sweet. "No! I would suggest we say nothing to be on the safe side!"

Chapter 16

Deployment

Jackson had just finished preparing the van to be loaded when Neil called him and now that was dealt with, he remembered that everything had to be loaded in a specific order, he then left the garage and was now on his way to buy the three extra mobile phones.

The weather was freezing cold when he arrived and he desperately needed to warm up, so he called into the local café. He bought a large cappuccino and two spicy cinnamon rolls and ate them as he walked down Rye Lane.

Coming to the mobile phone shop, he saw a special offer splashed in big letters across the shop window. "Apple Iphone 2G GSM Phones. Buy 2 get 1 Free!"

"That's a result! I'll save some money that might cheer him up!" He said to himself as he walked into the shop he saw the same man that he had bought five disposables from earlier that week.

"Ah Mr. Singh! Just the person, am I right in thinking that these Apple Iphone's can be used aboard domestic and international flights now? It's just that three of us are going abroad for a holiday tomorrow and we'd like to be able to talk to one another whilst we're in the air. Sorry I had better rephrase that! We would like to talk to one another from three different aircraft tomorrow!"

"That's nice! Hold on and I will go and check that out for you."

He went away to the back of the shop to check whether or not this information was correct but knowing the police were interested in this man, he also made a note of all three of the telephone numbers for the phones he was going to sell him.

As Jackson left the shop on his way back to the garage, but did he did not see, was Singh come outside the shop and watch him walk away.

When Jackson was far enough away, he rushed back inside to his office. It took him nearly ten minutes of searching amongst all the piles of rubbish on his desk, before he found the card that the two police officers had left him the other day.

Dialling the number on the card, he said. "Officer Cox, is that you? Good morning to you. It is Mr. Singh here from the phone shop in Rye Lane. That man that bought the disposable mobile phones, well he has just been back into my shop and bought three new phones. …… Pardon! Sorry, but I am having trouble with my hearing today. How long did you say that you would be? Okay, I will see you in twenty to thirty minutes. Thank you so much, Officer Cox."

Meanwhile Lawrence was sitting down at the small table in the flat going through the things that he needed to complete his task. Turning to McDonald and Dillon he said to them both.

"I think that it is advisable for the two of you to go out of the room for about an hour just whilst I finish things off here. Oh before you go, where is the empty soap powder box?"

McDonald pointed at the bottom of the wardrobe. "In there, along with the actual soap powder which is in a black bag."

Lawrence could see that neither of them needed a second invitation to leave the flat.

He had his notes in front of him, but the explosives bible was in his rucksack just in case he should need it. Picking up the mobile phone in his hands, he turned it over so the back was facing him.

Carefully removing the clips that held the front cover to the back, he was able to access the circuits of the phone then using a trace meter to confirm the ringing circuit.

He proceeded to connect the two different wires to it, when the wires were connected, he took the other two ends of the wires and connected them to a small bulb tester.

When he dialled the mobiles number, the phone itself rang for a second then the light bulb came on. He knew now that once he connected the wires to the detonator, it would be job done. Before he did anything else he put the phone back together and put a newly charged battery in it. Then carefully taking the two wires, he made the connection to the detonator cap.

He collected the soap powder box from the wardrobe and stood it on the large table.

Then he picked up the mobile phone, and wrapped it in a clear plastic bag, with just the two wires hanging out. Going back to the small table, he picked up the two rolls of black electrical vinyl tape and taped the mobile securely to the inside of the soap powder box.

Once he was happy with the security of the phone, he filled the box half up with the soap powder from the black bag in the wardrobe.

"Now comes the really dodgy bit!" He said to himself. "Connecting the detonator to the C4 explosives and the Uranium powder.

Taking his time, he fitted everything in place. Using the superglue that Jackson bought, Lawrence was able to seal the bottom of the soap powder box.

He turned the box over to its correct upright position, it looked as if it was brand new.

Walking down the stairs and into the public bar, he went and sat with McDonald and Dillon

"Your radio is fixed now? Whatever you do, don't drop it because it will break again. I have left my telephone number on the table, should you need to get hold of me. I will not be around though until 11:15am tomorrow at the earliest."

McDonald handed him an envelope, which Lawrence didn't even bother to look at. "Are you going to stay for a drink?" Asked Dillon.

"Sorry, things to do and places to go, speak to you both soon. Cheers!" Lawrence replied.

Looking at his watch, Dillon commented "It's nearly 11am, we had better give Shaun a quick call to find out if he's back yet?" Speaking to Jackson, McDonald asked.

"Where are you? Okay, how long do you think it will be before your back at the garage? Because James is just about to leave for the Transit Van hire place in the Old Kent Road, and I wanted to make sure that you would be back in time.

Did you get what you wanted? Good! Well give two of them to James when he meets you. What time is Dave Lansdale coming to pick the van up? Where's all your stuff that you need personally? Great, so you can leave for the airport as soon as you have cleaned out the garage."

With that he hung up and turned to Jackson, and said. "Right you had better get cracking! Shaun will be there by the time you reach the garage. It should take you no longer than an hour to rent the van and get back here."

With that sorted, He left to go and rent the van, McDonald meanwhile went back upstairs to the flat and for some reason very gingerly opened the flat door.

There on the large table in the middle of the room, the box of soap powder stood. The sunlight that shone through the window, made the lilac colour seem more vivid and intense.

For some reason he found himself walking towards it as if it was calling him. Snapping out of his self-imposed daydream, he walked over and picked it up. It was a lot heavier than he thought it would be.

Saying to himself. "Of course it would be you idiot! It's got five pounds of C4 explosive and Uranium powder inside." Confirmation of the telephone number for the detonation call was written on a piece of paper.

Meanwhile, Officer Simon Cox and Officer Glen Cox who by now were better known to everybody as Doris and George, had finally arrived at Singh's mobile phone shop.

"Good morning officers! How are you both today, well I hope? Right where was I? Oh yes! Today the same man that came and bought five disposable mobile phones from me, came back in today and bought three Apple Iphone 2G GSM Phones. They are on a very good deal today if you want to buy one yourself? Buy two get one free!"

"Doris" replied. "Mr. Singh, you were saying about the three new phones that he bought?"

"Ah yes, sorry, anyway, he said that he and his friends were going away today and he wanted phones that were capable of calling people whilst in an airplane!"

This time as if in taking turns. "George" replied. "Mr. Singh, the phones!"

"Oh yes the phones. So sorry! I sold him three phones, but what I remembered to do, was to take a note of the telephone numbers and to telephone you to come and get this information, did I do right?"

"Doris" then said to him. "Mr. Singh, it's a pity more people do not take the time and trouble to help us to help the community." Thank you so much!"

"George" added. "Mr. Singh we thank you so much, we will be in contact with you soon!" They then went to leave the shop when Singh suddenly became all agitated and said. "No…No… Don't go! I have found more information for you whilst you were coming here!"

Turning back to his desk he picked up an A4 sheet of paper. "This is a list of all of the twenty disposable mobile telephone numbers that we sold the same man. We sometimes get a list of telephone numbers for new phones and sometimes we don't. I was looking for something else for someone and I happened to come across this. Is it of any use?"

"Doris" turned to face Singh. "From now on Mr. Singh, if you have to call us, you can call me "Doris" and you can call him "George." We only let our friends call us that and today you have become the best friend we ever had, we cannot thank you enough!"

Outside the shop. "Doris" called Camberwell and told him that he needed to meet with him and Officer George at the Old School immediately. "The information that we have just been could blow the whole investigation wide open and I mean blow it wide open! Okay Sir, we will be as quick as we can."

Dillon was back within twenty five minutes and was drinking a cup of coffee. "Have you got everything that you need personally?" McDonald asked.

"Yes! As soon as I have finished with the van at the garage, I am coming back here with the phones. I had better get cracking, because I have to be at the airport by 4:40pm so as soon as I have finished here, I will be gone.

Followed by McDonald, Dillon carefully picked up the box of soap powder, and gingerly carried it down to the van. Putting it into the passenger seat, he put the vans seatbelt around it.

Turning to McDonald he said.

"Well I should be back in about thirty minutes. It will be about 12:30pm. Then I will collect my bag and be gone, that will give me three hours to get to the airport. I can check in up to an hour later, being business class but I would rather get there earlier, anyway, see you soon."

McDonald said to him. "Be careful, we don't want anything to happen on the way to the garage."

Whilst Shaun Jackson was waiting for Dillon, he had called for a mini cab to come and collect Dillon. Now that had been done, he had moved his van out of the way of the garage doors so that Dillon could just back in.

Checking his rucksack to ensure that he had everything that he needed for his flight, he had it all, apart from some new shirts and tops, which he was going to buy in the Burton's menswear shop in Crawley, so he would call in there before heading to the airport. He did not need to go back to the house, so it was just a case of getting to the airport for approximately 7pm.

Dillon pulled up to the garage gates right on time.

"Everything ready to go?"

Jackson just nodded. Dillon continued. "Take good care of this! Pack it carefully.

"Where's my package as time is very short and I need to get back?"

Jackson handed it to him then said. "The two numbers for you two are written in blue, the number for my phone is written in red. I have kept a copy of your two numbers. Go on you had better get going."

With that he gave Dillon a hug. As Dillon went to get into the cab that was waiting for him, he said. "Oh yes the contact number for tomorrow is in the envelope that was taped to the top of the soap powder box." With that he closed the cab's rear passenger door and it drove away.

When Dillon had gone, Jackson opened the rear doors of the van, turning round he saw that all the items were there laying out in delivery order on the floor, and more importantly to him they were ready to be loaded. After walking over to his desk, he started to sort out all the paperwork that would accompany the goods.

There would be two drops for Lansdale to make, the first place that needed delivering to was the Vale Public House in Grove Vale at East Dulwich. They had quite a bit to deliver but it should take no more than fifteen minutes.

They had ordered thirty boxes of mixed Walkers crisps, thirty sleeves of salted peanuts as well as the thirty sleeves of dry roasted peanuts. Lansdale had to be there by 2:30pm because he had to be at Kumasi Markets by 3pm to deliver the boxes of soap powder and the cigarettes.

Removing the box of soap powder from the front of the van, he put it in the corner with the others, he then picked up from the desk, six special offer tickets which he stuck on five of the normal boxes of soap powder and the other one on the doctored box. He had already agreed with the store owner that he could have them at a very special price of eight pounds each as long as they did not go on display until 11am in the morning. The special offer ticketed ones had to go at the front of the display, which had to be outside the shop, on the pavement.

Dave Lansdale was right on time as usual. Jackson went through the list of items that were to be delivered and to whom, taking his time explaining to him about the agreement with Kumasi Markets. "Remind them about the agreement and say that someone will be along tomorrow to check that the agreement was kept to." After they finished loading everything on to the van, Lansdale left for his first delivery.

When he arrived outside Kumasi Markets, he looked at his watch to check the time. He was pleased with himself, it was bang on 3pm as arranged! When he had finished unloading the van, he met with the shop's owner and ran through the agreement about the goods with him.

As he left the shop, he thought to himself. "What could I do with all this money?"

Chapter 17

Flight to Freedom?

James Dillon, you could see was obviously in quite a rush when he returned with the package that he had to give McDonald. "Here you go, Shaun says that the top number in blue is yours and the next blue one is mine, which obviously means the red number his is."

Grabbing his bag from just the other side of the bar, he said to McDonald. "Well tomorrows the day! Ralph's death will soon be avenged! And then it will have been worth all the effort, sorry Russ but I gotta go."

With that he gave McDonald a hug. "I have the number to call you tomorrow, about 11:16am, is that alright?" McDonald just nodded.

Dillon continued. "Tell Cathy and the kids that I send all my love and hope to speak to them soon." With that he was gone.

Shaun Jackson had ensured that there was no rubbish at all left in the garage, reversed his own van back in, leaving a note on the table at the back of the garage to Lansdale.

"Dave, it is okay to use the van whenever you need, but always return it back here overnight. Out of the money that you collected today, keep one thousand pounds of it as a gift for you and the missus. Please could you return the rental van back to its base in the Old Kent Road, the mechanic has mended our one now, so it will be okay to use next week. Not sure when I'll be back but make sure you keep upto date with everything. Any problems, you're in charge. Speak soon, Shaun."

With that he turned the lights out and locked up. Walking round the corner to South Croxted Road. He waited outside the same Lloyds Bank Branch in West Dulwich where Dillon had been arrested for armed robbery.

A number 3 bus soon came to take him to Crystal Palace Parade and then all he had to do was wait before catching the bus to East Croydon Railway Station. After the train took him to Crawley Station, he would go to the Burton's menswear shop buy a change of clothes for the flight, then return to Gatwick airport in time for his flight.

Police officers Simon and Glen Cox entered the classroom where Camberwell, Tomlin and John Nelson were waiting for them.

"Sir!" Simon said. "Mr. Singh from the mobile phone shop called us today and informed us, that Shaun Jackson, who bought the disposable mobile phones from him, came back to his shop today and bought another three phones."

Glen interrupted. "But these phones are ones with a difference. They were all Apple Iphone 2G GSM Phones!"

Nelson said quickly. "What is so special about them? A mobile is just a mobile isn't it?"

Simon answered. "What makes these phones so special, is that they are capable of making a telephone call to anywhere in the world from an aircraft that is flying. Even at 41,000 feet!"

Glen interrupted his brother then added. "The main thing about the three specific phones that he bought is that Mr. Singh took a copy of all three of the numbers, because he knew that we were interested in the suspect, and on top of that…."

He was cut short again by his brother Simon. "He managed to find a list of all twenty disposable mobile phones numbers that Jackson bought the other day." He handed the A4 sheet of paper that Singh had given them to Camberwell."

Camberwell took the sheet of paper and went and sat down and said. "Doris, George, you were not joking when you said dat dis may well blow the investigation wide open! Dis is such a good piece of investigative work it is untrue. "

Turning to Tomlin he added. "Take these two officers and let them help follow dis part of the investigation through to its completion." Tomlin knew full well what Camberwell had in mind.

Using his mobile to phone Collier at Thames House. "Collier! Tomlin here! Send a car down to the Old School, I want it to pick up two Police Officers, their names are Doris and George... Sorry Officers Simon and Officer Glen Cox. Yes Collier! I am aware that they have the same name! That is why they are called Doris and George! When they get back to Thames House you are to work with them, getting on to all the mobiles phones companies here in the UK and try and trace some telephone numbers. They will have all the details that you will need."

Camberwell gave Simon the list back and said. "Go and get dis copied and then bring the original back here to me. Then go and see the part of the investigation through to the finish and by the way boys! Well done to the pair of you!"

As both of them walked out of the classroom, they could be heard arguing as they walked down the corridor. "I told you I'm going to be the Metropolitan Police Commissioner one day!"

"After me fatboy! I'm going to be the Commissioner before you!" then once again they could be heard laughing at one another as they walked away.

Nelson queried. "Won't Dillon recognise McSloy? I mean he actually spoke to him twice, outside his flat?"

Tomlin replied that they had swapped both McSloy and Critchley over, so that it would not be a problem. Continuing he said. "Both of them have been told that all they have to do is point out their targets to the agents who will meet them in their final destinations."

"So if McSloy and Critchley are trailing Dillon and Jackson, who's going to be trailing McDonald?" Nelson once again asked.

Again Tomlin answered. "We have an agent in Banjul-Yundum. We feel that we don't need to trail him there, because we already have his wife and children under surveillance. If he goes somewhere else they will follow his family."

Camberwell called Critchley on his radio and asked him. "Are you at the airport yet? Dillon is on the move so he won't be long."

Critchley answered. "I am already here! I have managed to book the seat right behind him for the flight to Brussels. Then I am sitting right next to him on the flight to Slovenia. He hasn't arrived here yet but he can book in up to 15 minutes before departure as he is travelling business class, as soon as he arrives I will let you know."

Tomlin was already on the phone to McSloy asking about Jackson.

"Any sign of him yet? Okay, where are you sitting in relation to him? What do you mean they won't put you on the flight?" He said angrily.

McSloy explained that he had only just got there himself, but the airline were not playing ball. Tomlin barked down the phone. "Hang on don't move!"

With that he called Thames House again, this time though he was put through to the head of MI5, Andrew Parker.

Tomlin explained the problem that they were having with First Choice Holidays at Gatwick Airport. Now Andrew Parker is no mug and he doesn't like people taking the piss out of him, his staff and most definitely his beloved country.

He responded "Leave it with me and then get your officer to go back to the airlines desk in five minutes." With that he hung up. Tomlin was now talking back to McSloy.

"Go back to the airline desk and let me know what they say, but don't hang up! I want to hear exactly what they say!" Five minutes later McSloy arrived back at the First Choice Holidays check in desk, Tomlin heard someone say.

"Ah yes Mr. McSloy, please come straight through to the front of the queue, I am pleased to say that we have managed to find a seat, three rows behind a Mr. Jackson."

Meanwhile Russell McDonald was now sitting down in the public bar of the Ivanhoe Pub. He had from about midnight to 1 am in the morning before the limousine was due to arrive and take him to Manchester Airport.

Jackson was on his way, looking at his watch, it showed the time as 4.25pm. "James should at the East Midlands Airport very soon, and Shaun won't be that far off the airport as well." He thought to himself.

He ran through his entire plan in his head, the bomb had been delivered. All players were in play and going to their designated places, all three had phones that could do the job. Cathy and the kids were safely away from the danger zone. He had no other relatives that lived within the blast and fall out area.

Ticking everything off his mental task list the only thing left now was to wait for transportation to the airport and then three telephone calls. The very last thing to do was post a letter to the Times Newspaper group explaining why Prince Harry and the Duchess of Sussex were targeted and killed. He would do that when they stopped at a service station on the way to Manchester Airport.

Taking a mouthful of his beer, he looked up at the television and started to watch the pre match programme for the upcoming FA Youth Cup clash between the Arsenal youngsters and Queens Park Rangers.

His main reason for watching it was, because Sir Les Ferdinand was part of the commentating team. Ferdinand is now the director of football at Queens Park Rangers, so he wanted to watch the match to see if Sir Les had made any impact on the Q.P.R players

Dillon boarded his flight to freedom unaware that he was being shadowed every step of the way. As he sat down the stewardess came over and asked him ensure that his seat was in the upright position and his seat belt was on properly.

As he sat down, she pointed out to Dillon that he had not put away all his hand luggage. "Would you like me to put it in the overhead locker for you? Save you getting up!" She asked.

Dillon nodded politely and handed the carrier bag with his duty free spirits in to her, she struggled to open the locker which allowed Critchley to offer her some assistance and as he held the bag for her he managed to slip a very small tracer bug into it.

It was only the size of a match stick, but quite powerful. He would hand the tracing unit over to the agent he was meeting in Slovenia. Dillon who had put his headphones on was totally oblivious to what went on behind him.

Meanwhile Jackson was changing into the new top he bought at Burton's Menswear.

Exiting the toilets at Gatwick Airport, he made his way to the business class check in desk for First Choice Holidays, standing in the queue right behind him was McSloy.

Jackson was ushered forward, so he went to the counter. "Good Evening Sir! Please may I have your passport! Thank You. Do you have any luggage?" A lady asked from behind the counter. Jackson just nodded his head.

"Did anyone ask you to bring anything for them? Did you pack the bags yourself sir?" She asked.

He just simply replied. "No and Yes!"

Going easily through the X-Ray machine with no problem, at passport control he was asked the usual questions.

"Where are you going? How long will you be gone? When are you expecting to return? With that he was clear to continue on through, he then wandered off to see what duty free stuff was worth buying.

McSloy had a problem, he needed to attach the small tracer bug somehow to Jackson's bags but he had only checked in a small rucksack.

After checking in himself, he watched Jackson disappear past customs and passport control, so he knew where he would be.

Camberwell's mobile rang. Bob Marley for about the millionth time filling the room with One Love! "Can't you change that bloody ring tone? Or at least change the bloody song!" Nelson jokingly asked.

Camberwell never replied. "Camberwell here! …. Okay I will get someone from the airport to come and contact you and take you through to baggage and then you can attach the tracer to his rucksack."

Turning to both Nelson and Tomlin, he said. "Well dat is them two in play, all we need now is for McDonald to make his move. Nelson man! Is your passport up to date? Because you will need it very soon!"

Nelson never answered, instead he went to his jacket and removed his passport from the inside pocket. "Yes, I am fully prepared, to go anytime and anywhere!"

Nelson's mobile rang. "Hi Hilary! ….. Are you sure? No I have their number. Speak to you later, bye."

Turning to Camberwell and Tomlin he said.

" I have just been told the name of the limousine car company that is taking McDonald to Manchester airport. The wife's friend who works for them, she knows McDonald and when his name came up, she told Hilary.

Camberwell replied to Nelson and said. "No worries, now we know who is taking him, we can sort dat out with them."

McDonald was ready and waiting when the limousine turned up to collect him. "Are we going to stop on the way to the airport?" he asked.

The driver nodded and asked him if he had a preference of anywhere in particular.

"Newport Pagnell services would be good, I need to post a letter from there." He replied.

Before getting into the car he quickly went back upstairs to the flat and made sure that it was clean. Leaving through the public bar he stopped and spoke to the landlord.

"Well you know how much this has meant to me, your help and understanding is greatly appreciated." With that he shook the landlords hand and then he left.

The traffic through to the start of the M1 motorway was surprisingly busy but as soon as they reached the motorway proper, the driver then sped up and within what seemed no time at all, they were at the Newport Pagnell Motorway Services.

As McDonald left the car he asked the driver if he wanted a coffee or anything.

The driver just shook his head then picked up the newspaper that was laying on the passenger seat and started to read it.

As soon as McDonald was out of sight, the driver got out and went to the rear of the limousine and opened the boot.

Removing a small tracer from underneath the lapel of his jacket, he attached it to McDonald's luggage, as he straightened up he noticed that McDonald was coming back.

Quickly thinking on his feet, he said. "Champagne Sir?"

McDonald replied. "No thanks! I left my letter in my bag, and I need to post it! Are you sure you don't want anything?"

"Tell you what Sir, I will have a coffee, please."

Waiting until McDonald went out of sight again, he opened his mobile and called Tomlin.

"Hi Sir. McCarthy here! Just to let you know that the tracer on McDonald has been placed and it is now in play."

For McDonald, in his mind everything that needed to be done had been done. All he needed to do now was make a call. "And the rest as they say, would be history!"

Thinking to himself "I feel sorry for anyone who is innocent and suffers but the onus is on the British Government. People may say that it makes me as bad as them, but I can only fight my own battles, perhaps after this other people will seek out their own form of justice, then perhaps the government will listen."

Chapter 18

Detection

Collier and Officers 'Doris' and 'George' were at the computer consoles in Thames House. From the twenty disposable mobile phone numbers that they had on their list, they had managed to trace twelve of them, each one of them had only been used twice.

They found out that mobile phone service providers O2 and 3 had been extremely unhelpful in their requests for information. Of the three of them, O2 had seemed the worse, simply delaying any information that needed to be given.

Virgin Mobile had been the most helpful, which really was not that surprising. The company's founder Sir Richard Branson was extremely patriotic and if the staff at the head office had be unco-operative, then all hell would have broken loose and heads would have been rolling down the street.

'Doris's screen suddenly came with a flashing message, Virgin Mobile telephone number 07999 754444 was actually being used at this precise moment.

Scrolling down the screen it showed that the number it was calling 0161 191 9000, turning to Collier, 'Doris' asked. "Can you get a location on this telephone number? One of the four suspects was calling it right now! We need to trace the caller's position as well."

'George' interrupted. "Well it cannot be Dillon or Jackson because they are both in the air and these numbers are not from the G2 phones. We have no communication information for Lawrence so I'd guess that it is McDonald! Who the hell is he phoning at four in the morning?"

'George' laughed and said. "A Pizza parlour?"

Collier snapped at the pair of them. "Come on let's get back to work. I'll go and get this sorted. 'Doris', keep an eye on the call, let me know if he rings off!"

Collier came back less than a minute later. "Is he still on the line?" he asked.

'Doris' replied "Yes he is, hang on a second he has just rung off. Did you manage to trace his call? Who was he phoning?"

Collier's reply came as a bit of a shock. "Well, it is McDonald and he's on the motorway heading towards Manchester Airport. The shocking bit is that he was calling a Mrs. Nelson, who lives in Manchester's Openshaw district. We have dispatched a unit to her address to question her."

'George' then said. "We better tell Camberwell what is going on and if Nelson is still there, this will be a bit of a kick in the short and curlies, if it turns out to be a relative of his."

"George" phoned Camberwell and said. "Sir, we have just discovered that in the last five minutes McDonald has physically phoned a Mrs. Nelson in Openshaw, Manchester. He's on his way to Manchester Airport, The tracer bug is working well. The list? Oh the telephone list! Sorry sir. We have discovered that so far and including the phone that McDonald just used to call Mrs. Nelson, is that 13 of the numbers have now been used one way or another and none of them have been used more than twice."

Then he told Camberwell the telephone number that McDonald called. "Okay sir, when we get more information we will get back to you."

Camberwell turned to John Nelson and then just stared at him for a few moments, then said. "John, do you know anybody dat lives in Openshaw, Manchester?"

"Yes, my mother lives there, why?"

"Sorry to be a pain but can you tell me her telephone number please?"

Nelson replied. "0161 191 9000 why?"

Tomlin also said to Camberwell. "Why?"

"Well John, believe it or not, for some reason Russell McDonald has just phoned your mother!"

"What! What do you mean he's just phoned my mother?" Nelson just stood there almost in a state of shock, with that he grabbed a phone and called his mother.

"Mother! Did McDonald just phone you? … What did he say to you? … I don't care if there is a policeman asking you the same questions! Tell him to wait. Now tell me what McDonald just said to you when he called and I want you to tell me every single word he said, and I mean every single word!"

At the other end of the phone Mrs. Nelson was in tears. "What's happened to my Daniel?... Will people stop shouting at me? What the heck is going on? … Okay, Russell phoned me and all he said was.

"He was very sorry to hear about Daniel and when I asked why, what was wrong with him, he just replied that you would call and explain.

Then in the next breath he said that he had left instructions that I would receive a cheque for one million pounds, which would allow me to set up a trust fund in Daniel's name, he also said it should be enough money to set up a young black kid's music workshop in Manchester, and that you would get the same, to set one up in London."

With that she burst into tears. "John, what has happened to Daniel? I am really scared now, please tell me what has happened to Daniel?"

John Nelson then walked outside the classroom and you could sense that as he was talking he was just starting to cry.

When he was in the corridor he was heard saying. "Mum, Daniel has been involved in a terrible accident!" Then they could hear no more as he moved further away.

Camberwell turned to Tomlin then said. "We have about five to six hours to solve dis! We are so close but yet so far, it seems as if the solution is just out of our reach. We know who is plotting it but we cannot prove it, we don't even have enough evidence to arrest them. If we did they would be out within thirty minutes. Have we heard about the Prince's movements for today yet?"

Tomlin answered. "They told me that they would let us know right at the last minute, just in case anything should change. All I know at this particular moment in time is that they are leaving Clarence House at approximately 10:30 – 10:40 am. I have been still trying to get them to change their mind and not come, but so far, no luck!"

Dave Lansdale had been out on the tiles celebrating his new found wealth. Jackson leaving him the one thousand pounds and the use of the van whenever he felt like it, he'd been out making the most of it.

Whilst driving along the South Circular Road towards Forest Hill, he was singing along to Katy Perry's "Hot n Cold" record, as he passed the corner of Gallery Road.

Where the road becomes an S Bend, he lost control and smashed the van into the railings at the side of the road. The van flipped onto its side and then skidded down the road for nearly two hundred yards, hitting oncoming vehicles, including a motorhome!

When he came round he could hear sirens going off everywhere and he had obviously banged his head, as he had a stinking headache, the sound of all the sirens made it much worse.

He had been lucky, very lucky indeed! The Paramedics wanted to take him to the A&E department at Kings College Hospital for a check-up, but he refused to go. For some reason when he was approached by a Police Officer he decided to start singing "I did it my way!"

The female Police Officer was not impressed so asked him for a breath test, Lansdale refused.

"Do you not care that you have just killed someone! The person driving the motorhome was killed instantly by you smashing into him at sixty miles per hour. How does that make you feel?"

"I seem to have dropped some money somewhere, have you seen it?" was Lansdale's reply.

The officer angrily shouted at him. "I wish that you had been the one who died!" And with that he was put into the back of a police van and taken away.

When he arrived back at Peckham Police Station, he was finally breath tested and his blood alcohol level was so high that the machine recorded the highest level possible.

He was arrested for Drink Driving and causing a death by dangerous driving whilst under the influence, then put into a cell.

The booking desk sergeant said him. "You need to sleep it off, and then you will be questioned tomorrow."

Lansdale responded by starting to sing "Police and Thieves" by Junior Murvin.

The Officer in charge at the scene of the accident was reporting back to the control room at Peckham Police Station.

"We need a removal truck for a Fiat Carioca Motorhome, Registration Number NL2008 and a white Ford Transit Van, registration number SRJ 2008." The driver of the motorhome was killed instantly.

The control room officer stopped him in full flow.

"Did you just say the two registration numbers were NL 2008 and SRJ 2008?" "Yes why?" The officer in charge at the scene of the accident asked.

"Well those vehicles are being sought by Inspector Camberwell and the long streak of piss from MI5 or whatever cupboard he came out of!, Wait there, I am sure that he will send someone will come speak to you!"

Tomlin was in the classroom on his own, checking then rechecking the dry wipe board, trying to see once again if they had missed anything. The telephone rang and when he answered it, he was greeted with.

"Your missing vehicles, we have found them. Oops Sorry! I thought Inspector Camberwell would answer the phone. Is he there, please?"

"He's just popped out to the toilet, this is Tomlin from MI5, can you please repeat what you said about the vehicles?"

The control room officer from Peckham Police Station started to repeat the report, when Camberwell came back into the room. Tomlin said. "Hold on, Camberwell has just come back into the room, you had better tell him."

"Camberwell here! Who is dat? Oh hi, how are you? Where and how long ago did the accident happen? Do we know the name of the dead motorist yet? Neil Lawrence, Okay! Right and the other driver, Dave Lansdale, Okay! Is he still alive? Where is he now? What do you mean he's sleeping off a massive hang over? Right we are on our way, wake him up and pump him full of black coffee, we'll be five minutes."

Turning to Tomlin he said. "Grab Nelson and meet me in the car in two minutes, we need to go and we need to go now!" Tomlin walked into the courtyard only to find Nelson still on the phone to his mother.

"John, sorry to interrupt but we need to go right now, by the way, how's your mum?"

Tomlin asked. Nelson didn't answer for a few seconds, then after wiping tears from his eyes he answered.

"She is distraught, I hadn't got round to telling her about Daniel yet. There is a WPC with her and she called my sister who has come over to sit with them both. Do you know what he told my mum? He was sending a million pound cheque to her and one to me, so that we can set up young black kid's music workshops. One here in London and in Manchester in memory of Daniel! Russell McDonald is so dead when I catch up with him. I want to kill him so slowly it's untrue, the more painful the better. If I could I would use an old Japanese torture method. Stake him out standing up like a star then put a bamboo plant right underneath him then sit back and watch it grow right through him!"

Tomlin just simply replied. "Officially, I cannot say this, But! Nice, Very Nice! Put one there for me and Camberwell as well!"

In the car on the way to Peckham Police Station, Camberwell told the two of them what the phone call was about. "Lawrence is dead! They have the driver, who survived despite turning the van over and crashing into amongst others, Lawrence's motorhome at the junction of Gallery Road and The South Circular Road in West Dulwich. He is as drunk as a skunk! They should be pouring coffee down his throat like he's going out of fashion, he is the break in this case that we wanted. So we need to get all the information about his movements in the last couple of days."

Tomlin asked. "Where are they taking the vehicles? Because we will need to check them over as well."

Camberwell replied. "Well at the moment they are still at the scene of the accident. But I will get them taken back to the Old School car park, which is at least five times the size of the yard at the station. Your boys can give it them the once over there."

Tomlin got straight on his phone and told Collier to arrange the people to go to the Old School car park to check the vehicles out. "Any more news on the remaining telephone numbers yet?" He asked. Collier told him that they were now down to five numbers left to check.

As they pulled up outside the Police Station they were met by a waiting female uniformed officer.

"Sir, you cannot see him at the moment because he is with the doctor undergoing checks. His alcohol blood level is so high that there is a high risk of a fatal cardiac arrest due to the amount of alcohol that he consumed."

Nelson snapped at her harshly. "I couldn't care less if he dies as long as we get the information that we need, before he does."

Tomlin grabbed his arm and said. "Cool down, I need him to be awake and alert enough to help us with the information that we need. Trust me if he is one of the gang, I will wish him dead as well! But if he is not then we need to be careful otherwise we could lose him and the whole situation."

Camberwell asked the officer. "How long does the doctor think it will be before we can question him?"

The officer answered. "About an hour, I think?"

Nelson snapped again. "That will only give us about three to four hours to solve this. Is there no way that he can be compos mentis before then?"

"You'll have to speak to the doctor. He's in the detention block" The officer replied.

Chapter 19

Breakthrough

In the detention block all three of them were pacing the floor waiting for the doctor to come out and speak to them.

Camberwell looked at his watch it 7:30am. Out loud he said. "We have three and a half hours to solve dis, and all dis waiting is getting us nowhere."

With that he burst into the room where the doctor was checking Lansdale over. "Doc, how long is it going to be before we can speak to him? It really is a matter of life and death dat we can talk to him!"

The doctor looked at him and calmly said. "You may want to speak to him but you're lucky that he's even alive! The crash should have killed him and with the amount of alcohol that he has consumed, he should be dead as well. What's keeping him alive? I'll never now. So I suggest that you go outside and wait until he's fit enough to speak to! That is if he survives!"

Outside in the corridor he turned to both Tomlin and Nelson then stated. "It is pointless dat we all just sit here and wait, so dis is what I propose! Tomlin you stay here and the moment dat he is awake enough to question get in and question him! We will stay in contact every fifteen minutes with each other. John, you can come with me. I have something that you can do for us."

Tomlin, called the doctor out once Camberwell and Nelson had gone and said.

"Doctor, I want to question him at the earliest possible moment and to be honest if he keels over and dies afterwards I don't care. I don't want to wait until he is 100 per cent able to talk to us, I want 20 per cent if it means he can understand and talk to me. Is that understood?" The doctor just looked at him and after a few moments just nodded.

Camberwell and Nelson were on their way back to the Old School, when Camberwell said. "We are now getting close to the moment in time when we have to make our move. I want you to go to the row of shops opposite Peckham Square and speak to the shop workers and managers and double check dat none of them have had any contact with Jackson in the last twenty four hours."

Continuing he said. "Then take a walk around the square and use your eyes for the unusual things dat looks out of place, then let me or Tomlin know the slightest thing dat you're unsure or unhappy with. If anything our end comes up we'll let you know straight away."

Tomlin was getting really frustrated clock watching now. The doctor seemed no nearer in allowing him to question Lansdale. "8am. Three hours now! Come on Doc sober him up!" he said to himself, suddenly his mobile phone rang.

"Hello Tomlin here!" He answered. "Mr. Haverson, please tell me that everyone has come to their senses and the Prince is not going to come to Peckham today! Do you realize how much danger you lot are putting the innocent people of Peckham through? Hold on I'd better write this down. Okay ready. He's leaving Clarence House at 10am. Then he's stopping off for about twenty minutes to lay a wreath at the memorial stone for DC Morrison in Covent Garden."

Querying Haverson, he said. "Why is he going there? Oh okay, something about the anniversary of his death. Okay right! " He then started to write again.

When he had finished writing, he asked Haverson about contact with the motorcade should they need to abort? He was told that a plan was in place and he did not need to know what it was, all he had to do was keep the motorcade informed minute by minute. But the visit would go ahead irrespective.

With that Tomlin hung up fuming! Calling Camberwell he repeated the instructions that he had just been given. "He's laying a wreath for DC Morrison. He's then coming over Waterloo Bridge down Waterloo Road to the Elephant and Castle. Along Walworth Road towards Camberwell Green then left into Peckham Road. Finally to Peckham Square outside the library almost dead on 11am. Fifteen minutes with the kids and dignitaries then inside the library to open the new wing, they should be gone by midday."

When Camberwell said nothing for a few seconds Tomlin asked him. "Who is DC James Morrison?"

Camberwell again said nothing for a few seconds then said. "DC Morrison was fatally stabbed while he was off duty, attempting to arrest a thief in 1991. If my memory serves me correctly it was around dis time in December."

Again pausing for a second he added. "I am certain dat he was posthumously awarded the Queens Gallantry Medal. He was killed in Montreal Place, Covent Garden."

For what seemed the millionth time Tomlin looked at his watch, it was now 8am and he was really starting to panic.

Still they needed that little bit of divine intervention if they were going to save people's lives.

Opening the door to the cell where the doctor was still treating Lansdale, he said. "Come on Doc! You've got to give me something, at least some idea of a time that I can speak to him!" The Doctor just looked at him and shook his head.

Camberwell was back at the Old school when Tomlin phoned, after speaking to him he slammed the phone down hard, hard enough, that it cracked the phones plastic cover. In his rage he then clenched his fist and punched the classroom door, with so much force that he made a hole in it.

The sound of Bob Marley again started to fill the room, snatching it up off the table. "Hello Camberwell here! Officer Cox what have you got for me!" ...... What are the two numbers that are unaccounted for? Hold on! I'll write them on the dry wipe board."

1/. 07721 911102
2/. 07721 911114

"Brilliant stuff! Now get back here the pair of you as soon as possible!" With that he hung up.

"Tomlin here! Oh hi Camberwell! No Not yet? Hold on a moment here comes the doctor! Let me call you back in five minutes!"

"Well doctor can I go and speak to him now?"

The doctor answered. "It will be at least half an hour before he is ready to speak to him and if you are rough with him in your questions then you'll cause him to cardiac arrest."

Looking at his watch now seemingly every second, he replied. "Doc it is now nearly 9am and that now only gives us two hours."

The doctor looked at him then said, well it's your choice, try to make him talk now and he will die on you. If you wait for the 30 minutes you may stand a chance of getting the information that you want. Your call?"

Officers "Doris" and "George" Cox were on their way back to meet up with Camberwell at the Old School, when they got a message to ring Collier at Thames House. "Collier, what is so important that I had to ring you at all costs?" "Doris" queried.

Collier was speaking very fast and very excitedly. "We've found it, we've found it!"

"We've found what?" Cox replied. "The telephone number that will be used to detonate the bomb! We have accounted for the last used number two minutes ago but I have been unable to contact Tomlin or Camberwell. The last outstanding number is 07721 911114. Did you get that? The number to detonate the bomb is 07721 911114."

John Nelson was walking past the Subway sandwich shop at the bottom of Rye Lane, stopping occasionally to see if anything was untoward anywhere. There seemed to be loads of armed police marksmen walking around, he assumed that they were there for the visit of the Prince.

Looking at his watch, he saw that the time was now 9:15am. He continued to walk down the part of Peckham High Street, opposite Peckham Square.

He noticed that on a couple of the shop windows that there were notices telling the general public that due to the visit of Prince Harry, the shops would not be opening until about 1pm that day.

As he reached the junction of Peckham High Street and Peckham Hill Street he turned around and started walking back the way he came.

Something caught his eye, something was definitely was glinting on the skyline of the shops along the shops in that section of Peckham High Street.

So police marksmen were up there as well! He stopped and tried to count how many there were but gave up after reaching twenty. Restarting his walk back towards the Subway sandwich shop, he came across an Asian man who was opening the shutters of his shop.

For some reason his attention was drawn to the name of the shop. Kumasi Markets! The man spoke. "Good morning Sir! Do you like my new sign? It was only finished two days ago! Bit hip isn't it?"

Nelson answered. "Very Nice." Then he started to walk away.

"Tell you what sir! I can do you a very nice deal today! I have just taken delivery of a load of big boxes of soap powder, no rubbish mind you. Its Surf soap powder! For you twelve pounds per box. If you want to buy a bulk amount I have up to forty boxes. This is a once in a lifetime special offer, just for today only! "

"What did you just say?" Nelson asked.

The man repeated "I have just taken delivery of a load of big boxes of soap powder, no rubbish mind you. Its Surf soap powder no less! For you twelve pounds per box. If you want to buy a bulk amount I have up to forty boxes."

Nelson ignored him and immediately called Camberwell on the phone.

"Camberwell I have found the soap powder! Did you hear me? I have found the soap powder! All forty boxes of the stuff! Kumasi markets, one of the shops right opposite Peckham Square. Okay I will be here."

Turning to an armed police marksman that was walking past, he said. "In this shop we are certain that there is an unexploded bomb that is timed to go off when Prince Harry and the Duchess of Sussex gets here! The Inspector in charge of the case will be here in about ten minutes. Get your boss to meet us here right now!"

Ten minutes later bang on time both Camberwell and Metropolitan Police Assistant Commissioner Nick Ephgrave, who was the head of CO19, arrived at Kumasi markets.

Nelson told them both what he had found and also that the armed officer was now starting to close roads in the local area.

Ephgrave was not concerned that Nelson was a member of the public, he was just grateful the same as Camberwell and Tomlin that this information had been found out literally just in the nick of time.

At the detention block of Peckham Police Station, the doctor suddenly appeared at the door of the cell where he had been. He let out a massive sigh then spoke to Tomlin.
"It's no use! He's just died!"

Tomlin was stunned, suddenly the fury that had been building up inside of him exploded.

"What the hell do you mean he's just died? How the hell can he die just like that?"

The doctor just seemed to look straight through him, without compassion and without anger.

"His body just gave up, what with the accident and also the amount of alcohol he drank, there was nothing that we could do to save him, we tried our best but he just went!"

Tomlin who had been sitting on the edge of a desk just outside the cell door, stood up in his anger and fury then flipped the desk over like it was a piece of paper. "What the hell is happening?" He screamed out loud.

Suddenly the desk sergeant's phone rang. "It's for you Sir!" Snatching the phone off the desk sergeant. He ranted at all the staff that were just standing around looking at him with stunned faces.

"What the hell are you lot looking at! Get back to work, and call the bloody coroner?" Speaking into the phone mouth piece, he said. "Tomlin here! Okay I will be right there!"

Less than two minutes later Tomlin was outside Kumasi markets. Nelson took him, Ephgrave and Camberwell through the shop and showed him the stack of forty soap powder boxes.

"Do we know which one the bomb is in?"

Nelson replied. "No, we are waiting for bomb disposal to get here. They have sniffer dogs coming too."

"John" He said turning to Nelson. "Can you try to find out as much information from the shop owner as you can about the person or persons who sold him the stuff? Get him back to the detention block at the police station if you have to, I don't care how you do it but find out!"

Tomlin then walked back outside where both Camberwell and Ephgrave were waiting. Speaking to them both, he said. "It is 9:25am, if we try to evacuate now it will cause widespread panic and gridlock the local area. So this is what I propose!"

With that the dreaded sound of Bob Marley and "One Love" filled the air. Tomlin sneaked a look at Camberwell who was reaching for his phone. Camberwell looked in trepidation at Tomlin.

"Camberwell here!" Oh God! It was the wife and boy was she not happy!

Her anger and fury seemed to have reached a new level! "Am I expecting to go and watch out granddaughter present these flowers to Prince Harry and the Duchess on me own?"

She ranted down the phone at Camberwell in her strongest Jamaican accent she had. "You can't be bothered to come watch your Granddaughter in the greatest moment of her life!"

Camberwell answered. "Look Bab………!"

The phone seemed to shake as Marshita screamed down the phone. "Don't look baby me! I want to know will you be coming!"

Camberwell was so embarrassed that he hung up on her.

"Don't ask!" he said to Tomlin. "The damn woman has gone too far dis time!" Ephgrave made out he was looking at the floor.

Tomlin just stood there unsure whether to say anything or not, he looked at Camberwell and just as he was about to speak as Officers Simon and Glen Cox came running down the road, as fast as they could, calling out to all three of them.

When they were standing next to them, Simon said very breathlessly. "Sir, we tried to get hold of you by phone but for some reason the network seems to be snarled up."

Glen interrupted then added the killer blow that his brother did not find amusing. "We have the telephone number of the mobile phone that we believe will detonate the bomb!"

Handing over a piece of paper to Tomlin, he continued. "The number is 07721 911114. The reason we never got it before was because O2 spent hours stalling us, it seems that they finally woke up to the fact, is was a serious issue and gave it to us. They cost us over twenty four hours nearly with their stalling tactics."

The Bomb disposal units were already on their way, they are stationed at their Hyde Park Barracks headquarters in central London so they should be nearly here.

Ephgrave, the head of CO19, had called them in as soon as he knew that an actual device had been believed to have been found. Within twenty minutes of getting the call, they were at the scene. Tomlin looked at his watch for what seemed to be the thousandth time today. 9:55am.

The sniffer dogs were taken straight to the stack of soap powder boxes and then they were moved one by one by a Bomb Disposal expert who was wearing his protective suit. As each box was inspected one by one, they were removed by other officers in protective clothing.

The dog suddenly sat down at a box that had a special offer label on it. Leaving that box where it was he continued to check all the others until they proved harmless.

The bomb disposal officer then went outside and spoke to Camberwell, Tomlin and the head of CO19. Very calmly he said. "We have found the device, what can you tell me about it and I will need to know everything that you know about it. Everything!"

Tomlin spoke first. "Firstly we have just found out the telephone number of the mobile phone that was going too used as the detonation device!"

Immediately he was interrupted by the bomb disposal officer. "Right this is what we need to do! You immediately get on to the mobile phone's service provider and get them to block the signal to that telephone number, in fact what we want them to do is to take the number out of service! That way no one can use the phone at all and the suspects will be unable to connect either irrespective of wherever they are in the world."

Tomlin reacted by getting straight onto his phone. "Collier, listen to me and listen carefully! You are to contact the person you have been dealing with at O2 and have them take the telephone number for the bomb mobile phone out of service. It has to be out of service! Do you understand? If they give you any grief then tell then that within twenty minutes they will be shut down permanently. We will then get the military to go and do it. Is that understood?

Okay call me when they say that the number is offline"

Meanwhile Camberwell was in the middle of telling the Bomb disposal officer, the other information that they knew about the bomb.

"As I was saying, we believe dat there are four to five pounds of C4 explosive connected to the bomb."

"Plus four pounds of Uranium powder!" Tomlin added.

"Shit! The bomb disposal officer said. "Uranium powder is recognised the world over as being the most dangerous form that it can be. If it is Uranium 235 type that it will have come from a nuclear reactor somewhere!"

Turning to Camberwell he said. "Are we clear yet to attempt to diffuse it?"

Camberwell called on the control room on his radio, they told him that there was no chance of getting the whole area clear in time.

Camberwell turned to the bomb disposal officer and said. "Do It! we have no choice but to go with what we have. Tomlin, Ephgrave! We need to get to the control room and we can link up live from there!"

Peckham Police Station was literally five hundred yards away and by the time that Camberwell, Tomlin and Ephgrave got there, the bomb disposal officer had already started sending in the Cutlass robot into the back of the shop to bring the box out.

The Cutlass had been adapted to fire a high pressure but very fine jet of water, this would help avoid any accidental detonation from a munitions based defusing firing.

Chapter 20

Royal Visit

This time it was Camberwell looking at his watch. 10:15Am. Prince Harry would be leaving Covent Garden soon. Turning to speak to Tomlin, he said,

"The time to use the telephone to contact Haverson was almost upon them, we can afford to give it 10 more minutes then we have to make the call."

The robot was now carrying the box of soap powder in its claws out into the middle of Peckham High Street. It placed it down and very carefully sliced the bottom of the box all the way round with a robotic blade.

The claw, very slowly lifted top part of the box up away from the contents, as it started to lift the top of the box away, the soap powder very slowly started to spill out on to the road.

Moving centimetres at a time until the top of the box was off leaving the bomb exposed for all to see, its wires going to the mobile phone which was till stuck to the side of the box. Its operator sent the robots extendable camera in and had a good look round. Speaking to the control room he said,

"We are going to fire. Now! After moving five feet away from the box, its operator aimed water nozzle then fired.

Water seemed to spray everywhere. A fine mist made the monitor screen in the control room seem as if someone had shaken talcum powder everywhere. When the picture cleared, all that was left was the C4 explosive and a metal cylinder which had been separated by the water jet.

Panning round the scene, the mobile telephone could be seen broken in lots of different pieces about one hundred yards away.

Over the loudspeaker in the control room the words that they had all longed to hear, came through. "Device has been made safe! I repeat the device has been made safe!" The control room erupted in loud cheers and wolf whistles.

They made their way to the office of Borough Commander Simon Messinger, where the Metropolitan Police Commissioner Cressida Dick, the Worshipful Mayor of the London Borough of Southwark Councillor Sandra Rhule and all the other dignitaries were.

Camberwell asked the Commissioner if he and Tomlin could have a private chat with her, the Commander and the Mayor.

After going into another room Camberwell asked. "Sir, ma'am. As you know the bomb has been defused and now everything will go ahead as planned but we need to do a bit more than dat to catch the people behind it. It is now 10:30am and Prince Harry and the Duchess are due in thirty minutes, with your permission, I would like to put a story out to the world's media dat the assassination attempt on Prince Harry's and the Duchess's life was successful."

Tomlin butted in. "What he means is, that we need to convince McDonald and his cronies to that it worked! That way we can flush them out into the open, it would mean getting the assistance of Sky News and the BBC. They are both here already to cover the visit."

The Mayor said. "Can we not extradite them?"

The Commissioner Cressida Dick answered.

"Inspector Camberwell had kept me and the Chief Superintendent informed all the way along and I think that it is necessary to deal with these sorts of people!"

Dick had just taken over as the Metropolitan Police Commissioner from her predecessor Sir Bernard Hogan-Howe, had been fired by the new Mayor of London Sadiq Khan, so she was new to the game of being in overall control.

Then both she and the Borough Commander moved to the side of the room to discuss the options.

Dick said. "Do it and I will clear it with the Palace and the Prime Minister!"

Camberwell and Tomlin made their way back to the Chief Superintendents office. Tomlin addressed everybody there. "Ladies and Gentleman please could you make your way to Peckham Square in readiness to greet his Royal Highness Prince Harry and the Duchess of Sussex. You may all have lots of questions that need answering, but these will be dealt with after the visit has concluded."

While waiting for the office to clear, the Commissioner Cressida Dick had called the Prime Minister Boris Johnson and Buckingham Palace to confirm that the plan could definitely go ahead.

The Prime Minister had asked about other options, Dick replied "That there were none, they could not send a force in to eliminate them on foreign soil, so unless they return to Britain we are stuffed!"

As they all went to leave the office Camberwell and Tomlin pulled Sky News Sarah Hughes and the BBC's Justin Webb to one side and asked them to wait for a few minutes.

When everybody else had gone, into the room walked the Commissioner Cressida Dick, the Borough Commander Chief Superintendent Simon Messinger and the Mayor of Southwark Councillor Sandra Rhule.

Explaining to Sarah Hughes about what had happened and what they needed to happen now.

"We need to convince McDonald that his attack succeeded! We are aware that they have left the United Kingdom for countries with no extradition treaties with us, so we need to flush them out."

Sarah Hughes said. "I will need to talk to my editor about this, I can't make this call."

Justin Webb just said. "Let's do it, I'll clear it with the editor and the Director General of the BBC later!"

Leaving the room, Hughes went to call her editor, who in turn called his boss, who himself called her boss. She came back into the room ten minutes later and said. "They have agreed, we will keep the story up for two days after that we will reveal all!"

"Let's get it done then!" said Tomlin.

When everybody except the Met Police Commissioner and Tomlin had left the room, Camberwell asked. "Sir, my Granddaughter is one of those children who will be presented to Prince Harry and the Duchess in a few minutes. Now the thought of her dying is unthinkable to me, so if it is okay with you. Tomlin, Nelson and I, we need a holiday. We are thinking of a shooting holiday for say, seven days, with your permission of course Sir! We feel dat we really need a break!

Also could you see that these officers and members of the public are credited with so much assistance during the course of our enquiries? Without these people we probably would all be dead now!"

Cressida Dick looked at them quizzically then opened the piece of paper and read it.

WPC Maureen Lackey.
PC Simon Cox (Doris).
PC Glen Cox (George).
DI Paul McSloy.
DI Dave Critchley.
Scott Collier (Thames House)
John Nelson (Member of the public)

Rather than read the rest of the list, Cressida Dick looked at Tomlin and asked. "Do you agree?"
Tomlin just nodded.

Turning to them both he then added. "Have a nice holiday the three of you, and good hunting! By the way we only have five minutes before Prince Harry and the Duchess get here, so we had better get a move on!"

Camberwell and Tomlin made a detour on their way to Peckham Square, calling at the detention block, they collected John Nelson and together they made their way to watch the visit of the royal party.

As they were getting ready to watch Camberwell's Granddaughter presenting the Duchess of Sussex with a bouquet of flowers, Camberwell said. "Well as we have saved the whole of South London! Both Tomlin and I have decided to go on a shooting holiday tomorrow, would you like to come with us?"

"Depends where you're going as I have unfinished business first!" Nelson answered.

"Well we can take care of that while we are away. We have decided to go on a three country world tour, firstly we are thinking of going to Slovenia, after a day or so there, we're then going to Morocco and after another couple of days in the sunshine there we are paying a quick visit to the Gambia." Camberwell replied.

"Count me in!" Nelson added.

A phone rang and it was once again the sound of Bob Marley. Tomlin spoke first as all three men seemed to have been frozen by fear to the spot where they stood, But this time it was the sound of Buffalo Soldier.

"It's okay, it's my son Vance! Hello Vance! Tell your mum to give me a couple of minutes and I will be with her, Okay see you soon."

Turning to the other two men who were now standing there laughing at him, he added. "We have just saved the second in line to the throne, Prince Harry and his wife by defusing a dirty bomb and the three of us are more scared of my wife than that!"

They all started to laugh as they walked towards Peckham Square again.

Camberwell reached the spot next to Marshita just as their Granddaughter started to present the flowers to Prince Harry.

He suddenly froze with horror and dread, turning to look at both Bob Tomlin and John Nelson, he could see that they were both laughing so much that there were tears rolling down their faces, the music that the children had started dancing to was.

"One Love by Bob Marley and the Wailers."

Turning to his wife he planted a massive kiss on her cheek, and said to her softly. "One Love, One Love, Let's get together and feel alright!"

Marshita slowly turned her head and looked at him and said softly. "Paul McIntosh Your dinner is in the Microwave and has been there since you left to go messing around, after this me going bingo!"

Camberwell just simply said. "I Love You!"

Chapter 21

Premature Jubilation

Russell McDonald was on his plane heading to Gambia from Belgium, looking at his watch it read 11:09am UK time. Rising from his seat, he made his way to the toilet. Once he was in there he took out his phone, while dialling the number he was thinking to himself

"Ralph, this is for you and to all the innocent people that are about to die, please forgive me but the people to blame are the British Military and the British Government.

Again looking at his watch, the time read 11:14am UK time. He pressed the send button on the phones keypad, not hearing anything but a beeping sound, did not worry him at all, being a G2 phone you seemed to get a different ringing sound.

After 20 seconds he shut the phone lid down then placed it on the floor, smashing it with his foot. Picking up all the broken pieces he then flushed it down the aircrafts toilet. Back at his seat he put the radio onto the BBC world service news, then just sat back and waited.

He didn't have to wait for long! The radio barked out "This is the BBC World service newsflash. We have unconfirmed reports that Prince Harry and the Duchess of Sussex have been at the scene of a major explosion in the South East London Borough of Southwark, as soon as we get more information we will get it too you!"

McDonald was sitting back in his seat, when a sense of satisfaction and joy came across his body, other people on the flight had obviously heard the news and a really loud buzz of shock and excitement filled the whole of the airplane.

Everybody was discussing it, even the rather large and sweaty gentleman man sitting behind him, tapped on the shoulder and asked. "Have you heard about Prince Harry?"

Meanwhile both Dillon and Jackson although on different planes, were both sitting back in the comfort of their seats and toasting the success of their mission.

Again just like McDonald, when they had made their call, they had flushed their phones down the toilets. The BBC World Service delivered them the news that all three of them wanted to hear.

A new BBC report said. "We still have unconfirmed reports that Prince Harry along with his wife the Duchess of Sussex have been killed by an explosion in Peckham, South East London in England. I repeat that these are unconfirmed reports. Other important casualties are thought to include the Metropolitan Police Commissioner Cressida Dick and the Mayor of the London Borough of Southwark Councillor Sandra Rhule. According to our sources, a radioactive bomb detonated as they crossed the courtyard in front of Peckham Library."

Turning it over to Sky News, their Royal Correspondent Sarah Hughes was delivering the same speech.

Both Dave Critchley and Paul McSloy didn't know whether the news reports were true. They were in a position where they could not exactly be sure as to the truth in the reports.

McSloy rose from his seat and walked forward to the first class galley on the plane. Speaking to the chief steward, and said.

"My name is Paul McSloy. I am a police officer with the Metropolitan Police in London. Please could you go and ask the captain to radio London and get them to check with Inspector Camberwell who works from Peckham Police Station, what the correct situation with Prince Harry and the Duchess is, ask the Captain to give them this password. Then they will give you a response."

McSloy knew that they would return a coded message to him, depending on the reply, he would then make his next move. Good news nothing will change. Bad news, well he just hoped that it would be good news.

Dave Critchley on the other hand, used the Air Phone in the seat he was sitting in.

Again he called Peckham Police Station, and after giving a code word and receiving a coded answer, hung up then sat back and breathed a huge sigh of relief.

Turning to James Dillon he said. "What do you make of the supposed assassination of Prince Harry?"

Dillon responded somewhat coldly. "Well now the British Government and its Royal Family, will know the real feeling of pain and anger, for so long they have not only been ignorant to all of this, they have just ignored the pain and anguish those normal soldiers families have to live with on a daily basis. Normal soldiers who are not playing this game for fun like the Princes. They have had to put up with sub-standard training and sub-standard equipment. I bet you that when Prince Harry went to Afghanistan, he never had the wrong equipment or the wrong clothes, but I am just a man on the street and only read what the papers print, so what do I know?"

Critchley said to himself. "This cannot be the same man that Paul McSloy said that bought him out hot drinks and sandwiches to keep himself warm on the cold and wet night, not four days ago."

To him, he seems like a cold blooded killer. Would the real James Dillon please stand up! He thought to himself.

Meanwhile McDonald was sitting back with a sense of pride and duty at what he and the others had done. "The rest of the trip would be nice and stress free. I wonder if James and Shaun had heard the news." He thought to himself.

The Stewardess was suddenly alongside him. "Sir would you like something to drink?"

"Do you have champagne on board?" He asked.

"Yes Sir, we have Nicolas Feuillatte Rose Champagne at £97 per bottle." She replied.

"What can you tell me about it?" He asked.

"Well Sir, I don't know that much apart from the fact it comes from the Epernay region of Champagne, France. They use Pinot Noir grapes in the making process, but I have never tasted it."

He quickly responded by asking. "How many bottles do you have on Board?

"About 30 Sir!"

"Then please could you give a bottle to every business class and first class passenger!"

"Are you sure Sir? That's nearly fifteen hundred pounds!" She asked.

McDonald just looked at her and said. "That's no problem at all, then he gave her his credit card.

Upon arrival at Banjul-Yundum airport McDonald saw the posters proclaiming the death of Prince Harry and the Duchess.

What he didn't see was the person who removed the placard once he had cleared the flight arrival hall.

Outside in the glaring sun, Cathy and the kids were waiting for him. "Russ, did you hear the news? It's all over the news here! Prince Harry has been killed by an explosion in Peckham.

He just simply replied. "Yes I did, how awful must they feel!"

Just after midday the Times Editor James Harding opened the second batch of daily mail.

One particular envelope caught his eye, because it had Peckham Library written on the top left of it, as he started to read the letter, he became more and more shocked at what he was reading.

"Dear Mr. Harding.

My name is Mr. Russell McDonald. I alone am responsible for the death today of Prince Harry and the Duchess of Sussex and all other fatalities! Although I am responsible for today's actions, the blame has to be laid squarely at the feet of the British Government and the British Army.

My brother Ralph was left to die along with other members of his platoon in Afghanistan. They were cut off behind enemy lines and rather than send someone to save them, a civil servant from Whitehall, decided that their deaths were an acceptable facet of war. No one was sent to save them because (as we found out when the Prime Minister spoke about it to the Commons) it would upset the local Taliban Leader.

Would this civil servant still not have sent anyone if there were any of his relatives involved?

So although I am responsible. I am not to blame and all the people's blood is on their hands.

Perhaps now the Royal Family can instil a sense of anger and resentment into our military forces. Even if this costs me my life, I am sure that there will be other people waiting for the chance for justice!

Yours Sincerely
Russell McDonald."

Harding was frozen to the spot, this letter was dynamite. This letter was front page news it would knock off the pictures of the explosion to the inside of the paper.

What a scoop for the Times! Reaching for his phone he called the press office at Buckingham Palace.

Chapter 22

Recompense

The sun was burning bright and hot. The yacht was bobbing gently on the top of the waves. Sitting on a sun lounger on the foredeck, Russell McDonald was reading the Times Newspaper, which was dated 5 days ago.

The headline read "Prince Harry & the Duchess of Sussex survives an assassination attempt in Peckham. A bomb that was due to be detonated had been found just minutes before he arrived and safely disarmed.

With fury and rage reaching boiling point inside him McDonald threw the newspaper across the deck in absolute anger, shouting out loud "What went wrong? Ralph, what did we do to deserve this? Prince Harry had to die." It was the only way that McDonald could continue to live.

He swore to himself that "When I return to the UK, I will set in motion a plan to kill as many of the royal family as possible."

When he had calmed down, he bent down to pick up the newspaper again to finish reading the story, he found that the paper had fallen open on a page with the headline.

"British National Found Dead in Morocco." It continued. "A Mr. James Dillon was found dead in room 145 at the Sofitel hotel, Agadir, Morocco. Police believe that he had overdosed on heroin. Two native women were found dead alongside him, police sources state that they are not looking for anyone else in their enquiries."

He could hardly believe his eyes, he had to read the headline over and over again before it could sink in.

"Cathy! Cathy! Cathy, come here, it's urgent!" he shouted out loud.

His wife appeared from the galley of the yacht, her hands whilst covered in a brown mixture were carrying a large mixing bowl. "What is it? What's so important that I have to drop everything, you know that I am in the middle of making the curry goat!"

He screamed at her. "James is dead! James is dead! They say he apparently died of a heroin overdose!"

She looked at his face, there were tears streaming down from his eyes. She started to scream, the bowl dropped from her hands and shattered upon impact with the deck.

"Noooooo! It is not possible, not our James." Falling to her knees she started to cry, McDonald came and knelt beside her and cradled her head in his arms.

After a few moments his hurt and dismay turned to anger. "Dillon never touched drugs at all in his life. No never, something is wrong, very wrong." Getting up to turn the radio on to hear the news, his face was still streaming with tears.

Suddenly the radio boomed out.

"This is the BBC World Service Newsflash at 10:10am. Police are still hunting the people behind the assassination attempt on Prince Harry and his wife the Duchess of Sussex. Of the three people that the police are looking for, one of them James Dillon was found dead a few days ago in Agadir, Morocco. But they are still looking for Russell McDonald and Shaun Jackson, both of them are believed to be abroad. Interpol has been alerted.

Suddenly the radio boomed again. "Sorry, we have just received some more breaking news on this story! We are getting unconfirmed reports that one of the other two people that police are searching for in connection with the attempt on Prince Harry's life, Mr. Shaun Jackson, was today found dead in his room in at the Hotel Lev, Ljubljana in Slovenia. Police reports say that he basically drunk himself to death. Witnesses at the hotel bar have confirmed that he was drinking heavily and had drunk at least two bottles of local vodka along with a bottle of scotch."

Continuing the report said. "When he never came down for breakfast, the maid entered his hotel room and found him face down on his bed, a local coroner pronounced him dead and due to the high amount of alcohol empty bottles. Sources also say that they found two other half empty bottles of vodka. The autopsy later today will confirm the cause of death but police sources again say, that they are not searching for anybody else in connection with his death."

Silence fell between the two of them, but it was broken both from the sea.

Suddenly from over his right shoulder he heard a whooshing noise go past his ear, he heard Cathy let out a gargled scream.

Turning to face her, he saw that as she fell, her face was contorted with horror and pain and blood was dribbling out of a perfect formed hole, right in the centre of her forehead.

This time from over his left shoulder he heard the sound of two more bullets being fired. Turning and screaming at the same time for the kids to get back to the yacht, he saw that they were both laying face down in the sea.

Their arms and legs spread-eagled like a star, red blood mixed with the sea water to give a ghostly pinkish glow around them.

He just stood there rooted to the spot unsure and incapable of what, if anything he could do.

Suddenly he felt a sharp pain in the side of his neck, immediately clasping his hand to the area, he began to feel giddy, awkward and could not focus properly, he finally collapsed to his knees and passed out cold!

McDonald awoke with the stinging pain still in his neck and a really bad headache, struggling to see properly, he tried to stand up but couldn't, he fell back to the floor in a heap.

Suddenly a bucket of cold water was thrown over him. "Who are you?" he mumbled. "Why have you done this? Why have you killed my wife and family? Who are you? For God's sake, who are you?"

The voice coolly and calmly answered him back. "You know who I am and you know why I did what I did! Just as James Dillon and Shaun Jackson knew why! You killed my son and when he came to you for help, you just turned him away and left him to die. You took my life and now I am taking your life, just as I took theirs."

McDonald stared at him then screamed. "John, you killed them all?"

Suddenly he turned into a person that was unable to come to terms with what was about to happen. He began to beg. "I am sorry! But Prince Harry had to die! They killed my brother, they left him to die."

"Just as you left my Daniel to die! I want you to die as painfully as my Daniel did? I want to look in your eyes and see fear in them as you die."

As he readied himself to fire, the radio boomed out.

"We have just been given another breaking news story. Russell McDonald, the third person that police were searching for in connection with the assassination attempt on Prince Harry's life, has been found shot dead on his luxury yacht. His yacht was moored just off the coast near the Ocean Bay Hotel and Resort, Baku in Banjul-Yundum, Gambia. Police sources say that McDonald and his family were killed by local pirates who were trying to steal his yacht. Although police were unable to save McDonald and his family, the pirates were killed by police following a lengthy sea chase."

"Now for the rest of the news, Police today reported that!...."

With that he calmly lifted his right arm, aimed his gun at McDonald's head, and squeezed the trigger, without any tremor or hesitation. BANG! Was the very last thing McDonald ever heard.

John Nelson walked over to the radio, turned it off. Opened the lounge doors and walked down the stairs and through to the master bedroom and threw a lit Zippo lighter onto the bed. Shutting the door behind him and then just calmly walked away.

Once back on deck, he then stepped over the side railings and jumped back into the water. He swam to the beach and walked ashore, stopping for a few minutes to watch the now burning yacht, removing his wetsuit and oxygen equipment at the same time.

When he had finished, he started walking towards the road that ran alongside the small beach, as he walked, a car pulled up alongside. Nelson opened the boot and put his diving gear in.

Inside the car Camberwell and Tomlin were waiting for him. "It is done!" he said, as Tomlin drove down the road and away from the yacht, Nelson turned round to watch the flames burning the wheel house.

Camberwell and Tomlin said nothing, all they could hear was Nelson saying.

"That's for you Daniel, an eye for and eye!"

Special Mentions

98% of all the characters in this novel are real people, but their characteristics are totally fictional. The main characters are all friends that I have known for many years.

Inspector Camberwell is based on a man, who myself and my family called our second dad, so it was weird and even funnier to write about him this way as I wrote this novel.

There are some very special people to say thank you to and also pay respects to a few people, some of whom are no longer with us now.

1/. Michael Steward although not named in the novel, was involved in a situation in this novel that was extremely sad but very real.

2/. Peter Kiddle was the first person that came across the Clapham train crash in 1988, He received an award from the Automobile Association and Margaret Thatcher for it.

I again included this situation as a way of paying respect to him and to show people, that real heroes come in all different shapes and sizes and from different backgrounds.

3/. Whilst I was researching for this novel I came across that report of the tragic death of

DC James Morrison who was fatally stabbed in Covent Garden while off duty, attempting to arrest a thief in 1991. He was posthumously awarded the Queens Gallantry Medal.

4/. To all serving officials from the Metropolitan Police, Southwark Council, and The British Army Bomb Squad, both past and present, named in this novel, may I again thank you for all the hard work and dedication that you show to all the population of the United Kingdom.

We owe you all so much, and we can never repay the debt.

Printed in Great
Britain
by Amazon

Pearson's Canal Comp...
STOURPORT R...

BLACK COUNTRY RING   BIRMINGHAM CANAL NAVIGATIONS

Published by Central Waterways Supplies of Rugby
Tel/fax: 01788 546692 email: sales@centralwaterways.co.uk
Seventh edition 2007. ISBN 978 0 9 5491166 9

Karen Tanøiiv

Tillerman

Long after I have ceased haunting the canal and river banks covered in this guide, will my dwindling band of acolytes continue to aver that it was here and hereabouts that I was in my pomp, a born again Blackcountryman anxious to extol its virtues with a convert's zeal? Does not that arch canal blogger 'Granny Buttons' aver that I begin to lose my powers of description and, by inference, concentration when I stray too far from The Bratch, The Delph and Dudley Port? Yet nineteen years and seven editions after the *Stourport Ring Canal Companion* first slipped self-consciously on to the canal shop shelves I feel scarcely any closer to pinning down the region's transcendental hold on my heart. Lumbering along the towpath in the wake of its blistering pace of change I search in vain for old touchstones and benchmarks, and with each fresh edition the casualty list grows: traditional pubs which have given up the unequal struggle to compete with brash upstarts; corner shops killed by out of town retail parks; treasured views spoiled by rampant vegetation allowed to run amok; and a melancholy roll call of abandoned and demolished items of industrial archaeology - Stourbridge Ironworks, James Bridge Copper Works, Beans Foundry and the coal shutes at Smethwick being amongst the latest casualties. To think I used to poke gentle fun at the Black Country Living Museum - why pay the entrance fee, I joked, when its exhibits still ran lusty and wild beyond its perimeter fence? But, rhetorically, I was answering that question with increasing venom, bemoaning with each successive edition the emasculation of the Black Country, the remorseless character assassination of its soul incarnate; an ebb tide of individuality callously allowed to drown in a flood of mediocrity.

But be careful Michael, you are in danger of sounding like a parody of L. T. C. Rolt - 'old is good, new is bad' - and you will incite disillusion should you infer that all is lost, for it is the solemn duty of a guide book to enthuse and inspire. And heaven knows there remains enough throughout these pages to purr about: the Severn upstream of Worcester; the peerless Staffordshire & Worcestershire Canal on its sandstone wanderings around Kinver; the Trent & Mersey in the neighbourhood of Shugborough; and the Coventry Canal at Hopwas - waterway jewels each one, microcosms of England at its most enduring and inspirational. And even the BCN itself is not yet shorn of all its potency. The main line from Aldersley to Farmer's Bridge remains a latent hymn to the Industrial Revolution, far more compelling than any well-meaning museum. Explore them now, tease the essence out of them while it's still there to be extracted. Another edition or two and who knows, we may all be ghosts ...
Michael Pearson

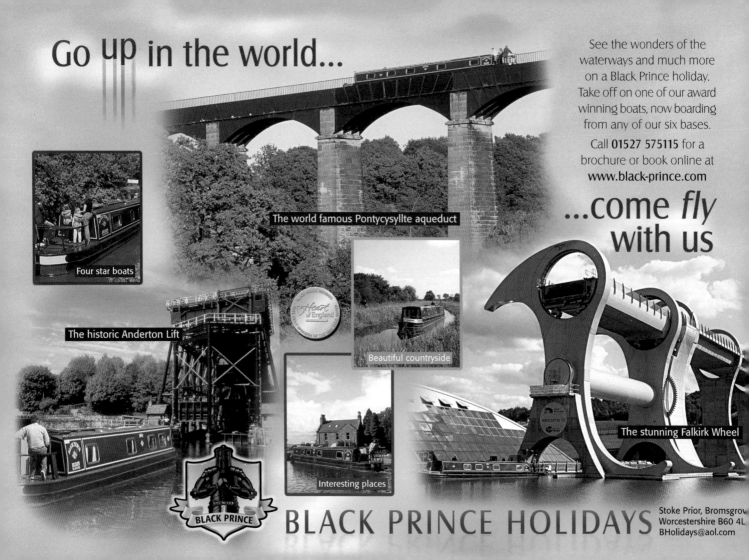

The Stourport Ring

FOR all practical purposes, STOURPORT marks the head of navigation on the Severn, and it is here that the through traveller by water exchanges the fluctuating currents of the river for the stolid waters of the Staffordshire & Worcestershire Canal. Stourport itself suffers from a personality disorder: half convinced that it's a seaside town; half a rich heritage of canal wharves, which are in the process of being regenerated. But whether you have come here for a ninety-nine and a knees-up, or to pay more serious homage to Brindley's basins, Stourport rarely disappoints. To moor in the Upper Basin, listening to time being measured by the quarter beats of the clocktower's sonorous bell, is one of the inland waterways' most magical experiences. And whatever entrance the boater makes - locking up from the Severn under the benign gaze of the Tontine Hotel, or descending into the dripping depths of York Street Lock from the canal - there will be few steerers able to resist exploration of the basins, shunting back and forth like some busy tug; turning in wide arcs or honing their reversing skills. The original and largest - known as the Upper Basin - opened in 1771, and connects through two wide-beam 'barge' locks with the river. These impressive (at least in narrowboater's eyes) chambers were built sturdily enough to withstand the Severn's perennial propensity for flooding, and capacious enough for the indigenous Severn Trows. Between the barge locks lies the smallest basin, thought to have been used as an assembly point and not as a wharf as such. A second link to the river, consisting of four narrow-beam locks in pairs of staircases, was opened in 1781. Here

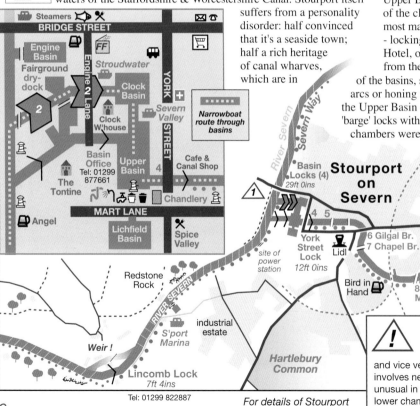

Narrowboat route through basins

For details of Stourport facilities turn to page 8

⚠ Advice for Boaters

The 'narrow boat' route through the basins at Stourport - from river to canal and vice versa - is indicated on the enlargement. It involves negotiating two staircase pairs which are unusual in that there is no need to ensure that the lower chamber is empty when going down.

6

again the locks are separated by a small basin from which a drydock extends. Manoeuvring a lengthy boat between the staircase pairs can be tricky, and it doesn't help one's sang-froid that there is often a sizeable crowd of onlookers. At the top of the narrow locks, and contemporary with their construction, lies the Clock Basin, interconnected with the Upper Basin. On a peninsula between these upper, boat-filled expanses of water stands the glorious Clock Warehouse, headquarters these days of the Stourport Yacht Club whose comparatively huge vessels migrate up-river to winter in the security of the basins.

Once there were two basins which lay to the east of Mart Lane. Known expediently as the 'Furthermost Basins', they dated from the early 19th century. The lower, reached through a wide lock, had a brief existence, closing in 1866 when the town gas works took over the site. The other basin flourished in an Indian Summer of commercial activity between 1926 and 1949 when coal boats for the power station discharged in it; their dusty black cargoes of Cannock coalfield slack being unloaded by electric grab and carried in hoppers along an aerial ropeway to the power station's furnaces. Subsequently it was infilled and a timber yard occupied its site, but now it is being re-excavated as a major focal point of the regeneration scheme - one trusts that it will be accessible by visiting boaters and not simply used for private moorings or, worse still, as a cosmetic water space.

Another important element of the redevelopment of Stourport Basins concerns the return to life of the Tontine Hotel, derelict for a decade or more. It derived its unusual name from a system of speculative life insurance, the last surviving member of its original group of investors gaining full ownership of the building: fuel for skulduggery one imagines and the possibility of a plot which would inspire most detective story writers. In its heyday it boasted a hundred bedrooms, a ballroom and formal gardens spilling down to the riverbank. It will be restored for use as housing.

The River

The Severn's official head of navigation is just upstream of Stourport Bridge where the Gladder Brook enters from the west bank, though occasional convoys of shallow-draughted diehards do journey upstream to Bewdley as part of a long term campaign to restore navigation to the Upper Severn all the way up to Shrewsbury; a relatively easy proposition were it not for

the distrust of riparian landowners. One waterway project which did not materialise was for a canal from Stourport to Leominster. A token sod was dug opposite the basins in 1797, but the ludicrously ambitious through route never came to fruition. Pending any progress with the Upper Severn scheme, then, LINCOMB LOCK is the highest on the Severn. It lies in a picturesque setting dominated by one of the sheer red sandstone cliffs which characterise the river in this part of the world. There is another such dramatic outcrop between Lincomb and Stourport known as Redstone Rock, a refuge, apparently, of outlaws in Cromwell's time. Opposite the rock, a well piled wharf marks the destination of the Severn's last commercial traffics above Worcester in the 1960s.

The Canal

Secretive, might be the best way to describe the Staffordshire & Worcestershire Canal's approach to (and departure from) its southern terminus at Stourport. Though sharing a wide enough valley with the Stour, the canal tends to be masked by trees and vegetation, and as a consequence has something of a reclusive character to it. Boaters not inclined to proceed beyond the confines of the canal are advised to moor above York Street Lock where 5-day visitor moorings are provided opposite the site of the canal company's workshops, redeveloped into not unattractive modern housing.

Leaving Stourport by the back door, the canal is soon curving beneath the old railway bridge which carried the Severn Valley Railway between Hartlebury and Bewdley. There used to be a canal/rail interchange dock at this point. Rusty mooring rings set into a high brick retaining wall recall busier times here, and on the towpath side you might spot a roller around which a line would be taken to aid access to and from the tightly-angled loading dock. Another distant echo of bygone trading days is encountered by Bridge 10A, through which a branch canal long ago led down by way of a lock into the River Stour for boats to reach Wilden Ironworks across the valley. Steel from South Wales and coal from Highley mine, north of Bewdley, would be transhipped at the aforementioned railway basin and taken the short distance to the ironworks by boat. It would be good to turn a bend and encounter such trade now instead of listening to the constant drone of lorries on the Stourport-Kidderminster road.

Stourport (Map 1)

Water on the brain has left Stourport under the illusion that it's a coastal resort. All the trappings are here: funfairs and fish & chips, steamer trips, paddling pools and amusement arcades. Day trippers pour in from the West Midlands to let their hair down and make believe they are really in Rhyl. Marginally more in touch with reality, us boaters can swagger about the town pretending that we've just come up with a cargo of oil from Avonmouth.

Eating & Drinking

THE ANGEL - riverside. Tel: 01299 822661. Lively local on the riverbank.

RISING SUN - canalside Bridge 5A. Tel: 01299 822530. Quaint little Banks's backstreet local offering good value meals.

CREATIONS RESTAURANT - High Street. Tel: 01299 871091. Cosy family run restaurant where the menu is a tad more sophisticated than most on offer in 'Stourport on Sea'.

SPICE VALLEY - adjacent York Street Lock. Tel: 01299 877448. Well appointed Indian by Upper Basin.

HOLLY BUSH - Mitton Street. Tel: 01299 879706. Real ale cornucopia. Food from 10am!

BIRD IN HAND - canalside between bridges 7 and 8. Tel: 01299 822385. Bar meals, outdoor seating beside the canal on summer days, bowling green.

OLDE CROWN - Bridge Street. Tel: 01299 825693. Wetherspoon pub with patio overlooking basins. Wide choice of food and real ales.

GOODNIGHT SWEETHEART - canalside York Street Lock. Tel: 01299 829442. Nostalgia tinged tearoom.

Numerous other eating and drinking establishments as befits this inland resort. More fish & chip bars than you would imagine sustainable.

Shopping

The town centre is large enough to support branches of Boots, Woolworths and W.H.Smith. There is a Lidl supermarket within easy reach of the canal. The Toll House Canal Shop stands alongside York Street Lock - Tel: 01299 821385.

Connections

BUSES - frequent services to/from Kidderminster, less intensive serices to/from Worcester via Holt Heath. Tel: 0870 608 2 608.

TAXIS - Pardoe's. Tel: 01299 824924.

Kidderminster (Map 2)

Famous for its carpets, its steam railway and its football team, 'The Harriers', Kidderminster is a working town with a definite, though difficult to define, appeal. A busy ring road divorces the

Caldwall Lock

canal from the town centre, but in the pedestrianised streets the roar of traffic soon dies down, and you can admire 'Kidder's' knack of remembering its most famous sons in statue form.

Eating & Drinking

THE WATERMILL - Bridge 13. Pleasant modern family pub, food. Tel: 01562 66713.

FRANKIE & BENNY'S - Weavers Wharf. Tel: 01562 741333.

KING & CASTLE - Comberton Hill. Instant nostalgia in the Severn Valley Railway's refreshment room. Guest beers and home made food. Tel: 01562 747505.

THE LOCK - canalside Bridge 20, Wolverley. Tel: 01562 850581.

McDonalds and Pizza Hut by Bridge 16.

Shopping

The shopping centre is lively and traffic free and has recently been boosted by the advent of the Weavers Wharf retail development which features a designer outlet housed in an imposing former carpet mill. There's a retail market on Thursdays and Saturdays.

Things to Do

SEVERN VALLEY RAILWAY - One of Britain's premier preserved railways, the SVR runs up the valley to the Shropshire market town of Bridgnorth, a delightful ride in its own right, never mind the fun of being hauled by steam. Services run throughout the summer and on most other weekends and holiday periods. Talking timetable on 01299 401001.

Connections

BUSES - Tel: 0870 608 2 608. Useful links with Wolverley and Stourport for towpath walkers.

TRAINS - frequent local services to/from Birmingham and Worcester etc. Tel: 08457 484950.

Taxis - Central Taxis. Tel: 01562 825522.

THE carpet-making town of Kidderminster has had its waterfront regenerated in recent years - all the usual suspects: fast-food outlets, supermarkets, ring roads and retail parks. Yet one or two of the old carpet factories remain intact, putting up with, if not exactly relishing, new 21st century uses as parodies of American restaurants and Designer Outlets.

South of the town two isolated locks, couched in the shadow of sandstone outcrops and bereft now of the lock-keepers' cottages which long ago accompanied them, are separated by a high viaduct over which steam trains of the Severn Valley Railway puff and pant their way between Kidderminster and Bridgnorth; a worthwhile excursion ashore for boaters who have time to spare.

Passing through the centre of town, the canal used to penetrate a deep canyon of factory premises, but these have been demolished, along with another carpet works which once stood above Kidderminster Lock. Now two supermarkets vie for boating custom and provide good moorings in the process, but personally we still prefer (during daytime at least) those at the old town wharf (on the offside above the lock) which are handsomely overlooked by the imposing parish church.

New housing is spreading out north of Kidderminster, but the canal quickly establishes its more obvious rural charms. Wolverley Court Lock lies in a seemingly remote parcel of scrubland in an area once extensively used for sand extraction. Wolverley Lock is overlooked by a quaint pub, with a canalside patio which has the potential of transforming your lock routine into street theatre; comedy or drama, it's entirely up to you. North of here, delving into glades of balsam and convolvulus, bluebells and foxgloves, the canal is at its most beguilingly attractive. You grow to wish it would go on for ever.

Until relatively recently the Elan Valley water pipe-line used to cross the canal between bridges 21 and 22, now it is culverted beneath it. Completed in 1907, this 73 mile pipe brings water from reservoirs in the Rhayader Mountains of Wales to the bathtubs of Birmingham and the Black Country. The pipe-line's construction at the turn of the century was a huge undertaking, and one of the last great adventures of the 'navvies': "rough, violent men, whose speech had foreign inflections and whose corduroys were caked with the mud of four counties," wrote Francis Brett Young in the preface to one of his most enjoyable novels, *House Under the Water* inspired by the project.

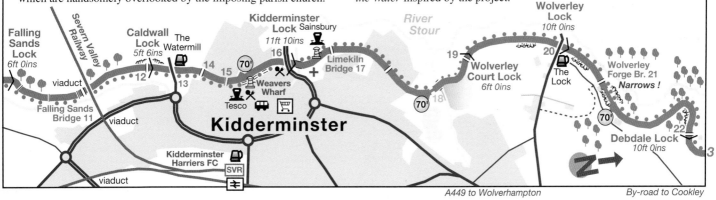

S there a prettier length of canal in the country? Rivals spring to mind, but none lovelier than the Staffs & Worcs, winding its wooded way from Cookley to Stourton past Kinver with its church perched high on Kinver Edge. There is a "Toytown" ambience about this whole canal which the Swiss would thoroughly approve of. Arguably the prettiest length of all lies between Hyde Lock and Dunsley's diminutive tunnel. Here, bordered by woods on one side, the canal glides past meadows backed by a conifer plantation. It would be difficult to imagine a more rural scene, yet a huge ironworks stood in the vicinity for two centuries. In its heyday twenty puddling furnaces produced wrought iron and the premises lined the canal for some distance. But only the manager's house remains, demurely situated beside the towpath above Hyde Lock. One is awestruck that such a massive undertaking can vanish so completely, until the realisation comes that the same process of change and renewal has recently taken place throughout

the neighbouring Black Country, as the traditional heavy industries of the region were replaced by urban forests and shopping malls.

Barely had the ironworks' pandemonium ceased, when a new interloper arrived on the Stour Valley scene, in the shape of a curious little narrow gauge railway operated with electric trams. The Kinver Light Railway opened in 1901 and lasted only twenty-nine years, but in its short existence brought thousands of day-trippers from the Black Country to Kinver, flaunted by the operating company as the "Switzerland of the Midlands". On Whit Monday, 1905, nearly seventeen thousand passengers were carried along the five mile line from Amblecote, near Stourbridge. The 3ft 6ins gauge track (along which through cars ran from as far away

Kinver Edge

Kinver

Kinver Lock 7ft 3ins

COOKLEY TUNNEL 65 yards

Worcestershire

works

Cookley

Rock Tavern

The Anchor

Austcliff Bridge 24

Clay House Br. 25

Caunsall Bridge 26

Whittington Lock 9ft 9ins

Whittington Horse Br. 28

Whittington Inn

Vine

29

Hyde Lock 10ft 0ins

Dunsley Hall

site of old ironworks

course of Kinver Light Rly.

DUNSLEY TUNNEL 25 yards

Stewponey Lock 10ft 31A

32

33

STOURTON JUNCTION

Stourton Locks 36ft 3ins

waterworks

Stourton Castle

Devil's Den

Stour Aq'duct

A449 to Wolverhampton

Staffordshire

The towpath is in excellent condition for a rural canal, and used by walkers and cyclists alike. Short walks abound in the vicinity of Kinver where good car parking is available or you can use the bus from Stourbridge and walk back via Stourton Junction.

For details of facilities at Cookley and Kinver turn to page 13

*Figures refer to Staffs & Worcs route, allow an hour for Stourton Locks etc.

as Birmingham) crossed the canal at Stewponey, ran alongside it at Hyde, and terminated at Mill Lane, Kinver where the pumping station now stands.

STEWPONEY was a focal point for boat traffic on the Staffs & Worcs. Facilities included a wharf, stables, toll office, workshop and employees' cottages. In recent years, the former toll house was home to a gift shop run by Paul De'Aaran, 'international clairvoyant', but this had closed down by the time of our most recent research trip: one trusts it wasn't due to unforseen circumstances. Even after the Second World War, in excess of fifty boat loads of Cannock Chase and Baggeridge Colliery coal was being worked through here to Stourport Power Station each week. But in 1949 the National Coal Board announced a florin surcharge on each ton of coal loaded on to boats. Not entirely surprisingly, the traffic rapidly transferred to rail. A few years of desultory day boat trading to Swindon Steel works, 'railway' boats off the Stourbridge Canal, and occasional cargoes of baled wool to Stourport from 'up north' followed, and then, without anyone really noticing, the working boats were gone.

Stewponey doesn't find its way on to Ordnance Survey maps, but is a name of local currency, thought to be derived from an old soldier, returning with a Spanish wife from the town of Estepona, who opened an inn here, the name of which was soon corrupted by Black Country vowels. The inn was rebuilt as a roadhouse in the Thirties, one of those huge joints which were honeypots in the early days of motoring when there was still an element of romance to be found on the roads; there was even a huge Lido in the grounds at one time. Architecturally it had a good deal going for it, even in the debased years of its long drawn out decline, so it is sad to discover that it has been demolished and replaced by housing completely devoid of any aesthetic ambition. Imagine for a moment that the Lido was still in use, and that you could still reach it in the jolly company of one of the Kinver Light Railway's trams, and then calculate just how much Progress has defaulted on the Past.

At STOURTON JUNCTION four chambers raise the Stourbridge Canal up on its way to the Black Country. Canal junctions don't come much more attractive than this and, even if your itinerary commits you to the Staffs & Worcs, you could do worse than spend a night in Stourbridge, little more than an hour and a half away as described on Map 33.

Austcliff

North of Stourton Junction, the canal - known colloquially as the 'Stour Cut' - bridges the river of the same name. The setting is idyllic, the river tumbling over a shallow weir just upstream of the double-arch aqueduct, and issuing from the adjoining bend, a broad pool. Close by, a peculiar cave is cut out of the rocks at water level. Known as "Devil's Den", it is thought to have been used as a boathouse by the Foley family of Prestwood Hall. Southwards from Stewponey, the river is the canal's constant companion, the man made waterway keeping pace with the Stour's gradual descent to the Severn by way of occasional, isolated locks of great charm. It is difficult to think of another canal bounded by so many trees, their presence broken only by occasional outcrops of Triassic rock. The most dramatic of these - a real cliffhanger if ever there was one! - is near Caunsall where the Bunter pebble beds of Austcliff Rock loom over a bend in the canal. Little less spectacular is the canal's burrowing beneath the old iron-making village of COOKLEY, its houses seemingly precariously poised over the northern portal of Cookley Tunnel.

THE countryside empties. Wales is only the width of an Ordnance Survey map away. These are the landscapes of Francis Brett Young, a writer recently rediscovered by paperback publishers, though still easily found on the shelves of secondhand bookshops. No-one has ever written better about the area between the Black Country and the Welsh Marches. You should try *Far Forest* or *Dr Bradley Remembers*; either would make admirable reading before 'lights out' on your cruise.

Smestow Brook, a tributary of the Stour, is now the canal's chief confidant and friend. In the woods below GOTHERSLEY LOCK stood a canal company roundhouse, a twin to that at Gailey (Map 31) now restored and used as a canalside shop. Both roundhouses date from the year of Trafalgar. The Gothersley one marks the site of an important canal wharf provided to serve a sizeable ironworks which existed here until the 1880s. The roundhouse itself, a gaunt ruin for many years, was storm damaged in 1991 and its base is now the focal point of a picnic site and visitor moorings. The ironworks has vanished as well, its forges, furnaces, tramways and wharves superseded by ivy, ash, balsam and butterbur.

GREENSFORGE is a delightful mooring place. Its name recalls the existence of another vanished forge, one which became a mill, the big, four square building which remains intact and glimpsed through the alders and willows lining the Smestow. Stroll down the lane and you'll discover its macey, long dry mill pond, an obvious declivity in the reed beds. Nearby an arm extends into ASHWOOD BASIN, now a marina but once an important interchange basin with the Kingswinford Railway, a colliery line dating from 1829 whose first locomotive, *Agenoria*, is now in the National Railway Museum's collection in York.

Between Greensforge and Hinksford locks the canal is bordered by the contrasting images of woodland and a huge static caravan park. Hinksford Pumping Station is one of several waterworks in this part of the valley. Yet another ironworks lined the canal at SWINDON. This one survived until as recently as 1976 and specialised in rolling silicon steel sheets for the electrical engineering industry. Not that you would credit it now, the site being covered - not by flora and fauna - but by the neat lawns, barbecues and conservatory extensions of modern housing. The works was owned at one time by the Baldwin family, of which Stanley became Prime Minister. Note how the towpath briefly changes sides so that it did not run through the works' precincts. Railway boats traded here with steel blooms from Stourbridge Basin.

BOTTERHAM LOCKS are a staircase pair, so remember to ensure that the top chamber is full and the bottom empty to start with. They raise or lower the canal over twenty feet. North of here the canal becomes temporarily embroiled with the industrial fringe of Wombourne.

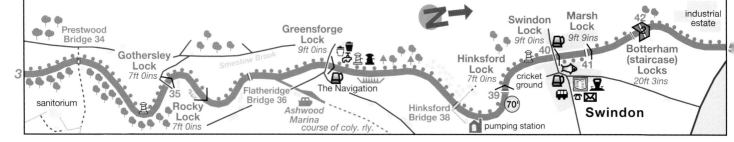

Cookley (Map 3)

A village with an iron-making tradition going back three centuries and where steel wheels are still made in canalside premises. Access from the canal is via a steep path at the northern end of the tunnel, and perhaps not for chronic asthmatics. There are two pubs: the Bulls Head (Tel: 01562 850242) with a prominent outdoor terrace high above the canal and the well-appointed Eagle & Spur (Tel: 01562 850184) whose tables spill out on to the pavement. A fish & chip shop (Tel: 01562 850554) and Tandoori take-away (Tel: 01562 850900) offer further options, whilst a post office stores (quaint, with ham slicer, and open daily EC Wed & Sun) butcher, Tesco Express (with cash machine) and newsagent make Cookley a useful and friendly port of call for the day's provisions. Buses run hourly (Mon-Sat) to/from Kidderminster.

Kinver (Map 3)

Kinver is well aware of its charms and flaunts them to the full. Visitors pour in during the summer months, filling car-parks at the rear of the pubs, restaurants and cafes which provide most of the fabric of High Street. But somehow Kinver preserves its appeal and repays the ten minute stroll from the canal. In any case, the village's main asset is its superb setting in the shadow of Kinver Edge, a dramatic wooded ridge rising to five hundred feet and the southern end of the 'Staffordshire Way' long distance footpath. For those with time and energy at their disposal, the climb to the top of The Edge can be recommended. On a clear day you can see - well almost, as the song says, forever - certainly over to Bredon Hill and The Cotswolds.

Eating & Drinking

THE VINE - canalside Bridge 29. Traditional pub with big garden. Food lunchtimes and evenings. Good choice of local beers - Kinver, Enville and Holdens. Tel: 01384 877291.
PLOUGH & HARROW - High Street. Unprepossessing 'local' worth patronising for the medal-winning Batham ales. Tel: 01384 872659.
WHITTINGTON INN - located on A449 and accessible from Bridge 28. Historic half-timbered inn with links to Dick. Fine choice of food and lovely walled garden.
Kinver boasts many other eating & drinking establishments, from modest cafes to expensive restaurants; there are two fish & chip shops and numerous fast food outlets.

Shopping

All the shops (and there's a good choice for such an apparently small village) congregate along the main street. Galleries and gift shops rub shoulders with a pair of 'Early-Late' shops. THE BUTCHERY offers a great range of sausages and hand-raised pork pies; just make sure you don't fall into the queue behind the charming but elderly and hard of hearing 'Stan'! Barclays *still* have a small branch here with a cash machine.

Hyde Lock

Things to Do

TOURIST INFORMATION - Just Petals, High Street. Tel: 01384 877756.
HOLY AUSTIN ROCK HOUSES - Comber Road. Tel: 01384 872553. The National Trust have recently restored these typical examples of local rock houses, and they are open to the public on Saturday and Sunday afternoons between March and November.

Connections

BUSES - successor to the light railway, but not half as romantic, there is an hourly bus link with Stourbridge. Tel: 0870 608 2 608.

Swindon (Map 4)

Not easily confused with its Wiltshire namesake - once you've seen it anyway - this Swindon barely amounts to more than a spattering of houses at a meeting of by-roads and a small housing estate occupying the site of a former steel works. To the west lies Highgate Common, threaded by the "Staffordshire Way", and, not far beyond - should you have the benefit of bicycles - Halfpenny Green and its vineyard.

Eating & Drinking

NAVIGATION INN - adjacent Greensforge Lock. Tel: 01384 273721. One of the most comfortable of inns on the southern half of the Staffs & Worcs Canal. Most boaters opt for this in preference to Swindon's four other pubs, though we have always had a soft spot for the GREEN MAN (Tel: 01384 400532) just west of Bridge 40. Fish & chips in Swindon itself.

Shopping

The only chance to shop between Kinver and the outskirts of Wolverhampton, Swindon offers a well-stocked convenience store. Boy, doesn't it feel good to be beyond the siren call of a supermarket for at least a day!

Boat crews only

Images of The Bratch

14

5 STAFFS & WORCS CANAL

Wombourne & The Bratch 5mls/7lks/3hrs

BELOW Bratch the canal skirts Wombourne, skirmishing with industry. The red scars of former sand quarries abound. Narrowboats carried sand from local wharves to Black Country forges for mould making in the casting process. Bumble Hole and Bratch sound like Dickensian characters. The latter form the canal's best known locks, a trio originally built by Brindley as a staircase, but later separated and provided with extended side pounds to eliminate water waste and traffic delays. Motorised visitors to Bratch have their own car park and picnic site but, apart from a limited length of offside moorings at the foot of the flight, visitor moorings have been sacrificed for a long line of permit-holder moorings to the north of the top lock. As well as the hugely picturesque juxtaposition of the three locks, the Bratch's other attractions include an elaborately ornate pumping station dating from 1895 and a dismantled railway converted into a bridleway and public footpath. The waterworks opened in 1896, its architectural style being flamboyantly Gothic. Coal came in by narrowboat to fuel a pair of steam engines affectionately referred to as Victoria and Alexandra. They fell out of use in 1960 but the former has been fully restored and the works is occasionally opened to an admiring public.

The Kingswinford Railway Walk occupies the trackbed of an old Great Western Railway line opened as late as 1925. Passenger trains lasted only seven years, but the station building at Wombourne (less than half a mile east of Bratch Locks) remains intact and is used as a tea room. Wombourne village, whose delightful green lies about a mile to the east, is worth seeking out if you have the time.

North of Bratch the countryside is open and attractively rolling and there are glimpses westwards of the Clee Hills. Working narrowboats are often to be seen moored at Dimmingsdale Wharf. The huge Art Deco style pumping station which was a landmark here for many years, and just as valuable as the one at Bratch, has regrettably been demolished.

Summary of Facilities

There are canalside pubs by bridges 43 and 45. The WAGGON & HORSES is a huge circa 1930s road house of mock half-timbering refurbished in a contemporary way - Tel: 01902 892828. The ROUND OAK is a Bank's all day, family orientated pub with a big canalside garden - Tel: 01902 892083. There are no shops within easy reach of the canal. For a taxi to civilisation call Wombourne Cars on 01902 324114.

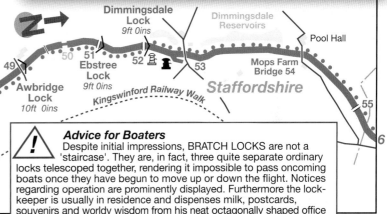

⚠ Advice for Boaters

Despite initial impressions, BRATCH LOCKS are not a 'staircase'. They are, in fact, three quite separate ordinary locks telescoped together, rendering it impossible to pass oncoming boats once they have begun to move up or down the flight. Notices regarding operation are prominently displayed. Furthermore the lock-keeper is usually in residence and dispenses milk, postcards, souvenirs and worldy wisdom from his neat octagonally shaped office on Bridge 48. At busy times do as he asks and be prepared to be patient.

WOLVERHAMPTON'S western suburbs are what estate agents would term 'residentially desirable' and they harbour little hint of Black Country industry. Moreover, the canal closets itself away from the most pressing overtures of urbanisation, masquerading its way through wooded cuttings to and from a conspirators' assignation with the Birmingham Canal Navigations at Aldersley Junction (Map 7). Evidence suggests that COMPTON LOCK was James Brindley's very first essay in narrow lock construction. It was rebuilt in 1986 and it is interesting to note that the top gate came from Bradley Workshops on the BCN, whilst the bottom pair were provided by British Waterways' depot at Northwich in Cheshire. The chamber is graced by one of the Staffordshire & Worcestershire Canal Society's charming wooden name posts. The lock also boasts one of the distinctive circular weirs peculiar to this canal. An impressive girder bridge carries the trackbed of the Wombourne branch railway (now a well-surfaced public right of

way) over the canal on the outskirts of Tettenhall. Another old railway bridge of interest remains intact immediately north of Bridge 62A. It carried a private line into Courtaulds' long demolished rayon factory which was also served by Cowburn & Cowpar chemical boats, trading to the adjoining wharf now occupied by a community centre. Another significant canal crossing sees Bridge 62 carry Telford's Holyhead Road. In this age of specialisation and anonymity, one can only marvel at one man's contribution to so many aspects of civil and industrial engineering. In the early years of the 19th century, communications between London and Dublin were appalling. Over twenty quite autonomous turnpike trusts were responsible for the road from London via Shrewsbury to Holyhead, the port for Ireland. Yet despite vociferous protests from travellers and the frequent failure of the Mail Coach to penetrate the wilds of Wales at all, matters were not brought to a head until the Act of Union between Britain and Ireland required the regular presence of Irish Members of Parliament at Westminster. Thomas Telford was invited to survey the route and plan improvements, which he did with characteristic thoroughness; recommending widening, resurfacing and numerous gradient modifications, as demonstrated nearby in the cutting through Tettenhall Rock. Telford's new road opened throughout with the completion of his famous bridge over the Menai Strait in 1826.

Wightwick Manor
Late Victorian Manor house strong on Arts & Crafts and the Pre-Raphaelites open Thursday, Friday and Saturday afternoons. The grounds (additionally open on Wednesdays) are gorgeous too, and there's a tea room, National Trust shop and pottery - Tel: 01902 761400.

Summary of Facilities
Both Compton and Tettenhall (but especially the former where the moorings are better) offer useful facilities within easy reach of the canal. Both feature pubs and takeaways, and frequent buses into Wolverhampton but it is difficult to resist paying culinary court to an intriguing little canalside restaurant at Bridge 59 called SINNERS & THINNERS - Tel 01902 759049.

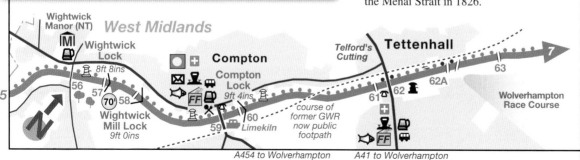

RINDLEY'S Birmingham Canal of 1772 encounters the proud and ancient manufacturing town of Wolverhampton. North of the town centre the canal negotiates a memorable flight of locks known colloquially as 'The Twenty-one'. At its foot lies an unexpectedly rural junction with the Staffordshire & Worcestershire Canal at ALDERSLEY. There is so much to see that the flight never becomes tedious. The 'Twenty-one' is well maintained and seems somehow less exhausting than one might expect. Brindley only provided twenty chambers, but the last was so deep that it caused water shortages. In 1784 the bottom lock was therefore reduced in depth and a short cutting excavated to carry the canal to a new lock built in the intervening pound. This extra lock - No.20 - gives its identity away by having only one bottom gate.

In working boat days the locks were the haunt of 'hobblers', men or boys who would help single-handed captains through the locks for a small consideration: occasionally, latter-day hobblers are on hand to provide the same service. Another feature of the flight were boat children apparently in the habit of riding horses bareback, at breakneck speed down to Aldersley to collect upcoming boats. Galloping equines are still encountered on the flight in the slightly different shape of racehorses on the neighbouring course; an almost unique juxtaposition - one can only think of Aintree and Ripon in comparison.

A Science Park borders the canal between locks 15 to 12 where Clayton tar boats used to ply to and from the gas works. Wolverhampton has always been a fascinating railway centre, and the once rival lines of the Great Western and London Midland & Scottish railways span the canal at several points, notably on a pair of fine viaducts. Lock 11 must have been a trainspotter's idea of heaven when the best of Swindon and Crewe puffed imperiously overhead. Between locks 9 and 10 the pit of an old turntable can still be discerned. Here stood the coaling stage of Stafford Road engine shed, home to a number of the Great Western Railway's legendary King and Castle classes of express locomotives.

Wolverhampton's refuse incinerator overlooks the middle of the flight. Sadly the nearby Springfield Brewery, a handsome conglomerate of Victorian buildings, has been almost irretrievably damaged by fire. Above the top lock - with its picturesque pair of BCN cottages - the canal widens into a landscaped area where handy visitor moorings are provided for overnight stops. The present Broad Street bridge replaces an earlier structure that had cast-iron balustrades and ornate gas lamps and which now graces the Black Country Living Museum. The adjoining warehouse was owned by the famous canal carriers, Fellows, Morton & Clayton.

continued over

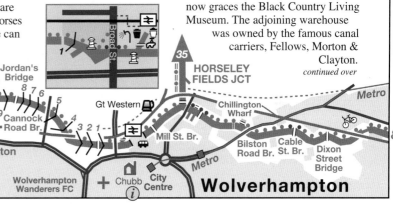

continued from page 17

Water, Elsan and refuse disposal facilities are obtainable by entering a short arm spanned by a cast iron bridge immediately south of Broad Street Bridge. More visitor moorings are provided on the opposite side to the towpath at this point: hard-by the busy ring-road, they offer a great sense of security, but no access to or from the outside world. Like a sizeable wedge of chocolate cake, Chubb's former lock-making works dominates the horizon. The arm was the original course of the canal before it was diverted through Wolverhampton Tunnel when the High Level railway station was built in 1850. Above the tunnel there's a multi-storey car park for rail users. It is said that Wolverhampton's 'ladies of the night' were in the habit of entertaining their customers in the twilight of the canal tunnel.

The canal proceeds through a redeveloped canyon of spanking new flats (all very un-Wolverhampton-like) to Horseley Fields and the junction of the Wyrley & Essington Canal route to Walsall. There were so many wharves and arms and basins in the vicinity that it would be impractical to go into them here. The emerging railways quickly grasped that development of short haul traffic, to and from the numerous works firmly established beside the densely knit canals, was in their best interest. One, of what amounted to over forty, railway owned basins, remains in surprisingly good condition at Chillington Wharf and has been given Grade II listed status. It was opened by the London & North Western Railway in 1902 on the site of an ironworks, and retains a marked degree of latent atmosphere.

South of Wolverhampton the BCN's main line pursues a winding course through a largely industrial area. Bilston Road Bridge carries the Metro tramway across the canal, and there is barely a dull moment as each bend in the canal intrudes upon a fresh variation on the Black Country's age old theme of 'metal bashing'. At Rough Hills Stop the canal narrows at the site of a former toll house.

Wolverhampton   *(Map 7)*

The Barnsley Bard, Ian McMillan, likened Wolverhampton to an auntie who's never been kissed, though in doing so inferred that there is much more to the city than meets the eye, a stance that the Canal Companions have firmly held throughout their existence. Wolverhampton had city status conferred upon it at the Millennium. Prior to that, it had tended to languish in shadows cast by Big Brother Birmingham. Wulfrunians will rapidly put you right. After all, their pedigree is more impressive than that of the upstart down the A41. Ethelred the Unready granted the town a charter in 985 - Birmingham had to wait two more centuries before being so recognised. In medieval times Wolverhampton was something of a wool centre, a way of life recalled by street names like Farmers Fold and Woolpack Alley, but the discovery of coal and iron turned Wolverhampton into a manufacturing town famous for lock making, notably Chubbs, whose huge triangular works overlooks the canal, though it is now in use (amongst other things) as an arts centre. Today, like everywhere else, Wolver-hampton has had to re-gear for the future, but steel is still processed in the periphery of heavy industry that still, to some extent, cloaks the town.

Eating & Drinking

GREAT WESTERN - Sun Street. Tel: 01902 351090. Adjacent old Low Level station. Easiest access from canal by Broad Street Bridge. Go under railway then turn right past old station (being redeveloped as the Station Plaza complex of restaurants, shops and bars) until the pub comes into sight on its cobbled street corner hemmed in by blue brick arches. Railway memorabilia, Holdens, Bathams, guest beers, Black Country cooking (at lunchtimes), what more could you want from a pub!

Shopping

The Mander and Wulfrun centres are modern precincts emblazoning all the inevitable names in plastic facia. But down sidestreets and up alleyways plenty of characterful local shops are waiting to be discovered by the discerning shopper. Try the faggots at any butcher's, they are a Black Country delicacy - really! There's a lively retail market on Tue, Wed, Fri & Sat and a Farmers' Market on the first Friday of the month.

Things to Do

TOURIST INFORMATION CENTRE - 18 Queen Square. Tel: 01902 312051.

ART GALLERY - Lichfield Street. Tel: 01902 552055. Imposing Victorian pile in the process of being reinvigorated to the tune of almost £7 million; will contain prestigious Pop Art collection.

Connections

BUSES & TRAINS - respective stations directly adjacent to the canal, access via Broad Street Bridge. Local services on 0121 200 2700. Treat yourself to a ride on the Metro tramway, a fascinating journey across what's left of the industrial Black Country and the opportunity to eavesdrop on oral history! Other trains 08457 484950.

TAXIS - Associated. Tel: 01902 420420.

O what do you think of it so far? - the BCN that is. Are you under its spell, or are you under psychoanalysis, still hyperventilating from its fulminating blend of inspirational industrial heritage and sheer downright ugliness? Love it, or loathe it, you're here now, so make the most of the BCN's Main Line as, between Wolverhampton and Tipton, in sinuous accord with the contours, it betrays its Brindley origins. Only on the cut through Coseley - engineered by Thomas Telford to by-pass the circuitous Wednesbury Oak Loop (partially retained to serve the maintenance workshops at Bradley) - do 19th century improvements deviate from the original route

of 1772. And if you are prepared to use your imagination, there will barely be a dull moment as the canal traverses an area of the Black Country where the traditional activities of the region are in retreat, their place taken by ubiquitous industrial units and innocuous housing estates. You are a symptom of this change. The relative popularity of boating and walking the BCN is largely a recent phenomenon, helped no little, in the former case, by the popularity of the "Stourport Ring". The recreational potential of canals, however, was recognised too late to save approximately one third of the BCN system from being abandoned during the Fifties and Sixties. Traces

continued on page 21

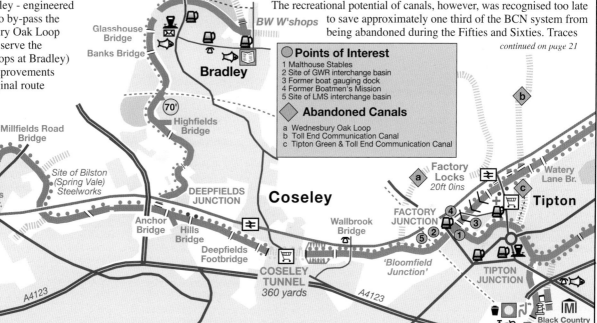

Points of Interest
1 Malthouse Stables
2 Site of GWR interchange basin
3 Former boat gauging dock
4 Former Boatmen's Mission
5 Site of LMS interchange basin

Abandoned Canals
a Wednesbury Oak Loop
b Toll End Communication Canal
c Tipton Green & Toll End Communication Canal

*No locks on Old Main Line

For details of Tipton facilities turn to page 20

Tipton

(Map 8)

'Teapton' - once islanded by canals - was nicknamed the 'Venice of the Midlands' long before the hackneyed analogy of Birmingham having more canals than Venice became common currency. And even with the relegation of the Tipton Green & Toll End Communication Canal to a landscaped pathway, Owen Street (the main thoroughfare) remains embraced by the old and new main lines. The little town's most famous son is William Perry aka 'The Tipton Slasher', England's champion prizefighter for seven undefeated years from 1850. His pugilistic years followed a period as a canal boatman; ideal preparation one imagines. His statue overlooks the canal by Owen Street Bridge.

Eating & Drinking

THE FOUNTAIN - Owen Street. Tel: 0121 522 3606. Once the Slasher's headquarters, now a Banks's pub offering food and a canalside beer garden.

THE PIE FACTORY - Hurst Lane. Tel: 0121 557 1402. Eccentric creation of former Little Pub Co.

PAPA PICCOLO'S PIZZERIA - dial a pizza on 0121 557 8555.

Two fish & chip shops and a Chinese takeaway.

Shopping

A handy little shopping centre easily reached from either of the main lines. There is an HSBC bank and a fair range of shops, including a Co-op and a branch of Firkins for those in dire need of a cream cake or two.

Things to Do

BLACK COUNTRY LIVING MUSEUM - Tipton Road, Dudley. Tel: 0121 557 9643 *www.bclm.co.uk* Admission charge. Each year the disparity grows between the real West Midlands and this little pocket of preserved in aspic, nostalgia-tinted Black Country. Located on

Railway boat at the BCLM

a 26 acre site, it'll take you at least a couple of hours to walk around the exhibits which include a village, colliery, pumping engine, boat dock and fairground. Rolfe Street Baths (which used to overlook the canal as it passed so dramatically through Smethwick) have been re-erected here as an excellent exhibition hall devoted to Black Country social history and industrial archaeology. Trams (and sometimes trolleybuses) offer rides from the main entrance to the village. An additional attraction is the operation of electric trip boats into Dudley Tunnel and its caverns - see page 94. Secure moorings (with facilities) are available for visiting boaters, access via Tipton Junction. Refreshments include a Canalside Cafe,

Fried Fish Shop (where the fish & chips are cooked in beef-dripping) and the Bottle & Glass Inn. Frankly, it would be ludicrous to boat along the BCN Main Line and not call in here!

Connections

BUSES - links from centre of Tipton to/from Dudley (an interesting town with a castle to visit) also calling at stops by the Black Country Museum, otherwise about 20 minutes walk from the railway station.

TRAINS - local services half-hourly between Wolverhampton and Birmingham.

Tel: 0121-200 2700 for details of local bus and train services.

continued from page 19

of these lost routes abound on this map, and it is difficult not to regret their going, and in doing so daydream of itineraries impossible to recapture afloat, if not on foot.

Utilitarian nomenclature abounds on the BCN, and at FACTORY JUNCTION, Brindley's "Wolverhampton Level" and Telford's "Birmingham Level" are seen to meet or divide, depending on your direction of travel. Boating towards Birmingham you have a choice (always assuming both routes are free of stoppages) between the directness of Telford's wide, embanked, twin-towpathed 'Island Line', twenty feet below through the three Factory Locks, and Brindley's original route which parallels it, hugging the 473ft contour in the shadow of the Rowley Hills. The latter affords access to the BLACK COUNTRY LIVING MUSEUM, where secure overnight moorings and boating facilities are available in the surreal environs of a 19th century time warp. Incorporated into the museum, an unusual vertical lift bridge, rescued from the Great Western Railway's Tipton interchange basin (2), gives access to a section of Lord Ward's Canal which led directly from the Old Main Line to a bank of lime kilns which still forms an attractive feature of the museum. Several historic boats are usually on display here, and there is a working boat dock where visitors can see some of the trades and techniques of Black Country boat construction taking place. Beyond the museum moorings is the northern portal of DUDLEY TUNNEL, first dug in 1775 to gain access to subterranean limestone workings. Ten years later it was extended through to join up with the Dudley Canal at PARKHEAD (Map 34). The sole preserve of electrically-powered trip boats for many years, Dudley Tunnel re-opened to general boating traffic in 1992, with the proviso that they be shafted and 'legged' through so as to avoid the creation of engine fumes, and that they meet the fairly restrictive gauge limitations. Life has been made easier by the introduction of a tug to haul you through: contact the Dudley Canal Trust on 01384 236275 for more details.

TIPTON, once waggishly known as the Venice of the Midlands, is rich in canal heritage, and a short circular walk based on the railway station, and incorporating the public footpath now occupying the course of the Tipton Green & Toll End Communication Canal, would provide an immediate, if not intimate, introduction. By FACTORY JUNCTION (named after a long vanished soap works) two interesting buildings survive.

Between the pub and the top lock stood a Boatmen's Mission (4), one of five such establishments on the BCN dispensing hot drinks, tobacco, washing facilities and a little transitory warmth and companionship. On the Sabbath the emphasis became more overtly religious, and Sunday School lessons were held for boat children. On the opposite bank of the top lock stands a former BCN gauging station (3) where the carrying capacity of boats was calculated for toll taking purposes. Craft gained access through two arches at the west end of the building. Beyond the junction, in the direction of Wolverhampton and on the far side of the modern road bridge, lay the entrance to the Great Western Railway basin (2). Railway owned boats would operate between these interchange points and 'boatage' depots which were wharves operated by the railways but without direct rail links. The London & North Western Railway also had an extensive interchange basin at nearby Bloomfield (5). Back at the junction, alongside the Old Main Line's route, former malthouse stables (1) have been given a new lease of life as a canoe centre - boaters should proceed with due care. Snaking round the corner, past "The Fountain" public house and under Owen Street Bridge, Brindley's route skirts the centre of Tipton, passing a small park where the local authority have erected a statue to Tipton's most famous son, the boxer, William Perry, aka 'the Tipton Slasher'! Opposite here, a fairly easily come upon pathway leads between houses along the course of the Communication Canal back to Telford's canal and the railway station. More to the BCN than you thought? You bet!

The Wednesbury Oak Loop

The new route opened in 1837 between Deepfields and Bloomfield junctions was just over a mile long, yet it replaced something like four miles of typical Brindley wanderings which then became known as the Wednesbury Oak Loop. Largely abandoned by 1960, a mile and a half remains in use from Deepfields connecting British Waterways' Bradley Workshops with the main line, a tempting diversion for those enamoured of backwaters. From the outset a real sense of exploration is engendered: the margins are reedy; the water turquoise coloured; whilst tethered ponies dolefully regard your passing. Be warned, however, that out of office hours you are requested to turn at the winding hole beyond Highfields Bridge because access to Bradley Workshops is denied.

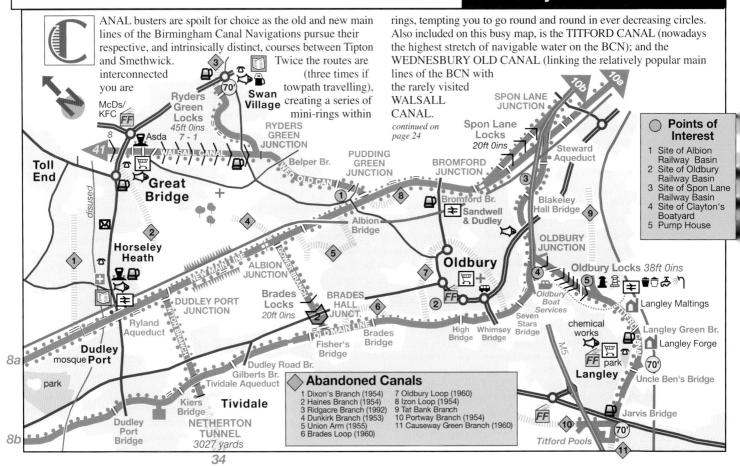

CANAL busters are spoilt for choice as the old and new main lines of the Birmingham Canal Navigations pursue their respective, and intrinsically distinct, courses between Tipton and Smethwick. Twice the routes are interconnected you are (three times if towpath travelling), creating a series of mini-rings within rings, tempting you to go round and round in ever decreasing circles. Also included on this busy map, is the TITFORD CANAL (nowadays the highest stretch of navigable water on the BCN); and the WEDNESBURY OLD CANAL (linking the relatively popular main lines of the BCN with the rarely visited WALSALL CANAL.

continued on page 24

Points of Interest

1. Site of Albion Railway Basin
2. Site of Oldbury Railway Basin
3. Site of Spon Lane Railway Basin
4. Site of Clayton's Boatyard
5. Pump House

Abandoned Canals

1. Dixon's Branch (1954)
2. Haines Branch (1954)
3. Ridgacre Branch (1992)
4. Dunkirk Branch (1953)
5. Union Arm (1955)
6. Brades Loop (1960)
7. Oldbury Loop (1960)
8. Izon Loop (1954)
9. Tat Bank Branch
10. Portway Branch (1954)
11. Causeway Green Branch (1960)

Map labels:

McDs/KFC · Ryders Green Locks 45ft 0ins 7 - 1 · Swan Village · RYDERS GREEN JUNCTION · Asda · WALSALL CANAL · Great Bridge · Belper Br. · WED OLD CAN · PUDDING GREEN JUNCTION · SPON LANE JUNCTION · Spon Lane Locks 20ft 0ins · Steward Aqueduct · Toll End · Horseley Heath · Albion Bridge · BROMFORD JUNCTION · Bromford Br. · Sandwell & Dudley · Blakeley Hall Bridge · NEW MAIN LINE · ALBION JUNCTION · OLDBURY JUNCTION · Oldbury · Oldbury Locks 38ft 0ins · Langley Maltings · Brades Locks 20ft 0ins · BRADES HALL JUNCT. · Oldbury Boat Services · Langley Green Br. · Langley Forge · Dudley Port · DUDLEY PORT JUNCTION · Ryland Aqueduct · OLD MAIN LINE · Fisher's Bridge · Brades Bridge · High Bridge · Whimsey Bridge · Seven Stars Bridge · chemical works · park · Langley · Uncle Ben's Bridge · mosque · Dudley Road Br. · Gilberts Br. · Tividale Aqueduct · Kiers Bridge · Tividale · NETHERTON TUNNEL 3027 yards · Jarvis Bridge · Dudley Port Bridge · Titford Pools

34

Oldbury (Map 9)

Redevelopment continues to alter the face of Oldbury, though here and there echoes of the old Worcestershire town bounce back at you. L. T. C. Rolt wrote: "Of Oldbury, with its mean, blackened streets, I can find no redeeming word to say," but then he had a horror of over industrialisation, whereas a lot of us have an acute nostalgia for many aspects of it now. The vast conglomerate offices of Sandwell MBC's civic headquarters dominate the town now, and the mind can only boggle at the army of bureaucrats employed in keeping tabs on the rest of us who actually have to make something useful in order to eke out a living.

Eating & Drinking
WAGGON & HORSES - Church Street. Standing defiantly opposite the civic offices, this CAMRA recommended pub has retained virtually all its Victorian character, right down (or should that be up) to a copper-panelled ceiling! Dispenses many of the region's best local ales plus a cycle of other guest beers. Food usually available Mon-Fri. 5 minutes walk from Whimsey Bridge on the old main line. Tel: 0121 552 5467.
McDONALDS - 'drive-thru' outlet adjacent Whimsey Bridge, though no loop provided for the boat trade as yet.

Shopping
The best canalside choice in shops between Wolverhampton and Birmingham. The centre is most easily reached from the old main line, but is also little more than half a mile from Telford's route at Bromford. SAINSBURY'S supermarket near Whimsey Bridge, branches of most banks and a small market on Tues & Sats. Some good Black Country butchers and bakers.

Connections
BUSES - bus station adjacent to Whimsey Bridge. Tel: 0121 200 2700.
TRAINS - InterCity and local services from Sandwell & Dudley railhead by Bromford Bridge. Tel: 08457 484950.

Great Bridge (Map 9)

The Spine Road has brought 21st century reality to Great Bridge - there are even KFC and McDonalds 'drive-thrus' - and we were saddened to see the exorcism of much of the town's time-warp atmosphere so prevalent when we last journeyed this way. Still, the West Bromwich Building Society continues to advertise itself ingenuously as 'the home of thrift' whilst Great Bridge remains a more than useful frontier post for stocking up on life's little necessities (Tunnocks caramel wafers for example) before heading off into the northern wastes of the BCN.

Eating & Drinking
THE EIGHT LOCKS - canalside top of Ryder's Green Locks. Food, pool, darts and a garden. Tel: 0121 522 3800.
Fish & chips from FRYDAYS or THE BLACK COUNTRY CHIPPY. McDONALDS and KFC outlets adjacent Lock 8.

Shopping
Access between locks 7 and 8 to main thoroughfare of shops including: Barclays Bank, Kwik Save and Firkins, famous for their imitation cream slices. ASDA supermarket and BOOTS pharmacy adjacent Lock 7.

Langley (Map 9)

The Black Country's heart still beats faintly in little communities like Langley. It feels just like a village; albeit a village surrounded by chemical plants and foundries. There are canalside pubs by Langley Green Bridge and Jarvis Bridge, but perhaps the most visitor friendly at present is THE CROSSWELLS on Whyley Walk (Tel: 0121 552 2626) which has recently been provided with a conservatory restaurant. Meanwhile, at THE TEA POT (on the main street) the all day breakfast will set you back just £3! However it's Langley's shops which really capture the imagination: ELAINE'S intriguing 'discount store'; BASTABLE'S car spares outlet (much of its contents being of use to boats as well); MELLOR'S old-fashioned cobblers; and the VILLAGE BAKERY.

Smethwick (Map 10)

High Street was sliced in half to make room for the expressway. What remains is more Asian than Anglo-Saxon, but all the more intriguing for that. If you enjoy cooking Indian then this is the place to stop for authentic ingredients; the sweet shops are mouthwatering! Otherwise Smethwick's attractions lie very much in the past, and anyone with an interest in canals and/or industrial archaeology will revel in the panoramic sweep of Brindley's and Telford's split level canals.

Things to Do
GALTON VALLEY CANAL HERITAGE CENTRE - Brasshouse Lane. Tel: 0121 558 8195. Former pub converted to display exhibits and interpretive material relating to Smethwick's fascinating canal history. Access at most times to the adjoining pumphouse. Guided tours arranged for parties booking in advance.

Connections
TRAINS - frequent services between Rolfe Street station and Birmingham New Street and between Galton Bridge and New Street and Snow Hill. Tel: 0121 200 2700.

continued from page 22

The Old Main Line

Brindley's route tends to be less boated than Telford's. Duckweed encroaches on the channel whilst moorhens and coots are confident enough in being undisturbed to build precarious nests midstream. East of Tipton the Old Main Line (aka the Wolverhampton Level) runs through council housing, passes beneath the mothballed South Staffordshire Railway - earmarked for re-opening as part of the Metro tramway system - then finds itself in the much changed environment of 'Tividale Quays', a housing development incorporating a large canal basin, underlining the significant role that the BCN has played in the regeneration and 'greening' of the new Black Country; though there will be some who feel that a considerable amount of character has been lost in the process. If this feeling of being short-changed applies to you, then you need to get yourself down to the reference library and study old, large scale maps of the area to grasp the hive of industry which once existed here. Trace the Wolverhampton Level's route past colliery basins, iron foundry basins and brick-works basins and you begin to gain some conception of the canal's former importance. As detailed as we like our maps to be, there was simply no way that we could do justice to the plethora of arms and basins which once branched off the old main line between Tipton and Oldbury.

TIVIDALE AQUEDUCT carries the old main line over the Netherton Tunnel Branch. There is no waterway connection here, but a path links the two levels. Netherton's northern portal looks intriguing and sepulchural when seen from the vantage point of the aqueduct, as though it might somehow lead you into the past, if only you had the courage to go there. At BRADES HALL JUNCTION the Gower Branch descends through the BCN's solitary 'staircase' lock to join Telford's main line, half a mile to the north. More new housing precedes Oldbury, though there are occasional glimpses south towards the Rowley Hills and Dudley Castle.

Vestiges of the Brades and Oldbury loops - which marked the original, even more convoluted course of Brindley's original route - are discernible to the diligent explorer, but the canal's course through Oldbury now is as blandly neat and as instantly forgettable as a meal from the adjoining fast food drive-thru.

OLDBURY JUNCTION (egress point of the Titford Canal) suffers the indignity of being located beneath the M5 motorway. This was the site (between 1935 and 1966) of a boatyard belonging to another carrying company inseparable from the history of this area's canals. Thomas Clayton specialised in the transport of bulk liquids. With a fleet in excess of eighty boats to maintain, this yard presented a busy scene, a distinctive aspect of which were two mobile slipway shelters which provided some protection from the weather while craft were being repaired. Clayton's best known long distance traffic was the carriage of oil from Ellesmere Port to Shell's depot at Langley Green, a contract which lasted from 1924 until 1955; some of the boats remaining horse-drawn until virtually the end.

Southwards from Oldbury, Clayton boats - with their distinctive decked holds and river names - served gasworks at Oxford, Banbury, Leamington and Solihull, but the bulk of their trade was of a more localised nature, notably the carriage of gas works bi-products such as tar. Their last cargo - carried aboard the now preserved motor *Stour* - arrived at Midland Tar Distillers, Oldbury from Walsall Gasworks on 31st March, 1966. Faced with diminishing cargoes (brought about largely by the advent of North Sea gas) and the disruption brought about by construction of the elevated section of the M5, Thomas Clayton called it a day as far as canal transport was concerned. In 2006 a number of preserved Clayton boats gathered at a boat rally on the Titford Canal to mark the 40th anniversary of the end of the fleet.

Playing hopscotch with the elevated motorway, the old main line proceeds towards Smethwick. Blakeley Hall Bridge possibly recalls the existence of some long-vanished mansion. The simple, hump-backed character of the bridge contrasts starkly with the overhanging motorway's concrete ceiling. In dramatic sequence, the canal passes beneath the Birmingham to Wolverhampton railway, crosses Telford's route by way of STEWARD AQUEDUCT, and meets Brindley's original route to Wednesbury at SPON LANE JUNCTION. The aqueduct's impact is somewhat diluted by the hefty pillars of the motorway towering above it. Interestingly, the iron lattice footbridge immediately south of the railway is numbered as a railway and not canal structure, undoubtedly because it was part of the adjoining interchange basin with the London & North Western Railway.

The New Main Line

Whilst Brindley's canal winds about the foot of the Rowley Hills reciting poetry to itself, Telford's gets to grips with the business of reaching Birmingham in a no nonsense manner which accountants would approve of. For almost three miles the canal runs as true as a line on a balance sheet, crossing great open expanses of wasteground where large craters recall past quarrying and brickmaking. These areas have been designated for development as urban woodland. Inexorably the Black Country is becoming green again, going full circle back to its pre-industrial origins.

Junction after junction - some vanished, some intact - keep the adrenalin flowing. The short Dixon's Branch served the Horseley Iron Works foundry which moved from its earlier site at Tipton in 1865. Three aqueducts carry the canal across two roads and a railway. The most notable, RYLAND AQUEDUCT, is a concrete rebuilding of 1968. A short loop railway once crossed the canal here, used by the 'Dudley Dodger' push & pull train which ran from the town station at Dudley to connect with main line trains at Dudley Port. The rusty, overgrown tracks of the old South Staffordshire Railway betray its lack of use now, all a far cry from the days when Palethorpe's nearby 'sausage siding' was shunted on a daily basis.

At DUDLEY PORT JUNCTION the Netherton Branch makes a bee-line for its famous tunnel. Opened in 1858 to relieve pressure on the parallel Dudley Tunnel route, it was the last canal tunnel to be built in Britain, going into the record books - at 3027 yards - as the eighth longest. Subsequent closures have rendered it fourth only (in navigable terms) to Standedge on the Huddersfield Narrow Canal, Dudley itself, and Blisworth on the Grand Union. TIVIDALE (location of the largest Hindu temple in Europe) used to be considered a safe place to moor, but British Waterways have apparently withdrawn the boating facilities hitherto present, whilst the BCN cottages by the Old Main Line aqueduct have been boarded up for some time*. In any case, the last time we passed by coincided with reports of gangland shootings in the local media, so perhaps this is not the best spot for an overnight stop.

Watching the trains go by, you come to ALBION JUNCTION where the Gower Branch links up with the old main line and 'Wolverhampton Level'. A former toll island all but fills the width of the new main line; an 'eye of the needle' job for nervous steerers. Two more junctions tempt you

*Being refurbished as we went to press!

in quick succession. From PUDDING GREEN the door swings open to the under-boated waters of the 'northern half' of the BCN via Brindley's original Wednesbury Canal (see page 28), whilst at BROMFORD JUNCTION there's a link with the old main line through the trio of Spon Lane Locks. These locks are quite possibly the oldest working chambers in the country, and enjoy listed status. Here, between 1861 and 1890 the evangelist John Skidmore held weekly, open air revivalist meetings each summer, with attendances peaking at an incredible twenty thousand souls. According to Skidmore's diaries, the throngs assembled on slag heaps bordering the middle lock. 'Thousands worshipped God in the open air ... rich and poor, old and young, well-dressed and ragged, drapers, grocers, butchers, tailors, publicans, ironmasters, clerks, magistrates, puddlers, coalmasters, mine agents, colliers, navvies, boatmen, roadmen, labourers, sweeps, a goodly number of Frenchmen from the Glass House (Chances - see below), the aged and infirm, the lame and the blind, men of all creeds and no creed at all.' Skidmore had been inspired to hold meetings when, whilst out distributing tracts, he had come upon a gathering of colliers and ironworkers at Spon Lane engaged in cockfighting and dog-fighting, gambling and whippet-racing. Through sheer force of personality the then youthful missionary persuaded these rough diamonds to attend an evangelist meeting on the spot the following Sunday. The meetings continued for nearly thirty years until the canal company reclaimed this lawless land. Negotiating the flight now, you need all the imagination you can muster to visualize the al fresco congregation, moved, in turn, to laughter and tears by Skidmore's oratory. There must have been times when they made as much noise as the crowd at West Bromwich Albion's nearby Hawthorns football ground. Nowadays the noise comes from the incessant roar of traffic on the elevated section of the M5 motorway. The top lock is all but engulfed by the road, its tiny, cantilevered, cast iron tail bridge provoking piquant contrast with the motorway's massive concrete pillars and girders.

Meanwhile Telford's route keeps to the 'Birmingham Level' and passes beneath the M5 and STEWARD AQUEDUCT, entering a vast cutting of blue-brick retaining walls between the railway on one side and what's left of Chance's glassworks on the other. The works was known world-wide in its prime as a manufacturer of, amongst many other things, glass for lighthouses.

Bromford Junction

Steward Aqueduct

Galton Bridge

26

Engine Arm
Aqueduct

Winson
Green

Galton
Bridge

The Wednesbury 'Old' Canal

Pudding Green ought to be the name of some picturesque village snuggled deep in the Sussex Weald. Instead, it's an incongruous gateway to and from the northern waters of the BCN; though we did discover wild poppies and lupins flowering bravely along the towpath yards from the junction itself. But flora and fauna - other than the ubiquitous rosebay willowherb and Canada geese - are otherwise none too conspicuous as the canal winds through an area of metal and chemical works past the site of the old Albion railway basin; the inspiration for an atmospheric night-time interior painting by Brian Collings included as a plate in Tom Foxon's evocative memoirs of a working boatman *Number One*. Reference to the Godfrey Edition Ordnance Survey reprint for Greets Green in 1902 illustrates the layout of Albion Basin and, indeed, the full course of the Wednesbury Old Canal to its present truncated terminus at Swan Bridge. Though not as built upon as now, the canal's course is accompanied by numerous side basins and arms - twenty or more at a rough count - emphasising the canal's vital role in the industrialisation process of an area of once wild heathland.

At RYDERS GREEN JUNCTION the Walsall Canal descends through a flight of eight locks to Great Bridge. The Haines Branch at its foot was associated with bricks and coal, but although abandoned officially in 1954, it was briefly used by Willow Wren boats with consignments of timber from Brentford Docks in the early 1960s. Veering to the right, Brindley's original canal carries on for another half mile or so to Swan Bridge until petering out where the Black Country Spine Road controversially - in canal circles at any rate - brought about closure of the canal. Historically the canal continued from here to Swan Bridge Junction where one arm, known as the Balls Hill Branch, wound its way to Hill Top, terminating amidst colliery shafts beside the Holyhead Road. A second arm, called the Ridgacre Branch - trifurcated into the long forgotten Dartmouth, Halford and Jesson extremities. This is a real backwater, even by BCN standards; the water in the navigable section becoming more and more like pea soup as its foreshortened terminus is approached. Where they have not already been reduced to mounds of rubble, the works on its banks are increasingly silent, their chimneys replaced by telecommunication masts.

The Titford Canal

Arguably the BCN's greatest adventure - especially as far as boaters are concerned, for water supply seems perennially problematical - the Titford Canal packs a good deal of interest into its mile and a half journey from the motorwayed enclave of Oldbury Junction to the wildfowl-filled expanses of Titford Pools.

Half a dozen locks - nicknamed 'The Crow' - lift the Titford up to its 511ft height above sea level, nowadays the BCN's loftiest pound. The chambers have single-leaf gates at both top and tail, and the short intervening pounds feature extended side ponds to increase water capacity. With no reservoir, as such, to feed its summit, the Titford Canal relies largely on precipitation to maintain a navigable depth.

The canal's surroundings are overwhelmingly industrial, whilst an acrid smell - part chemical, part burnt offering - seems to hang permanently over the proceedings. A refurbished engine house (used as an appropriate meeting room by the Birmingham Canal Navigations Society) marks the junction with the old Tat Bank Branch, now replete with moorings and boating facilities, its far end an unlikely sanctuary for water voles.

Passing under the Great Western Railway's Langley Green-Oldbury branchline (closed to passengers as long ago as the First World War, though only relatively recently to goods) you reach the Wolverhampton & Dudley Brewery's handsome Langley Maltings. The canal water becomes as clear as a see-through blouse; though the contents of the canal bed thus revealed are not quite so desirable as the analogy suggests.

Langley Forge continues in business; though the thumping presses fondly associated with previous visits appear forebodingly still. By Uncle Ben's Bridge, Slade's Coal Wharf was supplied by boat until 1967. A neat little park (from which the strains of Langley Prize Band are sometimes to be heard) precedes a length of canal embalmed in suburbia before the junction of the old Portway and Causeway Green branch canals (gradually abandoned between 1954 and 1960) heralds the end of navigation; a rather eldritch, road-noisy terminus if the truth were known. Brave boaters can toy with exploration of the coot-haunted, debris-filled Titford Pools, navigating beneath the cylindrical concrete support columns of the M5 motorway; though there are shallows to contend with, together with terrapins if not crocodiles.

REALISATION of the impact made by Thomas Telford's new main line comes with exploration of the lengthy loops it superseded. By the end of the 18th century Brindley's canal had become a victim of its own success; water was short and traffic congested. Telford was called in to suggest improvements and discovered 'a canal little better than a crooked ditch'! The original towing path had deteriorated to the extent that horses frequently slid and staggered into the water, tow lines entangled when boats met, and boatmen quarrelled over precedence at locks. The canny Scot devised a bold improvement plan cutting through the Smethwick summit. The work took five years and was completed in 1829. It reduced the distance between Wolverhampton and Birmingham by a third. A local historian found the new route "unsurpassed in stupendous magnificence"!

It is difficult to this day not to be impressed by the puissance of Telford's engineering; though just as easy to be beguiled by Brindley's peregrinations. The old loops retained their local traffics, serving works firmly established along their banks. And so the Oozells Street, Iknield Port and Soho (though not the Cape nor Soho Foundry) loops remain navigable to this day, functioning - as does a greater part of the BCN - as storm drainage channels and linear reservoirs for industry. Included in the itineraries of Birmingham's trip boats, they are worth investigating as dreamy alternatives to the unequivocal, focussed concentration of the new main line.

Westwards from SMETHWICK JUNCTION the old and new main lines forge their separate routes to and from Tipton. The earlier canal ascends through three locks to reach its 473ft summit. Originally its course lay even higher at 491ft, traces of which can be discerned along the embankment above the canal as it proceeds west of Brasshouse Lane Bridge. An even better viewpoint is the footbridge straddling the railway just west of Rolfe Street station.

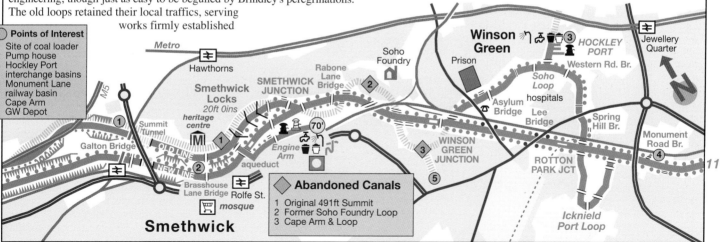

Points of Interest
1 Site of coal loader
2 Pump house
3 Hockley Port interchange basins
4 Monument Lane railway basin
5 Cape Arm GW Depot

Abandoned Canals
1 Original 491ft Summit
2 Former Soho Foundry Loop
3 Cape Arm & Loop

*Three locks and an extra half hour via Old Main Line

29

From this point there is a grandstand view of the two main lines as they sweep past Smethwick, a scene without equal anywhere else on the inland waterways system; though being Pearsons, and infamously reactionary in outlook, we cannot help but mourn the disappearance of the Brasshouse Lane foundry (and particularly the Sikhs amongst its labour force who would habitually cool off in the canal), transformed, heaven help us, into Wimpey Homes' 'Brindley Village', its honest housing marred by a sequence of hideous descending terraces which would be more at home at West Bromwich Albion's nearby Hawthorns football ground.

Access to the celebrated ENGINE ARM is through the tiny arch of a stone side bridge adjacent to Smethwick Top Lock. The arm spans the new main line by way of a wonderfully Gothic iron bridge, a real treasure in the context of its industrial setting. Boating is busier on the arm since British Waterways provided mooring, boating facilities and, most pertinently, a winding hole at its far end. The arm was built to serve as a feeder from Rotton Park Reservoir at Ladywood, and if you scale the grassy bank opposite the junction with the Soho Loop at Winson Green you can see the remnants of its narrow brick channel. The Engine Arm derives its name from James Watt's 'Smethwick Engine' of 1779 which was introduced to pump water up the original flight of six locks. Even when three of these were by-passed in 1790 the engine continued its work for another century until the pumping engine at Brasshouse Lane was commissioned. The 1892 pump house has been refurbished by the local authority in conjunction with the adjoining Canal Heritage Centre. West of here the old main line, running along the course engineered by Smeaton (of lighthouse fame) penetrates an unexpected oasis of water plantain and rosebay willowherb. For a moment it is possible to make believe you are deep in the countryside, but any rural illusion is shattered by the so-called SUMMIT TUNNEL, an ugly concrete tube covered by the high embankment of a dual carriageway.

Beyond the tunnel the canal is embraced by a deep and swarthy cutting and overlooked by the high rises of West Bromwich. The railway line into Snow Hill crosses the canal adjacent to the site of coal loading apparatus regrettably demolished in 2006 on the grounds that it might collapse and pose a threat to public safety. A totemic concrete structure,

it had once been used to load boats with coal brought down by cable tramway from the Jubilee Colliery in Sandwell, and its removal broke yet another tenuous link with the BCN's working past. A regular run from here was to Kings Norton (Map 12) with coal for the furnaces of the paper mill.

In contrast with the old line's excursions over the summit, Telford's route lies in shadows cast by extensive earthworks; dank corridors of blue engineering brick retaining walls and precipitous banks of bracken and bramble. The scale of these 19th century works, accomplished by navvies totally without sophisticated machinery, can be overwhelming. But the climax is Telford's astonishing GALTON BRIDGE; hidden in both directions by other structures until the last dramatic moment, and done no favours by rampant vegetation: it behoves the powers that be to consider the importance of sight-lines amidst their perennial initiative packages.

Between Smethwick and WINSON GREEN the old and new main lines are one, sharing the same route through an industrial heartland of foundries and railway sidings. Much of the fun to be had from exploring the BCN derives from piecing together clues to its past. Railway boats would ease out of the Cape Arm's tunnel-like exit with nuts and bolts from GKN destined for the railway basin at HOCKLEY PORT; now a centre for residential moorings. Earlier still, near Rabone Lane Bridge, Matthew Boulton and James Watt opened their Soho foundry, the first factory in the world to be lit by gas so that work could continue after darkness had fallen. Visited by Boswell in 1776, Boulton boasted: 'I sell here, sir, what all the world desires to have - power!'

Adjacent to the western junction of the SOHO LOOP (and again beneath the Engine Arm aqueduct) stand the bases of former toll houses. These octagonally shaped offices were strategically sited to keep account of the numerous short-haul traffics which operated throughout the BCN. Now only the bases remain, but a replica has been erected at Smethwick Top Lock, enabling you to judge how interesting these buildings used to be. It would be both rewarding and entertaining if they would complete the job by employing a suitably clothed character actor to issue from its confines demanding to know the nature of your business and the measure of your cargo ...

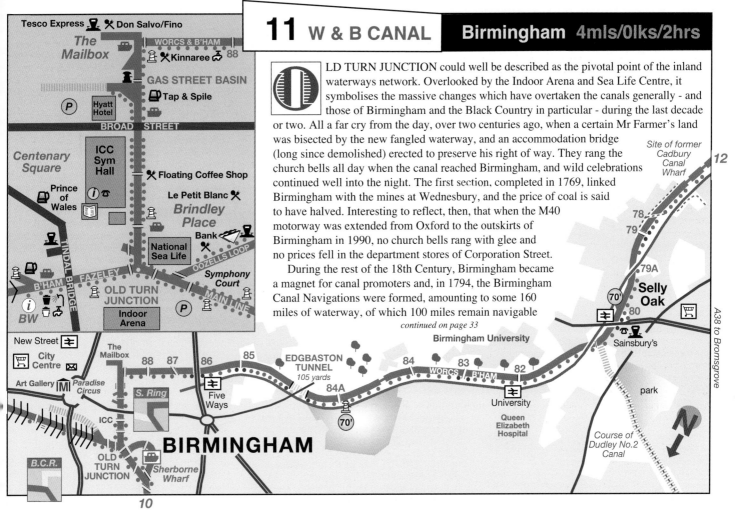

Tesco Express — Don Salvo/Fino
The Mailbox
WORCS & B'HAM
Kinnaree 88
GAS STREET BASIN
Tap & Spile
Hyatt Hotel
BROAD STREET
Centenary Square
ICC Sym Hall
Prince of Wales
Floating Coffee Shop
Le Petit Blanc
Brindley Place
Bank
National Sea Life
OOZELLS LOOP
Symphony Court
TINDAL BRIDGE
B'HAM FAZELEY
OLD TURN JUNCTION
BW
Indoor Arena
MAIN LINE

New Street
City Centre
Art Gallery
Paradise Circus
ICC
The Mailbox
88 87 86 85
S. Ring
Five Ways
EDGBASTON TUNNEL
105 yards
84A
84 83 82
WORCS B'HAM
University
Queen Elizabeth Hospital
Birmingham University
BIRMINGHAM
OLD TURN JUNCTION
Sherborne Wharf
B.C.R.
Course of Dudley No.2 Canal
park
Site of former Cadbury Canal Wharf
78
79
79A
70'
Selly Oak
80
Sainsbury's
A38 to Bromsgrove
70'

LD TURN JUNCTION could well be described as the pivotal point of the inland waterways network. Overlooked by the Indoor Arena and Sea Life Centre, it symbolises the massive changes which have overtaken the canals generally - and those of Birmingham and the Black Country in particular - during the last decade or two. All a far cry from the day, over two centuries ago, when a certain Mr Farmer's land was bisected by the new fangled waterway, and an accommodation bridge (long since demolished) erected to preserve his right of way. They rang the church bells all day when the canal reached Birmingham, and wild celebrations continued well into the night. The first section, completed in 1769, linked Birmingham with the mines at Wednesbury, and the price of coal is said to have halved. Interesting to reflect, then, that when the M40 motorway was extended from Oxford to the outskirts of Birmingham in 1990, no church bells rang with glee and no prices fell in the department stores of Corporation Street.

During the rest of the 18th Century, Birmingham became a magnet for canal promoters and, in 1794, the Birmingham Canal Navigations were formed, amounting to some 160 miles of waterway, of which 100 miles remain navigable

continued on page 33

10

12

31

Birmingham *(Maps 11 & 20)*

Canal boating holidays come low enough in the kudos stakes, and Birmingham as a destination lower still. But any sympathy your friends can muster will be wasted. Let them bake on some beach. There is more character in Birmingham's big toe than the whole of 'The Med' put together. The city centre is only a brief stroll from the visitor moorings radiating from Old Turn Junction, and its sophisticated character and traffic-free thoroughfares may surprise those with preconceived notions of an ungainly, uncouth city where everyone speaks through their nose and has something to do with the motor trade. But cars have lost their pole position in 'Brummagem's' scheme of things and the city continues to recover from its crass submission to traffic which ruined it a generation ago. Centenary, Chamberlain and Victoria squares set the tone for the canal travellers' perambulation of the city. The first revitalised with the opening of the Convention Centre in 1991, the other two dominated by imposing Victoriana, including the Art Gallery and the Town Hall. There are deeper oases of calm and character to be discovered too. Churches like St Philip's Cathedral and St Paul's (the 'Jeweller's Church'), the bustling markets of the rebuilt Bull Ring, and the quiet backwaters of the Jewellery Quarter. These are the bits of Birmingham you should make it your business to see.

Eating & Drinking

BANK - Brindley Place. Tel: 0121 633 4467. Award-winning restaurant with sister establishments at The Aldwych and Westminster in London. Terrace overlooking the Oozells Loop. Breakfasts Mon-Fri from 7.30am.
DON SALVO / FINO - The Mailbox. Tel: 0121 643 4000. Waterside Italian with resident gondola.

FLOATING COFFEE SHOP - Water's Edge, Brindley Place. Tel: 0121 455 6163. Coffees and light meals aboard a narrowboat called *George*.
KINNAREE - Holliday Wharf (opposite The Mailbox at what used to be known as Salvage Turn. Tel: 0121 665 6568. Elaborately decorated Thai restaurant.
LASAN - James Street (off St Paul's Square. Tel: 0121212 3664. Highly thought of Indian.
LE PETIT BLANC - Brindley Place. Tel: 0121 633 7333. Cordon bleu cuisine Francais.
LOS CANARIOS - Albert Street (within easy reach of the Digbeth Branch. Tel: 0121 236 3495. Spanish cooking by a family from The Canaries.
PRINCE OF WALES - Cambridge Street. Tel: 0121 643 9460. Nearest unspoilt pub to the canal. Real beer, faggots and peas etc.
TARNISHED HALO - Ludgate Hill. Tel: 0121 236 7562. Plush restaurant bar overlooking the eleventh lock down on the Farmer's Bridge flight.
WONGS - Fleet Street. Tel: 0121 212 1888. Atmospheric Chinese adjacent Saturday Bridge between locks 4 and 5 on the Farmer's Bridge flight.

Shopping

Canallers in a hurry - if that's not a contradiction in terms - will find convenience stores adjoining the Oozells Loop and Tindal Bridge by Farmer's Bridge Junction. Otherwise you'll find all the facilities of a major city within easy reach of the canal. The BULL RING markets (located on Edgbaston Street beyond New Street station) are a famous focal point of Midland merchandising. The Bull Ring Shopping Centre - a painful lesson in the excesses of concrete architecture dating from the Sixties - has been redeveloped, the landmark Rotunda having escaped by the skin of its Grade II listed teeth, so that it now rubs shoulders with the likes of Kaplicky's shimmering Selfridges store. THE PALLASADES (above New Street Station) and THE PAVILIONS development in High Street are predictable precincts. New Street and Corporation Street burgeon with department stores and multiple chains.

Things to Do

ROTUNDA TOURISM CENTRE - New Street. Tel: 0870 225 0127.
INTERNATIONAL CONVENTION CENTRE - Broad Street. Tel: 0121 200 2000. Even if you are not a delegate, worth visiting to admire its confident new architecture, or perhaps to enjoy a concert in the splendid SYMPHONY HALL whose Box Office is on 0121 780 3333.
INDOOR ARENA - King Edward's Road. Tel: 0121 200 2202. Sports events, concerts etc.
NATIONAL SEA LIFE CENTRE - Brindley Place. Tel: 0121 633 4700. Fish & stuff!
IKON GALLERY - Oozells Sq, Brindley Place. Tel: 0121 248 0708. Contemporary art venue.
MUSEUM & ART GALLERY - Chamberlain Square. Open daily, admission free. Recently boosted by opening of Gas Hall extension. Rivals Manchester in the richness of its Pre-Raphaelite collection.Tel: 0121 303 2834.
MUSEUM OF THE JEWELLERY QUARTER - Vyse Street (Hockley). Open Mon-Sat. Quarter of an hour's walk from Farmer's Bridge but well signposted. Open Mon-Sat. Tel: 0121 554 3598. Housed in former jewellery factory. Shop & refreshments.
THINKTANK - Curzon Street. Tel: 0121 202 2222. Science can be fun! Home to Watt's Smethwick Engine and Stanier's *City of Birmingham*.

Connections

Local bus & train hotline: 0121 200 2700. Nationwide trains: 08457 484950.

continued from page 31

in an area bounded by Wolverhampton, Walsall, Dudley and Tamworth.

There *were* celebrations, however, in 1991 when the Convention Centre opened alongside the canal, and Birmingham, here, has something to be proud of. Delegates from all over the world are wooed to convene in Birmingham instead of Brussels or Baltimore, and who knows what magic of the BCN might rub off on them.

BRINDLEY PLACE lies at the centre of things now. Here are 24 hour moorings overlooked by a plethora of cafe bars and restaurants - for once the hackneyed analogy of Birmingham with Venice seems almost understated, even disingenuous, and you cannot help but think that of all the British cities to see virtue in revitalizing their canals, Birmingham has made the best fist of it. From the piazzas of the Convention Centre the canal leads through Broad Street tunnel to GAS STREET BASIN, the epitome - and for many the lost soul - of Birmingham's waterways.

In fact Gas Street had come to symbolise the BCN to such an extent that it was often forgotten that the actual terminal wharf and offices of the Birmingham Canal lay to the east of here. Two arms terminated at the rear of the BCN company's handsomely symmetrical offices on Suffolk Street which, sadly, were demolished in 1928. Demolition controversially took its toll of the Gas Street canalscape in 1975 as well, by which time the planners should have known better, and British Waterways have never really been forgiven for razing their rich heritage of 18th century waterside warehouses to the ground in a calculated move to sidestep a preservation order.

For a time nothing was done to fill the void. Gas Street might have ceased to exist but for a community of residential boats which lent a splash of colour and humanity to a decaying canalscape. A decade elapsed before the developer's proposals were realised in bricks and mortar, and the biggest irony of all is that the new pubs and offices emerged in a warehouse vernacular style of remarkable similarity to the bulldozed originals. The only post Seventies interloper unsympathetic to the scale of the original Gas Street is the towering, shimmering, slippery, silvered edifice of the Hyatt Hotel. What do its sybaritic guests make of the little boats miles below their air-conditioned eyries? Do they see them as 'local colour', as archaic as the sampans of Hong Kong harbour?

The Worcester & Birmingham Canal

Work began on the Worcester & Birmingham Canal from the Birmingham end in 1794, but it was not until 1815 that the route was completed throughout. Fearful of its water supply disappearing down into the Severn, the Birmingham Canal Company at first refused to be directly linked with the newcomer, and so laborious transhipment of through traffic took place across an infamous divide known as the 'Worcester Bar'. Eventually, however, a stop lock was provided between the two waterways, affording the BCN some measure of protection, yet enabling through passage of boats.

Quickly extricating itself from the wine bars and nightclubs of downtown Birmingham, the Worcester & Birmingham Canal turns right-angle past The Mailbox development (soon to have a new neighbour called The Cube) and makes for the sylvan suburbs of Edgbaston. It was this cloistered, arboreous entrance to and exit from the city that prompted Robert Aickman to express the aphorism: "Canals stretch green fingers into towns." He might have added yellow and purple to his palate, for by late summer the borders of the canal and adjoining railway are a riot of rosebay willowherb and golden rod. But we can't help but share his enthusiasm, for this is a lovely stretch of canal, given its proximity to the city centre, and its towpath is increasingly used by walkers and cyclists as an alternative to the choked carriageways of the A38.

In cahoots with the old Birmingham West Suburban Railway, opened in 1876, and now heavily trafficked with sleek green electric units interspersed with Virgin Voyagers, the canal skirts Birmingham University, whose Italianate tower stabs the sky. At SELLY OAK there are plans for part of the former Dudley No.2 Canal to be re-opened in conjunction with a massive retail development scheme led by Sainsbury's. Journeying southwards, the Worcester & Birmingham reaches the outskirts of the chocolate making centre of Bournville. Again there are scant remains of the canal's heyday, when its east bank was a busy point of interchange for Cadbury's fleet of narrowboats and its internal railway system shunted by its own fleet of perky tank locomotives painted in a dark red colour inspired by the company's cocoa tins.

COMMERCIAL activity on the canal is sadly no longer considered a viable proposition, but leisure boating does bring its fair share of visitors to Cadbury World (see page 37) notwithstanding the slightly intimidating nature of the security fenced moorings provided alongside Bournville railway station and that accompanying recommendation that you leave no valuables on board because 'thieves operate in the area'!

Bournville's garden village owes its existence to the altruism of Quakers Richard and George Cadbury, who built a chocolate factory on a greenfield site in the vicinity in 1879. It was George in particular who had vision's of a worker's paradise, commissioning the architect Alexander Harvey to design artisans dwellings on a 120 acre site. Each house was to have a garden with fruit trees and a vegetable patch to provide an element of self-sufficiency - one cannot live on chocolate alone!

Between bridges 75 and 73 the towpath swaps sides, not on a whim, but because the Midland Railway once operated a transhipment basin on the west bank of the canal. At King's Norton the Stratford Canal comes in to join the Worcester & Birmingham, a route described in the *Severn & Avon Canal Companion*. A sizeable paper mill formerly overlooked the canal junction and large quantities of coal were brought here by narrowboat from Black Country mines: nails, screws and coins were other busy facets of local industry long vanished. Now the main landmark is the old Junction House, backed by the soaring steeple of St Nicholas, the notable parish church of King's Norton.

At 2,726 yards, WAST HILL TUNNEL is the Worcester & Birmingham's longest. It takes around half an hour to pass through and, whilst appearances can be deceptive, rest assured that there *is* room to pass oncoming craft inside its gloomy depths. Like all Worcester & Birmingham tunnels (except Edgbaston), it has no towpath. The lads

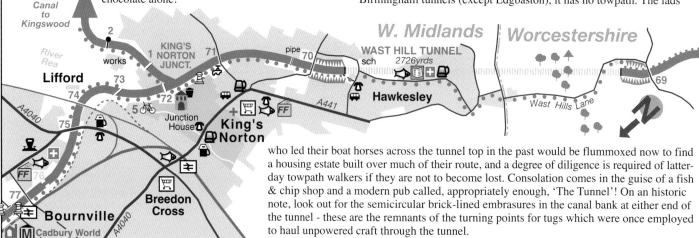

who led their boat horses across the tunnel top in the past would be flummoxed now to find a housing estate built over much of their route, and a degree of diligence is required of latter-day towpath walkers if they are not to become lost. Consolation comes in the guise of a fish & chip shop and a modern pub called, appropriately enough, 'The Tunnel'! On an historic note, look out for the semicircular brick-lined embrasures in the canal bank at either end of the tunnel - these are the remnants of the turning points for tugs which were once employed to haul unpowered craft through the tunnel.

For details of facilities at Bournville and King's Norton see page 37

POST-WAR Alvechurch overspills up its hillside to impinge upon the canal, but barely deflects from its dreamy, lockless progress above the valley of the River Arrow. There are panoramic views eastwards towards Weatheroak Hill crossed by the Roman's Ryknild Street. A feeder comes in from Upper Bittell Reservoir beside an isolated canal employee's cottage near Bridge 66. The Lower Reservoir, rich in wildfowl, lies alongside the canal and is given a gorgeous wooded backdrop by the Lickey Hills. Only the Upper Reservoir feeds the canal, the Lower was provided to compensate millers whose water supplies from the Arrow had been detrimentally affected by construction of the canal. A short section of the canal was re-routed in 1985 to accommodate construction of the M42 motorway.

Bridge 62 carries the electrified commuter line from Redditch through Birmingham to Lichfield. A seventy-five minute train journey - three days by boat to the nearest canal settlement at Fradley Junction. But time is an irrelevance on the canals, so relax and savour the charms of Shortwood Tunnel, its approach cuttings so suffocated by the odour of wild garlic that you feel as if you are being embraced by an over enthusiastic Frenchman. All that's missing is the tang of Gauloise, but then you may be able to provide that yourself.

As with all other Worcester & Birmingham tunnels (Edgbaston excepted) the towpath isn't subterranean, but the old horse-path across the top remains well-defined, and it is pleasant to wander across the top, fantasising that you've a horse to lead while your boat is hauled through the earth beneath your feet by one of the erstwhile tunnel tugs as described so evocatively by Tom Foxon in his regrettably long out of print book *Number One*.

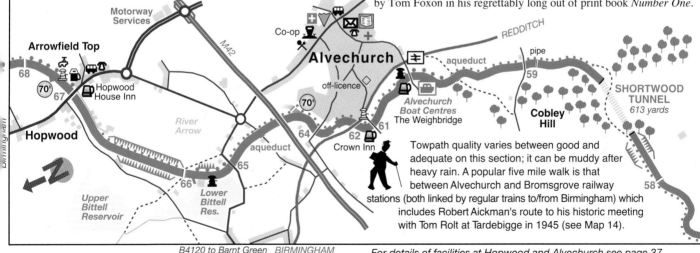

Towpath quality varies between good and adequate on this section; it can be muddy after heavy rain. A popular five mile walk is that between Alvechurch and Bromsgrove railway stations (both linked by regular trains to/from Birmingham) which includes Robert Aickman's route to his historic meeting with Tom Rolt at Tardebigge in 1945 (see Map 14).

For details of facilities at Hopwood and Alvechurch see page 37

14 WORCESTER & BIRMINGHAM CANAL

Tardebigge 4mls/36lks/7hrs

TARDEBIGGE represents a boater's Rite of Passage. Once you have tackled this flight which, coupled with the neighbouring six at Stoke, amount to thirty-six locks in four miles, other groups of locks, however fiendish, however formidable, pale into insignificance. The thirty chambers of the Tardebigge flight raise the canal over two hundred feet, the top lock - somewhat removed from the rest - being, at 14 feet, one of the deepest narrowbeam locks on the system; it replaced a lift prone to malfunction and water wastage. Well maintained and surrounded by fine countryside, with wonderful views to the Malvern Hills, Tardebigge Locks are there to be enjoyed, not dreaded. And in the summer months you'll have plenty

direct result of their meeting the Inland Waterways Association was formed. A plinth adjacent to the lock tells the story, along with a supplementary plaque correcting the date to 1945 - as Pearsons had maintained all along!

Only the briefest of pounds separates the Tardebigge and Stoke flights. Room enough, just, for half a dozen boats to moor for an overnight breather. The picturesque lock-keeper's cottage between locks 31 and 32 is available for holiday lets from the admirable Landmark Trust (Tel: 01628 825925) a body devoted to the rescue and refurbishment of worthwhile buildings in all shapes and sizes. It was the demolition of the junction house at Hurleston, on the Shropshire Union Canal, which 'maddened' the Trust's founder, John Smith, into creating the organisation in 1965.

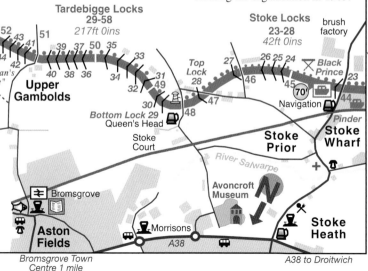

of fellow travellers with whom to share the experience, not to mention the work! Tardebigge's 18th century church, with its slender 135ft spire, is an inspirational landmark: 'belatedly baroque' in the words of James Lees-Milne in his pithy 1964 *Shell Guide to Worcestershire*.

Tardebigge holds a special place in the story of the inland waterways movement. It was to here that Robert Aickman and his wife made their way from Bromsgrove railway station to meet Tom and Angela Rolt aboard their narrowboat home *Cressy* which had been moored above the top lock throughout the Second World War. As a

36

Bournville (Map 12)

Use of a BW Yale key provides access from the secure offside moorings opposite Bournville railway station to suburban shops and take-aways and CADBURY WORLD, whose opening times etc can be obtained by telephoning 0121 451 4180.

King's Norton (Map 12)

KING'S NORTON provides the most easily accessible facilities for canal travellers in this area. 48 hour moorings are provided between bridges 71 and 72 and it's only a short uphill walk to the centre of this busy suburban settlement grouped about a pretty green and overlooked by the imposing spire of St Nicholas' Church. Facilities include: a pharmacy, Spar shop, newsagent, off licence, post office and Lloyds TSB bank with cash machines. There's an Indian restaurant and takeaway and two pubs.

Hopwood (Map 13)

The HOPWOOD HOUSE INN (Tel: 0121 445 1716) is a large, refurbished roadhouse alongside Bridge 67. There's a garage with shop across the road.

Alvechurch (Map 13)

It's one thing strolling down from the canal, but an altogether different matter struggling back with shopping bags. Nevertheless, Alvechurch is a pleasant village with some worthwhile facilities, though if you are not up to the trek a modest range of provisions is obtainable at the boatyard shop in addition to a good choice of canalia.

Eating & Drinking

THE WEIGHBRIDGE - canalside Bridge 60. Tel: 0121 445 5511. Part of Alvechurch Boat Centres boatyard, and the 'weighbridge house' for a coal wharf in days gone by. Tillerman's Tipple is brewed for them by Weatheroak. Home cooked food lunchtimes and evenings; breakfasts by prior arrangement.

THE CROWN - canalside Bridge 61. Tel: 0121 445 2300. An unspoilt canalside pub.

Shopping

Alvechurch lies twenty minutes walk down from the canal but boasts a useful range of shops: Co-op, post office (with newspapers) pharmacy, butcher, off licence, and bakery, but no bank. There is also a Chinese (Tel: 0121 447 8085) takeaway and an Indian restaurant (Tel: 0121 445 5660). Real ale enthusiasts may like to seek out Weatheroak Ales off licence just down the road from Bridge 61 - Tel: 0121 445 4411.

Connections

TRAINS - half-hourly service to Redditch and Birmingham (Tel: 08457 484950).

Aston Fields (Map 14)

Aston Fields, a suburb of Bromsgrove, has a number of useful shops - notably BANNERS deli and hot food outlet established as long ago as 1906 (Tel: 01527 872581) as well as the town's railway station. For Taxis contact Bill's of Bromsgrove on 01527 832594

Stoke Wharf (Map 14)

Canalside pubs include the QUEEN'S HEAD by Bridge 48 (Tel: 01527 877777) and the NAVIGATION by Bridge 44 (Tel: 01527 870194). AVONCROFT MUSEUM, a mile north of Bridge 48, houses a wonderful collection of buildings saved from demolition (Tel: 01527 831363). The LITTLE SHOP by Bridge 44 (Tel: 01527 876438) deals in Calor Gas, coal and chandlery.

Stoke Works (Map 15)

The BOAT & RAILWAY (Tel: 01527 831065) is a Banks's pub with a nice canalside terrace, good choice of beers and a wide range of bar meals (not Sundays) and a skittle alley. The Worcester & Birmingham Canal Society regularly meet here. There's a butcher and a post office stores on a housing estate half a mile north of Bridge 42.

Hanbury Wharf (Map 15)

At Hanbury Wharf the EAGLE & SUN (Tel: 01905 770130) is perennially popular with boaters, perhaps on account of the generously-sized bar meals that are served. Shops are conspicuous by their absence hereabouts, although a range of basic provisions is available from the boatyard along with guides, maps and postcards.

Dunhampstead (Map 16)

The quiet hamlet of Dunhampstead is able to offer both a canalside craft shop and a well-appointed pub called THE FIR TREE INN (Tel: 01905 774094) which serves tasty food and Hook Norton within its designer interior, and you can also learn about the dastardly Oddingley Murders.

Tibberton (Map 16)

Tibberton's amenities include a post office stores which also sells newspapers (lunchtime closing and early closing Wed, Sat & Sun) and two Bank's pubs, the BRIDGE INN (Tel: 01905 345684) is the more canal orientated, having a large waterside garden and offering a good choice of food; however the SPEED THE PLOUGH (Tel: 01905 345602) can also be recommended. Buses connect the village with Worcester - Tel: 0870 608 2 608.

OWADAYS, Britain's salt industry is largely confined to Cheshire but, as the name Droitwich suggests, this part of Worcestershire was once a centre of salt making too. The salt obsessed Romans built a special road between Droitwich and Alcester to carry this valuable commodity. Similarly, the Worcester & Birmingham built the short Droitwich Junction Canal from Hanbury Wharf to carry the same cargo. Barely two miles long, it included seven locks and passed briefly into the River Salwarpe before meeting the previously established Droitwich Canal at Vines Park near the town centre. Both the Droitwich canals had lapsed into dereliction before the end of the Thirties. In recent years they have undergone varying degrees of restoration: at Hanbury Wharf the first three locks have been restored and the top pound of the Junction Canal has been re-watered and is in use as private moorings. The summit of the widebeam Droitwich Canal is also in water and a day boat is available for hire from the Droitwich Canal Company - see page 95. Full restoration is earmarked for 2009.

At the end of the 18th century, John Corbett, son of a local boatman, discovered large deposits of brine at Stoke Prior and developed one of the largest saltworks in the world on the site. It made his fortune. He met an Irish woman in Paris, married her and built a replica French chateau for her on the outskirts of Droitwich, a town he transformed from one of industrial squalor into a fashionable spa. In its heyday the canalside works at Stoke was producing 200,000 tons of salt a year. The company had a fleet of narrowboats and hundreds of railway wagons. Corbett died in 1901 and is buried at the pretty little church of St Michael's, Stoke Prior (Map 14). His vast works, later part of ICI, was demolished in the 1970s.

Attractive countryside returns at ASTWOOD LOCKS, as canal and railway drift lazily through lush farmland overlooked by the wooded slopes of Summer Hill to the east. Westward views encompass Abberley and Woodbury hills beyond the River Severn. Closer at hand are the twin 700ft high masts of Wychbold radio transmitting station. Opened in 1934, its call sign "Droitwich Calling" became known throughout Britain and in many parts of Europe. During the Second World War Droitwich's long range transmitter broadcast the 'voice of freedom' throughout occupied Europe.

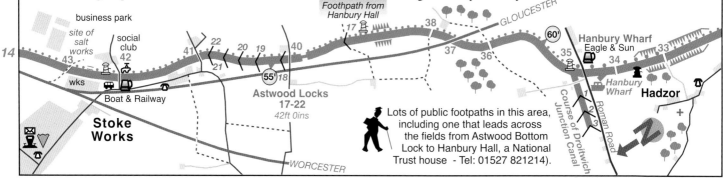

For details of facilities at Stoke Works see page 37

THE canal skirts the mellow settlements of Shernal Green, Dunhampstead, Oddingley and Tibberton and, in spite of being sandwiched by the railway and motorway, seems remote and untouched. High clumps of sedge border the canal, swaying with the passage of each boat and somehow emphasising the loneliness of the landscape. At Shernal Green the Wychavon Way - a 42-mile long distance footpath running from Holt Fleet on the River Severn to Winchcombe in Gloucestershire - makes its way over the canal. 'Severn & Avon Ring' boaters will encounter the path again at Cropthorne where it crosses the River Avon by way of Jubilee Bridge.

DUNHAMPSTEAD TUNNEL is tiny compared to the 'big three' to the north, but like them it has no towpath, forcing walkers to take to the old horse-path through deciduous woodlands above. A hire base adds traffic to the canal at this point, whilst a craft shop and convivial country pub provide an excuse to break your journey.

ODDINGLEY consists of little more than an ancient manor house, a tiny church and a level-crossing keeper's cabin of typical Midland Railway style. Murder was done here in 1806!

TIBBERTON is a long straggling village of mostly modern housing with a useful (if modestly stocked) post office stores and a pair of pubs. Well piled visitor moorings are provided west of bridge 25. A deep cutting and the M5 motorway separates Tibberton from OFFERTON LOCKS. Boating northwards you can now take a breather. Southbound the locks begin again as the Worcester & Birmingham completes its descent to the Severn.

Worcester's industrial fringe makes its presence felt; rugby players stomp across the footbridge at the tail of Lock 11, whilst Hindlip Hall (4934 to fans of the old GWR), headquarters of the County Constabulary and refuge, in its original Elizabethan guise, of two members of the Gunpowder Plot, dominates the nearby ridge.

Two aspects of this canal's working practice were remarkable. Boats kept left when passing each other and pairs of donkeys were widely used in place of horses to haul the boats. The animals worked well together as long as they 'knew' one another, but the introduction of a new donkey would cause considerable ructions. One of the last traders on the Worcester & Birmingham Canal was Charles Ballinger of Gloucester. He was still using horse-drawn boats as late as 1954, carrying coal from the Cannock area to Townsend's mill at Diglis. Occasionally he would have an 'uphill' cargo as well: matches from Gloucester to Birmingham, or flour from Worcester to Tipton; but by the beginning of the Sixties trade had deserted the canal.

By-road to Droitwich *For details of facilities at Dunhampstead and Tibberton see page 37*

WATERSIDE Worcester has always enjoyed a flagrant love affair with the Severn, but in recent times the canal has come into its own. From Tolladine down, the towpath is designated a 'pedway' and popular with pedestrians and cyclists alike. Burgeoning industrial estates accompany the canal but do little to spoil it. Cadbury's once had a busy wharf at Blackpole linked by water transport to their premises at Bournville and Frampton-on-Severn. A leisure centre and municipal golf course border the canal above Bilford Upper Lock. Worcester City, a non league football club, have a substantial ground, signposted by tall floodlights, beside Bridge 12. North of Bridge 11 school playing fields are overlooked by an imposing pavilion.

A shapely railway bridge spans the canal by

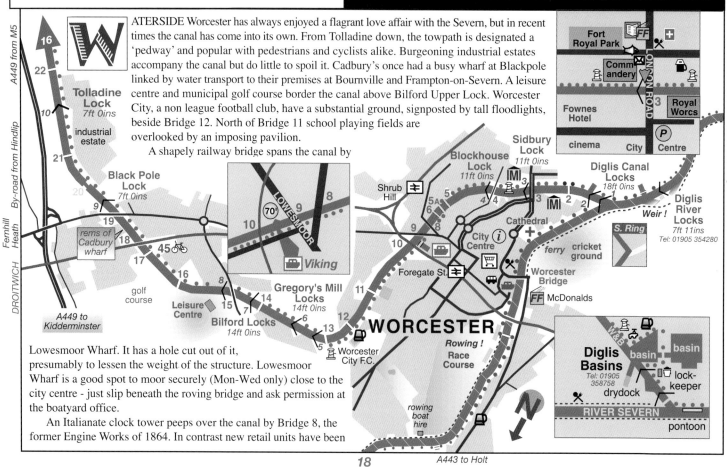

Lowesmoor Wharf. It has a hole cut out of it, presumably to lessen the weight of the structure. Lowesmoor Wharf is a good spot to moor securely (Mon-Wed only) close to the city centre - just slip beneath the roving bridge and ask permission at the boatyard office.

An Italianate clock tower peeps over the canal by Bridge 8, the former Engine Works of 1864. In contrast new retail units have been provided with a linking footbridge numbered 5A. Fownes Hotel was once a glove factory. Almost opposite stands The Commandery. Charles II used this building as his headquarters during the Civil War Battle of Worcester in 1651, though it was originally a hospital and dates from as early as the 15th century. There is space here for some half a dozen boats to moor overnight within mellifluous earshot of the cathedral clock. Sidbury Lock lies near the site of a gate in the city wall where a thousand Royalist troops are said to have been killed. Cromwell's men had captured the nearby fort and turned its canons on the escaping Cavaliers. The elevated fort is a pleasant park now, easily reached from the Commandery moorings. A panoramic plaque identifies major incidents of the Battle of Worcester and the gardens offer a marvellous view over the city.

Industry reasserts itself as the canal passes the famous Royal Worcester porcelain works and Townsend's Mill. The latter, refurbished for accommodation, was once an intensive user of water transport, via both canal and river, but nowadays the only traffic hereabouts is of the pleasure variety, all regular trade on this waterway having ceased by the Sixties.

DIGLIS BASINS opened in the 19th century to facilitate transhipment of cargoes between river and canal. Redevelopment has largely eroded the latent atmosphere of this inland port, but it would be carping to criticise British Waterways too much for cashing in on the inherent value of such sites - they need all the income they can muster to keep the canals ticking over. Two broad locks separate the basins from the river. They are closed overnight, re-opening about eight in the morning when the lock-keeper comes on duty. Mostly he doesn't get involved in operating them, but it's good to know he's about should you require his help or advice. Entering or leaving the river can pose problems, especially if the current is flowing quickly, and getting your crew on or off for the locks needs careful consideration. One of the easiest access points is the pontoon immediately downstream of the lock entrance.

Downstream the river heads for Tewkesbury and Gloucester through Diglis River Locks as covered in our *Severn & Avon Canal Companion*.

Upstream, 'Sabrina' flows beneath the great west window of the Cathedral, the juxtaposition of the noble building and the wide river being one of the great inland waterway scenes. Antiquated wharves and warehouses line the east bank of the river south of WORCESTER BRIDGE. Widened in the 1930s, the old parapet found its way into Edward Elgar's garden, so enamoured was the composer of anything associated with his home town. On summer Sundays a ferry operates in the vicinity of the Cathedral, and trip boats ply this reach as well, so keep a weather eye open for sudden manoeuvres. Limited official moorings are available on the city side between the old road bridge and the ornate, cast iron railway bridge which carries the Malvern and Hereford line across the river. A third bridge spanning the Severn is of modern origin, being a stylish pedestrian link between the city centre and the west bank suburbs: the Severn Way swaps sides at this point. Passing rowing clubs, the racecourse, and some enviable riverside properties, the river traveller heads upstream for more rural locales.

Worcester Racecourse

Worcester   (Map 17)

Descending from Birmingham to Worcester, the West Midlands are left intuitively behind, and you find yourself in streets where the patois has a distinct West Country burr. 'Royal' Worcester suffered more than most at the hands of the developers during the Sixties (Ian Nairn, the late architectural writer and broadcaster, was incensed, and James Lees-Milne got into hot water for permitting his *Shell Guide to Worcestershire* to be too critical) but much making of amends has been done in recent years to enhance the city's fabric. The Cathedral, gazing devoutly over the Severn, belongs - along with Gloucester and Hereford - to a golden triangle of ecclesiastical paragons which share Europe's oldest music festival, 'The Three Choirs'. From the deep well of Worcester's history you can draw inspiration from almost any era that captures your imagination. This was the 'faithful city' of the Civil War from which Charles II escaped following the final defeat of the Cavaliers. It was the home, for much of his life, of Sir Edward Elgar. Home too of the manufacturers of Royal Worcester porcelain and that ensign of the empire, Lea & Perrins sauce. And here you'll find one of the country's loveliest cricketing venues, Worcestershire's New Road ground - Tel: 01905 748474. So in any boating itinerary, Worcester deserves to be allotted at least half a day in your schedule, and ideally rather more.

Eating & Drinking

BROWNS RESTAURANT - Quay Street. Tel: 01905 26263. Worth blowing the budget here for the ambience of this former riverside mill, let alone quality of the cooking.

BENEDICTO'S - Sidbury. Tel: 01905 21444. Italian on the Cathedral side of Sidbury Lock.

HODSON - High Street. Tel: 01905 21036. Long established cafe restaurant near the Cathedral and Elgar's statue. Ideal for morning coffee.

DIGLIS HOUSE HOTEL - Riverside. Tel: 01905 353518. Best to moor in basins and walk back for good bar and restaurant meals; nice views over the Severn.

DRAGON INN - The Tything. Tel: 01905 25845. *Good Beer Guide* recommended real ale, cider and perry paradise located just north of Foregate Street railway station. Lunches Mon-Sat.

SALMON'S LEAP - Severn Street. Quiet real ale pub within easy reach of Diglis. Tel: 01905 726260.

THE ANCHOR - Diglis Basin. Tel: 01905 351094. Down to earth Banks's boozer for prodigious Swallowers and Amazons; lunches and takeaway baguettes from 9am: a last redoubt of the old Diglis!

Shopping

Worcester is an excellent city in which to shop. Two refurbished shopping areas are The Hopmarket and Crown Passage. The Shambles, Friar Street and New Street feature numerous fascinating little shops and small businesses. Crown Gate is the main shopping precinct with adjoining street markets on Tue, Wed, Fri & Sat. If you are making the *faux pas* of boating through non-stop, then a butcher, post office and pharmacy stand within seconds of Sidbury Lock.

Things to Do

TOURIST INFORMATION CENTRE - The Guildhall, High Street. Tel: 01905 726311.

Worcester appears to have more visitor centres than any other provincial city of its size. A thorough list defies our space limitations, but obvious highlights are: THE COMMANDERY (canalside by Sidbury Lock - Tel: 01905 361821) which was Charles II's headquarters during the Civil War; CITY MUSEUM & ART GALLERY (Foregate Street - Tel: 01905 25371), ROYAL WORCESTER (Severn Street, near Sidbury Lock again - Tel: 01905 746000), the porcelain and bone china makers; THE GUILDHALL (High Street - Tel: 01905 723471); and THE CATHEDRAL (Tel: 01905 611002, dating from the 11th century and the burial place of King John.

Connections

TRAINS - stations at Foregate Street and Shrub Hill. Services to/from the Malverns and on through the hopyards to Hereford, a nice idea for an excursion; Droitwich, Kidderminster, Birmingham etc. Good service also to and from London Paddington via Oxford and the picturesque Cotswolds line. Tel: 08457 484950.

BUSES - Tel: 0870 608 2 608.

TAXIS - Cathedral Cars. Tel: 01905 767400.

Bevere   (Map 18)

THE CAMP HOUSE - riverside downstream of Bevere Lock. Tel: 01905 640288. Peacocks in the garden, Bathams beer and rabbit pie render this isolated riverside inn a veritable heaven on earth. Limited moorings for customers.

Holt Fleet   (Map 19)

Good place to stop on the Severn, a reasonably lengthy pontoon being provided by BW between the tail of the lock and the bridge. There are also customer moorings at THE WHARF INN (Tel: 01905 620289) and a general store. The pretty village of Ombersley lies 2 miles to the east, but the road thence is abysmally busy. Other riverside pubs between Holt and Stourport include the LENCHFORD INN (Tel: 01905 620229) and the HAMPSTALL INN (Tel: 01299 822606); both have limited customer moorings.

THE Malvern Hills come into view in the neighbourhood of Bevere, glimpsed on the south-west horizon behind the spire of Hallow church. Queen Elizabeth I is said to have hunted for deer hereabouts. Another historical figure, albeit a peripheral one, with associations in the area was Napoleon's brother, Lucien Bonaparte, who lived in exile near Grimley for a period of time.

Make the most of your brief encounter with the Severn. For unless you choose to tie up, perhaps - if there is room - at Bevere or Holt locks, or at one of the riparian hostelries, like the incomparable Camp House - the three or four hours spent on the river between Worcester and Stourport are apt to flash swiftly by, leaving you with just a treasured blur of alder and willow fringed banks broken by occasional outcrops of sandstone; caravan parks and static homes; cattle or anglers flank or thigh high in the river margin; kingfishers skimming like low flying aircraft over the water's surface; and the unruffled routine of the automated locks.

A loop in the river forms the three acre island of Bevere, a place of refuge for the good burghers of Worcester in medieval times when war or plague threatened. Just upstream the little River Salwarpe enters unostentatiously from the east, having risen on the slopes of the Lickey Hills and wound down through Bromsgrove and Droitwich to meet the Severn. Alongside, between two houses mostly hidden by foliage, lie the remains of the bottom lock of the Droitwich Canal. Opened in 1771 and surveyed by Brindley - though actually engineered by John Priddey - the canal flourished during the 19th century as an export route for the salt industry, an activity carried out in the vicinity of Droitwich since Roman times. When salt making declined this 'barge' canal fell into decay and was disused by the First World War, its horse-drawn trows just a memory. In 1973 a trust was formed to restore the canal, and, so far, the summit pound and a sizeable basin in central Droitwich have been returned to water. Further progress must wait until more funding is in place, though 2009 has been pencilled in as a possible date for reopening.

The village of Grimley sits well back from the river, though anglers make use of the bumpy lane down to the water's edge to reach their perches in amongst the musky clumps of balsam.

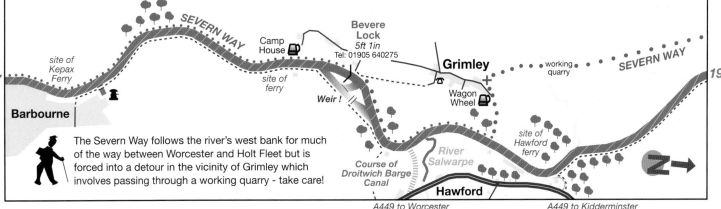

The Severn Way follows the river's west bank for much of the way between Worcester and Holt Fleet but is forced into a detour in the vicinity of Grimley which involves passing through a working quarry - take care!

43

"ANYONE so disposed could forget the present in Shrawley Woods," wrote L.T.C. Rolt in his 1949 topographical guide to the county of Worcestershire, going on to evoke two halcyon summer days moored on *Cressy* along this most beautiful of upper navigable Severn reaches between Holt and Lincomb locks. Disregard for the present implies a nostalgia for the past, and it is intriguing to discover that Dick Brook - emerging almost imperceptibly out of the shadowy trees on the west bank of the river - was once made navigable in the 17th century to serve a forge located deep in the woods. Two or three lock chambers were cut out of the sandstone, and barges trading up from the Forest of Dean conveyed cargoes of pig iron along the narrow stream to the doors of the forge.

The Holts provide vestiges of civilisation alongside the river's otherwise remote course: Holt, Holt Heath, Holt Fleet and, just off the edge of our map, Holt Who Goes There? A rash of caravan parks and shanty-like chalets mar otherwise unspoilt riverside meadows for everyone but their proud owners. Luckily this manifestation of mankind's capacity for destroying the very tranquillity he desires is confined to those parts

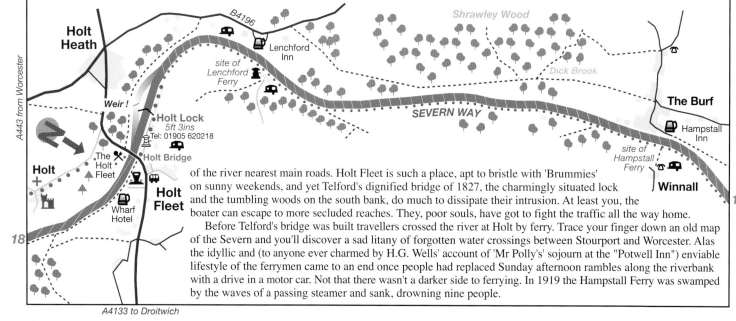

of the river nearest main roads. Holt Fleet is such a place, apt to bristle with 'Brummies' on sunny weekends, and yet Telford's dignified bridge of 1827, the charmingly situated lock and the tumbling woods on the south bank, do much to dissipate their intrusion. At least you, the boater can escape to more secluded reaches. They, poor souls, have got to fight the traffic all the way home.

Before Telford's bridge was built travellers crossed the river at Holt by ferry. Trace your finger down an old map of the Severn and you'll discover a sad litany of forgotten water crossings between Stourport and Worcester. Alas the idyllic and (to anyone ever charmed by H.G. Wells' account of 'Mr Polly's' sojourn at the "Potwell Inn") enviable lifestyle of the ferrymen came to an end once people had replaced Sunday afternoon rambles along the riverbank with a drive in a motor car. Not that there wasn't a darker side to ferrying. In 1919 the Hampstall Ferry was swamped by the waves of a passing steamer and sank, drowning nine people.

The Black Country Ring

Fradley Junction

45

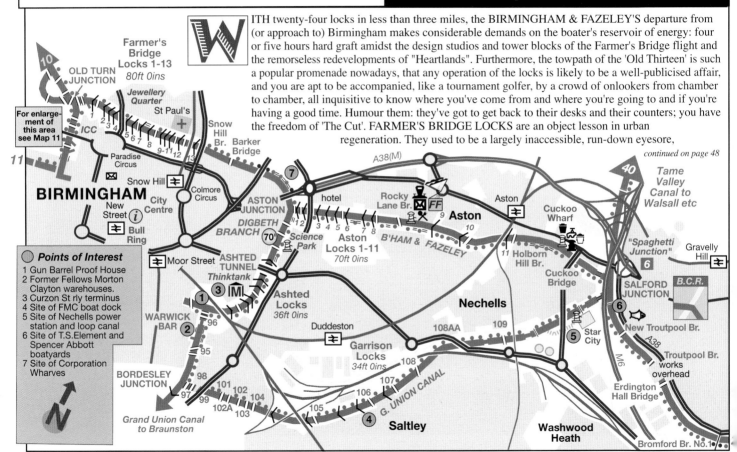

WITH twenty-four locks in less than three miles, the BIRMINGHAM & FAZELEY'S departure from (or approach to) Birmingham makes considerable demands on the boater's reservoir of energy: four or five hours hard graft amidst the design studios and tower blocks of the Farmer's Bridge flight and the remorseless redevelopments of "Heartlands". Furthermore, the towpath of the 'Old Thirteen' is such a popular promenade nowadays, that any operation of the locks is likely to be a well-publicised affair, and you are apt to be accompanied, like a tournament golfer, by a crowd of onlookers from chamber to chamber, all inquisitive to know where you've come from and where you're going to and if you're having a good time. Humour them: they've got to get back to their desks and their counters; you have the freedom of 'The Cut'. FARMER'S BRIDGE LOCKS are an object lesson in urban regeneration. They used to be a largely inaccessible, run-down eyesore,

continued on page 48

BIRMINGHAM

Farmer's Bridge Locks 1-13 80ft 0ins

OLD TURN JUNCTION

Jewellery Quarter

St Paul's

ICC

Paradise Circus

For enlargement of this area see Map 11

Snow Hill Br.

Barker Bridge

Snow Hill

City Centre

Colmore Circus

New Street

Bull Ring

ASTON JUNCTION

DIGBETH BRANCH

Moor Street

ASHTED TUNNEL

Thinktank

Science Park

hotel

Rocky Lane Br.

FF

Aston

Aston Locks 1-11 70ft 0ins

B'HAM & FAZELEY

A38(M)

40

Tame Valley Canal to Walsall etc

Cuckoo Wharf

"Spaghetti Junction"

Gravelly Hill

6

B.C.R.

SALFORD JUNCTION

Holborn Hill Br.

Cuckoo Bridge

New Troutpool Br.

Nechells

Star City

Troutpool Br. works overhead

Erdington Hall Bridge

WARWICK BAR

Ashted Locks 36ft 0ins

Duddeston

Garrison Locks 34ft 0ins

Saltley

Washwood Heath

Bromford Br. No.1

BORDESLEY JUNCTION

Grand Union Canal to Braunston

G. UNION CANAL

Points of Interest

1 Gun Barrel Proof House
2 Former Fellows Morton Clayton warehouses.
3 Curzon St rly terminus
4 Site of FMC boat dock
5 Site of Nechells power station and loop canal
6 Site of T.S.Element and Spencer Abbott boatyards
7 Site of Corporation Wharves

N

*Figures relate to Old turn Junction - Bromford Bridge via Salford Junction.

Farmer's Bridge Flight

continued from page 46

a boil on Birmingham's bottom, suffering from years of neglect following the demise of commercial carrying in the early Sixties. In 1984 a programme of renewal got under way sponsored by the Birmingham Inner City Partnership. Using Gas Street to Aston as a prototype, BICP set about resurfacing the towpath, improving and increasing access, landscaping, lighting and general restoration at the then not insignificant cost of a million pounds. The scheme's impact was considerable. It introduced Brummies to a well-kept secret aspect of their city, and they came to discover it in droves, so that now it hooches with shop and office staff on warm weekday lunchtimes and family groups on postprandial Sunday walks. Joggers relish it too, extending their limbs and expending their energy up and down the ribbed brick surfaces of the refurbished towpath in a distant echo of the hurrying boatmen of the past.

Farmer's Bridge Locks

Farmer's Bridge Locks pass dramatically beneath the commercial core of the city. Each time we visit here more change has accrued - redeveloping the redeveloped one might put it. Locks 10 and 11 lie in a cavern beneath British Telecom's communications tower. There's access here over an easily vaulted wall on to Ludgate Hill and the calm oasis of St Paul's Square, nicknamed the 'Jeweller's Church' because of its connections with the adjoining Jewellery Quarter, a fascinating corner of old Birmingham. Between Locks 12 and 13 the canal negotiates a huge vault under Snow Hill railway station; closed and subsequently demolished at some cost in 1972, but re-opened and rebuilt at more cost (though less style) just fifteen years later.

Lock 13 marks the foot of the flight and is overlooked by a Salvation Army hostel. Two streets away from the mobile-phone-wielding go-getters of Ludgate Hill are the derelicts of Old Snow Hill - the Good Lord giveth and the Good Lord taketh away. Between Snow Hill and Aston the canal, clear of locks for a brief respite, widens and is less claustrophobically engulfed by the high canyons of industry and commerce. The most significant feature of this section - apart from the switchback side bridges which formerly gave access to the Corporation wharves - is the handsome BARKER BRIDGE, a graceful span of cast iron supported by brick piers and abutments dating from 1842.

Aston Locks

A Horseley Iron Works cast iron roving bridge marks the junction of the Birmingham & Fazeley Canal with the Digbeth Branch at Aston. Its elegance, amounting almost to a misleading fragility, is in marked contrast to the overpowering concrete edifice of the adjacent Expressway. Time and time again exploration of the BCN emphasises the great gulf in aesthetic achievement between the civil engineering of the last century and this. Time alters perception, but it does seem inconceivable that any age will ever be able to indentify beauty in the Aston Expressway - but then again!

Rocky Lane Bridge offers access to useful shops and take-aways. Up the road at Aston Cross the iconic HP sauce factory has closed with production being transferred to the Netherlands.

Access to and from the canal has been provided at Holborn Hill Bridge. Easy, then, to use Aston railway station as a staging post: a five minute train ride out from New Street followed by a healthy hour's walk back along the towpath to the city centre. Nearby, one of the earliest main line railways crosses the canal by Lock 11. Opened in 1839, only fifty years after the canal, it linked Birmingham with the North-west. Moorings and boating facilities are provided by Cuckoo Bridge.

Salford Junction

Only a fraction of the stressed-out motorists, fighting their way around the confusion of Gravelley Hill Interchange (aka Spaghetti Junction) are aware of the older, less frenzied meeting and parting of ways engulfed in the concrete gloom below. But such is SALFORD JUNCTION, where the Grand Union Canal's 'Saltley Cut' and Tame Valley Canal - both dating from 1844 - form a canal crossroads with the Birmingham & Fazeley Canal. It's a sobering spot for contemplating Man's contribution to the landscape. Monstrously compromised, the River Tame churns despondently through artificial channels beneath successive generations of civil engineering. Tier upon tier of roadway spirals above you. Little groups of earnest middle management, self-conscious in safety helmets, huddle over calculators, extrapolating infinity.

Whilst ASTON LOCKS represent the most obvious, time efficient route for boaters tackling the "Black Country Ring", a fascinating alternative for diehards (or indeed as part of a self-contained circular itinerary on foot or afloat) can be made up out of the Digbeth Branch and Grand Union Canal via Bordesley and Saltley as described below.

The Digbeth Branch

Opened in 1799, the Digbeth Branch descends through half a dozen locks from Aston Junction to Warwick Bar, terminating now in a pair of foreshortened basins once lucratively busy with trade to and from Digbeth's many food factories like Typhoo Tea and HP Sauce. It's a secretive section of urban canal of unique character and appeal. All but the top lock have extended side pounds, whilst the chambers have single gates top and bottom as per BCN practice. 48 hour visitor moorings are to be found in the relative security and calm of Aston Science Park with a handy winding hole nearby.

Below the bottom lock the original sandstone arch of the Grand Junction Railway's line into Curzon Street station provides a portal into a curvaceous, sepulchral 'tunnel' of railway lines, beyond which the canal opens out to Digbeth (or Proof House) Junction. The alternative name - also used by the adjoining maze of railway tracks - reflects the proximity of the Gun Barrel Proof House of 1813, a strikingly handsome building, with a Jacobean air, overlooking a cobbled courtyard. Above the entrance door is a colourful, three-dimensional military sculpture and the inscription: "Established by Act of Parliament for Public Security." Another nearby building of immense significance is the old Curzon Street station, terminus of the London & Birmingham Railway, whilst the Thinktank science museum is also readily accessible.

Warwick Bar & Bordesley Junction

Whereas the 'Worcester Bar' at Gas Street lies on a well-trodden tourist trail, the 'Warwick Bar' in Digbeth lies off the beaten track in a 'backstreet' Birmingham still replete with cast iron urinals and pubs offering beer at less than £2 a pint. Here a stop lock was constructed to separate the valuable waters of the Birmingham & Fazeley (later BCN) and Warwick & Birmingham canal companies, and it has recently been cosmetically reinstated to illustrate the deadly rivalry which existed between the two

companies. But whilst the environs and towpath have been much refurbished, the location still has an 'out on a limb' feel, resonantly retaining the ambience of its working past. Alongside the remains of the stop lock stands a warehouse with an awning supported by cast-iron pillars over an arm lying parallel to the narrows. At one time it was leased by Geest the fruit importers and earned the sobriquet 'Banana Warehouse'. Earlier still it belonged to Pickfords, canal carriers of some importance before they made their name with heavy road transport. Nearby is New Warwick Wharf, marked by the tall curved wall of Fellows, Morton & Clayton's warehouse built in 1935 following modernisation of the canal from London. This confident 'Art Deco' style of architecture - emblazoned with the company's name along Fazeley Street to this day - was not rewarded by a significant increase in trade, and, having been for a number of years used by HP Sauce, it now houses a conglomeration of small businesses. Likewise FMC's adjoining Fazeley Street depot, separated from the newer building by an aqueduct over the turgid waters of the River Rea. Built of alternate courses of red and blue brick, and equipped with weatherboarded elevators and an attractive saw-tooth valanced canopy over a side arm, this older grouping of warehouses has been redeveloped as 'The Bond', a centre for graphic art based businesses. Directly opposite the towpath rises and falls over a side bridge spanning an arm which once led into one of the City of Birmingham's Salvage Department basins. Horsedrawn rubbish boats operated between here and the Small Heath destructor until 1965. The high arch of a ruined railway viaduct frames the canal near Bridge 95.

The Saltley Cut

Surrounded by gloomy factory walls, BORDESLEY JUNCTION is spanned by a graceful roving bridge cast by Lloyds & Fosters. Immediately southwards the Grand Union Canal commences the climb to its Olton Summit via Camp Hill Locks, a route covered in our *South Midlands Canal Companion*. Likewise the Saltley Cut, barely industrial now as neat blocks of new housing overlook a towpath burgeoning with poppies, cranesbill, dog rose and daisies: a fecundity derived from generations of boat horse dung perhaps. Visitor moorings have been thoughtfully - if a tad irrationally - provided in Nechells to give easy access to Star City, a pleasure dome of Kubla Khan proportions.

INWORTH used to mark the frontier between open country and the West Midlands conurbation, but the building of a high tech business park on the towpath side between Minworth Green and Wigginshill Road bridges has blurred the once distinct boundary. Cornfields remain defiantly agricultural on the opposite bank, but the more cynical may feel that it is only a matter of time before the prices for building land outweigh the marginal profits of the annual harvest.

If, then, you want to avoid overnight mooring in a built-up area, you would be advised to tie up no further west than the "Kingsley" steak bar by Wigginshill Road Bridge. A pleasant stroll can be had from here up past the Jacobean gabled farmhouse of Wiggins Hill Farm and beyond to where you come upon a picturesque (if converted) barn built of brick and timber.

Not that the stretch of canal between Bromford and Minworth is uninteresting. Reference to three twentieth century maps revealed a steady cycle of change. In 1916 the tyre makers Dunlop built a huge works on a 400 acre greenfield site which became known as Fort Dunlop. To transport the workforce to and from this new plant, the company operated a small fleet of passenger carrying narrowboats between Aston and Bromford until the neighbouring Tyburn Road was laid with tram tracks. Apparently the two and a half mile, lock-free journey took around half an hour and each boat could seat a hundred passengers. The imposing Cincinnati Machine Company's premises by

Minworth Top lock manufactures lathes and profiling equipment.

In 1938 the fields east of Fort Dunlop were occupied by one of the 'shadow' munitions factories as Britain armed for war. During the next seven years over eleven thousand Spitfires were built at the plant. The works was handily placed for test flights, for across the Chester Road stood Castle Bromwich Aerodrome which had hosted Birmingham's very first flying demonstration in 1911. After the Second World War the aerodrome was run down and replaced, in the early Sixties, by the sprawling estate of Castle Vale.

In his book *Number One*, former canal boat captain, Tom Foxon, wrote in detail of his experiences on the Birmingham & Fazeley in the mid 1950s. At that time substantial tonnages of coal were still being carried by canal from the collieries of North Warwickshire to the factory furnaces of Birmingham aboard 'Joey boats', boatman's parlance for narrowboats used for short-haul work and not designed for living aboard. The men who worked these largely horse-drawn boats knew this canal as the 'Old Cut' and in his book Tom describes the working practices of the era, commenting wryly that this was the most depressing route experienced in his boating career. You'll just have to take it from us that matters have improved since those days - well relatively! Near Minworth Green narrowboats used to unload ash for use in the filter beds of the adjoining sewage plant.

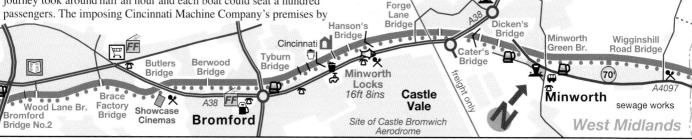

For details of facilities at Minworth turn to page 53 By-road to Water Orton

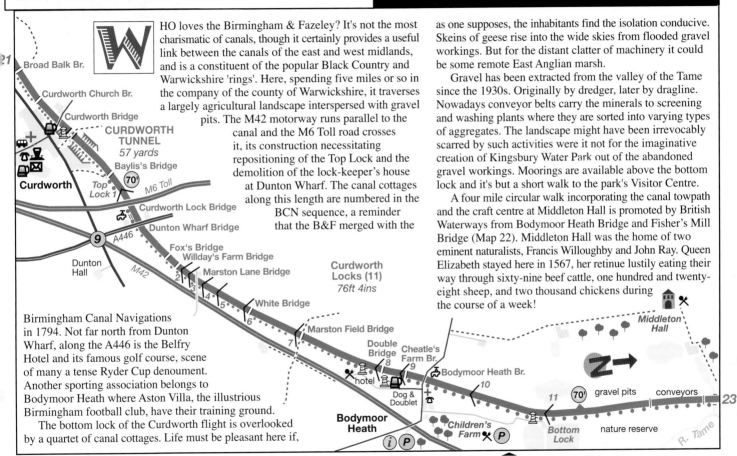

WHO loves the Birmingham & Fazeley? It's not the most charismatic of canals, though it certainly provides a useful link between the canals of the east and west midlands, and is a constituent of the popular Black Country and Warwickshire 'rings'. Here, spending five miles or so in the company of the county of Warwickshire, it traverses a largely agricultural landscape interspersed with gravel pits. The M42 motorway runs parallel to the canal and the M6 Toll road crosses it, its construction necessitating repositioning of the Top Lock and the demolition of the lock-keeper's house at Dunton Wharf. The canal cottages along this length are numbered in the BCN sequence, a reminder that the B&F merged with the Birmingham Canal Navigations in 1794. Not far north from Dunton Wharf, along the A446 is the Belfry Hotel and its famous golf course, scene of many a tense Ryder Cup denouement. Another sporting association belongs to Bodymoor Heath where Aston Villa, the illustrious Birmingham football club, have their training ground.

The bottom lock of the Curdworth flight is overlooked by a quartet of canal cottages. Life must be pleasant here if, as one supposes, the inhabitants find the isolation conducive. Skeins of geese rise into the wide skies from flooded gravel workings. But for the distant clatter of machinery it could be some remote East Anglian marsh.

Gravel has been extracted from the valley of the Tame since the 1930s. Originally by dredger, later by dragline. Nowadays conveyor belts carry the minerals to screening and washing plants where they are sorted into varying types of aggregates. The landscape might have been irrevocably scarred by such activities were it not for the imaginative creation of Kingsbury Water Park out of the abandoned gravel workings. Moorings are available above the bottom lock and it's but a short walk to the park's Visitor Centre.

A four mile circular walk incorporating the canal towpath and the craft centre at Middleton Hall is promoted by British Waterways from Bodymoor Heath Bridge and Fisher's Mill Bridge (Map 22). Middleton Hall was the home of two eminent naturalists, Francis Willoughby and John Ray. Queen Elizabeth stayed here in 1567, her retinue lustily eating their way through sixty-nine beef cattle, one hundred and twenty-eight sheep, and two thousand chickens during the course of a week!

AZELEY JUNCTION isn't anywhere near as pretty as Fradley, but it exudes a certain grubby grandeur, lent added gravitas by a big old textile mill which quite plausibly might have escaped from Oldham or Rochdale. The Birmingham & Fazeley reached here in 1789 and the following year Sir Robert Peel (father of the Prime Minister) opened a mill for cotton spinning and calico printing. It was powered by the waters of the Bourne Brook which joins the Tame nearby. A second mill, of five towering storeys, was erected in 1883 for the weaving of haberdashery and upholstery. Both mills remain more or less intact for the entertainment of the industrial archaeologist, but the handsome junction house, which we have both admired and coveted for many years had been inexplicably mothballed and boarded up on our most recent visit.

East of Fazeley Junction the Coventry Canal heads off for Nuneaton, Hawkesbury and Braunston as covered by our *South Midlands Canal Companion*. South of Fazeley lies one of the 'little wonders' of the inland waterways, the exotic Drayton footbridge, where two Gothic towers encase spiral staircases and support an otherwise pretty ordinary open iron span; a delightful functional folly: have your camera ready.

British Waterways regional offices overlook the canal at PEEL'S WHARF, along with adjoining housing, the sale of which presumably paid for the offices. More new housing has materialised on the opposite bank, whilst a new dual-carriageway section of the A5 has effectively vanquished the former peace and quiet of the broadwater by Bonehill Road Bridge. There are glimpses to the north of Tamworth Castle and the imposing parish church of St Editha, before the canal escapes the clutches of the retail parks and loses itself in and amongst the cabbage fields - which it is often called upon to irrigate - on the way to Hopwas.

To the west looms a tall transmitting mast at Hints, erected as long ago as 1956 to broadcast the then fledgeling ITV Channel to the west midlands. Nearby, a new section of the A5 carves its way through the adjoining escarpment with scant consideration for the equilibrium of this otherwise rural locality. In the woods above Hopwas stands the unusual Arts & Crafts church of St Chad's.

Middleton Hall

22

Fisher's Mill Br.

Drayton Brick Br.

Drayton Manor Park

Drayton Foot Bridge & Swivel Bridge

B.C.R.

Debbies Daydoats

River Tame

FAZELEY
BW Office
WATLING STREET
FF

Coleshill Road Br.
Mill Marina

mills

Tolson's Foot-bridge

Peel's Wharf

Staffordshire

Fazeley

Ball's Bridge

Dunstall Farm Bridge

Dunstall Bridge

R. Tame

Bonehill Road Bridge

Sutton Road Br.

Sainsbury's

FAZELEY JUNCTION

ASDA
FF

Coventry Canal to Hawkesbury A5 Southbound Tamworth Town Centre

Bj404 to Hopwas

A5 to Lichfield

Minworth (Map 21)

A pleasant enough suburb on the edge of the West Midlands conurbation with a handful of useful shops bordering its green, Minworth is known chiefly for the huge sewage works which once boasted an internal narrow-gauge railway system, remains of which can be seen on the road to Water Orton.

Eating & Drinking

THE BOAT - pub by Dicken's Bridge advertising 'English' food. Tel: 0121 240 9696.

KINGSLEY - canalside by Wigginshill Road Bridge. Modern pub/steak bar on the county boundary where urbanisation and countryside collide. Tel: 01675 470808.

Curdworth (Map 22)

The village street is reached by crossing the busy A4079. Curdworth is one of the oldest settlements in this part of the world and gets its name from Crida, first King of Mercia. Facilities include a post office stores (Tel: 01675 470259) and two pubs, one of which, the WHITE HORSE (Tel: 01675 470227), is adjacent to the canal.

Bodymoor Heath (Map 22)

DOG & DOUBLET - canalside adjacent Cheatle's Farm Bridge. Tel: 01827 872374. Rambling Georgian pub with attractive interiors and garden with dovecot. Good moorings.

MARSTON FARM HOTEL - adjacent Marston Field Bridge. Tel: 01827 872133.

Things to Do

KINGSBURY WATER PARK - Over six hundred acres of waterside and woodland walks. Cycle hire (Tel: 01827 284646), miniature railway, cafe and gift shop, Tel: 01827 872660.

BROOMEY CROFT CHILDREN'S FARM - Not so much a new approach to child-rearing, more a fun day out for the family. Tea rooms. Tel: 01827 873844.

MIDDLETON HALL & CRAFT CENTRE - Former home of Sir Hugh Willoughby the Tudor explorer. Open to the public on selected dates. Craft Centre with refreshments Wed-Sun. Tel: 01827 283095.

Fazeley (Map 23)

Now by-passed by the A5, Fazeley seems somewhat less frenetic than in the past, and there are useful facilities in what, because of its junction status, has always been a popular overnight mooring point.

Eating & Drinking

PARTRIDGES - adjacent Tolson's Foot Bridge. Tel: 01827 739277. Cosy cafe for cooked breakfasts, lunches and cream teas in quaint location alongside one of Fazeley's mills.

THREE TUNS - Watling Street. Canalside pub with offside moorings for customers. Wide choice of homely food. Tel: 01827 281620.

IVORY TUSK - Tel: 01827 285777. Stylish Indian restaurant on Coleshill Road within a couple of minutes walk of the junction.

PENINSULAR - Atherstone Road. Tel: 01827 288151. Chinese restaurant with take-away outlet.

Shopping

There's a TESCO EXPRESS (with cash machine), pharmacy and post office in the village centre. Bike shop for beleagured cyclists! From Bonehill Road Bridge a footpath leads under the A5 to a nearby retail park featuring ASDA and SAINSBURY supermarkets and a MCDONALDS.

Things to Do

DRAYTON MANOR PARK - open daily Easter to October. Admission charge. Access on A4091 adjacent to Drayton footbridge. Tel: 01827 287979. Family theme park, amusements, zoo, farm park, nature trail and woodland walk.

Connections

BUSES - frequent connections with Tamworth and its railhead.

Hopwas (Map 24)

TAME OTTER - canalside Lichfield Road Bridge. Attractively renovated pub with an entertaining pun to its new name. Good food, families welcome. Tel: 01827 53361.

RED LION - canalside at Lichfield Road Bridge. Tel: 01827 62514. Food served daily from 10am.

Whittington (Map 24)

Attractive village retaining three pubs: THE SWAN (Tel: 01543 432269) canalside by Bridge 80; BELL INN (Tel: 01543 432372) on Main Street; and DOG INN (Tel: 01543 432252) at the far end of the village which offers bed & breakfast. There is additionally a Chinese take-away - Tel: 01543 433397. Shopping facilities include a Co-op store, pharmacy, post-office/newsagent and antiques outlet. Bus service 765 runs hourly (bi-hourly Suns) to both Lichfield and Tamworth.

Huddlesford (Map 24)

THE PLOUGH - canalside Bridge 83. Tel: 01543 432369. Revamped in the modern mould, though no less pleasing for that.

Taxis - Dial-a-Cab. Tel: 01543 255155.

Fradley (Map 25)

THE SWAN - canalside, Fradley Junction. Tel: 01283 790330. This well known former boatmen's pub plays a leading role in the social life of Fradley Junction. Additionally, refreshments available from British Waterways' cafe (Tel: 01283 790236) and the Kingfisher Holiday Park - Tel: 01283 790407.

TAXIS - Alrewas Taxis. Tel: 01283 790391

NOT generally thought of as a beautiful canal, the Coventry nevertheless becomes almost picturesque in its wandering between Fazeley and Huddlesford; particularly as it ghosts through the brackeny woodlands of Hopwas, where red flags warn of military manoeuvres. Glibly we call this the Coventry Canal, but actually - and by now the presence of nameplates and not numbers on the bridges should have quickened your suspicions - the canal between Fazeley and Whittington was built by the Birmingham & Fazeley company. The Coventry Canal received its Act of Parliament in 1768, but seventeen years later it was nowhere near completion; primarily through a shortage of capital, but also, historians suspect, because some of the directors had interests in the Warwickshire coalfield and were worried by the thought that their through route, were it to be finished, would boost trade from the North Staffordshire pits at the expense of their own. In frustration the Trent & Mersey and Birmingham & Fazeley companies undertook to jointly build the canal between Fazeley and Fradley. The two met at Whittington in 1790, at a point graced with a plaque provided by the local branch of the I.W.A. commemorating the bicentenary of the joining.

So pleasant scenery, polytunnels and canal history mingle as you negotiate the lower valley of the Tame; passing Fisherwick, where the houses face the canal in Dutch fashion, rather than turning their backs on it as is more often the case in England; and arcing round Whittington, where one of the canalside gardens is graced with its own decorative lock. As we researched this edition the West Coast Main Line railway was in the process of being quadrupled, a civil engineering project of considerable cost and complexity, all very admirable in its way, perhaps, though we couldn't help wondering if the budget might not have been better spread re-opening some of the routes bludgeoned to death by Beeching.

A signpost at Huddlesford points hopefully towards Ogley, anticipating restoration of the Wyrley & Essington Canal abandoned half a century ago before the canal system's renassaisance for leisure gathered momentum. Championed by the Lichfield & Hatherton Canals Trust, the project envisages reinstatement of seven miles of canal including four detours from the orginal route in response to post-abandonment developments. Work has already commenced at a number of sites but the provision of expensive culverts beneath the A38 and A5 trunk roads remains a major challenge; though the erection of an aqueduct over the M6 toll road in 2003 illustrates the strength of commitment locally to such a potentially exciting scheme.

For details of facilities at Hopwas, Whittington and Huddlesford turn to page 53

Whittington Polytunnels

55

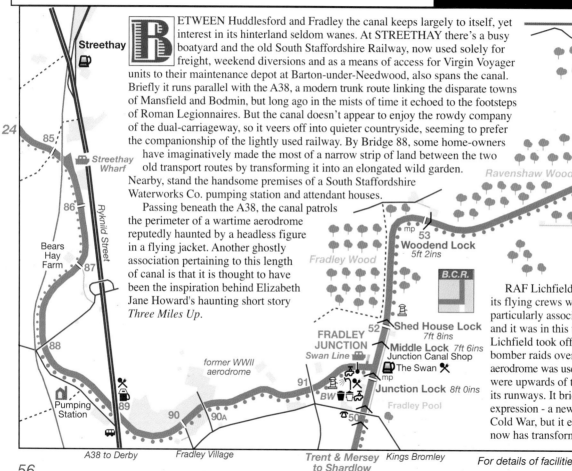

BETWEEN Huddlesford and Fradley the canal keeps largely to itself, yet interest in its hinterland seldom wanes. At STREETHAY there's a busy boatyard and the old South Staffordshire Railway, now used solely for freight, weekend diversions and as a means of access for Virgin Voyager units to their maintenance depot at Barton-under-Needwood, also spans the canal. Briefly it runs parallel with the A38, a modern trunk route linking the disparate towns of Mansfield and Bodmin, but long ago in the mists of time it echoed to the footsteps of Roman Legionnaires. But the canal doesn't appear to enjoy the rowdy company of the dual-carriageway, so it veers off into quieter countryside, seeming to prefer the companionship of the lightly used railway. By Bridge 88, some home-owners have imaginatively made the most of a narrow strip of land between the two old transport routes by transforming it into an elongated wild garden. Nearby, stand the handsome premises of a South Staffordshire Waterworks Co. pumping station and attendant houses.

Passing beneath the A38, the canal patrols the perimeter of a wartime aerodrome reputedly haunted by a headless figure in a flying jacket. Another ghostly association pertaining to this length of canal is that it is thought to have been the inspiration behind Elizabeth Jane Howard's haunting short story *Three Miles Up*.

RAF Lichfield opened in 1941 and many of its flying crews were Australian. The base was particularly associated with Wellington bombers, and it was in this type of aircraft that crews from Lichfield took off to take part in the first 1000 bomber raids over Germany. After the war the aerodrome was used for storage - at one time there were upwards of two thousand aircraft cluttering its runways. It briefly enjoyed - if that's the right expression - a new lease of life at the outset of the Cold War, but it eventually closed in 1957, and now has transformed itself into a trading estate;

Streethay

24

85

Streethay Wharf

86

Bears Hay Farm

87

Ryknild Street

88

Pumping Station

89

90

90A

A38 to Derby

Fradley Village

91

FRADLEY JUNCTION
Swan Line

BW

50

Fradley Pool

Trent & Mersey to Shardlow

Kings Bromley

former WWII aerodrome

Fradley Wood

52

Shed House Lock 7ft 8ins

Middle Lock 7ft 6ins
Junction Canal Shop

The Swan

Junction Lock 8ft 0ins

mp

53

Woodend Lock 5ft 2ins

B.C.R.

Ravenshaw Wood

mp

54

Kings Bromley Wharf

Kings Bromley Wharf

garden centre

Rileyhill

For details of facilities at Fradley turn back to page 53

though some 'blister' hangars remain to lend eerie tribute to the pathos of the past.

FRADLEY JUNCTION came top in a recent inland waterways magazine readership poll to find correspondents' 'favourite' canal junctions, though the fact that they were interviewed just a few miles along the Trent & Mersey may have bearing upon the result. But canal junctions - as we have long maintained - do not come much more charming than this. Here, remote from any other settlement, the canal authorities created a self-contained community to house their employees at a point where the 'Coventry Canal' met with the Trent & Mersey. Two centuries on the simplicity still beguiles: with no local landowner to mollify, mock heroics are absent from the architecture. Solely in the Georgian junction house - home to the Company's 'man' - does style depart from the functional; though even then the effect is soberly restrained.

East of Fradley Junction, the Trent & Mersey Canal passes through woods richly coloured by rhododendrons in May and June. Wood End is the southernmost point of the canal in its 92 mile journey from Shardlow, by the Trent, to Preston Brook, near the Mersey. For a moment the woods recede to reveal the three spires of Lichfield Cathedral aka the 'Ladies of the Vale'. By Kings Bromley Wharf stand the buildings of an old creamery which once relied upon water transport in much the same way as that at Knighton on the Shropshire Union Canal.

Handsacre (Map 26)

THE CROWN - canalside Bridge 58. Tel: 01543 490239. A congenial local where the locals' repartee is apt to be as frothy as your pint.
MICHAELS - adjacent Bridge 58. The length of the queue testifies to the quality of fish & chips.
SELWOOD HOUSE - adjacent Bridge 58. Tel: 01543 490480. Homely little cafe self-confidently offering 'the best breakfasts in Staffordshire'; accommodation also available.

Armitage (Map 26)

Offside moorings provide access via an alleyway to a number of shops on the main road, including a good butcher/bakery.

Eating & Drinking
PLUM PUDDING - canalside Bridge 61a. Tel: 01543 490330. Award-winning brasserie which has dropped considerably below the level of the canal because of subsidence, but the outdoor patio remains commensurate with the canal. Customer moorings on offside and accommodation also available.
SPODE COTTAGE - Restaurant housed in a 17th century farmhouse. Tel: 01543 490353.

ASH TREE - canalside Bridge 62. Tel: 01889 578314. Refurbished pub offering 'two for one' food.

Rugeley (Map 27)

A resilient little town, well versed in the vicissitudes of existence, life here being lived on the cheap, though with a certain deadpan dignity. Here in the tight-knit streets, and on the old Coal Board estates, are thrift and graft and a perverse civic pride, whilst a consoling beauty is to be found up on the nearby Chase.

Eating & Drinking
GEORGE & BERTIES - Albion Street. An unusual cafe with a central bar around which customers sit perched on high stools as if this were somewhere in Belgium. Tel: 01889 577071.
LA TERRAZZA - Italian restaurant housed in an old chapel on Lichfield Street. Tel: 01889 570630.
INFINITY - Market Square. Tel: 01889 576727. Chinese buffet restaurant.

Shopping
Moor north of Bridge 66 for easiest access to town centre: Morrisons supermarket and Aldi nearby. Market on Tue, Thur-Sat; most banks and several good cake shops.

Connections

BUSES - services throughout the Trent Valley and Cannock Chase. If you have time to spare, take the Green Bus to Cannock, a magical mystery tour up and over The Chase. Tel: 0870 608 2 608.
TRAINS - two stations (Town and Trent Valley) support an hourly weekday service between Stafford, Walsall and Birmingham. Sparse but potentially useful link with Lichfield for towpath prowlers. Tel: 08457 484950.
TAXIS - Sixty-one. Tel: 01889 586061.

Wolseley (Map 27)

Moor by Bridge 70 and you can visit a garden centre, gallery, antiques showroom and craft units, whilst the WOLSELEY ARMS (a meeting place for the T&M's promoters) is a pleasant country pub offering a wide choice of food. Tel: 01889 575133. The neighbouring SHIMLA PALACE Indian restaurant and takeaway caters for spicier tastes. Tel: 01889 881325. THE WOLSELEY CENTRE - Tel: 01889 880100. Staffordshire Wildlife Trust visitor centre located in revitalised garden park.

BETWEEN Fradley and Handsacre the canal winds through a village-less tract of country, comprehensively agricultural now, but betraying signs of the wild heathland it must once have been in its sandy soil, gorse, bracken and gnarled oaks. From Bridge 58 it's but a short stroll to the old High Bridge across the Trent. It's been by-passed by progress and unsightly girders support its once graceful cast iron span, but its interest lies in the fact that it was made at Coalbrookdale in 1830.

Armitage and Shanks are synonymous with toilet plumbing, their trade marks are emblazoned on public conveniences throughout the world. Once they were separate firms - they merged in 1969 - but the site alongside the canal at ARMITAGE dates back to 1817. Sanitaryware became a speciality in the 19th century under the management of Edward Johns - the origin of the Americanism 'going to the John'. Today the factory is huge and convincingly prosperous, and Armitage Shanks are a public limited company apparently flushed with unlimited success. A path worth exploring leaves the towpath between bridges 60 and 61 and leads beneath the railway and over the Trent to the isolated settlement of Mavesyn Ridware. Not that there are any facilities when you get there, but sometimes you just feel an urge to turn your back on the canal!

Connections are apparent with another famous earthenware firm at Spode House and Hawkesyard Priory. Josiah Spode, a member of the North Staffordshire pottery family, left his house to a Dominican Order in 1893 and the monks proceeded to build a priory in the grounds. The buildings now house a day spa whilst the grounds have been converted into a golf course.

Passing beneath the A513, the canal narrows and negotiates a rocky cutting. One-way working is the order of the day. This was formerly the site of Armitage (or "Plum Pudding") Tunnel, a dramatic, unlined bore through the rock face. Subsidence, brought about by coal mining, necessitated opening out of the tunnel, and concrete lining of the canal banks. Not that mining is any longer an activity associated with the area. Lea Hall Colliery, which stood canalside by Bridge 63 since opening in 1960, had been a modern showcase pit for the NCB, much of its output making the shortest of journeys to the adjacent power station, but it closed in 1990 and was rapidly demolished, an industrial estate being developed on its site. One aspect of the mining life they couldn't entirely eradicate, however, was its workforce, and it is not unusual when boating the Trent & Mersey or walking its towpath in this vicinity to overhear the accents of Lanarkshire and Northumberland, counties from which many miners 'emigrated' to Rugeley.

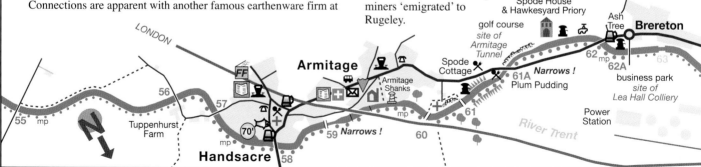

For details of facilities at Handsacre and Armitage turn to page 57   Footpath to Mavesyn Ridware

HE river's slow influence pervades the canal, and the pair wander across the landscape like indolent lovers on a long afternoon, chaperoned at a discreet distance by the recumbent mass of The Chase. Several big houses were built by prosperous landowners in this enchanting countryside. The stuccoed facade of Bishton Hall overlooks the canal. Nowadays it is a prep school with a cricket ground shaded by ancient chestnut trees bordering the water. Another mansion, Wolseley Hall, stood opposite on the far bank of the river. It was demolished long ago, but the grounds have become home to a garden centre. Wolseley Bridge has graced the Trent here since 1800. It was designed by John Rennie, best known in canal circles for his work on the Kennet & Avon. The Staffordshire Way joins the towpath at Bridge 68 and follows the canal as far as Great Haywood, before disappearing off into the grounds of Shugborough on its way to the southernmost tip of the county at Kinver Edge. This is also the route of the Millennium Way which runs from Newport (Staffs) to Burton-on-Trent: waymarked walking routes are all very well, but do you not sometimes worry that we are in danger of removing 'self-initiative' from the equation?

RUGELEY gets a bad press from most guide-books which condescend to mention it at all, but we have always had a soft spot for this down to earth little town, once home to the notorious Victorian poisoner, William Palmer, and also remembered as the scene, in 1839, of the canal murder of Christina Collins. In years gone by Rugeley was the location of a malodorous tannery, but it is the power station which dominates now, and still coal-fired, though now this fuel is railed in from open-cast workings in Ayrshire or even abroad as opposed to being dug in the immediate locality. At Brindley Bank the canal suddenly stops running parallel to the Trent and turns sharply to cross it, as though Brindley had been screwing up his courage to bridge the river. Once there was a transhipment wharf here where flint was swapped between canal and river vessels for the short run down to Colton Mill by Trent Valley railway station. By Bridge 68 a short reedy arm adjacent to the railway provides a useful turning point for lengthy craft. It occurs to us that this may have been used as a transhipment basin in the fledgling days of the railway, perhaps for the conveyance of building materials.

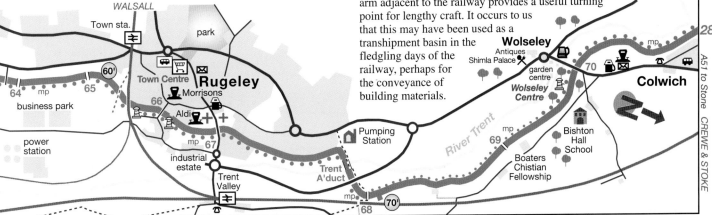

For details of facilities at Rugeley and Wolseley turn back to page 57

BRINDLEY always found it easier to follow river valleys, and Great Haywood was an obvious choice of location for a canal junction designed to establish his scheme for a 'Grand Cross' of man made waterways linking the four great English estuaries: Humber, Thames, Severn and Mersey. With the completion of the Staffordshire & Worcestershire Canal in 1772, and the Trent & Mersey five years later. Haywood became a canal junction of major importance, as significant to transport in the 18th century as any motorway interchange today. One is only left to marvel at the simplicity of it all - two quiet ribbons of water meeting beneath a bridge of exquisite beauty - and compare it sadly with transport interchanges of the 21st century, acres of concrete, noise and pollution. Where did we go wrong? History may have taken some wrong turnings, but there is little chance for the canal traveller to make a mistake, for a prominent fingerpost directs one concisely enough to "Wolverhampton", "The Trent", or "The Potteries". Between here and Colwich the TRENT & MERSEY is at its most memorably beautiful as it skirts the boundary of Shugborough. On one bank beechwoods tumble

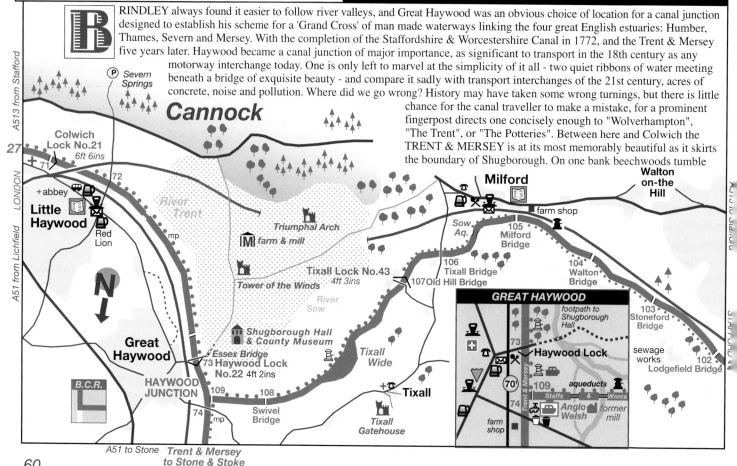

60

down to the water's edge. On the other, across the Trent, there are glimpses of the curious statues, antiquities and follies which pepper the grounds of this famous home of the Anson family. Colwich Lock lies in an attractive setting between the village church, a picturesque farm, and a bend in the river. From Bridge 72 you can take an idyllic walk to Severn Springs, a wonderful springboard for exploring Cannock Chase.

The Staffordshire & Worcestershire Canal

Through the arch of Bridge 109 - an 18th century fusion of functional engineering and enduring loveliness - the Staffordshire & Worcestershire Canal commences its 46 mile journey down to the Severn at Stourport. Two aqueducts carry it across the Trent and a millstream. A couple of miles further on it crosses the Sow. Between these river crossings the canal suddenly casts off its inhibitions and widens into a broad lake of quite un-canal-like proportions, bordered by thick reedbeds inhabited by a gorgeous array of wildfowl. Boaters will find their craft looping the loop out of sheer exuberance. This is Tixall Wide or Broadwater and there are two theories for its surprising existence. Some maintain that the canal was widened into

an artificial lake to placate the owner of Tixall Hall. Others that the expanse of water predates the canal, that it was naturally formed, and that Izaak Walton learnt to fish here. Whichever explanation suits you, don't miss the extraordinary Elizabethan gatehouse which overlooks the Wide. The hall itself, where Mary Queen of Scots was imprisoned for a fortnight in 1586, was demolished long ago. The gatehouse is let for holidays by the Landmark Trust - Tel: 01628 825925.

West of Tixall's solitary lock the canal meanders enchantingly through the valley of the Sow. A plethora of trees adds lustre to the landscape. The river is crossed by way of a typical low-slung Brindley masonry aqueduct. Bridge 105 is a handsome turnover affair from which there is access under the railway to the village of Milford. Between here and Baswich the canal runs through fields between the river and the railway whose southbound trains are quickly gobbled up by the decorated portal of Shugborough Tunnel. Those of a railway bent may be intrigued to learn that Francis William Webb, the great locomotive engineer of the London & North Western Railway, hailed from Tixall, where his father was Rector for over half a century.

The Haywoods (Map 28)
The villages of Great and Little Haywood are separated by the long, high brick wall of the Shugborough estate. Dormitory housing has inevitably expanded both populations, but the centres remain peaceful and largely unspoilt; especially so in the charming lane leading from Great Haywood, under the railway and over the canal, to the Essex Bridge, one of the finest examples of a packhorse bridge imaginable. Tolkien convalesced in Great Haywood after catching trench fever during the Battle of the Somme, and it is thinly disguised as 'Tarvobel' in *The Tale of The Sun and The Moon*.

Eating & Drinking
LOCK HOUSE - adjacent Haywood Lock. Tel: 01889 881294. Popular tea rooms and licensed restaurant. A pair of pubs in either village.

Shopping
Little Haywood has a post office stores (with cashpoint) and a newsagent. Great Haywood has two general stores (one with a butcher's counter), a pharmacy, post office, and a farm shop alongside the junction.

Things to Do
SHUGBOROUGH - access via Haywood Lock and Essex Bridge. Open daily April to December. Admission charge. Attractions include mansion, county museum, working farm, brewery, watermill, gardens, National Trust shop and cafeteria. A visit to the farm can be particularly recommended for families. Special events and a regular point of departure for hot air balloons.Tel: 01889 881388 www.shugborough.org.uk

Connections
BUSES - Arriva service 825 operates half-hourly Mon-Sat (bi-hourly Sun) between Stafford and Lichfield via Rugeley. Tel: 0870 608 2 608.

Milford (Map 28)
A motorist's gateway to Shugborough and The Chase unlikely to hold too much attraction for canal travellers. Throughout the summer its 'village green' is covered with parked cars. Facilities, however, include a steak bar, Britain's most long-lived WIMPY fast food outlet, post office store, newsagent and farm shop. Access from either Bridge 105 or 106. On Brocton Road MILFORD'S (Tel: 01785 662896) is a busy cafe celebrated for its cooked breakfasts and fish & chips.

Stafford (Map 29)

One of England's lesser-known county towns, Stafford has always seemed too self-effacing for its own good; though there are signs that in recent years it has begun to wake up to its tourist potential. Unfortunately for canal folk, the centre lies over a mile from Radford Bridge. But there are frequent buses, and those with time at their disposal will find Stafford a rewarding place to visit. First stop should be the Ancient High House in Greengate Street - the main thoroughfare. Dating from 1595, it's thought to be the largest timber-framed town house remaining in England. Inside there's a heritage exhibition tracing Stafford's history since 913 when Ethelfleda, daughter of Alfred the Great, fortified the settlement against marauding Danish invaders. King Charles I stayed at High House in 1642, and in later years Izaak Walton visited relatives who owned it. An alleyway beguiles you off Greengate Street to discover the town's large parish church of St Mary, much restored by Gilbert Scott in the 1840s and containing the bust of Izaak Walton. Elsewhere, some impressive buildings reflect the town's administrative status, lending it on occasions an almost metropolitan air.

Eating & Drinking

RADFORD BANK - canalside Bridge 98. Pub and carvery. Tel: 01785 242825.

THE SOUP KITCHEN - Church Lane. Quaint, sprawling and recently extended eatery (enhanced by attentive waitresses) serving coffees, lunches and teas. Tel: 01785 254775.

STAFFORD ARMS - Railway Street. Real ale buff's pub serving Stoke-on-Trent brewed "Titanic" beers. Food and accommodation. Tel: 01785 253313.

Shopping

Good shopping centre featuring all the well known 'high street' names plus many attractive individual shops tucked away down twisting side streets. Large ASDA and TESCO supermarkets. Indoor market Tue, Thur, Fri & Sat. Farmers' Market on the second Saturday in the month. CO-OP 'Convenience Store' accessible from Bridge 100 at Baswich if you're just passing through.

Things to Do

TOURIST INFORMATION - Market Street. Tel: 01785 619619 www.visitstafford.org

ANCIENT HIGH HOUSE - Greengate Street. Tel: 01785 619131. Local history and gifts.

SHIRE HALL GALLERY - Market Square. Tel: 01785 278345. Exhibitions, crafts and coffee bar housed in an imposing late Georgian building overlooking the Market Square.

STAFFORD CASTLE - Tel: 01785 257698. Well preserved Norman castle on town's western outskirts.

Connections

BUSES - Tel: 0870 608 2 608.

TAXIS - AJ's Tel: 01785 252255.

TRAINS - Important railhead with wide variety of services. Tel: 08457 484950. Useful links with Penkridge and Rugeley for towpath walkers.

Acton Trussell (Map 29)

THE MOAT HOUSE - canalside Bridge 92, Acton Trussell. Four star hotel in former moated farmhouse: restaurant and bars, lovely gardens, customer moorings. Tel: 01785 712217.

Penkridge (Map 30)

Quite easily the best place to break your journey on the northern section of the Staffs & Worcs. Five minutes walk from the wharf will take you to the narrow main street, a pleasant spot to shop and saunter. At its foot stands an impressive church of sandstone, formerly a collegiate church, considered second only to a cathedral in ecclesiastical status.

Eating & Drinking

CROSS KEYS - canalside Bridge 84. A once isolated pub, described by Rolt in Narrow Boat, but now surrounded by a housing estate, though that doesn't diminish its popularity with boaters and motorists alike. Tel: 01785 712826.

THE BOAT - Bridge 86. Tel: 01785 714178. Canalside pub with an incongruous sign featuring a tanker barge on the Aire & Calder!

FLAMES - Mill Street. Tel: 01785 712955. Contemporary Eastern cuisine.

Shopping

We sensed a downturn in the fortunes of Penkridge's independent retailers on our most recent visit, but the outdoor market on Wednesdays, Saturdays and Bank Holiday Mondays beside the river still apparently thrives.

Connections

BUSES - to Cannock, Wolverhampton and Stafford. Tel: 0870 608 2 608.

TRAINS - to Wolverhampton and Stafford. Tel: 08457 484950.

Coven (Map 32)

Coven's village centre is less than ten minutes walk from Bridge 71, but do take care crossing the A449!

Eating & Drinking

FOX & ANCHOR - canalside north of Bridge 71. Tel: 01902 798786. Flourishing Vintage Inns establishment offering a wide choice of food and drink. Fish & chip shop in the village centre and visitors welcome at the local golf course club house.

Shopping

Two food stores, pharmacy, post office, butcher, greengrocer and bakery.

LARGELY unmolested, the canal slips quietly through the outskirts of Stafford. The county town stood an aloof mile to the west of the Staffs & Worcs Canal which, in true Brindley fashion, followed the easy contours of the Penk Valley. Plans to construct a branch were dropped in favour of a simple lock down into the Sow, the river being dredged and realigned to take boats as far as a terminal basin at Green Bridge in the centre of Stafford. The navigation was opened in 1816 and in use until the end of the First World War. A footpath follows the riverbank into the town, but it is difficult to imagine how seventy foot narrowboats ever got up there: all the old navigation needs now is a determined restoration society!

Baswich church once stood as isolated on its hillside as Acton Trussell's does still, but now it is surrounded by a housing development, though those with an interest in ecclesiastical architecture can easily reach it from Bridge 100. Note the spelling of the village's name with a 'k' on the bridgeplate. There was a substantial wharf by Radford Bridge, but its site is now somewhat less interestingly occupied by a car showroom following demolition of the original warehouses in the Philistine Seventies.

Stafford Boat Club - with their impressive club house and welcome to visiting boaters - occupy a former brickworks arm near Hazelstrine Bridge. Most of the works's output was despatched by canal. Bridge 97 has disappeared completely, there being not even any tell-tale narrowing in the canal's channel where it once must have stood. Hereabouts the inherent other-worldliness of the waterway undergoes strange, paradoxical fluctuations in fortune. Nowhere could be more apparently remote than Deptmore Lock, where the reclusive inhabitant of the rose-clad cottages commutes to the outside world by dinghy. Elsewhere, however, the M6 threatens to intrude like an unwelcome caller on your afternoon off; whilst Acton Trussell, which you'd expect with such a name to be a picture book English village, disappoints with its banal modern architecture. Similarly Wildwood, which ought to be the home of friendly, furry little creatures straight out of some children's tale, has become a housing estate on a hill. But when vapours rise off the Penk, and its marshy meadows ooze sponge-like with excess water, a return to an older, more elemental existence seems somehow tangible, and man's scars upon the landscape recede into the mists of time.

Acton's houses attract a following of ducks. The solitary building on the towpath side used to be a boatman's pub. Present day boaters, however, slake their thirst in the old moated house by Bridge 92, opened a few years ago as a bar and restaurant set in charming grounds. It is said that Brindley actually used the old house's moat for a few yards when building the canal.

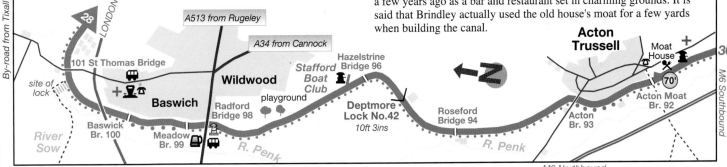

By-road from Tixall

28 LONDON

A513 from Rugeley

A34 from Cannock

101 St Thomas Bridge

site of lock

Wildwood

Baswich

Hazelstrine Bridge 96

Stafford Boat Club

playground

Deptmore Lock No.42
10ft 3ins

Roseford Bridge 94

Acton Trussell

Moat House

70'

Acton Moat Br. 92

Acton Br. 93

River Sow

Baswick Br. 100

Meadow Br. 99

Radford Bridge 98

R. Penk

R. Penk

M6 Southbound

30

public footpath to Stafford

A34 to Stafford town centre 1 mile

M6 Northbound

Penkridge Scenes

64

30 STAFFS & WORCS CANAL

Penkridge 4mls/7lks/3hrs

A S the canal ascends to (or descends from) its summit level, the locks come thick and fast. The motorway retreats, only to be replaced by the housing estates which cling-wrap the otherwise agreeable little town of Penkridge. Yet, a mile on either side, the countryside is characterised by rolling farmland lifting to the bulwark of Cannock Chase.

The towpath between bridges 90 and 86 is hi-jacked by the "Staffordshire Way" which seems forever to be bumping into canals and appropriating towpaths in the course of its 92 mile journey from Mow Cop to Kinver Edge. Its route has come down off The Chase and crossed Teddesley Park. Teddesley Hall was the seat of Sir Edward Littleton, one of the chief promoters of the Staffordshire & Worcestershire Canal. Indeed, the family remained involved with the canal company until its nationalisation in 1947. The hall itself was demolished by the army (!) in the mid Fifties (having been used as a prison camp for German officers during the Second World War) but the estate farm remains, hidden from the canal by some woodland known as Wellington Belt in commemoration of a visit to the hall by the Iron Duke. Bridge 89 once had ornate balustrades commensurate with its importance as the gateway to the hall, but sadly these have been infilled by brickwork.

PENKRIDGE WHARF is quieter than of late, no longer being the location of a busy boat hire base. Boats still pause here to take on water, however, and there is usually room to moor up for a visit to the town. The Littletons had fingers in many pies, not least the local colliery, which at one time employed over a thousand men. A huge basin, now covered by the motorway, was constructed to enable boats to be loaded with coal from a raised pier by gravity. The chief traffic flow of Littleton coal by canal in later years was down to Stourport power station as noted on Map 1.

Rodbaston Lock had a keeper until the motorway was built. A special bridge was built over the new road to maintain access to his lockside cottage, but the noise of the ensuing traffic was so bad as to cause him to leave and find new accommodation, the cottage subsequently being demolished. West of the canal between Otherton and Rodbaston lies a college of agriculture.

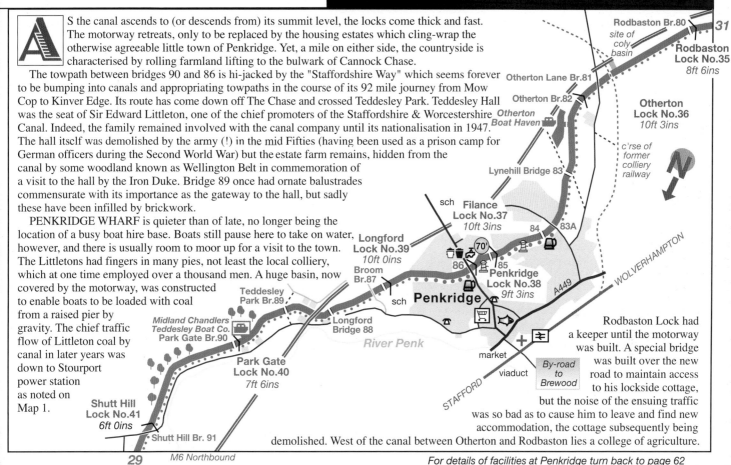

For details of facilities at Penkridge turn back to page 62

65

ALF HEATH is a strangely isolated tract of country, pancake flat and crossed by a grid of sullen little roads, with here and there a huddle of houses, gathered reassuringly together like something out of Van Gogh's early potato field paintings. The canal all but boxes the compass of this gravel pit-riddled landscape, so that The Chase with its communications tower and the chemical works with its phalanx of flaring chimneys, appear to move about you, teasing you into geographic insecurity, like a game of Blind Man's Buff.

The Staffs & Worcs Canal's summit - from Gailey to Compton (Map 6) - lies at more or less 340 feet above sea level. If you've climbed up from Penkridge and beyond it's a relief to be done with locks for the time being, though for those on an anti-clockwise "Black Country Ring" itinerary the prospect of the Wolverhampton 'Twenty-One' can be quite daunting. Industry lines the canal at Four Ashes. The old tar works here was once served by Thomas Clayton boats.

The last load of Cannock coal came off the Hatherton Branch in 1949 and it was abandoned a couple of years later. However, the illusion of a junction remains, because the bottom lock (of what was once a flight of eight in three miles) is still used to provide access to moorings. The Lichfield and Hatherton Canals Restoration Trust is actively seeking restoration of the branch with the intention of linking it with the northern waters of the BCN at Norton Canes. It is envisaged that the new link of six miles and sixteen locks will join the Cannock Extension Canal at Grove Basins (Map 37), and there is little doubt that its opening would prove a great filip to the under-boated northern extremities of the BCN.

Watling Street crosses the canal at Gailey. The most significant feature here is the 'round house', originally a toll clerk's office but now a splendid canal shop run by mother and daughter team, Eileen and Karen Lester. A short walk along the A5 will take you to Gailey Pottery, a small gallery and showroom housed in a former church. The pottery was established in 1976 by Paul Gooderham following his training at Wolverhampton Art College.

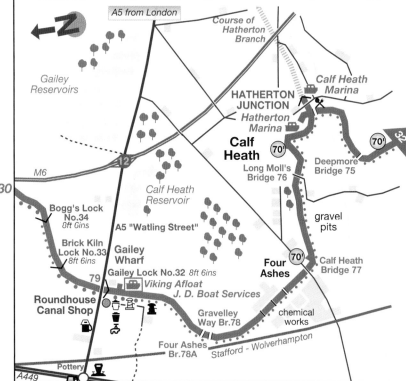

THE canal exchanges the loneliness of Calf and Coven heaths for the industrial and suburban outskirts of Wolverhampton; the M54 to Telford forming an obvious, though not intentional, boundary. At Cross Green a former boatman's pub called "The Anchor" has become the "Fox & Anchor", a popular restaurant bar, and many boaters choose to moor here overnight. As it passes beneath the M54 the canal crosses the county boundary between Staffordshire and the West Midlands, one of the new counties which had its origins in the local government changes of 1974. Many people still mourn the old counties. It must have been galling, for instance, to have lived in Lincolnshire all one's life and wake up one morning in South Humberside. West Midlands was possibly the dullest of all the new names, and sounds as though it must have been the compromise of a committee. Black Country would have been a far more appropriate and resonant title. You can imagine its inhabitants espousing a perverse pride in such a name, no-one could possibly show a flicker of interest in anyone who admitted to coming from the West Midlands! The most significant feature of this length is "Pendeford Rockin", the old boatmen's name for a shallow, but tellingly narrow cutting hewn by Brindley's navvies through a solid belt of sandstone which breaks through the clay strata at this point. The cutting, half a mile or so long, restricts the channel to such a degree that you begin to wonder if you have lost concentration and taken a wrong turn. There are, however, one or two passing places - as on a single lane road - where oncoming boats can be successfully negotiated without losing one's temper. Similar narrows occur on the Shropshire Union north of Autherley as that canal encounters the same difficult rock.

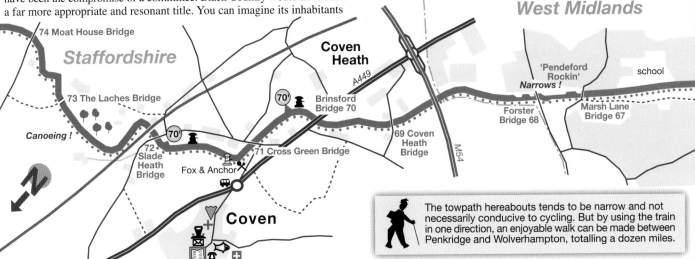

The towpath hereabouts tends to be narrow and not necessarily conducive to cycling. But by using the train in one direction, an enjoyable walk can be made between Penkridge and Wolverhampton, totalling a dozen miles.

A449 to Stafford   *To Brewood*   *For details of facilities at Coven turn to page 62*

Dudley & Stourbridge Canals

Gosty Hill Heron

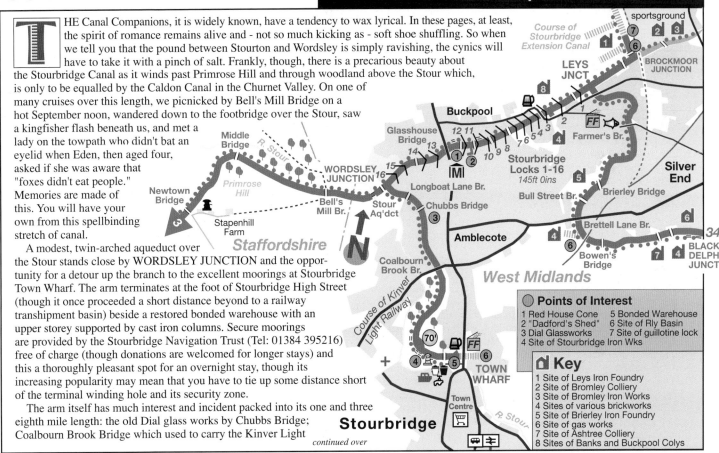

THE Canal Companions, it is widely known, have a tendency to wax lyrical. In these pages, at least, the spirit of romance remains alive and - not so much kicking as - soft shoe shuffling. So when we tell you that the pound between Stourton and Wordsley is simply ravishing, the cynics will have to take it with a pinch of salt. Frankly, though, there is a precarious beauty about the Stourbridge Canal as it winds past Primrose Hill and through woodland above the Stour which, is only to be equalled by the Caldon Canal in the Churnet Valley. On one of many cruises over this length, we picnicked by Bell's Mill Bridge on a hot September noon, wandered down to the footbridge over the Stour, saw a kingfisher flash beneath us, and met a lady on the towpath who didn't bat an eyelid when Eden, then aged four, asked if she was aware that "foxes didn't eat people." Memories are made of this. You will have your own from this spellbinding stretch of canal.

A modest, twin-arched aqueduct over the Stour stands close by WORDSLEY JUNCTION and the opportunity for a detour up the branch to the excellent moorings at Stourbridge Town Wharf. The arm terminates at the foot of Stourbridge High Street (though it once proceeded a short distance beyond to a railway transhipment basin) beside a restored bonded warehouse with an upper storey supported by cast iron columns. Secure moorings are provided by the Stourbridge Navigation Trust (Tel: 01384 395216) free of charge (though donations are welcomed for longer stays) and this a thoroughly pleasant spot for an overnight stay, though its increasing popularity may mean that you have to tie up some distance short of the terminal winding hole and its security zone.

The arm itself has much interest and incident packed into its one and three eighth mile length: the old Dial glass works by Chubbs Bridge; Coalbourn Brook Bridge which used to carry the Kinver Light

continued over

Points of Interest
1 Red House Cone
2 "Dadford's Shed"
3 Dial Glassworks
4 Site of Stourbridge Iron Wks
5 Bonded Warehouse
6 Site of Rly Basin
7 Site of guillotine lock

Key
1 Site of Leys Iron Foundry
2 Site of Bromley Colliery
3 Site of Bromley Iron Works
4 Sites of various brickworks
5 Site of Brierley Iron Foundry
6 Site of gas works
7 Site of Ashtree Colliery
8 Sites of Banks and Buckpool Colys

*Figures refer to main line between Newtown Bridge and Black Delph Junction. Allow half an hour in each direction for the Town Arm.

continued from page 69

Railway (Map 3); and the rubble-strewn site of Stourbridge Iron Works where the first steam locomotive to operate in the USA was built. Named *Stourbridge Lion*, it puffed its way through Pennsylvania in 1829. The works had been founded by John Bradley in 1798. His name appears on the southernmost roving bridge, a diminutive structure of cast iron construction dated 1873. By this final bend the canal widens, arrowhead flourishes and there is plenty of room to manoeuvre a turn in easier conditions than the crowded end of the arm.

The Stourbridge Sixteen

On a former trip, we came down the Sixteen in a respectable two and a half hours, with a crew of two adults and two children and not another boat in sight. It was two days before Tamar's eleventh birthday and she heroically coped with the flight's stiffish paddle gear. Lockwheeling ahead, it was 'Dad' who had the most problems, with the badly balanced bottom gates of Lock 15, which refused to stay shut simultaneously. He had suspicions of being 'set-up' as he closed one gate, then ran round via the top of the lock to try and shut the other before the first swung back open. Asking an elderly gentleman for help proved fruitless." 'E's not touching that lock," growled his wife - a belligerent Jack Russell of a woman - "'E's just had an 'art attack!" The flight is characterised by reedy side ponds aiding and abetting water supply. Furthermore it is accompanied by the spirits of the long deceased industries - coal, clay and iron - whose trade made it so prosperous in its heyday. Most of the evidence of these trades is confined to old maps, but two classic survivors remain in the form of "Dadford's Shed", a former transhipment warehouse built of timber and now partially used by a boatbuilder; and the massive Red House Cone (or kiln) which dates from the end of the 18th Century and which is now incorporated into a glass-making heritage centre. Both of these dinosaurs reside in the vicinity of Lock 12, whilst nearby stands "The Dock", a general store and off licence with a tradition of serving boatmen past and present. Locks 9 and 10 are telescoped together like a mini-Bratch, and were similarly once a true staircase. By Lock 4 is the "Samson & Lion", a popular free house, whilst the old "Bottle & Glass", now preserved at the Black Country Living Museum, used to stand on the opposite side from the towpath above Lock 3.

Leys Junction - Black Delph

Leys Junction may not be much to look at now, but it is effectively the custom post to the lost worlds of the Fens Branch and Stourbridge Extension Canal. The SEC was opened in 1840, enjoying six brief years of independence before being absorbed by the Oxford, Worcester & Wolverhampton Railway. Its goal was the coal and ironstone deposits at Shut End, two miles to the north-west. Navigation is feasible as far as Brookmoor, where secure offside visitor moorings were recently installed. But the setting is lugubrious to say the least, and one imagines that walkers will derive most pleasure from exploring these forgotten routes. Try and get hold of a copy of Ian Langford's *Towpath Guide to the Stourbridge Canal* published by Lapal in 1992 if you want more detail than we have space for here. The main line, however, veers east essaying a serpentine course through housing zones and echoes of industry past and present. Hereabouts - as we remarked in an earlier edition - realisation comes suddenly that you are no longer a holidaymaker, but rather a traveller in the strictest sense of the term, as adventurously off the beaten track as if you were mountain-busting in darkest Peru.

The Stourbridge has a celebrated niche in the story of the post-war canal revival. Trade had largely vanished from this route by the late Fifties and the canal decayed to the point of dereliction. In 1962 the IWA held their National Rally on the Town Arm against the wishes of British Waterways. A series of absurd hostilities ensued which would have furnished the plot of an Ealing comedy. The authorities refused to dredge the canal so the enthusiasts decided to do it themselves. The late David Hutchings recalled confronting a BW deputation on the towpath as his dragline was poised to break the choked waters of the arm. Reaching an impasse, both parties repaired to nearby telephone kiosks to seek the advice of their respective solicitors. Hutchings was advised to proceed in 'his usual piratical manner' and, to coin a phrase, British Waterways ended up with mud all over its bureaucratic face. The Stourbridge Rally was a success in its own right and, five years later, after much work had been carried out jointly by BW and volunteers, the Stourbridge Sixteen was re-opened.

At BLACK DELPH JUNCTION the Stourbridge Canal makes an unheralded and imperceptible end-on junction with the Dudley No.1 Canal, and the next part of your journey is covered by Map 34.

Stourbridge *(Map 33)*

From the canal wharf, it's but a short walk through the underpass beneath the ring-road (which encircles the glass-making town of Stourbridge like a boa constrictor) to the town centre. And how unexpected! For Stourbridge is not yet another Black Country industrial community, but rather a market town with a profusion of shops and some not uninteresting architecture. Even the usually restrained Pevsner was moved to label the former Grammar School (on your left as you ascend the High Street) 'picturesque', whilst a little further on stands the town clock; imposing, fluted-columned, cast in the local iron works in 1857, and equipped with a match-striking plate (a typical piece of Victorian thoughtfulness and ingenuity) for passers by.

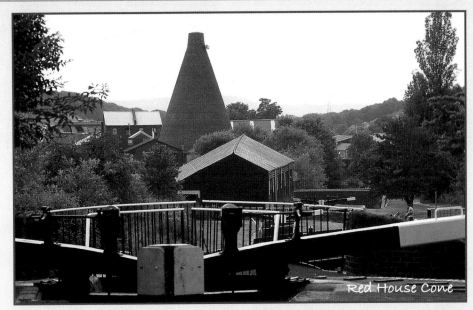

Red House Cone

Eating & Drinking

MOORINGS TAVERN - Cosy local on main road to rear of town wharf. Chinese takeaway next door. Tel: 01384 374124.

CELLARS - High Street. Indian restaurant within easy reach of the basin. Tel: 01384 44482.

FRENCH CONNECTION - Coventry Street (opposite the town clock). French cooking in the Black Country is rather rare and this little bistro makes a pleasant exception. Tel: 01384 390940.

ROYAL EXCHANGE - Enville Street. Batham's tied house offering only snacks to deflect from the serious business of downing this wonderful Black Country brew. Tel: 01384 396726.

SAMSON & LION - canalside Lock 4 of Stourbridge flight. Banks's and Marston's beers, good food and a friendly atmosphere. Skittle alley and garden with aviary. Accommodation. Tel: 01384 77796.

Shopping

Stourbridge has a daily market, whilst two precincts play host to all the major chain stores.

Make your way to the FRENCH CONNECTION delicatessen on Coventry Street where you'll find a mouthwatering selection of meats and regional cheeses on sale. Also noteworthy is NICKOLLS & PERKS wine merchants established as long ago as 1797.

Things to Do

RED HOUSE GLASS CONE - adjacent Lock 12 of Stourbridge flight. Self guided audio tours, including ascent of spiral staircase within the hundred foot high cone itself. Crafts, gifts, refreshments etc. Special moorings for boating visitors. Tel: 01384 812750. Stuart (Waterford) Crystal shop on site as well. Tel: 01384 342701.

STOURBRIDGE NAVIGATION TRUST - Tel: 01384 395216. Administrators of town wharf and bonded warehouse. Contact for long term mooring details, hire of hall etc.

Connections

BUSES - services throughout the area from bus station at top of High Street.

TRAINS - shuttle service on Britain's shortest branch line between Stourbridge Town and Stourbridge Junction for connections to Birmingham and Worcester. Tel: 0121 200 2700 for bus and train timetable information.

TAXIS - Falcon Taxis.Tel: 01384 393939.

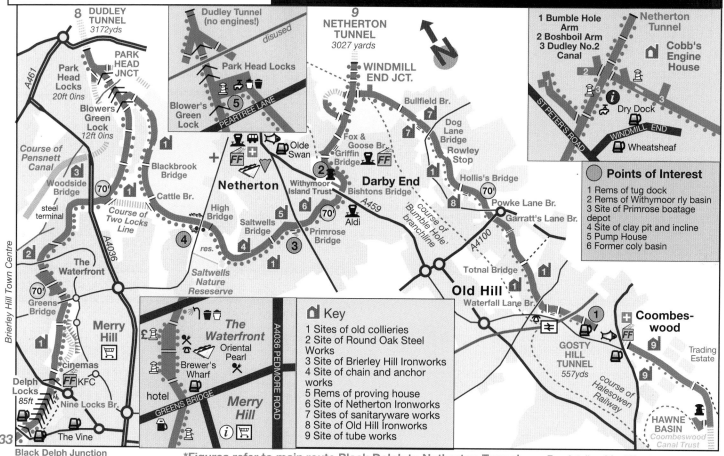

34 DUDLEY CANAL

Delph - Parkhead - Windmill End 5mls/9lks/3hrs*

8 DUDLEY TUNNEL 3172yds

PARK HEAD JNCT

Park Head Locks 20ft 0ins

Blowers Green Lock 12ft 0ins

Course of Pensnett Canal

3 Woodside Bridge

steel terminal

70'

Blackbrook Bridge

Cattle Br.

Course of Two Locks Line

Dudley Tunnel (no engines!) disused

Park Head Locks

5

Blower's Green Lock

PEARTREE LANE

Netherton

High Bridge

Saltwells Bridge

res.

4

5

Primrose Bridge

4

3

Saltwells Nature Reseserve

FF

Olde Swan

Withymoor Island Trust

2

Aldi

9 NETHERTON TUNNEL 3027 yards

WINDMILL END JCT.

Fox & Goose Br.
Griffin Bridge

FF

Bishtons Bridge

Darby End

6

70'

Bullfield Br.

7

Dog Lane Bridge Rowley Stop

7

Course of 'Bumble Hole' branchline

Hollis's Bridge

8

Powke Lane Br.

Garratt's Lane Br.

70'

1 Bumble Hole Arm
2 Boshboil Arm
3 Dudley No.2 Canal

Netherton Tunnel

Cobb's Engine House

2

3

Dry Dock

ST PETER'S ROAD

WINDMILL END

Wheatsheaf

Points of Interest

1 Rems of tug dock
2 Rems of Withymoor rly basin
3 Site of Primrose boatage depot
4 Site of clay pit and incline
5 Pump House
6 Former coly basin

Totnal Bridge

1

Old Hill

Waterfall Lane Br.

A4100

A459

1

1

GOSTY HILL TUNNEL 557yds

1

Coombeswood

FF

9

Trading Estate

9

course of Halesowen Railway

HAWNE BASIN
Coombeswood Canal Trust

Brierley Hill Town Centre

A4461

Course of Pensnett Canal

A4036

2

The Waterfront

70'

Greens Bridge

1

Merry Hill

cinemas

FF KFC

Delph Locks 85ft

Nine Locks Br.

The Vine

33

Black Delph Junction

The Waterfront

The Waterfront

Oriental Pearl

Brewer's Wharf

hotel

GREENS BRIDGE

A4036 PEDMORE ROAD

Merry Hill

Key

1 Sites of old collieries
2 Site of Round Oak Steel Works
3 Site of Brierley Hill Ironworks
4 Site of chain and anchor works
5 Rems of proving house
6 Site of Netherton Ironworks
7 Sites of sanitaryware works
8 Site of Old Hill Ironworks
9 Site of tube works

*Figures refer to main route Black Delph to Netherton Tunnel

For details of facilities turn to page 78

72

THOUGH amalgamated with the Birmingham Canal Navigations as long ago as 1846, there is about the Dudley Canals an independence of style and spirit which marks them apart from the bulk of the system on the other side of the Rowley Hills. Mid 19th century improvements - by-passing some of the more circuitous loops; construction of Netherton Tunnel; substitution of the original nine locks at The Delph by eight new ones - left their legacy of BCN characteristics. But crossing the 'invisible' junction at the foot of Delph Locks, or emerging from the gloom of Netherton's southern portal, you can almost grasp the change in atmosphere; a new variation on an old theme.

Black Delph - Park Head

THE DELPH was known in the 19th century as 'Black Delph' because of the proliferation of collieries in the vicinity. Nowadays 'Green Delph' would be a more appropriate sobriquet, for barely a vestige of industry remains. Delph Locks consist of eight chambers, of which six are in close proximity, carrying the canal from the 356ft level of the Stourbridge Canal to the 441ft contour of the Dudley No.1 Canal. The flight is one of the most spectacular anywhere on the canal system, but because of its location on the esoteric BCN it tends to be less celebrated than the likes of Bingley, Foxton and Devizes. On the off-side of the locks a series of overflow weirs cascade spectacularly when water levels are high. When the canal opened in 1779 there were nine locks. The top and bottom are originals, but in 1858 the present central six were built to replace seven earlier locks, traces of which can be explored to the east. A Horseley Iron Works roving bridge spans the original course of the canal below the top lock. In the middle of the flight a former block of canal horse stables is leased to the BCN Society and is occasionally open to the public.

Having acclimatized yourself to the 19th century environs of Black Delph, the next bend in the canal opens out to reveal the 21st century vista of the MERRY HILL CENTRE, one of the out of town shopping developments akin to Sheffield's Meadowhall or the Metro Centre at Gateshead which we gladly seem to have grown out of. The canal has

recently been slightly rerouted and one benefit of this work is the provision of mooring rings for boaters intending to moor up and visit the centre; though many of you will doubtless have taken to the water to escape such manifestations of modern life.

THE WATERFRONT, a billion pound development mixing commerce with leisure, occupies the site of the once vast Round Oak steel works. Aesthetically it is barely an improvement on the past: arguably the most satisfying building of the development is the pub, a pastiched cross between an East Anglian watermill and a Black Country foundry with plenty of mock weatherboarding and reconditioned brick; there must be a moral in that somewhere. Pre-book pontoon 'pay moorings' with electricity and water laid on are available if you're so inclined, a facility more likely to appeal to private boaters rather than hirers - telephone 01384 487911 for further details.

Passing the former junction of the Two Locks Line at Woodside Junction, the canal reaches the 12 feet deep Blower's Green Lock and PARK HEAD JUNCTION. Here the two Dudley Canals met, the No.1 Canal proceeding up the Park Head flight to the portal of DUDLEY TUNNEL. Re-opened in 1992 after a long period of neglect, we were looking forward to researching this route - even if it meant 'legging' the boat through so as to avoid making fumes - only to be thwarted by the restricted loading gauge of Dudley Tunnel. Considering that our boat on this occasion was a traditional tug, well-ballasted and tanked full with water to render it as low in the water as possible, we were disappointed to discover that it wouldn't fit. Since then, the Dudley Canal Trust have introduced a tug service (free of charge, though donations are welcome) to haul boats through their Aladdin's Cave of a tunnel; though of course the size limitations still apply. The Trust can be contacted on 01384 236275 for advice and further details, and the more advance warning they get of your intended passage the better. It is rewarding, however, to visit Park Head, if only to admire the handsome pump house - which the Trust have developed as an educational centre - and to take in the canal scene as a whole, and we can recommend mooring here and strolling up to view, not only the southern portal of Dudley Tunnel, but the interesting remains of the Pensnett Canal and Grazebrook Arm as well.

Nine Locks Bridge

Delph Locks

Park Head

74

Wordsley Junction

Windmill End

Cobb's Engine House

Park Head - Windmill End

The Dudley No.2 Canal once totalled eleven route miles, linking the Dudley No.1 Canal at Park Head with the Worcester & Birmingham Canal at Selly Oak (Map 11). It was completed in 1798 and included Britain's fourth longest canal tunnel at Lapal (3795 yards), a daunting towpath-less bore subject to a unique system of operation whereby a steam pumping engine produced an artificial bi-directional current through the tunnel to aid the momentum of boats passing through.

Between Park Head and Windmill End the canal describes a wide arc, clinging to the 453ft contour at the foot of Netherton Hill. Once upon a time industry congregated beside its banks: collieries, claypits, furnaces, limekilns and ironworks. But now this is coot country and the reeds seem as abundant as any Broadland river. At Blackbrook Junction the other end of the Two Locks Line is still evident through its roving bridge, even if subsidence caused it to be abandoned in 1909. Clothed in gorse and hawthorn, Netherton Hill stands behind the erstwhile junction, climbing to a 600ft summit topped by St Andrew's church where cholera victims are buried in unmarked common graves in the churchyard. The surrounding environs offer generous views over the southern extents of the not so Black Country and the distant wooded tops of the Clent Hills rising to a thousand feet southwards beyond Halesowen; it's a view the west midlands author Francis Brett Young must have known and held close to his heart.

A housing estate occupies the site of Doulton's once extensive clay pit linked to the canal by a tramway incline. Boats would carry this clay along the Dudley Canal to the firm's works at Darby End. High Bridge spans a rocky cutting where originally the canal builders built a short-lived tunnel. Nowadays the exhaust from your boat reverberates and rebounds between the sheer sandstone slopes of the cutting. No wonder the old boatmen nicknamed this 'Sounding Bridge'. Lodge Farm reservoir, used for watersports, gleams like antimony in its cup of land between the canal and Saltwells Nature Reserve. Footpaths penetrate its hinterland, threading their way through swampy pools down to Cradley Heath.

We've seen elsewhere on the BCN how the railways developed a network of interchange basins and boatage depots. Two examples of this are encountered hereabouts. Primrose Boatage Depot provided the LMS Railway (and its antecedents) with water access to an area otherwise dominated by GWR lines. LMS boats traded between here and the company's interchange basins at Bloomfield (Map 8) and Albion (Map 9). In recent years the site has been occupied by a builders merchant who has progressively erased all evidence of the past. When we first encountered the basin in the mid-1980s, we could still read the words 'London Midland & Scottish Railway' in faded paint on a gable end. Half a mile away, by Bishtons Bridge, the Great Western Railway's Withymoor Basin was one of the most extensive interchange points between rail and canal in its heyday. Withymoor opened in 1878 and closed in 1965. Its last regular transhipment cargo was chain from Lloyds Proving House by Primrose Bridge. Sadly its transhipment sheds and canopies have been demolished, but its arm survives in water, providing useful residential moorings for the Withymoor Island Trust.

Mention of chain recalls Netherton's landbased involvement in maritime engineering. Did you know that the *Titanic's* anchors were cast here? Each anchor required a team of twenty-four horses to tow it out of Netherton. There was a tradition of chain and anchor making in this unlikely corner of the Black Country. Much of the chain-making was done by women packed tightly in small premises which became so hot that they habitually worked bare-breasted. Would that the Black Country had had an artist of the calibre of Joseph Wright of Derby to do justice to such scenes. The workshops of the new estates which fringe the canal seem nebulous in comparison. Hingley's, owners of Netherton Ironworks, were instrumental in the establishment of Midlands & Coast Canal Carriers following the demise of the Shropshire Union fleet in 1921.

WINDMILL END is arguably the epitome of the Black Country canal scene, and given its location at the centre of the inland waterways system, together with the public open space which lines its canal banks, it's not surprising that it serves from time to time as an ideal venue for major boat rallies. The gaunt outline of Cobb's engine house, silhouetted against the Rowley Hills, above a profusion of Toll End Works roving bridges, forms one of the Black Country's most potent post-industrial images. Would, though, that the 'Bumble Hole' push & pull train still steamed back and forth between Dudley and Old Hill. Admirable as it undoubtedly is, the Visitor Centre is little consolation to connoisseurs of forgotten branch lines; though Windmill End station was immortalised in Flanders &

Swann's lovely, and outrageously neglected song *Slow Train*.

Cobb's engine house contained a stationary steam engine which pumped excess water from coal mines in the vicinity and discharged it into the canal. Built in 1831, the engine kept the pits dry and the cut wet for well nigh a century, until the local collieries were all worked out. The engine subsequently went for scrap, but the engine house remains, adorning the landscape as if somehow transmuted from a Cornish cliff top. The old colliery precincts surrounding Windmill End are now known as Warren's Hall Park; a haunted countryside to saunter in, to go roaming in the gloaming in, imagining the pandemonium of its industrial past.

Three cast iron roving bridges span the waterways radiating from Windmill End Junction. Originally the Dudley No.2 Canal ran east to west here, following the course of what became quaintly known as the 'Boshboil' and 'Bumble Hole' arms after the loop was cut off by the improvements of 1858 associated with the opening of Netherton Tunnel. The tunnel's southern portal stands to the north of the junction through the arch of a blue-brick overbridge which carried a colliery tramway.

NETHERTON TUNNEL provokes piquant contrast with Dudley Tunnel's ancient confines. High, wide and equipped with twin towpaths, it now lacks only the lighting once generated by a turbine fed from the high level old main line at Tividale (Map 9). It takes roughly half an hour to walk (preferably with a torch) or boat through this monument to the last fling of the canal age. We counted seven airshafts providing 'air-raids' of rainwater, but we've met wetter tunnels on our canal travels.

Windmill End - Hawne Basin

Lapal Tunnel's closure in 1917 severed the Dudley No.2 Canal's route between Windmill End and Selly Oak, but this end of the canal remained in commercial use right up until 1969 to serve the giant tube making works at Coombeswood on the far side of Gosty Hill Tunnel. Thereafter the canal might easily have deteriorated but for the emergence of the Coombeswood Canal Trust who developed the railway interchange basin at Hawne, on the outskirts of Halesowen, into a flourishing centre of Black Country leisure boating. The journey down to Hawne is continually engrossing if less than edifying. Old basins abound and 19th century large scale maps illuminate the density of industry here.

The canal still narrows at Rowley Stop, but these days no one materialises to take the tolls, so you proceed beneath Hollis's Bridge and on past a roving bridge under which an arm once extended into Old Hill Ironworks. Opposite here, we were gratified to learn, stood Pearson's Colliery, but if we were counting on the shares as part of our inheritance, we are in for a disappointment.

By Powke Lane stands the substantial Rowley Regis crematorium and cemetery and suburban Blackheath occupies the adjacent hillside. At Old Hill a series of overbridges pass in quick succession as the canal approaches the stygian delights of GOSTY HILL TUNNEL. In the early years of the 20th century the BCN operated a tug service through the tunnel and the remains of its dock can be seen beside the northern portal. The tunnel's confined, towpathless bore is infamous in boating circles. Working boatmen were content to abandon the tiller and spend the time it took to pass through the 557 yards long tunnel in their boat cabins, whilst, as snugly as a piston in a cylinder, the boat made its own way from one end to another.

You used to emerge from Gosty Hill Tunnel into the eerie precincts of a massive tube works. The canal traversed a canyon of sheer brick walls and passed beneath a sequence of mysterious corrugated iron clad overbridges and pipes whispering loquaciously with escaping steam. Some of the last commercial activity on the area's canals survived here. All this now, however, has vanished and been redeveloped into a trading estate of soulless units, inscrutable behind their ubiquitous cladding and characterless trading names. Beyond these interlopers, the canal runs at the foot of Mucklow Hill, a pleasant open landscape threaded by public footpaths, before abruptly reaching the old transhipment basin at Hawne. Visiting boaters are welcomed but not intruded upon, and this is definitely one Black Country mooring where the nightmare of vandalism won't disturb your slumbers. As to the remainder of the Dudley No.2's route, its future lies in the capable hands of the Lapal Canal Trust - founded in 1990 - torchbearers with a long term interest in restoration of the canal and Lapal Tunnel to their former glory. Recent achievements include the reinstatement of a massive embankment at Leasowes.

Merry Hill (Map 34)

Of course Merry Hill is really Brierley Hill, but so much does the massive retail complex dominate the vicinity now, that it seems more appropriate to refer to it thus. In common with its peers - Meadowhall, Metro, Trafford Park and Bluewater -you either love this sort of thing or loathe it. "Over 200 shops and stores" shrieks the publicity blurb: "two and a half miles of marbled halls - a uniquely enjoyable experience" - much like the BCN itself you might justifiably retort!

Eating & Drinking

The Waterfront boasts numerous bars and restaurants, and you are likely to find something to suit most tastes. Two alternatives to consider are, however:

ORIENTAL PEARL - Tel: 01384 78868. A bustling, value for money, Chinese restaurant just down from Greens Bridge.

THE VINE - Tel: 01384 78293. Better known as the 'Bull & Bladder', Batham's brewery tap is one of the great Black Country pubs. It stands on Delph Road about 5 minutes walk east from the foot of Delph Locks. Lunch time snacks, families welcome and, of course Batham's wonderful, wonderful beer which the family have been brewing for five generations. The Vine, one of only ten tied houses, has a Shakespearian quotation emblazoned across its frontage at roof level. *Several other pubs congregate on Delph Road: THE DOCK & IRON, BLACK HORSE (Enville Ales), TENTH LOCK and THE BELL but the 'Bull & Bladder' is by far the most atmospheric.*

Shopping

If the prospect of Merry Hill's two hundred plus shops is more than you can bear, then head in the opposite direction for Brierley Hill's beleaguered but traditional High Street. Note also the existence of a UCI Multiscreen cinema adjacent to the canal south of Green's Bridge.

Connections

BUSES - but no trains - connect Merry Hill with every conceivable Black Country town. TAXIS - Newline Taxis. Tel: 01384 480001.

Netherton (Map 34)

Netherton was literally and metaphorically built on coal. The parish church of St Andrews stands 600ft above sea level on a bare hillside once extensively mined. From its summit there are views across the intervening valley, traversed by the Dudley Canal, to Brierley Hill and the distant horizon of The Wrekin. The sturdy church itself, surrounded by tombstones which tell their own Black Country story of industrial triumph and personal misery, was locked, but we could see that it contained a gallery supported by cast iron columns as well as some interesting stained glass.

Eating & Drinking

The lamentable demise of Colm & Sheena O'Rourke's 'Little Pubs' took the wind out of the sails of their eccentric creations. Most of the pubs themselves, like THE DRY DOCK (Tel: 01384 235369) here at Windmill End, have passed into alternative ownership and are pale shadows of their heyday: comic creations need tender loving care just like the rest of us. But another firm favourite in the vicinity has returned revitalised from a period in the wilderness, and a ten minute walk into central Netherton will land you on the beguiling doorstep of THE OLDE SWAN (Tel: 01384 253075). Older regulars still lovingly call it 'Ma Pardoe's' after a former landlady. Once again they brew on the premises and a lovely pale, fruity beer the bitter is too. Additionally a wide choice of food is available lunchtimes and evenings; whilst, if you've timed it right, you might enjoy a sing-along with the mighty organ in the lounge!

Shopping

It must be hard being an independent shopkeeper in the all pervading thrall of Merry Hill, but Netherton's shops evince character and courtesy with Black Country wit never far from the surface. There's an excellent butcher selling home made pies at the top of Cradley Road, morale boosting cakes are obtainable from FIRKINS the West Bromwich bakers, and ALLANS discount store remains worth visiting: "every seasonable line imaginable - no nonsense prices." Meanwhile, no self-respecting cowpoke would miss the chance to visit the RANCH HOUSE Western Store - "complete Western & Line Dance outfitters."

Things to Do

BUMBLE HOLE VISITOR CENTRE - Tel: 01384 814100. Interesting and friendly centre devoted to Windmill End and its haunted environs.

Connections

BUSES -frequent services to/from Dudley etc. Nearest railway station at Old Hill. Tel: 0121 200 2700.

Old Hill (Map 34)

The sole railhead on this map, and though there are a couple of pubs, there are no shops within easy reach of the canal.

Coombeswood (Map 34)

Handy facilities above the southern portal of Gosty Hill Tunnel include both a fish & chip shop and Chinese take-away and a pharmacy. THE LIGHTHOUSE at the top of well worn steps is an intriguing outpost of the Cardiff brewery Brains, does food, welcomes families and boasts a beer garden - Tel: 0121 602 1620.

B.C.N. Backwaters

Olinthus Bridge

MEANDERING in best tradition of a contour canal, the Wyrley & Essington lives up to its nickname - "Curly Wyrley." It opened, independently of the Birmingham Canal, in 1797; extending for 24 miles from Horseley Fields, Wolverhampton to Huddlesford Junction on the Coventry Canal (Map 24) near Lichfield. Its fidelity to the 473ft contour was absolute until Ogley (Map 37) beyond which there were no less than thirty locks in the seven mile stretch down to Huddlesford. Several branches were built, so that by the mid 19th century there were half a dozen or more important junctions adding traffic to what had become a route of much importance. The W&E merged with the BCN in 1840.

After the disappearance of trade from this canal, it fell into neglect. Technically it remained navigable, but it was too ugly to appeal to all but the most hardened of pleasure boaters. And to all intents and purposes, despite the march of redevelopment along its banks, together with a general mellowing in atmosphere, the 'Curly Wyrley' remains an unloved canal, and one rarely boated, as evidenced by the algae gathering on its surface all summer long: indeed, there are enough lilies floating on its surface to capture the imagination of budding Black Country Monets.

Apart from the roving bridge at its erstwhile junction all trace of the Bentley Canal (which linked the W&E with the Walsall Canal at Darlaston (Map 41) has vanished under a retail park development. At Lane Head the arm which served Holly Bank Colliery basin is still in water, though no longer do the mineral trains come clangorously down from Hilton Main.

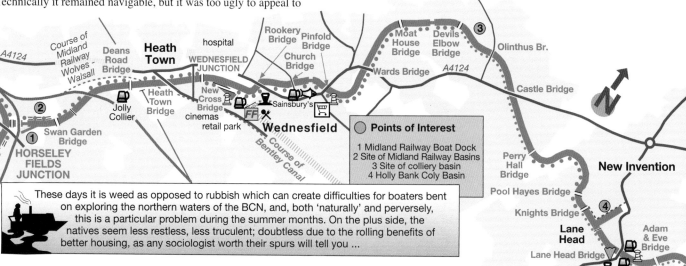

These days it is weed as opposed to rubbish which can create difficulties for boaters bent on exploring the northern waters of the BCN, and, both 'naturally' and perversely, this is a particular problem during the summer months. On the plus side, the natives seem less restless, less truculent; doubtless due to the rolling benefits of better housing, as any sociologist worth their spurs will tell you ...

Points of Interest
1 Midland Railway Boat Dock
2 Site of Midland Railway Basins
3 Site of colliery basin
4 Holly Bank Coly Basin

Goscote

Coal Pool

Arboretum

Hildick's Br.

Coal Pool Br.

Goscote
Hall Bridge

7

Goscote Works Bridge

Harden

Walsall

Little Bloxwich

Holland's Bridge

Teece's
Bridge

Freeth's
Bridge

Forest Foot
Bridge

Town
Centre

Leather Museum
B4210

Little
Bloxwich
Bridge

aqueduct

Pratt's Mill Bridge

Art Gallery

Town
Wharf

FF

37

site of
Keays's
Boatyard

6

70'

Walsall
Locks 8
65ft

wc

**BIRCHILLS
JUNCTION**

A34

1 2 3 4 5 6 7 8

A4148

Rolling
Mill St
Bridge

41

5

Sainsbury's

FF

Stubbs
Bridge

FF McDonalds

A S bedraggled Black Country crows fly, it's little more than
a mile from Rough Wood to Birchills Junction, but, true
to form, the desultory W&E manages to treble the distance.
ROUGH WOOD is a public open space reclaimed from
19th century coal workings. Mining here proved difficult because of
a geological feature known as the Bentley Faults. From SNEYD
the erstwhile Wyrley, Wyrley Bank and Essington branch
canals once proceeded northwards to remote
colliery basins; all 'grist' to the BCN's
invariably entertaining 'mill'. Nowadays

CANNOCK

Stoke's
Bridge

4

Wall End Bridge

3

Brick Kiln Br.

Key
1 Site of Wood Farm Colliery
2 Site of Bloxwich Colliery
3 Site of Hatherton Brickworks
4 Site of Hatherton Furnaces
5 Site of Birchills Power Station
6 Site of Staffordshire Ironworks
7 Site of copper works

school

Edward's Br. M6

Sneyd
Wharf

2

70'

1

*Course of
Wyrley Branch
Abandoned 1954*

**Short
Heath**

*Rough Wood
Chase*

Bentley
Wharf
Bridge

Sneyd Wharf is something of a centre for canoeing. Secure
moorings are available here on an overnight basis. Between Sneyd
and Birchills the canal pursues a largely turbid course bounded
by housing and pockets of industry. Stoke's Bridge has been
imaginatively repainted to reflect local heritage, in contrast to many
BCN bridges imaginatively repainted to reflect local sexual activity.
BIRCHILLS JUNCTION marks the egress of the W&E's
Walsall Branch. The local power station, for many years
the dominant feature of the branch and source of
considerable trade in coal boats, has been demolished and
the inevitable retail park has expanded in its place.
Whether afoot or afloat, it's worth making the detour

For details of facilities at Walsall turn to page 84

A4124 to Wednesfield

35 *Figures refer to Wyrley & Essington - allow 1.5 hours for Walsall Canal

to the top of the Walsall flight at least. The generating plant brought considerable traffic to the canal. A sizeable unloading basin was serviced by overhead travelling cranes whose grabs lifted considerable tonnages out of fleets of Joey boats.

The Walsall Branch terminated, prior to the construction of the Walsall Junction Canal and its flight of eight locks, at Birchills Wharf. Here, in 1900, a Boatmen's Mission or 'Rest' was built under the aegis of the Incorporated Seamen & Boatmen's Friendly Society. Its function was similar to that at Tipton (Map 8) but at Birchills an upper storey provided considerable dormitory facilities for day boatmen as well. Unfortunately, although the building had been used as a canal museum for a number of years, it closed due to lack of local authority funding.

Walsall (Locks & Town Arm)

WALSALL LOCKS were first mooted to link the Wyrley & Essington and Walsall canals in 1825, but the W&E and BCN companies were suspicious of each other's motives and proposal was followed by counter-proposal for fifteen years before the canal and its flight of eight locks, rising 65 feet, materialised. The flight seems characteristically morose and lugubrious, as evinced by the crucifix overlooking Lock 5. Alongside Lock 7, fronting Wolverhampton Road, an until recently busy flour mill has been converted into stylish apartments. An arched loading bay covers a side pond beside the lock chamber. Lock 6 is unique to the flight in having mitred bottom gates; the rest being more typical of BCN design with single leaves.

Following many years of decay and dereliction, the WALSALL TOWN ARM has been impressively revitalised, and creates an off-beat gateway to the town's new art gallery; a £21m project designed by Peter St John and Adam Caruso. The gallery's hundred foot high, terracotta-tiled tower forms a fitting new climax to the canal arm. Further redevelopment is being undertaken by Urban Splash - one trusts they'll retain the quaintly juxtaposed premises of Pleck Boxing Club and its adjoining Body Repair Shop. In the far off days of commercial carrying, several basins extended off the arm serving two iron works, the town's original gas works, and the corporation wharf. The Walsall Canal between Walsall and Great Bridge is described in the text accompanying Map 41.

Birchills - Little Bloxwich

Unsympathetically overlooked by new offices, sunken wooden narrowboat hulls lie in the reeds east of Birchills Junction, eloquent testimony to the BCN's busy past. There are no tangible remains, however, of the boat docks which once stood by Pratt's Mill Bridge - which, before being rebuilt in the 1930s, carried one of Walsall's tramway routes. Bowaters and Worseys - both famous Black Country boatbuilders - had premises here. In latter years the yard west of the bridge - now covered by housing - was operated by Peter Keay & Son, one of the last specialist wooden canal boat builders. Keays went into business after the Great War, based at first on the Daw End Branch, and were also known as canal carriers by virtue of their fleet of tugs which towed 'Joey' boats down from the Cannock coalfield. Joey was a BCN colloquialism for day boats without living accommodation used for short haul work. Tugs would pull 'trains' of these unpowered craft, or they might be worked singly by horses. They were equipped with transferable helms for bi-directional working, saving the need to turn in space-restricted basins. Long gone, Pratts Mill itself received narrowboat cargoes of wheat all the way from Ellesmere Port, and was known as the regular scene of Saturday night fights between rival boat families.

An aqueduct carries the canal over the Walsall to Cannock railway. The original course of the canal was by-passed when the railway cutting was excavated, thus allowing the aqueduct to be built without disrupting canal trade. Through Harden, Coal Pool and Little Bloxwich housing estates border the canal. Pilfering was commonplace when the coal boats passed by. Boater captains were apt to turn a blind eye however flagrant the theft. The easiest approach was to board a boat at one bridge-hole, fill a bag with the black stuff, and alight at the next. Coal Pool Bridge used to carry the wires of one of Walsall's late, lamented trolleybus routes.

Pigeon lofts clutter a significantly high proportion of the canalside gardens, but you don't need us to evoke analogies between the mental imprisonment of their owners and the bird's airborne freedom. At FREETH'S BRIDGE eastbound canal travellers wriggle free from the suffocation of the suburbs and escape into an open, level countryside which seems doubly beautiful in the light of what has gone before. Paradoxically, the working boatmen of the last century would be passing from farmland into an area of coal mining.

Walsall Vignettes

APOLLO

83

Wednesfield (Map 35)

The big brick church of St Thomas, topped by a gold cockerel weathervane, lures you off the cut into Wednesfield's busy main street. Strange how these tangential Black Country communities contrive to stay so purposeful and relevant. This town's particular contribution to the industrial revolution was in the painful art of trap-making, though you must in turn not fall into the trap of underestimating its facilities, which are more ambitious than you'd think: banks, a retail market on Tue, Fri & Sat, at least two good Black Country butchers flying in the face of Sainsbury's by Rookery Bridge. BENTLEY BRIDGE retail park offers eating places, a cinema complex, and visitor moorings alongside a new-build pub called THE NICKLEODEON. More traditional in outlook, however, is THE BOAT by Church Bridge with KING FRYER fish & chips handily placed next door.

Walsall (Map 36)

You cannot go far in Walsall without discovering the town's stock in trade, leather goods; especially saddle making. Walsall is also a centre for lorinery (saddle ironmongery) and is esteemed throughout the world for such equipment, particularly in South America, where no self-respecting Pampas gaucho would be seen dead without an elegant pair of spurs cast in this North Black Country metropolis. Walsall is inordinately proud of two former citizens. A statue on 'The Bridge' (which recalls that Flean Brook once flowed visibly through the town) salutes Sister Dora, an Anglican nun who arrived in Walsall in 1865. She found the medical facilities primitive, many industrial accidents turning to fatalities for the want of treatment. She devoted the rest of her life to local people, rushing to the scene of industrial disasters, coping with a smallpox epidemic, and providing solace and succour to the working men and their families to such an extent that she has never been forgotten. Her statue is notable in being the first in England erected to a woman other than a monarch. The base features copper friezes depicting her work against suitably satanic industrial backdrops. Walsall's other hero is Jerome K. Jerome who was born in the town, but whose family was forced to move following his father's bankruptcy when JKJ was only two. Jerome didn't return to Walsall until he was sixty, coming first to collect material for his autobiography, and then to receive the Freedom of the Borough. A man capable of the delicious humour of *Three Men in a Boat* must have enjoyed the gentle irony of that moment; many larger towns have done less to honour greater men. When the nights draw in, West Midlanders leave summer behind with a barely perceptible sigh and turn their thoughts to the 'Walsall Illuminations'. Quarter of a million Black Country folk pour into the Arboretum, where 40,000 light bulbs temporarily transform 35 acres of parkland into a carnival atmosphere rivalling Blackpool's with delicious dollops of irony.

Eating & Drinking

THE WHARF 10 - canalside Town Wharf. Lively cafe/bar beside the refurbished basin and overlooked by the new, much vaunted art gallery. Tel: 01922 613100.

NEW ART GALLERY - cultured and cost-effective cafe providing breakfasts, lunches and teas with big glass window views over the canal basin. Tel: 01922 654400.

THE GEORGE STEPHENSON - canalside, Birchills. Risibly misnamed (on account, one assumes, of the neighbouring trackbed of the Midland Railway's long defunct Walsall-Wolverhampton line) modern all-day pub offering 'Wacky Warehouse' and 'Family Feast'. Tel: 01922 630458.

Shopping

Walsall's thriving market dates from 1219 and attracts shoppers from all over the region. There are several busy precincts burgeoning with all the usual chain stores. The Guildhall has been attractively converted as a centre for craft and gift shops, as has the nearby Mews in Goodhall Street. A new retail park abuts the canal terminus. Look out also for the VICTORIAN ARCADE.

Things to Do

TOURIST INFORMATION - St Paul's Bus Station. Tel: 01922 625540.

WALSALL LEATHER MUSEUM - Wisemore, Walsall. Open Tue-Sat 10-5, Sun 12-5, plus Bank Hol Mons. Tel: 01922 721153.

WALSALL MUSEUM - Lichfield Street. Tel: 01922 653116.

THE NEW ART GALLERY - Gallery Square. Open Tue-Sun admission free. Tel: 01922 654400. Spanking new gallery with a surprisingly cosmopolitan range of exhibits by the likes of Cezanne, Van Gogh, Renoir and Picasso.

JEROME K. JEROME BIRTHPLACE MUSEUM - Bradford Street. Open Tue-Sat admission free. Tel: 01922 728860.

Connections

BUSES - Services throughout the region from striking new bus station. Useful towpath-walking links with Brownhills etc.

TRAINS - local services to/from Stafford, Wolverhampton and Birmingham. Details of buses and trains on 0121 200 2700.

Little Bloxwich (Map 36)

Two housing estate pubs, a canalside Chinese take-away and a Spar store make this a useful little outpost.

THE canals depicted (overleaf) on Map 37 consisted - in their heyday - of the Wyrley & Essington Canal together with seven arms or branches, three of which remain navigable. At Ogley Junction the Wyrley & Essington continued in an easterly direction, skirting Lichfield on its way to join the Coventry Canal at Huddlesford (Map 24). The Lichfield & Hatherton Canals Restoration Trust plans to restore this missing link as part of a revived route between the Staffordshire & Worcestershire Canal at Hatherton (Map 31) and Huddlesford. As for the arms and branches, the majority of them: Lord Hays Branch and the Gilpins, Slough and Sandhills arms, are long gone; but the Cannock Extension Canal (or at least a mile and a half of it), the Anglesey Branch and the Daw End Branch remain.

The Cannock Extension Canal

The Cannock Extension Canal opened in 1863 to tap the Cannock coalfield. It was five miles long, lockless, and terminated at Hednesford, a colliery town at the very foot of Cannock Chase. En route there was a junction at Bridgtown, where a precipitous flight of thirteen locks linked with the Hatherton Branch of the Staffs & Worcs Canal. The Cannock Extension was revered as the scene of the 'Black Country Tide', a canal water bore caused by the simultaneous movement of convoys of narrowboats. Perhaps fifty boats at a time would converge on Pelsall Junction from the Walsall and Brownhills directions, and their passage up the Extension would raise the water level by half a foot. Ironically, mining subsidence brought about abandonment of the Cannock Extension above the A5 at Norton Canes in 1963, though by this time the coalfield's dwindling output was mostly railborne in any case. The old basins which served Grove Colliery are bosky moorings now, but may well be given new relevance when the Lichfield & Hatherton Canals Restoration Trust scheme comes to fruition, for a new section of canal will require digging at this point along the course of a former mineral railway.

The Extension was probably the last narrow gauge canal of any significant length to be built, and it has a distinctive character. Even in its decay, it retains a commercial sense of purpose. Blue 'Utopia'

engineering bricks line its banks; BCN concrete fencing posts can be glimpsed in the undergrowth; and hefty, name-plated overbridges - more railway-like than canal - parenthesise its passage across the moody, returning to nature landscape. Two old BCN cottages (No.s 211 & 212) adjoin the massive proportions of Friar Bridge. Opposite are old stables retaining the framework of their stalls. Wasteland extends westwards across Wood Common, a heathery, pock-marked site of a huge ironworks.

Pelsall - Ogley

PELSALL JUNCTION is the scene of occasional boat rallies, but at other times few boats pass by, let alone negotiate the junction and head for Norton Canes. A shame, because this really is a nice place to moor overnight, soaking up the haunted setting of post-industrial inactivity; all fir trees and ponds where once there were slag-heaps and mineral railways. A big public open space encourages the stretching of boating-stiff limbs, whilst hearty appetites and thirsts can be appeased at one or other of the adjoining pubs.

East of Pelsall the canal becomes an aquatic corset, keeping the housing estates at bay. Only occasionally does the whalebone burst as urbanisation spills across the cut. The Gilpins and Slough arms were disused by the end of the 19th century; the latter had two locks leading to a short summit fed by local springs and colliery pumping. A public footpath - part of a local nature trail - follows its course now. The defunct "Jolly Collier" inn had stabling for canal horses.

Two abandoned railways crossed the canal either side of Cooper's Bridge. The South Staffordshire line bridge is still in place, its cast iron parapets of exactly the same design as the company's bridge at the foot of the Ryder's Green flight (Map 9). You have to be even older to remember the Midland Railway's branch to Brownhills Watling Street in action, the high abutment of its former bridge across the canal provides the lost route with a crumbling memorial: do the denizens of all these new houses hear ghost trains in the night?

A rewatered arm extends into the former railway interchange basin at BROWNHILLS. A canoe centre provides boating facilities and visitor moorings. Clayhanger Common incorporates ninety acres of colliery waste redeveloped as a public open space including a Site of Importance for Nature Conservation. CATSHILL JUNCTION is overlooked by tower

continued on page 87

Triangle

A5 from Shrewsbury

Norton Canes

course of Cannock Extension Canal

ANGLESEY BASIN

Chasewater Reservoir

Chasewater Heritage Railway

course of LNWR Norton Branch

Burntwood Road Bridge

M6 Toll

Canal Transport Services

WATLING STREET

Little Chef

Wulfrun Way

Freeth Bridge

aqueduct
Middleton Br.

B4155

course of Wyrley & Essington

Anglesey Br.

OGLEY JUNCT

A3 to Tamworth

suggested new course of Hatherton Canal

Staffs

West Mids

Brownhills Nature Trail

Holland Park

Miner's Statue

course of South Staffordshire Rly.

Brownhills

FF

Tesco

course of Sandhills Arm

A461 to Lichfield

Key
1 Rems of Brownhills (Grove) Coly.
2 Sites of various collieries
3 Site of iron & spelter works
4 Site of Walsall Wood Coly.
5 Ogley Hay Steam Flour Mill
6 Site of chemical works

B4154

Engine Lane
Wulfrun Way

Wyrley Common

course of Slough Arm

course of Mid. Rly Brownhills Watling Street branch

Becks Bridge

CANNOCK EXTENSION CANAL

Wyrley Grove Bridge

Green Bridge

Pelsall Common Br.

High Bridge

Jolly Collier Bridge

Cooper's Bridge

Clayhanger Bridge

A452

B5011

The Anchor

CATSHILL JUNCTION

Lord Hays Branch

Friar Bridge

Yorks Br.

A4124

PELSALL JUNCTION

Royal Oak

Yorks Foundry Bridge

Clayhanger

Points of Interest
1 Valve House
2 Rems of coly basin
3 Site of rly/canal interchange basin
4 Rems of boat horse stable
5 Site of Brownhills Watling Street station

Shire Oak

Pelsall Works Bridge

Free Trade

N

36

Pelsall   Crse. of Gilpins Arm

38

A461 to Walsall

A452 to Castle Bromwich

A449 to Lichfield

continued from page 85

blocks and is graced by an attractive sculpture. Both routes narrowed here to facilitate toll taking. The W&E proceeds from Catshill to Ogley passing the long vanished course of the Sandhills Arm, known to working boatmen as the 'Apple Arm' because it traversed an area of orchards. These have gone, but farmland falls bucolically away to the east as the canal enters a shallow cutting of bracken and broom to reach Ogley Junction. Mining subsidence caused a breach here in 1983 which, were it not for the importance of water supply, would probably have resulted in abandonment.

The Anglesey Branch

Chasewater Reservoir was opened in 1799 to supply the Wyrley & Essington main line with much needed water. Fifty years later, with the development of coal mining in the area, the feeder to Ogley was upgraded to navigable standards. Nowadays the branch represents the furthest north you can travel on the BCN. Come this far and you can assume you've won your spurs. There are views north-east beyond the M6 Toll of the three spires of Lichfield Cathedral. An aqueduct carries the canal over the trackbed of the South Staffordshire Railway. Tom Foxon wrote evocatively of ANGLESEY BASIN in its days as a centre for the loading of coal boats in *No.1*, a classic account of life amongst working boatmen in the early Fifties. He described how the colliery wagons were upended and their contents carried by conveyor belt to a loading gantry spanning the canal. The gantry consisted of two chutes: one for large lumps of coal which could not be dropped from a great height for fear of damage to the boat holds. Typically the coal would leave in 'trains' of five loaded day boats hauled by a tug, destined perhaps for Birchills power station or the GEC works at Witton. The last coal was loaded at Anglesey in 1967 and only some contorted lumps of metal recall the existence of such complicated apparatus. The basin is green now, an expanse of water of lake-size proportions considered, in its heathland environment, to be a Site of Special Scientific Interest. Here, in the environs of Chasewater Country Park are moorings as remote as any on the inland waterways. At weekends (and on summer Wednesdays) the sounds of steam locomotive whistles echoing around the rim of the reservoir recall the past heyday of numerous mineral railways in the neighbourhood.

Brownhills (Map 37)

Brownhills's new miner's statue (30 feet high and of stainless steel) towers over the town like a Soviet Bloc sculpture of Stalinist proportions, reminding us all (very necessarily now) why the town was built here in the first place. The long main street exemplifies its era, the lacklustre shop frontages harbouring no ambitions above the monotony of two storeys, save at Catshill where monolithic high rise flats also echo Eastern Europe. A rash of churches and chapels - Catholic, Jehovah's Witness, Spiritualist, Nonconformist et al - provide all the entertainment the inhabitants of Brownhills were ever likely to be offered. And yet, on Tuesdays and Saturdays the canalside market throbs with activity, the car parks are crammed and buses packed with people who you would have thought more plausibly to have done their business in Walsall or Cannock.

Eating & Drinking
MARIO'S FISH BAR & RESTAURANT - High Street. Tel: 01543 371487. THE ANCHOR - Chester Road (by Anchor Bridge near Catshill Junction). Tel: 01543 360219. Modern Wolverhampton & Dudley pub offering all day menu. *Additionally there are several fast food outlets of varying ethnicity to be located along the lengthy High Street.*

Shopping
Besides the market, there are Tesco and Aldi supermarkets adjacent the canal's Silver Street visitor moorings; a couple of butchers and various banks.

Things to Do
CHASEWATER HERITAGE RAILWAY - Tel: 01543 452623 *www.chaserail.com* Trains operate on Sundays throughout the year and on Saturdays and Wednesdays in summer along two miles of former colliery railways, remnants of a once extensive system centred on the Cannock Chase coalfield. The main station, Brownhills West, lies less than 10 minutes walk from Anglesey Basin. FOREST OF MERCIA INNOVATION CENTRE - Tel: 01543 308860.

Connections
Both Brownhills's railway stations having closed (in 1930 and 1965), buses offer the only means of public transport. Frequent links with Walsall, Aldridge and Rushall are a boon for towpath explorers. Tel: 0870 608 2 608.

Rushall (Map 38)

Two pubs of contrasting style and atmosphere can be found adjacent to Daw End Bridge: THE BOATHOUSE (Tel: 01922 615032) is a newly built all day pub; the MANOR ARMS (Tel: 01922 642333) much more traditional in outlook. Half a mile down the B4154 are shops and a McDonalds.

THE navvies who laboured to build the DAW END BRANCH of the Wyrley & Essington Canal probably wouldn't recognise it now. When it opened in 1800, as a link to the limestone quarries at Hay Head, it was a typical contour canal, crossing a district largely innocent of industry and urbanisation. But it soon became apparent that the hinterland of Brownhills was rich in clay deposits, and brick and tile making became the staple activities of the area. Coal mining prospered too, bequeathing a legacy of subsidence which wrought havoc with the canal bed, necessitating continual heightening of its banks, so that it came to resemble a Fenland river. So it's likely that old-stagers would furrow their brows in amazement to see their cut twisting and turning high above the rest of the crumbling landscape, whilst today's canal travellers find themselves somewhat

burying dangerous wastes in the former clay pits. More memories are evoked at Hopley's Bridge where Duckham's canalside works was the recipient of the ill-fated Birmingham & Midland oil consignments from Ellesmere Port in 1970; perhaps the last long distance narrowboat cargo of note; poignantly, the mooring rings are still there. Two of Walsall MBC's imaginative nature reserves can be found alongside the Daw End Branch: at Park Lime Pits and Hay Head, both sites formerly worked as limestone quarries.

At LONGWOOD the Daw End Branch turned eastwards to reach the limestone workings at Hay Head, and there was no canal link southwards until the merger of the BCN and W&E in 1840. The Rushall Canal was an offspring of this union though, maintaining the connubial metaphor, there is reason to believe that the resultant waterway was by way of being an accident of careless family planning. Apparently the BCN began to have doubts about the viability of the proposed link, only to be reminded that Government money borrowed under the Act of Union with the W&E would have to be returned should the Rushall Canal not be built!

voyeuristically at bedroom and bathroom level of houses lining the canal at WALSALL WOOD: some of those wallpapers are hard to take seriously. In Tom Foxon's day Walsall Wood was the location of 'The Traveller', probably the last pub in England to offer stabling for canal horses. The Utopia blue bricks we discovered on the Cannock Extension were apparently made in a canalside works near Northywood Bridge. These days the local industry seems more concerned with

For details of facilities at Rushall turn to page 87

B4154 to Rushall
(McDonalds, shops etc)

B4151 to Walsall

39 RUSHALL & TAME VALLEY CANALS

EVEN the most committed BCN diehard would admit that the canals featured on this map hardly represent the system at its most scintillating. Suffocated by suburbia and motorways, unrelievedly straight - and therefore lacking the inherent 'mystery' of the classic winding canal - they lack the dynamism of the industrialised BCN at its best. Such criticisms, though, are relative, and it would be an unimaginative canal explorer who failed to find something, at least, of interest in the characters of these two routes. RUSHALL LOCKS were nicknamed 'The Ganzies' by working boatmen, reputedly because of the thick Guernsey style sweaters favoured by steerers on this windswept cut. In the pound between locks 6 and 7 stood Bell Wharf, one of the few predominantly agricultural basins to be found on the BCN.

Half on embankments, half in cuttings, the TAME VALLEY CANAL's most dramatic incident is its crossing, on an imposing three-arch aqueduct, of the Grand Junction Railway; a rare case (possibly unique) of a railway pre-dating an adjoining canal. We were intrigued by the proliferation - west of Stone Cross - of side bridges. Our trusty 1904 6" Ordnance map showed them to have spanned arms serving sandpits and small collieries.

HOLLOWAY BANK BRIDGE carries Telford's Holyhead Turnpike road across the canal at Hill Top. Apparently the road here was so steep that passengers had to climb the hill on foot whilst the horses strained to haul their carriages up unloaded. The region's new Metro system also crosses the canal here, its brightly painted modern trams emphasising the archaic nature of passing boats. Scarcely anything remains of the Balls Hill Branch abandoned in 1960. In typical Brindley fashion a boat would literally have to box the compass when navigating this early waterway. The first cargoes of Wednesbury coal were loaded at its terminus in 1769.

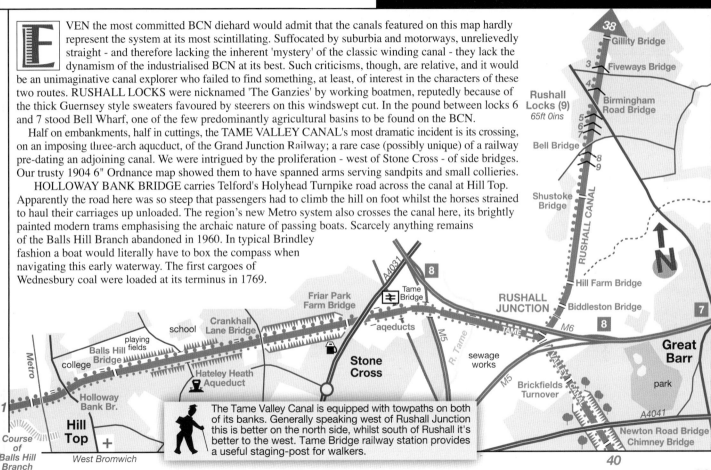

The Tame Valley Canal is equipped with towpaths on both of its banks. Generally speaking west of Rushall Junction this is better on the north side, whilst south of Rushall it's better to the west. Tame Bridge railway station provides a useful staging-post for walkers.

NCE upon a time, before the navvies dug this latecomer, the Tame must have been a pretty enough watercourse, skipping gaily down off the Black Country ridge to its confluence with the Trent above Tamworth. Not that the canal can be blamed for the urbanisation of the valley. Save for Hamstead Colliery (whose basin by Gorse Farm Bridge was linked by tramway to the pit head) the Tame Valley Canal attracted little industry to its banks hereabouts, being built primarily - and remaining useful throughout its commercial life - as a by-pass route, enabling through traffics to avoid the centre of Birmingham. No, these fields were filled by the phenomenon of the housing estate which, from the late Thirties onwards, crept northwards from burgeoning Birmingham, creating subtopias out of Perry Barr, Witton and Hamstead. Fortunately, all these Englishmen's castles fail to smother the canal which, either hides in rocky, wooded cuttings reminiscent of 'The Shroppie', or rides upon embankments with views southwards over the Second City. From here it doesn't look far - but it's the best part of a day's boating away!

Two aqueducts of differing design carry the canal above the rooftops of HAMSTEAD. The local colliery closed in the early Sixties. In 1908 there was an underground fire at the pit which claimed the lives of twenty-five miners. One of the trapped groups, anticipating their doom, chalked their names

on a nearby door together with the poignant inscription: "The Lord preserve us for we are all trusting in Christ." Rescue teams with special breathing apparatus were sent from the Yorkshire coalfield, and one of these men, John Welsby, lost his own life, heroically searching for the trapped men. He is commemorated by a street named after him on the estate which now covers the site of the mine.

PERRY BARR LOCKS - colloquially known as the 'New Thirteen' (as opposed to the 'Old Thirteen' at Farmers Bridge (Map 20) - lie adjacent to Perry Park with its impressive athletics stadium. The chambers are fitted with double bottom gates throughout. Interesting relics of the recirculating pumping system, which returned water lost through lock-usage to the top of the flight, are still to be seen: the 'Grid House' at the foot of Lock 13; 'No.1 Reflux Valve' by Lock 11; 'No.2 Reflux Valve' by Lock 7; and the 'Gauging Weir House' at the top of the flight. By the time the foot of the flight has been reached, the canal finds itself re-entering Birmingham's industrial zone. Travelling southbound, the suburban dream is over.

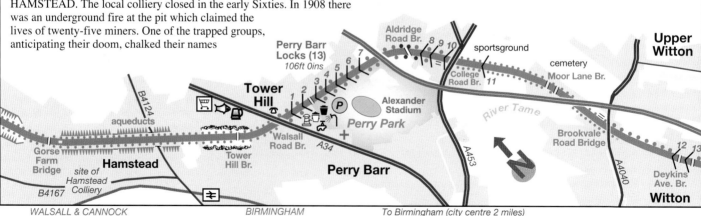

T's not just a boat or a bicycle or a stout pair of walking boots which you need to do justice to the Walsall Canal, it's a time machine as well. When Pearsons first charted these waters circa 1988 we noted that 'this canal plummets to levels of unsavouriness that anyone reading this guide from the comfort of an armchair can only simulate by going outside and sitting in their dustbin'. Perversely, though, we and like-minded diehards, cherished the 'Woebegone Walsall's' potential for masochistic adventure, a challenging assault course of a canal at the nadir of its fortunes. 'Decay', we opined, 'like old age, has a way of tugging at your heart strings, as if there were some mute urgency in disintegration to escape the parameters of time.' Twenty years later, we would give anything to have the old

continued on page 92

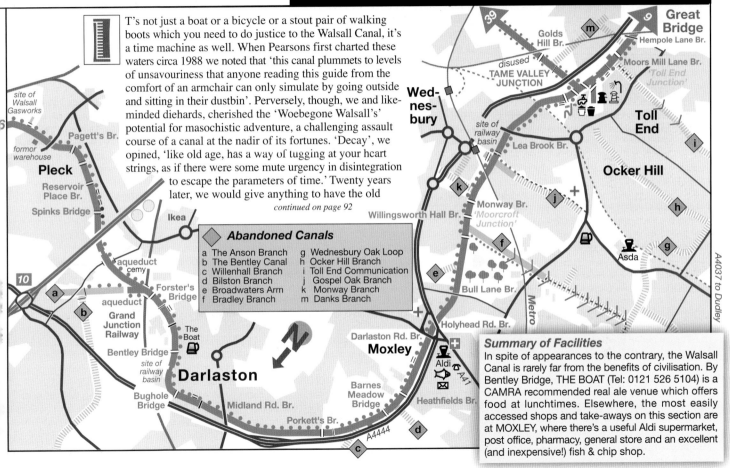

Abandoned Canals

a The Anson Branch
b The Bentley Canal
c Willenhall Branch
d Bilston Branch
e Broadwaters Arm
f Bradley Branch
g Wednesbury Oak Loop
h Ocker Hill Branch
i Toll End Communication
j Gospel Oak Branch
k Monway Branch
m Danks Branch

Summary of Facilities

In spite of appearances to the contrary, the Walsall Canal is rarely far from the benefits of civilisation. By Bentley Bridge, THE BOAT (Tel: 0121 526 5104) is a CAMRA recommended real ale venue which offers food at lunchtimes. Elsewhere, the most easily accessed shops and take-aways on this section are at MOXLEY, where there's a useful Aldi supermarket, post office, pharmacy, general store and an excellent (and inexpensive!) fish & chip shop.

continued from page 91

irascible Walsall back, its brave new, brightened-up, 21st Century manifestation being the palest shadow of its progenitor. The Black Country Spine Road accompanies the Walsall Canal for much of its length now, and virtually all the old, 'haunted' ambience of the canal has been eradicated. The Walsall Canal of the twenty-first century has assumed a cosmetic role within a regenerated zone of business parks, housing schemes, and retail centres. All good clean fun, though just a bit too clean, one suspects, for it to any longer pump the adrenalin of canal enthusiasts. The towpath is well-surfaced, and its banks are becoming overlooked by neat houses, and the threat of hooliganism recedes. But - and to our mind it's a 'Big Woolwich Butty' of a but - what dyed-in-the-wool canal buff, head full of fantasies of carrying coke to Coseley and timber to Tipton, is going to derive any satisfaction from walking or boating along a concrete-banked waterway threading its way through housing estates and retail parks and accompanied by a dual-carriageway? Yes chums, we've come to bury the Walsall Canal, not to praise it.

Bearing generally southwards from Walsall - generally, that is, in the context of a contour canal - the Walsall runs through the suburb of Pleck, passing the site of Walsall gasworks, a relatively late user of canal transport; coal in and waste products out. In fact, Thomas Clayton's very last run was from here with crude tar to Oldbury on 31st March, 1966 aboard the motor boat *Stour*. The canal slips through Pleck in a sandy cutting and then passes the levelled site of James Bridge copper works. Emerging from beneath the M6 motorway it rides upon a considerable embankment carrying it over a by-road and the infant River Tame. To the north-west other lofty earthworks can be seen. This was the Anson Branch - still partially in water - which connected with the Bentley Canal abandoned in 1961 (Map 35).

The canal crosses the Grand Junction Railway and essays a loop around the old metal-bashing town of Darlaston. By Bughole Bridge the Spine Road makes itself known to southbound canal travellers for the first time - you are not expected to become bosom pals. Pipes, pylons and Poundland's gargantuan warehouse are poor substitutes for the riproaring past, and you find yourself wondering who exactly Mr Porkett was, and what would he think of the vacuous present. Moxley was the location of Ernie Thomas's rubbish tip. Day boats stacked with refuse were worked here from Birmingham and all over the Black Country to have their malodorous

contents tipped into an old sand quarry. The remains of a roving bridge, and rough ground beyond, still bear evidence to this long lost trade. Redevelopment has eroded much of the latent atmosphere of the canal as it reaches MOORCROFT JUNCTION. Until its closure in 1961, the Bradley Branch lead off from here to the Wednesbury Oak Loop, ascending to the Wolverhampton Level through a flight of nine locks. A footpath follows the course of this interesting route under the Metro tramway and up into a public open space circling housing estates to Bradley itself.

The Monway Branch once served a complex of iron and chemical plants, including the vast Patent Shaft Steel Works. The Gospel Oak Branch led to Willingsworth furnaces. Opposite its reedy remains, shot like a green arrow into the entrails of a housing estate, a roving bridge spans the entrance to the Great Western Railway's Wednesbury rail/canal interchange basin. It didn't take long for reorganisation-prone British Waterways to vacate their new office and visitor centre overlooking TAME VALLEY JUNCTION, and the welcome visitor moorings on the Lower Ocker Hill Branch - opened in 1785 to feed water to pumping engines at Ocker Hill via a tunnel in the hillside - have become primarily residential moorings. The Tame Valley Canal egresses eastwards, offering alternative routes to Brownhills and Birmingham. To the south another through route has been lost. The Tipton Green & Toll End Communication Canal doesn't exactly roll off the tongue, but until 1960 it 'communicated' with the main line at Tipton, easing congestion in the heyday of the BCN when boats were apt to be choc-a-bloc at Ryders Green. You can walk its course as far as the A461, beyond which it is fenced off.

Alan Godfrey's reprint of the 1902 Ordnance Survey Map for Great Bridge & Toll End depicts in all its fascinating complexity the stretch of canal between Toll End Junction and Ryders Green Bottom Lock. Here the Danks Branch made its dog-leg connection with the Tame Valley Canal, whilst the South Staffordshire Railway spanned the Walsall's main line. It still does (though its tracks haven't seen a train in years - and await the clarion call to become part of the Metro system, linking Walsall with Dudley) but virtually all trace of the extensive London & North Western rail/canal interchange basins have vanished into a swampy undergrowth abutting the Spine Road. Hempole Lane Bridge is date-stamped 1825 in Roman numerals - strap us into our time machines ...

How to use the Maps

There are forty-one numbered maps whose layout is shown by the Route Planner inside the front cover. Maps 1-19 show the route of the STOURPORT RING; and Maps 7-10 and 20-32 the route of the BLACK COUNTRY RING. Maps 33/34 cover the Stourbridge and Dudley Canals, whilst Maps 35-41 cover the northern area of the Birmingham Canal Navigations.

The maps are easily read in either direction. The simplest way of progressing from map to map is to proceed to the next map numbered (in blue figures) from the edge of the map you are on. Figures quoted at the top of each map refer to distance per map, locks per map and average cruising times. An alternative indication of timings from centre to centre can be found on the Route Planner. Obviously, cruising times vary with the nature of your boat and the number of crew at your disposal, so quoted times should be taken only as an estimate. Neither do times quoted take into account any delays which might occur at lock flights in high season.

Using the Text

Each map is accompanied by a route commentary which highlights items of interest, past and present, along the course of the waterway. Details of most settlements passed through are given, together with information of the facilities likely to be of interest to canal users. Regulars will be familiar with our approach, tried and tested for over quarter of a century!

Towpath Walking

The simplest way to go canal exploring is on foot. It costs largely nothing and you are free to concentrate on the passing scene; something that boaters are not always at liberty to do. With the exception of the River Severn, all the waterways

Information

covered by this guide are equipped with towpaths. Over the years we have walked every yard of these, and we try to keep our towpath information as up to date as possible. We recommend the use of public transport to facilitate 'one-way' walking and suggest that this is used on the outward leg of an itinerary so that you are not necessarily pressured to complete the walk within a certain time limit. We also stress the advisability of using our quoted telephone numbers to check up to the minute details of bus and train services.

Towpath Cycling

Cycling canal towpaths is an increasingly popular activity, but one that British Waterways - the nationalised body responsible for the upkeep of the bulk of Britain's navigable inland waterways - is only slowly coming to terms with. The goalposts keep moving, but as we went to press it was still necessary for cyclists wishing to use towpaths to acquire a permit (albeit a free of charge one) from one of the British Waterways offices listed opposite.

Boating

Boating on inland waterways is an established, though relatively small, facet of the UK holiday industry. There are over 25,000 privately owned boats registered on the canals, but in addition to these numerous firms offer boats for hire. These companies range from small operators with half a dozen boats to sizeable fleets run by companies with several bases.

Most hire craft have all the creature comforts you are likely to expect. In the excitement of planning a boating holiday you may give scant thought to the contents of your hire boat, but at the end of a hard day's boating such matters take on more significance, and a well equipped, comfortable boat, large enough to accommodate your crew, can make the difference between a good holiday and an indifferent one.

Traditionally, hire boats are booked out by the week or fortnight, though many firms now offer more flexible short breaks or extended weeks. All reputable hire firms give newcomers tuition in boat handling and lock working, and first-timers soon find themselves adapting to the pace of things 'on the cut'.

Navigational Advice

LOCKS are part of the charm of canal cruising, but they are potentially dangerous environments for children, pets and careless adults. Use of them should be methodical and unhurried, whilst special care should be exercised in rain, frost and snow when slippery hazards abound. We have no space here for detailed instructions on lock operation: trusting that if you own your boat you will, by definition, already be experienced in canal cruising; whilst first time hire boaters should be given tuition in the operation of locks before they set out.

Apart from the basin locks at Diglis, Worcester and the automated locks on the River Severn between Worcester and Stourport, all the locks on the canals covered by this guide are of the familiar narrow-beam variety. All gates should be closed on leaving each chamber (unless courteously leaving them open for an approaching boat) and all paddles wound down.

The River Severn locks at Bevere, Holt and Lincomb are mechanised and manned. One prolonged blast on the boat horn should be enough to alert the keeper that you wish to use the lock, though in most cases he will already be aware via the lock-keeper's grapevine of your approach. Be guided by the colour light signals, but wait for the signal to turn green and the gates to open before approaching too closely. The chambers of these locks are large and you may be sharing with other craft. Steadying straps and chains are attached to the chamber walls and these can be hand held to control your boat if there is any turbulence. Always follow the lock-keeper's advice. He will be in his control cabin as you pass through the lock.

The basin locks at Worcester and Stourport are only open during timetabled hours - as indeed are the river locks mentioned above. Hire craft are likely to have up to date timings in their boat manuals, but private boaters can obtain details from British Waterways, Llanthony Warehouse, Gloucester GL1 2EJ. Tel: 01452 318000.

MOORING on the canals featured in this guide is per usual practice - ie on the towpath side, away from sharp bends, bridge-holes and narrows. An 'open' bollard symbol represents visitor mooring sites; either as designated specifically by British Waterways or, in some cases, as recommended by our own personal experience. Of course, one of the great joys of canal boating has always been the ability to moor wherever (sensibly) you like. In recent years, however, it has become obvious, particularly in urban areas, that there are an increasing number of undesirable locations where mooring is not to be recommended for fear of vandalism, theft or abuse. We hope, therefore, that you find our suggestions both pleasant and secure. But do bear in mind that the absence of a bollard symbol from any particular location does not necessarily imply that it is unsuitable or not

to be recommended.

FLOODS can occur on the River Severn at any time of year at short notice. Officials should be on hand to help and advise at such times. If you are already on the river you must tie up at the nearest official moorings and remain there until further notice. At times of flood you may be denied access to the river. Boat hire companies are familiar with the Severn's moods and will be sympathetic to genuine delays.

CLOSURES (or 'stoppages' in canal parlance) traditionally occur on the inland waterways between November and April, during which time most of the heavy maintenance work is undertaken. Occasionally, however, an emergency stoppage, or perhaps a water restriction, may be imposed at short notice, closing part of the route you intend to use. Up to date details are usually available from hire bases. Alternatively, British Waterways provide a recorded message service for private boaters. The number to ring is: 01923 201401/2. Stoppages are also listed on British Waterways'internet site: www.waterscape.com

TURNING. Turning points on the canals are known as 'winding holes'; pronounced as the thing which blows because in the old days the wind was expected to do much of the work rather than the boatman. Winding holes capable of taking a full length boat of around seventy foot length are marked where appropriate on the maps.

Emergencies
British Waterways operate a central emergency telephone service. Call them free of charge on 0800 47 999 47.

Useful Contacts
British Waterways Central Shires - Peel's Wharf, Fazeley, Tamworth, Staffs B78 3QZ. Tel: 01827 252000.
Customer Service Centre - Birmingham. Tel: 0121 200 7400.

Canal Societies
Inland Waterways Association was founded in 1946 to campaign for retention of the canal system. Many routes now open to pleasure boaters may not have been so but for this organisation. Membership details may be obtained from: Inland Waterways Association, PO Box 114, Rickmansworth WD3 1ZY. Tel: 01923 711114 www.waterways.org.uk
Birmingham Canal Navigations Society www.bcn-society.co.uk
Dudley Canal Trust is based at the Blowers Green Pumphouse, Peartree Lane, Dudley, West Midlands DY2 0XP Tel: 01384 236275. www.dudleycanaltrust.org.uk
Staffordshire & Worcestershire Canal Society www.swcs.org.uk
Worcester & Birmingham Canal Society www.wbcs.org.uk

Acknowledgements
Thanks, as ever, to Brian Collings for the signwritten cover - his forty-fourth for us, we think!; to Karen Tanguy for additional research and photography; to Mark 'our man in the midlands) Smith of Halesowen; to Toby Bryant of Central Waterways Supplies; and to Hawksworths of Uttoxeter for handling the printing side of things. Mapping reproduced by permission of Ordnance Survey (based mapping) on behalf of The Controller of Her Majesty's Stationery Office, Crown copyright 100033032.

Hire Bases

ALVECHURCH BOAT CENTRES - Worcester & Birmingham Canal Map 13. Scarfield Wharf, Alvechurch, Worcestershire B48 7SQ. Tel: 0870 835 2525 www.alvechurch.com

ANGLO WELSH WATERWAY HOLIDAYS - Worcs & Birmingham Canal Map 17 and Staffs & Worcs Canal Map 28. 2 The Hide Market, West Street, Bristol BS2 0BH. Tel: 0117 304 1122 www.anglowelsh.co.uk

BLACK PRINCE HOLIDAYS - Worcester & Birmingham Canal Map 14. Stoke Prior, Bromsgrove, Worcestershire B60 4LA. Tel: 01527 575115 www.black-prince.com

BROOK LINE - Worcester & Birmingham Canal Map 16. Dunhampstead Wharf, Oddingley, Droitwich, Worcs. WR9 7JX Tel: 01905 773889.

SHERBORNE WHARF - BCN Maps 11 & 20. Sherborne Street, Birmingham B16 8DE. Tel: 0121-455 6163 www.sherbornewharf.co.uk

TEDDESLEY BOAT COMPANY - Staffs & Worcs Canal Map 30. Teddesley Road, Penkridge, Stafford ST19 5RH. Tel: 01785 714692 www.narrowboats.co.uk

VIKING AFLOAT - Worcs & Birmingham Canal Map 17 and Staffs & Worcs Canal Map 31. Lowesmoor Wharf, Worcester WR1 2RS. Tel: 01905 610660 www.viking-afloat.com

WATER TRAVEL - Staffs & Worcs Canal Map 7. Oxley Moor Road, Wolverhampton WV9 5HW. Tel: 01902 782371 www.water-travel.co.uk

Boatyards

ASHWOOD MARINA - Staffs & Worcs Canal, Map 4. Tel: 01785 257717.

CALF HEATH MARINA - Staffs & Worcs Canal Map 31.Tel: 01902 790570.

CANAL TRANSPORT SERVICES - Cannock Extension Canal Map 37. Tel: 01543 374370.

Boating Directory

HANBURY WHARF CANAL VILLAGE - Worcs & Birmingham Canal Map 15. Tel: 01905 771018.

FAZELEY MILL MARINA - Birmingham & Fazeley Canal Map 23. Tel: 01827 261138.

JD BOAT SERVICES - Staffs & Worcs Canal Map 31. Tel: 01902 791811.

KINGS BROMLEY WHARF - Trent & Mersey Canal Map 25. Tel: 01543 417209.

LIMEKILN NARROWBOATS - Staffs & Worcs Canal Map 6. Tel/Fax: 01902 751147.

OLDBURY BOAT SERVICES - BCN Map 9. Tel: 0121 544 1795.

OXLEY MARINE - Staffs & Worcs Canal Map 7. Tel: 01902 789522.

OTHERTON BOAT HAVEN - Staffs & Worcs Canal Map 30. Tel: 01785 712515.

PINDER & SONS - Worcs & B'ham Canal, Map 14. Tel: 01527 876438.

SEVERN VALLEY BOAT CENTRE - Staffs & Worcs Canal Map 1. Tel: 01299 871165. Fax: 01299 827211.

STREETHAY WHARF - Coventry Canal Map 25. Tel/Fax: 01543 414808.

STROUDWATER CRUISERS - Staffs & Worcs Canal Map 1. Engine Lane, Stourport, Worcs DY13 9EP. Tel: 01299 877222.

SWAN LINE CRUISERS - Trent & Mersey Canal Map 25. Fradley Junction, Alrewas, Burton-on-Trent DE13 7DN. Tel: 01283 790332.

Day Boat Hire

ANGLO WELSH - Tardebigge, Worcester & Birmingham Canal, Map 17. Tel: 01527 873898. Great Haywood, Staffs & Worcs Canal, Map 28. Tel: 0117 304 1122.

DEBBIES DAY BOATS - Birmingham & Fazeley Canal, Map 23. Tel: 01827 262042.

DROITWICH CANAL CO - Droitwich Barge Canal. Tel: 01905 458352.

PITCHCROFT BOAT STATION - River Severn, Worcester, Map 17. Tel: 01905 27949.

SHERBOURNE WHARF - Birmingham Canal Navigations, Map 11. Tel: 0121 455 6163.

STREETHAY WHARF - Coventry Canal, Map 25. Tel: 01543 414808.

SWAN LINE CRUISERS - Trent & Mersey Canal Map 25. Fradley Junction, Alrewas, Burton-on-Trent DE13 7DN. Tel: 01283 790332.

Trip Boats

DUDLEY CANAL TRUST - trips into Dudley Tunnel, Map 8. Tel: 01384 236275.

FELLOWS, MORTON & CLAYTON - trips along the Stourbridge Canal, Map 33. Tel: 01384 375912.

PARTY BOATS - canal trips in central Birmingham, Map 11. Tel: 0121 236 7057

RIVER SEVERN CRUISES - river trips from Worcester, Map 17. Tel: 01905 611060.

SECOND CITY CRUISES - canal trips in central Birmingham, Map 11. Tel: 0121 236 9811.

SHERBOURNE WHARF - canal trips and waterbus services in central Birmingham, Map 11. Tel: 0121 455 6163.

SOW VALLEY CRUISES - canal trips from Great Haywood, Map 28. Tel: 01785 663728.

STOURPORT STEAMER CO. - river trips from Stourport, Map 1. Tel: 01299 871177.

Nine Good Reasons for Exploring the Canals with Pearsons

8th edition - ISBN 978 0 9 5491168 3

8th edition - ISBN 0 9549116 0 1

7th edition - ISBN 0 9549116 3 6

8th edition - ISBN 978 0 9 5491169 0

6th edition - ISBN 0 9549116 5 2

7th edition - ISBN 978 0 9 549 1166 9

6th edition - ISBN 0 9549116 2 8

3rd edition - ISBN 0 9545383 4 X

2nd edition - ISBN 978 0 9 5491167 6

Pearson's Canal Companions are published by Central Waterways Supplies. They are widely available from hire bases, boatyards, canal shops, good bookshops, via the internet and the Inland Waterways Association. For further details contact CWS on 01788 546692 or sales@centralwaterways.co.uk